Thornfalcon

Thornfalcon

Matthew W Harrill

For Tricia, my wife, who always has faith that one day one of these books will make it.

Thanks go to Marie and Lynzie for their editing, and teaching me a thing or three, and Carrie, my always-vocal proofreader.

Chapter One

Clarity is one of those paradoxical phenomena. It seems to make sense to get a good look at something close up, but in truth it is time and distance that truly illuminate.

Her eyes were open for the first time in years. Samantha Scott crouched, balancing on one hand, squeezing the beach sand between her fingers with the other. A thousand micro points of pain began, with a network of assaults on individual nerves as miniscule specks of shell and stones dug into her skin, the sum no more than a tingling. The discomfort barely registered as another portion of her life slipped away. Behind her, a companion raged against their failures. *How could she have been used for so long,* she wondered?

She heard the roar of celebration in the distance, smelled the faint waft of distant fumes, but pushed it away. She had given too much already. This would be her own little dig at her mother's greatest achievement.

It was already late afternoon; she felt the sun on her face, tasted the salt carried on the light breeze to the edge of her tongue. She imagined the sky sling, the culmination of a decade of international co-operation spearheaded by the brightest minds on the planet—noting the pull on the ocean as preparations were underway. Was there nothing humanity could not alter?

"Sammy, you should see this," urged one of her companions.

"What?" The wind whipped her voice into strands.

"This sight is the only success you'll have today if you don't concentrate."

Luke? Lance? Her mind was scrambled, as it always was when she drew blood. Lucas. The young man was the latest in a long line of sycophants—devil worshippers. He, and the three bootlickers cowering behind him, was a distraction. Her priorities had changed and with that came a black cloud of responsibilities. Her head swirled with confused energy, like lightning randomly erupting.

She opened her clenched palm, examining the laceration stretching from the base of her forefinger to the heel of her hand. Skin deep, the wound had stopped bleeding as soon as it started; grains of the coarse sand now stuck in what would become another scar on the latticework already there. She wiped the laceration on the faded grey of a once-black t-shirt bearing the word 'Disturbed', the sand spilling onto tight jeans of a similar hue.

She looked up at Lucas and the others, "It's not why you came. This is why you're here. All of you." Samantha pointed at the sand beneath. Waves lapped at the edge of a circle with symbols etched within. As the seawater spilled into the furrowed shoreline, the mark faded, taken back by the sand and ocean; here there would be no scar.

"Give her time, Lucas," one of the three girls whispered, her voice shaking. She stared at him, then cowered, scuttling along the solitary beach on the island of Brusnik.

Samantha took everything in; the acrid taste of jet fuel caught in the back of her mouth, the Adriatic had been forever spoiled by the enormity of Hunter's Ridge. The salt air scent forever gone.

A tiny black lizard scampered across the beach and then darted into a volcanic outcrop, one of many on Brusnik covered by the followers and sycophants of Lucas and his trio. Brainwashed believers in the Devil, or those along for the sheer rebellion against one of the world's greatest and yet most secret organisations. Fifty metres across, the shoreline and the lapping blue sea became Samantha's refuge amidst this gathering of the lost. But behind her, the strange technological behemoth, whose birth she had ushered in, dominated the skyline. The revolving spaceport and two miles of runway loomed. Twin vapour trails traced the heavens, a rocket at their head, bearing a satellite into space roared over the cheering masses.

My mother is likely there, celebrating, she thought. Both of them had been catapulted into the upper echelons of society and legend, but Samantha now wanted no part of it. This gathering would drive her nuts.

All her life, Samantha Scott had been dragged from place to place, country-to-country, in her mother's wake; Eva Scott worked for Anges de la Résurrection des Chevaliers—ARC. Twenty years ago, she had stopped the demons. Because of that, the world saw her mother as a saviour, so of course there was no time for a young daughter. Besides, Samantha was not like her older sister Nina, who dutifully followed in their mother's footsteps. Nonetheless, Samantha had not been completely neglected; she was well educated, had acquired skills … still, she rebelled.

"Unique parentage," her mother explained, refusing to offer additional details. She and Nina had unusual skill sets. Nina, for instance, could communicate with no more than a look, and Samantha suspected that she could also pull thoughts from anyone in her vicinity. It was the only thing she envied about her sister. Samantha's particular talent differed, although it too centered on communication—she could, in fact, summon the Devil. *Who wouldn't want that,* she mused?

"Do you want to try again?" Lucas urged. Leather-clad, in a long black trench coat, Lucas Rossi's long, greasy hair hung loose about his face, the waft of a seldom-washed body threatened to overpower her more than the menace in his voice.

It was in Geneva at the age of fourteen that Samantha first discovered her *skill*, the ability to call forth an image of a demon. The book she had used, a gift from her sister Nina, was full of arcane instruction. Fascinating. The first time she carved the symbols into the ground and cut her hand, spilling her own blood into the pattern, filled her with such immense euphoria she almost fainted. Power pulsed through her. Discovery. Her very own secret. Before long she rebelled; descending into the lowest common denominator, she styled herself as a priestess, gathering a flock of wannabe worshippers—little more than goths with attitude. It was two years ago, as she turned twenty that Lucas attached himself to her. The three girls: Tamsyn, Donna and Tracey, were his latest trio, his *coven*. The rest of the crowd contained those wishing or even plotting to take his place. They followed him aimlessly, living from moment-to-moment, devoid of any self-esteem or personal goals.

Lucas stayed, mostly because he had access to Samantha's unlimited funds, to which he regularly helped himself. He and his pathetic *coven* contented themselves in ritual sex, drugs and booze. Now all waited, excited, expectant.

Although Samantha had fallen, she had not slipped into the slime of wanton sex, money and meaningless rituals. None of it held any interest for her. As life went on, she became more and more disassociated from the world into which she was born.

"If I must," she muttered. The apathy was for his benefit. She wanted this. It was the only way she felt anything. Kneeling, she carefully redrew the summoning glyphs in the sand, hoping the water would remain calm now that the satellite was in orbit—her mother's crowning glory.

Strawberry-blond curls draped over her shoulder, obscuring her view; she took a moment to tie her hair back. She drew the familiar work from rote, the intricate markings magically rising out of the sand.

Lucas leaned in, fanatically checking her design. He leaned over her shoulder and Samantha tried not to recoil. He seldom brushed his teeth, leaving his breath putrid. She was his prize, and it pissed off her mother.

"Give me the knife," she instructed, raising her hand aloft.

He pressed the hilt into her palm with a flourish, playing to his crowd. Wooden, bound with string, it housed a blade of black conchoidal obsidian tinged with red. Razor sharp, never losing its edge, the blade could have been used to perform surgery. Rotating her hand Samantha used the point of the blade to score her scarred palm, bringing blood to flow across her hand and drip as she squeezed her fingers into the cut. She felt nothing.

Lucas began to chant an ancient language as her blood spilled into the complicated sand carving. She had long given up the rite of summoning, content to allow Lucas to impress his women. The three girls, made brave by the confident chant, crept closer, the crowd edging in behind. Samantha ignored them, watching for signs that the spell was a success.

The sand swirled—satisfaction —it had worked. She tightened her lips, bored with *any* sign. The downside was that her mother would know where she was—under her nose, spiting her with this act of insurrection.

A body that prevented a demon incursion two decades ago produced one capable of returning demonkind to earth. Samantha studied all the reports. Access to the full ARC database had given her information the average man would pale to consider. There she discovered the darkest secret—her father was a demon.

Now it was her secret; her companions could never know. The truth was that Samantha's father was *the* demon.

Samantha discovered his earthly name, as well—Madden Scott. He had taken the mantle as the protector of the nether realms. Through his own choice he had risen, or fallen, to become Satan.

Samantha wondered, *Was he a hero, or the ultimate villain?*

In the shadow of Hunters Ridge the sigil she formed in the sand turned from yellow to darker brown, and then to sullen red. The circle pulsed with her heartbeat, the base of her skull throbbed—she had succeeded. She knew she was close to drawing the likeness of the most-unholy himself.

Samantha glanced at Lucas, seeing the lust in his eyes for both the rite and the women around him. But she could feel his desire was mostly for her.

She knew she was sacrosanct, beyond his reach while she was in control. The other girls were his only outlet and he flaunted his dominance over them as if to impress Samantha with what she was missing.

What they both knew was that he could never conduct this rite. It was not in his blood.

With the glow, many of the crowd began to edge away, furtive glances seeking the easiest route back to the flotilla of speedboats anchored to the far side of the island. They came for the thrill, but now it had become a reality.

Lucas rose from a mutter to a shout as his chant reached its climax. "He comes," roared Lucas as he spread his arms wide.

Samantha ignored his theatrics, concentrating on the glowing circle of sand. Waves hissed into steam where they touched the edge of the circle, seaweed catching fire and leaving a fishy stench in the air. A steady red light glowed in the shade of the late afternoon, the vapour whirled, caught in the spell. The background roar of celebration, like a call from Hades, heightened the drama and in that moment, a form materialised into being.

To Samantha, it was nothing new. Since learning her power, she had seen the image of her father many times. She understood others saw what he wanted them to see, and on this evening, Samantha watched in silence as the body coalesced into a form not quite human.

Glowing yellow eyes and curled black horns of polished onyx sat atop a body with combat boots, black trousers and a well-muscled torso. For a moment this was it. No change. Behind her, Lucas and the trio were on their knees, foreheads pressed to the ground. Glowing yellow eyes and curled black horns of polished onyx sat atop a body with combat boots, black trousers and a well-muscled torso. For a moment this was it. No change. People were rooted still. Some gasping, others screaming. Behind her, Lucas and the trio were on their knees, foreheads pressed to the ground.

"Command us, Lucifer, mightiest of Hell's army," Lucas announced in grand tones.

"Idiot," Samantha muttered, shaking her curls loose in disgust. "Lucifer is quite someone else."

Turning back to the form held by her blood, she shrugged. "They never learn."

The horns shimmered, the eyes darkened. Time seemed to slow about her, as had always happened with the spell. Lucas' voice lowered, his movements sluggish. In place of the evil perceived by others, a man's face looked back at her from the sullen ruby glow, A long dark ponytail hung behind. The pain returned, crushing her. Every time their eyes met she wished for death, to be by his side. Her father, in a place she couldn't reach him. Stubble framed a look of concern, or maybe exasperation. It seemed to say, *And yet, you bring them to me, time after time.*

"What can I do?" Samantha asked. "It's the only way I get to see you. Mom never arranged proper visitation rights. Seeing you impresses his flock, keeps him off my back."

What would you have me do?

"Take me with you, Dad. There's nothing for me here. I miss you."

That's not an option. However, it's about time you walked away from them, daughter.

A smile crept round the edges of her mouth. "Do you have something in mind?"

Satan grinned, and winked.

She chuckled. She was not a cruel person but her father had proven on many occasions that he needed no more than a look. Satan, it seemed, had quite an impish sense of humour. *It's time to move on. You know what to do. What you should be doing.* Unspoken words were delivered with an inclination of his head. Time moved normally once again.

"Stand," she commanded, silencing Lucas and his gibbering. "Stand and behold the true face of your Lord and Master."

Lucas scowled at the assumption of her authority but the three girls stood, obedient to anybody with a will stronger than their own.

Samantha witnessed no change as her father gazed upon the four parasites as they began to pale, their eyes fixed on his face.

"What is he doing?" Tamsyn cried out. "Those teeth, the blood. Those eyes — I." Her hands shook, as did her legs, and losing her balance, Tamsyn began to scream, with Tracey and Donna joining the hysteric chorus. Around them the crowd gave a similar reaction, the ear-splitting screams held immobile by his gaze.

Lucas was mute, his eyes wide, tracking the demon with his shaking head. He cried out, the scream strangled in his throat.

The crowd, given their freedom at last turned and bolted as one. The three girls ran, gibbering and howling back up the beach, followed by their master.

Samantha smiled at her father.

He raised his eyebrows. 'Job well done' was the satisfied impression he gave. A nod, and a wistful look and he was gone.

The air teemed with sorrow, with regret. Satan, or as Samantha longed to call him, Pop, disappeared, leaving a knot in her stomach. All that remained of the summoning was a feeling of emptiness and a circle of charred rocks. Samantha turned away, touched unexpectedly by the game. Could there be another way?

She followed the four sets of footprints leading up the beach, listening to the screams mixed with cries and incoherent shouting. The island was only a few hundred meters wide; she watched Tamsyn and Donna for a while, their backs turned away. After such an unmanning, Lucas would avoid her until his lust for power overcame his fear of the consequences. She didn't know where Tracy had gone. The growl of boat engines in the distance meant some of the gibbering mass had made it off the island.

Samantha sat in the sand, watching the sunset. The sky softened with the onset of distant mists. The dark at the edge of the horizon was familiar, a moody counterpoint to the emptiness she felt within.

A plane flew toward her. Chaff exploded in three directions, dropping vertically as the military celebrated with their own *angel*, as it was called. Wings of smoke from the flares expanded. *If there were angels*, Samantha thought, *they kept well away from humanity.*

She heard footsteps in the sand behind her and turned, seeing the fear-ravaged face of Lucas above her. His eyes were wide, haunted, the flesh of his cheeks withered as if recoiling from the face he had witnessed. His hands clawed, reached toward her.

"What … what did you do to … to me?"

"Do to you? Don't you mean what have I done for you? The same thing I've always done for you, Lucas: Brought your demons to life. Is that not my role? To make you look good in front of your followers?"

His clawed hands were now fists, as anger rose out of Lucas, dominating his will. His neck mottled with a fresh flush of blood, he took a step closer, a waft of stale body odour assaulting her nostrils. An all-too-familiar face presented itself, that of the man she knew to have bullied his way through those who did not accede to his wishes. And of course she knew it was all her fault; he had told her so too many times. She waited for the accusation, "You made that happen."

With a casual deliberateness, Samantha stood. While not as tall as Lucas, she made a much tougher target when on her feet. "Funny. I remember you chanting the rite of summoning. What's the matter, Lucas? Finally see something you didn't like?"

"Tracey ran straight into the sea. She kept running, right off the cliffs back there." Lucas threw his hand up behind him. "The rest of them. My followers. Gone. What did you make them see? Tracey lost her mind. This is your fault."

Samantha followed his hand. Spume sprayed up as waves hit the rocks beyond, specks moistening her face. "This shouldn't have happened to her, Lucas. You know the risk involved. People see what they see. This isn't some parlour trick, some childish fantasy."

He stepped into her space and slapped her hard across the cheek.

She fell onto the sand, the world reeling around her. She tasted the coppery salt of blood, as Lucas stood over her, gloating.

"The risk is now your responsibility. You fail me again and you … unhnnn…"

Lucas collapsed to the ground, the twin electrodes of a Taser protruded from his chest. As he spasmed, Samantha rolled to avoid contact, finding herself looking at a pair of black leather combat boots. She shook her head. Busted.

"It comes to something when ARC sends the head of Global Security out to look for a mere girl."

John Wolverton reached down, offering a hand up. "You were never a mere girl, Sammy. Playtime's done. You're overdue to meet your mother."

Chapter Two

They're always watching me. Will I ever be alone? Samantha wondered, reaching for Wolverton's outstretched hand and pulling herself up, hand being crushed in an iron grip.

Although Past sixty, Wolverton retained a commanding presence, a giant bear of a man. While those around him expected suits and formality, cargo shorts and tank tops for him were *de rigueur*, the tattoos on his arms and legs still bright despite age. He was a fighter with muscles once extensive, now lean and tight. It seemed he would always be strong, never going to fat. Bald with a bushy beard that young Samantha had tugged many times over the years, he was a father figure to her, continually training and teaching her. She had learned to fly under his tutelage, and when she had crossed swords with her mother, John had patience for her, even if he did not agree with her actions. She confided in him, and he held her secrets sacrosanct. He was the only father she'd had, the only man of integrity around that had given her his time with no expectations.

Behind him, several black-clad ARC operatives waited, three aiming machine guns in the direction of the remaining stragglers. The fourth retrieved the taser from the still-prone Lucas, now squawking as the electrodes were jerked from his chest.

"I'm only worth four?" Samantha asked, nodding in the direction of the operatives. What she didn't say was that she would have run had there been fewer commandos.

"Only room for you, me, and four in the boat."

Samantha grinned, nodding to Lucas and the two girls who lingered, "Maybe they can get back the way we came. I did all the navigation, anyway."

Leading the small team to the black speedboat moored against the volcanic outcrop, Samantha jumped in without waiting for assistance. She was a capable woman despite her outward faults, not waiting for others to pass sentence on her actions, nor caring whether they did if she felt she was right. When their opinion didn't matter to her, she dismissed them out of hand. The only person who persisted in making judgement was her mother.

As John gunned the throttle of the speedboat, seagulls shrieked in protest at the noise from the engine and the air traffic in the distance as they swirled above. Samantha stared at the superstructure of Hunters Ridge looming and expanding on the horizon. Several miles out in the Adriatic, the only way in or out was by air or sea. Planes were taking off from the runway amid ships; the celebrations concluded. Samantha shifted her balance as the boat skipped over the surface of the water.

"What does she want this time?" She sounded weary and she knew it.

Wolverton scanned the water between Brusnik and the nearby superstructure. One distant tanker from the cargo port of Trieja, the only port allowed to send traffic to the ARC project, was preparing to dock.

"She worries about you, Sammy. She might not show it but your stunts scare her. You girls are the only link to your father she has left."

"It's not like she had many to begin with," Samantha retorted. She knew that her mother's primary concern was not for her; her mother's demands were always about what she needed or wanted.

Wolverton didn't answer.

They passed under the outer edge of the superstructure. Massive concrete supports plunged into the water around them like the legs of some squatting monstrosity resting on the bedrock. Above, the control centre, a building the size of a football stadium, rotated on its mechanical base. Her mother had said, "The view of the Adriatic is too good to waste on a runway and a launchpad."

Wolverton eased the boat to into a dock built inside one of the supports lit with industrial lighting. It seemed alien in contrast to the beautiful sunset. The boat bobbed as it was tied off and as soon as it was secured, Samantha jumped onto the bolted walkway which stretched from pillar to pillar. She watched the waves lap through the honeycombed metal. "Come on then, old man," she taunted her guide and protector.

Wolverton snorted and pulled himself up behind her. "Not too old to put you in your place, young lady."

They followed the walkway up as it spiralled around the inside of the structure until they came to a pair of doors. Two operatives with machine guns, loosely held, manned the entrance. They nodded to Wolverton and opened the doors.

To Samantha, it seemed an imposing route for any would-be assailant, but whatever. She peered over the railing at the lapping water and the blue-green algae a hundred feet below while John summoned the lift, the metal cold and unyielding. Anybody who might try to gain entrance from the sea would surely fail. This wasn't just a technological miracle; it was a fortress.

A bleep and the lift door opened, as John tapped her shoulder and nodded. The two guards remained stationary while Samantha passed.

"Just try to be polite," John advised as they rose through the superstructure. "She might not show it but your mother only wants the best for you."

Samantha scowled. "I'm only doing this out of respect for you. Mother only wants what's best for mother. They have no time for me, nor I for them. The sooner you and the rest accept that, the better we'll all be. I'm going in there and coming straight back out. Mark my words." It was hard to love and respect someone as distant and cold as her mother, as hard as she had tried, and she hoped John would finally admit she was right; they'd had this conversation too often before. Instead, he huffed and sighed. She saw the frustration flash in his eyes.

"You're too much like Daniel. The time will come when you have to accept responsibility and grow up."

As much as John was right, the comparison to the elderly head of ARC irritated her. She rounded on him. "Grow up? Accept responsibility? John, I'm twenty-three years old. I have a degree in International Diplomacy from MIT. I fly planes and helicopters, too, and I speak three languages. How much more growing up do I need to do? Besides, Daniel Guyomard has no time for protocol and he runs the entire organisation. I don't want any part of this. What more do I have to do to prove this to everybody round here? If Pop were around —"

"Your father would tell you the exact same damned thing, girl. There's more to this world than your own wants and needs." John frowned, a tightness around his eyes. He was keeping something from her. "There's a difference between learning skills and applying them, Sammy. It's a skill when you fly a plane for pleasure. It's responsibility to fly one to further someone else's purpose. If you gave your mother a chance instead of flying off the handle every time you meet, you might understand that."

"Like Nina has?" As she spoke the words, Samantha knew she was behaving badly. She loved her sister, yet resented Nina being so compliant—never questioning, always acceding to their mother's wishes.

The lift stopped, opening onto the edge of the runway, with a stunning sunset and a brisk wind. The red sun dipped into the sea where Italy lay over the edge of the horizon. She caught her breath as her hair blew back, and despite her scepticism Samantha couldn't help admiring the sheer size of the construction.

She stepped out onto the hot runway, the day's heat radiating off the asphalt, filling her nose with fumes from the painted markings underfoot. Far above, more seabirds floated on the thermals, out of reach of the air traffic chaos. Instinctively, Samantha ducked as a twin-engine Cessna Citation roared past. She shielded her eyes against the glare of the dazzling runway lights. Apparently, more dignitaries were leaving for home. She imagined them in the executive offices atop the control tower, elegantly dressed, clinking champagne glasses as the rocket lifted skyward.

The less elite guests were at the other end of the runway, queuing up to board small business planes along with larger carriers and even a private Boeing 747.

Not speaking, John ushered Samantha across the runway, hurrying her into a waiting transport as ground crew frantically waved them out of the way. The noise was deafening and Samantha held her hands over her ears until they reached the rotating mass of the control tower.

As she disembarked Samantha said, "I'll try to control myself in there, but I'm making no promises, John."

"See that you do, girl," he growled. "What you did today was deliberately goading your mother, and because of that, ARC itself. There are only so many second chances. You've had more than most." He pressed the call button, and the glass door slid open for Samantha. "Go on up. There are a lot of important people up there."

Stepping into the slowly rotating structure, Samantha watched the old man disappear into the distance. She felt the whirl of the building at the edges, where she could see the rest of the runway, then turned to face the enormity of the cavernous control centre.

Well of course there would be a lot of important people. On a day like today everybody would want to party. She looked at her reflection in the glass and saw an athletic figure framed in strawberry blonde curls. *They'll just have to take me the way I am. This isn't my party, after all.*

The lobby of the control centre was palatial. Tropical plants topped out at three times Samantha's height, nourished by subfloor water and lighting intended to mimic daylight. Glass sculpture, *objects d'art*, and water features designed by world-renowned artists refracted the light, occasionally creating rainbows. ARC named the lobby the 'Orbiting Tropical Gyratory', but Samantha called it 'Fairyland'. It was all for show, an aspect of ARC the dignitaries appreciated and understood. The politicians and relations experts in the organisation brought everybody here. World leaders mingled with the high and mighty in business and social circles.

None of that impressed Samantha; she ignored it all. It was an extension of her mother, an attempt at a calming influence. Something the world sorely needed. What mattered stayed out of the public eye and that was where she headed.

She noted the lingering VIPs gawking at her in alarm or outright disgust as she passed. She smiled and walked past; if a roughed-up rock chick was part of the celebrations, so what?

She made her way to the central column rising from the middle of the building, this one constructed of opaque glass. Behind the demure door were offices with a receptionist behind a small desk. The middle-aged blonde in a couture black trouser suit waited, scanning the surroundings.

"Miss Turner," Samantha nodded and smiled. She certainly had authority issues with her mother but she was perfectly capable of being polite.

"Miss Scott," Hollie Turner's face broke into a knowing smile. A long-time acquaintance of Samantha's Aunt Clare, Hollie had been part of ARC for as long as Samantha could remember. Nonetheless, her role was precise—trusted to guard the gate but never enter the realm. "The suits are sure gonna love that get-up."

Samantha glanced down once more at her bedraggled state. "Oh this? I just threw it together, last minute. You know how it is."

Both women burst out laughing.

Hollie pressed a button below the desk, then cautioned "Be good in there."

"Whose in?"

"All of them."

"What is this? Some sort of court?"

Hollie shrugged. "No idea, love. I just man the gate." Hollie waved Samantha on as two panels in the glass cleared and retracted, revealing a doorway.

Feeling a wave of anxiety, shaking hands and dry mouth, Samantha left the opulence behind and entered a glass corridor walling off a bank of computers. Not a person in the rooms, just unending technology. The brains of the global organisation were in stark contrast to this palace of perfection. It was dark, except for the countless red lights to the waiting elevator, its doors agape. The air was not the usual stale reek, something she and her mother clashed over. At least this issue would not test their wills. No doubt there would be something else.

She stepped in and instantly the doors clicked shut. Sudden upward force made her legs buckle as it raced up five floors to the top of the control tower. It took only moments but uncertainty loomed large, as did the face of Lucas. He was vengeful and she had deserted him on Brusnik. Security would see him safe but at what cost to her?

Samantha was still considering the ramifications of her actions when she realised she was not alone. The lift doors opened and a roomful of people turned, staring at her.

She gazed back at the suited, formal group looking at her with disdainful expressions and gestures. A figure pushed through, separating them with gentle hands. "Excuse me, ladies and gentlemen, the guest of honor is here," Nina Scott said in a commanding voice.

The stunned press of bodies parted, leaving Samantha staring at her sister. Only a year apart in age, Nina nonetheless appeared many years older with her severe ponytail of platinum-blond hair, maroon leisure suit, and thick-rimmed glasses. She was the archetypal corporate sort, embracing this world of secrets. Samantha felt little in common with Nina. Other than blood and slim bodies passed on from their mother, they did not share commonality. Samantha's curly hair reflected her wild nature. According to those who had known him, she had too much of her father in her, while Nina was her mother's daughter in every way.

"There you are," Nina said, her tone neutral, though to Samantha it rang of disapproval. She was, at least, present. "Been playing on the beach again I hear."

"Not that anybody here cares," Samantha muttered. "Lucas and my friends had to leave."

Nina placed an arm about Samantha's shoulders, steering her through the press of the murmuring exclusive. Samantha nodded to Gila Byron, one of the ARC Council with whom she was familiar; An Egyptian with grey streaks in her otherwise black hair and a flawless olive complexion, the ageless Gila and her mother were close friends. The story was that Gila was instrumental in her mothers' rise within the organisation. Other than Gila, Daniel and John Wolverton, the rest of them Samantha barely knew.

"You might be surprised how much these people care," Nina countered. "Our family has a legacy here. It's time you embraced it."

"Maybe. I always felt this place did nothing for me. There's so much more out there."

"Like hunting down strange rituals in Indonesia?"

"Papua New Guinea," Samantha corrected her sister on reflex, realising she had just been baited. "At least those people live within their traditions. This organisation erases most beliefs and rituals through technology."

Nina's face went flat, a quick flash of anger in her eyes.

"Really, Samantha—that tired argument again? You know what this place is, what they hope to achieve. You know our history. You are just as much a part of it, whether you acknowledge this or not."

"Oh, I understand. I'm not sorry, Nina."

Nina led Samantha to the front of the assembled group, pressing a button on another set of glass doors.

"Ladies and gentlemen if you will be so kind as to follow me please?" It smacked of an order rather than a request.

Samantha followed her sister to the front row of plush blue office chairs lined up in ranks. A woman sat three seats along, facing forward. Her grey streaked brown hair was tied back into a ponytail, exactly in the same way as her daughter's hair. It was easy to tell that Nina followed Eva Scott in habit and mannerism.

Nina sat next to their mother, squeezing her hand in affirmation. Samantha had no words for the moment, and sat beside her sister, squirming to get comfortable on the thin cushioning. Something was up. Her mother kept her face forward but there was a distinct reddening around her eyes. Samantha leaned forward to comment but Nina forestalled her with a warning glance.

Whatever your game, now is not the time. Her sister's voice sounded in her head. Nina's gift. Samantha could summon her father's image but Nina could speak directly into the mind. They were both offspring of a demon, but Nina was dealt the best hand.

The final few sat, John Wolverton closing the doors behind them, and a sombre shaven-headed man with a slight paunch stepped up to the podium. Eyes normally strong and full of confidence were sunken. Swanson Guyomard regarded them all, sparing a hollow glance for Samantha, as he looked each person, one by one, in the eye.

His voice was subdued as he leaned forward. He cleared his voice and said, "It is with utmost regret that my beloved uncle and head of the ARC Council, Daniel Guyomard, has passed away."

Samantha gasped.

Chapter Three

It was one of those moments that defined a person: The end of an era.

A gasp rose as one from the gathered notables. Samantha's own cry of loss was lost among the tide. People began to weep, reaching for handkerchiefs. Many expressed their disbelief. If John Wolverton had been her father, Daniel Guyomard had been her grandfather. A wicked sense of humor akin to her own, he had always been welcoming to her. She had imprinted him as she grew up. His lack of regard for protocol was infectious.

In front of them Swanson raised his hands to quiet the audience. His voice was shaky. "There are protocols in place for this event. His death occurred only moments ago, although it was not, in the grand scheme of things, unexpected. My uncle was neither a healthy, nor a young man. There will be a proper time for mourning, but at present we require continuity. In this place, especially in this place it is important to remember that ARC has a responsibility to the past, to the future. To mankind."

Samantha glanced about her. Nina placed her arm about Samantha's shoulders, her head bowed. Feeling compassion for her sister, Samantha squeezed Nina's hand, not making eye contact for fear they might both break down. Instead she concentrated on Swanson as he tried to reassure everybody; he was focussed on nothing else. Nearby an elderly lady she had never met sobbed into her hands. Daniel had been a regular part of her mother's life as part of the ARC Council.

A kindly man with a rebellious streak, his own appointment occurred during an emergency; a flood had hit Geneva when Nina was born and countless had died. He was a man loved by many, respected by all. Worshipped by her. Samantha's eyes welled up.

Samantha knew the history: The Guyomards had a special claim on the rite of succession within ARC due to the organisation being formed by Swanson's ancestor Jerome.

A face caught her eye from a few seats down the row behind her. Thorsten Guyomard winked at her and grinned. Only a few years older than her, he was added to the ARC council at the behest of the man now speaking. Cocksure, bordering on arrogant, Thorsten wrung every drop of benefit out of his position. Samantha couldn't help but like the man. With his sun-bleached blond hair and infectious nature it was hard not to. Yet now, his disregard for the sombre news ate at her.

"...as such it is only proper that we hold a ballot for the next Chair of the council," Swanson concluded.

Murmurs raced through the audience. It was hard for Samantha to pick up on individual words, but 'succession' and 'dynasty' were prevalent.

"If I may," said John Wolverton from where he stood just inside the door, "there is a simple solution here." He crossed to the podium, standing next to Swanson and holding the lectern on both sides with his immense hands. Samantha could feel the tension. Was this a coup?

"Let me say on behalf of the entire Council and senior staff how sorry we are, Swanson. Your uncle was a man of many talents, and he led the organisation well." John turned toward him. "But this is not the time for radical decisions and wholesale change. The council functions efficiently as is. The staff know their roles and there is clarity between all. Everybody in this room knows what happened when you invoked clause three of the charter of the Council of Anges de la Résurrection des Chevaliers: In time of imminent demonic threat, a member of the family Guyomard may assume the role of Council Chair, independent of the vote of the Council. There is no imminent demonic threat. The world is safe. But I insist that you now take up the role which you should have had twenty years ago. Take the chair, Swanson. Take the chair."

The chant began immediately. Samantha wasn't sure who started it, either Thorsten, or Gila, but both stood, repeating, "Take the chair, take the chair."

Moments later, her mother joined in, the faces all around her still streaked with tears, although she had not openly wept. Samantha watched, fascinated by the momentous turn of events?

Swanson held his hands aloft, entreating the room for silence. "Is there anybody who objects to this course of action?" Strangely, he looked directly at Samantha.

She shrugged.

"Consider the motion carried," John announced. "Long live the king."

The room chuckled.

"Thank you for coming, Swanson continued. "It makes the hardship of losing my uncle that much more bearable that you are all behind me. Will the councilmembers please remain? We have matters to discuss."

With the dismissal, Samantha started to rise only to find a hand clamped above her elbow.

"Not you," Nina said. "You stay this time. There are things you need to hear."

The room emptied around her, only a dozen or so people remained.

"If you would, please," motioned Swanson, opening a door to the council chamber.

One factor was consistent in the world of ARC. No matter where they had a conference room, it looked just like Geneva. 'A home away from home' is how many referred to such places with its oval glass table and pale blue lighting, all of it Spacious and airy. To Samantha, it was bland and repetitive.

She took a seat next to Nina near the door, along with a tall woman she didn't recognise, and a man in a sharp black suit.

"Alexander, how many more times do I have to remind you that your place is at the table now?" Swanson held out a hand and flicked it toward the table where there were two free seats. Her mother sat opposite her, regarding Samantha in silence. There was disapproval in that gaze, and a steely resolve.

"I'm sorry, sir," the sharp black suit said, standing next to the tall woman, as he rose. "I was taught never to presume."

"By your father, no less." Swanson paused to smile. "We all miss him."

"That's Alexander Steadman?" Samantha's hushed tones reached her sister's ears.

It is. His father was a legend in ARC, saving the archives in Geneva from destruction.

"I remember Mom telling the story," Samantha whispered. "He was a hero."

Nina nudged her. Several of the Council members were glancing their way. *Just nod.*

Samantha let a small smile creep across her face.

Swanson had turned to sign the ancient ARC charter on the council table as Steadman took his seat. "Your reasons for being here are threefold. First, we have an empty seat at this table. Are we agreed on the choice for candidate?"

Heads turned as the council looked to each other.

"I don't think there is any dissention this time," said an elderly American woman with white hair.

"Good. Bring her in." Swanson waved at the door, which slid open. Samantha's mouth dropped. "Aunt Clare?"

Clare Rosser winked at her and strode into the room, pausing only to nod to the woman seated to Nina's left. Clare was their mother's half-sister and was introduced to them only ten years ago. Apparently she was recruited into the organisation before Nina was born. She was well-loved by everybody, a consummate professional with a tenacious knack of rooting out oddities in the world. A former forensic analyst, she left nothing uncovered. Moreover she had accomplished her great feats while learning to live with type-1 diabetes.

Taking the final seat and brushing a stray lock of hair over her ear, Clare said, "Thank you for the opportunity."

"You deserve it, Clare," Swanson cooed. "You've produced results consistently and above expectations and built a formidable team. Many people in this world are safe because of you and your people. We may yet authorise a new branch of ARC - covert hunters or some such."

Clare smiled. "That doesn't even begin to describe us."

"As things stand you will be a non-sitting member of this Council. We can hardly tether you to Geneva."

"Fine. Charlotte Benson there will run things when you need me."

At mention of her name, the identity of Nina's neighbour was revealed and she stood. An imposing figure, Charlotte Benson was a woman perhaps of forty, standing a good six feet tall. "We will be fine," she reassured the council, and took her seat.

"I have no doubt. Now Clare it is custom for me to introduce the Council. First, the sitting members, the permanent base. Gila Byron is my new deputy and Council co-ordinator."

Gila flashed a welcoming smile. The two knew each other well.

"Next, Swanson continued, "well, you know most of the council already. Tricia Pelirrojo and Gaspard Antroobus are all sitting members alongside John Wolverton and your sister "Some of our non-sitting members may be new to you. Forrest Kyle is ex-Shikari and works closely with Eva on our technology wing. Alexander Steadman heads up Biblical Interpretation. Mohammed El-Rafi is head of Grail, our artifact research wing. Jeanette Gibson, our media relations boss, I am sure is familiar to you, and our last councilmember is my cousin Thorsten."

Samantha raised her hand. "Why are we here? Nina and I aren't councilmembers."

This interruption earned Samantha a look of venom from her mother and an amused smile from several of the other notables.

"Ladies and gentlemen, I believe you all know Nina Scott and her younger sister Samantha," Swanson spoke with barely-contained amusement, which served to additionally irritate Eva.

Swanson's face turned serious once again. This was clearly no time for levity. "We're here for several reasons, Samantha. Firstly to fill the spare council seat—"

"But there are only supposed to be five sitting members."

"Sammy!" her mother warned, getting visibly angry as her eyes widened in a glare.

"No, Eva, that's a justified question. One that shows young Samantha has as good a claim to be here as anybody. In answer I would say to you that due to the age and role of many here, we need a larger permanent council body in place. The time has come for expansion."

Samantha ground her teeth at being referred to as 'young'. She was about to retort when Swanson got there first.

"Secondly, as the Sky Sling has been successful in placing our satellite in orbit, the time has come to unveil it to the world. We shall get to that in due course. What is a more pressing matter is your behaviour, young lady. The time has come for you to account for your actions."

"And just what exactly is that supposed to mean?" Samantha stood, coming to the edge of the table between Gaspard Antroobus and Tricia Pelirrojo.

"It means the days of you attempting to raise demons are at an end," her mother said from the far end of the table. "It means that one way or another, your rebellious streak is about to be curbed. ARC has need of you."

This wasn't a reprimand. Her mother's tone was in earnest. Eyes wide and pleading, she was serious. "I don't want any part of this," Samantha replied, defiant. "I didn't want to know when I was growing up and my life was being decided for me. Nothing's changed."

"Sammy, there's much more at stake than you know." Nina stood, crossing the conference room to stand behind their mother.

Samantha felt completely alone facing all the silent accusations from across the glass table. She had committed her fair share of misdemeanours. Daniel's death put it all into perspective. There was no longer any excuse to fall back on. She took a deep breath, closed her eyes, willing her heart to slow. "Nothing's changed," she repeated.

"What do you demand of me that the all-powerful ARC cannot accomplish? You have the foremost experts in the world, governments at your beck and call. You don't need me."

Her response caused raised eyebrows among some. Eva sighed, her face drawn. Samantha felt the same impasse she always had.

Nina turned to Swanson, who picked up a remote from the lectern. One click of a button locked the door, sealing them in. A second click turned off the lighting. A screen came into view. A picture of bloody carnage filled the screen, dozens of rats missing parts of their heads.

"Rats with their faces chewed off," Swanson emphasised.

"So?" Samantha challenged, still ready to question, unwilling to bend to their will.

"They chewed off each-other's heads. The natural order of things has been upset. That's not all. Since the incursion twenty years ago, we've monitored and ended any number of threats." The screen changed to a dust-covered farm. Rickety fences were held together by rusting nails, steel drums cut in half to make food troughs and a very perplexed farmer looking on.

"Here in Africa we have a case of a cow feasting on sheep. Nothing could tempt the cow. Normal feed, water had no effect. The animal wouldn't touch it. But it was left alone in a pen with a sheep and the following morning the sheep was dead with the cow feeding from its corpse."

"What has any of this to do with me?" Samantha asked. "Oddly behaving animals? Doesn't that warrant your attention?"

Her Aunt Clare stood, brandishing a handful of documents. She began to toss them across the table toward her. "Goats eating chickens. People claiming dinosaurs are clawing their way out of the ground. Look at these, Sammy."

Samantha rose and crossed to the table. She opened the covers as the documents slid to her. "Jellyfish slime coating rocks?"

"Not just rocks, an entire fjord in Norway went purple with this stuff. And not just in Norway. Across the planet, at exactly the same time. Thailand, Darwin, Krestovaya in Russia, and there are reports of this happening in Lake Victoria in Uganda."

"And they don't get jellyfish there?"

"Sammy, the species is saltwater, and it's filling a landlocked fresh-water lake in the middle of a continent. This is only the natural phe-nomena. I came here straight from hunting Voydanoy."

This meant nothing to Samantha.

Clare threw another folder at her. This contained a photo of a hu-manoid creature with a wide, froglike mouth and pale green skin covered in warts. "People don't want to believe in this stuff, and so we keep it quiet. That's why we seldom reveal the real purpose be-hind this organisation. Do you understand? It's also why we don't go around raising images of demons—Voydanoy, Viruñas, Imps, Sprites, and Nuns that can absorb people's sins from their bodies. We have been dealing with a global catastrophe in the making for the last twenty years. You're here because, like it or not, you and your sister are deeply involved in the cause and consequence of one immutable fact."

"And that is?"

Clare leaned forward, placing her hands on the table, one atop Eva's, and said, "Religion is dead."

Chapter Four

Samantha dropped the files to the table, now further annoyed. This entire gathering seemed more and more like a set-up, an intervention to try and teach her a lesson. They didn't know a damn thing about her—not really. Was Clare suggesting somehow the fault of waning belief was at Samantha's feet?

"You're trying to pin the fact that people don't go to church on me? Samantha's voice was low, cautious. Why don't you throw in the Holocaust and tidal waves while you're at it?"

"Samantha, you misunderstand." Her mother finally spoke. There was not a lot of emotion in those words. Frustration perhaps. Regret? Maybe. "Now she speaks. Why don't you enlighten me, Mother? How exactly should I interpret those words?"

Eva remained seated, her eyes hard. "Since before you were born, there's been a gradual disregard for religion. The secular nature of the world has come to define much of what we say and do. It was always accepted that some would always consider themselves spiritual. ARC is an organisation based on the melding of religion and technology. Swanson and Gila are Coptics, for example. I, as you know, once practised aspects of psychology. We take the best of both worlds."

"Some might say you still practise what you preach," Samantha accused; she noted her sister's frown.

"The same people, were they to see your ploys, might start saying similar of you," Eva retorted. "You have to understand why your distractions could have such dire consequences. When the darkness fell, when demons tried to colonise the earth, it was my blood—" Eva looked to Nina, taking her hand, "Our blood—that was the key. Our blood could have opened the gates of Hell, but events proved otherwise. Your blood runs the same as your sisters. Like it or not, Samantha, you're a person of religious significance."

"I have no idea what you mean." Samantha realised how stupid she sounded as the words slipped past her lips. She snorted a laugh. "I'm sorry. Of course I do. I speak to the dead because the living aren't interested."

Her mother stood, removing her suit jacket. An angry star-shaped scar was noticeable on her forearm as she reached over to tug at her collar. A five-pointed mark, a replica of the scar, was on the skin of her neck.

Nina pulled up her sleeve, revealing a six-pointed star. Samantha bore an identical mark on her right thigh. "We both have these, Sammy. You know it means we are scions of the House of David."

"I'm not Jewish," Samantha hissed. "I'm not anything."

"And therein lies the problem," Swanson concluded.

Samantha stepped back from the desk. She could make no sense of what they were saying to her. "This meeting's been convened because you've decided I need to get religion?"

Mohammed El Rafi moved to speak but Alexander Steadman stood, shifting the focus in the room to himself. "If I may, Council?" He didn't wait for permission. "Samantha, what your mother and these preeminent members of the Council are trying to put into words is, in fact, quite different, yet at the same time, is exactly that. You are not being requested to don a cassock, so to speak. The rest of the world is shedding their vestments. Literally. They are losing faith."

El Rafi stood to join his new colleague. An old friend of her mother's, Samantha was inclined to ignore him, but Steadman's words intrigued her. "Won't you take my seat?"

"I'm happy where I am," she stated. "I'll have a seat here."

Those beside her made room as Clare brought a seat to the table for her. There was no way she was going to sit that close to her mother.

"You understand my position within this Council, yes?"

"Head of Biblical Interpretation," Samantha replied. "You take what happens in the world and apply it to texts and scrolls for meaning."

Steadman nodded in approval. "Good. Mohammed heads up Grail, which looks for physical evidence of religion. Our departments have similar remits, although differing methods. What we tend to agree on is the current interpretation of the world. What happened twenty years ago precipitated this current state of affairs. Although we were saved from disaster, there is a lingering aftertaste, a festering sore that has not healed."

Samantha glanced at her mother. Eva's worn face could not hide the pain as she stared down at the table. The spark of a once vibrant and energetic woman had dimmed. This was all about her father.

"That being the death of religion?"

"Exactly." Steadman's face was animated as he elaborated. "Imagine, if you will, a physical link between Heaven and Earth, a conduit through which prayer is heard. Sever that conduit and what happens?"

"If you are correct, prayers are no longer heard."

"And in some cases, not answered where once they were."

Samantha leaned back in her seat. It was not hard to understand their logic. She had grown up hearing snippets of her father's great sacrifice. "You think Dad was responsible?"

Steadman shook his head. "No, I do not. He was not the only one to make a sacrifice. We lost many in that ill-feted journey, including—

"Metatron," Eva finished for him. "He said his name was Metatron."

"Who?"

Eva looked up at her. The pain of loss still shone in her mom's eyes. "A man we met once. He helped us. He called himself Janus. He took the fight to those beyond."

Samantha looked around the table. Not one face registered surprise. "You all know of this?"

"If you didn't distance yourself behind distractions you would know too," Nina chided her. "What do you know of the name?"

"An angel. Called the Scribe by some. The Voice of God by others. Are you saying he is the reason this is all happening?"

"We can't be sure," Mohammed stood, pacing around the room. "What we do know is this: In the two decades since the demon incursion—yes, a demon incursion is what happened—ARC has gone a long way to silencing the rumours. People forget, move on, dismiss what is incredible, and live for the mundane. Yet as they accept that reality, changes still occur. They are small at first, but with increasing frequency, they become noticeable. And then they gather a following. The oddities: The jellyfish, the strange animal behaviour. It's just the start. Religions starts to splinter, attendances fall. This might not appear much to the person on the street, but religious attendance globally has reduced by thirty percent. All religion—Catholic Mass, Muslim prayer—you name it; the numbers don't lie."

"There are some that say numbers are as close as you get to the handwriting of God," commented Tricia Pellirojo.

"You could be right," Mohammed agreed. "To be honest, we are running out of ideas. But as religion wanes, these strange occurrences increase."

Clare added, "I'm here because the occurrences are physical in nature too. Monsters out of legend, creatures that can suck a person dry of their sins, bizarre scientific experiments on horses that should not be physically possible. I've investigated them all. The Voydanoy are a prime example. Water creatures with frog-like faces who steal children?"

"Sounds considerably far-fetched," Samantha dismissed the example.

"And yet not only do we have one in our lab, we have at this table a dissenter who raises images of demons for kicks," Clare argued back. "This lack of interest in religion is reaching epidemic proportions."

Samantha listened and watched as the arguments flew across the room like flies batted with swatters—first Mohammed...

"This is more than a lack of interest. This is a forced increase in apathy. Do you have the coverage, Jeanette?"

Jeanette Gibson, head of media, swatted back, "I do." She dialed a few buttons into the conference table console, and a series of stills followed, the black and white photos showing groups of people surrounding rocks and other items as if praying to them. "A marked resurfacing of Pagan rituals. People are disappearing into mysterious cults of their own free will and never being seen again. These cults are no longer clandestine. They're actively recruiting. As religious attendance decreases, the interest in pre-religion increases. The world is slowly reverting. Mankind craves ritual and ceremony, looking to worship idols if they believe religion doesn't hold the answer. The names are many: Xris, Vodec, Drue, Lost, Heaven's Gate. We are struggling to understand their draw. As the years have gone by, one group, though quiet at first, has been making increasing noise—Aeon Fall."

A picture of a hiker flashed on the screen. He stood atop a hill staring off into an infinity of mountainsides. In the sky above him hung bright red letters that read, 'Your God is dead'. Hanging over a lower path, the words 'Aeon Fall' were printed in neat white letters.

Samantha frowned. "It looks like a war propaganda poster. Who are they?"

"Nobody knows," Jeanette replied. "At first nothing more than rumours of an underground organisation, nothing more than a collection of conveniently-placed street messages. Graffiti on churches and the like. They were no threat. That was ten years back. Soon we started hearing from multiple sources of the formation of a leadership structure."

Samantha drummed her fingers on the conference table, setting off another of the interactive panels under the glass. The bright blue glare startled her back to the present. "So? What has that to do with all these strange occurrences? With ARC?"

"It became clear to those that chose to take notice, there was a problem with religion beyond filling churches and temples. We attempted to mitigate the negative effects, but Aeon Fall picked up on the crisis as well. They encouraged it and aren't attempting to hide from the public eye either."

The screen flickered. Numerous propaganda posters came into view, the words 'Salvation', 'Follow', 'Together' were heavily emphasised.

"So what do you want me for?" Samantha challenged. "It seems you have a mysterious organisation that wants to manipulate the public, encouraging a belief you might not agree with. Sound familiar to anybody?"

Her mother shot to her feet. "How dare you lay that accusation at our door? We've been protecting mankind."

The fly swatting became a crescendo.

Samantha watched each of the councilmembers lose their way. They were desperate, reeling with hollow looks on their faces. These were the people who held the fate of the world in their hands.

"From whom are you saving mankind?" Samantha demanded. "I know the history. ARC was formed to monitor and counter the threat of demons. I've read the documents, been through the archives. Yet how many demons have appeared on earth in the last two decades?"

She opened her hands, spreading them apart, inviting comment. None came. "You're the saviours of mankind and you cannot live with the aftereffects of your great victory. Does it not strike you that for whatever reason, Aeon Fall know this as well? Maybe they have the answer." Then it hit her. "Your satellite. Your technological marvel. Mother, what does it do?"

"If you had been here, you would know."

"But I wasn't," Samantha snapped back. "You made it abundantly clear that you were preoccupied with my sister over there." She watched Nina's face fold into a frown, and thought, *she looks like her true self.*

Samantha raised her finger in warning to Nina. "Don't you even think of projecting thoughts into my head," and pivoted back to the council. "Did you bring me here to make me account for my transgressions or to apologise for yours? If you want my obedience, lock me up, because that's the only way you will get it. Do you want my help? If so, you have to give a little back. What does the sky sling do?"

"It will open a portal," Her mother provided.

"To heaven? You're seeking to reconnect with God?"

Nobody answered.

There was a strange feeling of tension in the air, of guilt. "No, that's not it, is it? Samantha challenged.

"It will open a portal to Hell."

Her mother's voice rang out; Samantha heard the clear, ominous, authoritarian timbre.

"One we can control, unlike what you've been doing the past few years. Lock you up? Your skills have been the basis of our entire effort. There's technology down there that surpasses anything we've been able to develop. Behind it, there's an energy source of indescribable proportions."

The words sounded too rehearsed. Whatever her mother's real reason, this was not it. "You brought me here to tell me you're opening a gateway you nearly sacrificed everything to close? Because I can do the same?"

"I've brought you here to understand why."

Samantha rose, walking away from the conference table. "Because if you can convince a massive doubter like me, you can convince anybody—correct?"

Eva slammed her hand on the table. "Because you're my daughter too. Because you've been irresponsible, a tearaway. Like it or not, you have responsibilities."

"And the time for playing games is over, right?" Samantha smiled. There it was: that omniscient authoritarian voice her mother mostly kept in check. She waited for more.

"Your attempts at lashing out are at an end, Samantha. Your followers are being dispersed as we speak. Do you believe the knowledge you gained growing up would be allowed to escape into the public domain? If you had let anything slip you would have been locked away. Only I kept you from that fate. Remember, daughter, at the end of the day your name is Scott and that means something. The very word is the modicum of sacrifice. Because your father sacrificed himself for all of us." Eva sat back down. "He paid for our sins."

"Mom, I think you're looking in the wrong direction in terms of who paid for our sins."

Eva stood, red-faced, ready to go toe-to-toe with her own daughter.

"Why don't we please just take it down a notch?" Swanson suggested. "Everything's just a little too heated. Sammy, yes we want you to understand the gravity of the situation. Also we can't have you acting like a maverick and creating your own cult, which, like it or not you were, in fact, doing through the use of your friend."

"I had no such intentions," she countered. How ridiculous they all were!

"He did," supplied John Wolverton. "We highly suspect Lucas Rossi is a member of Aeon Fall too. If they ever reveal themselves we will know quickly. We are not without resource."

"You don't know the upper echelons of an organisation you're clearly worried about, yet you can tell all this about Lucas?"

"Some people aren't as discreet about their affiliation as others," the big man replied, shifting in his seat. "If you think I'm going to jump up and get all hysterical, you're grossly mistaken. Look at it this way, Sammy. When there's a big movie coming out, the studio doesn't want to be held responsible for direct leaks. They want the information to hit where it will have the most impact. They find one of the less-discreet members of the cast, put him in front of the camera and let nature happen. You have to admit, your Lucas isn't the most rational of guys."

"He's not my *anything.*"

"That's not what he thinks," Wolverton contradicted. "Eva, do we have the footage to hand?"

For the first time in this grand confrontation, Samantha watched her mother's reluctance, holding her breath as she stared back at her daughter. "We, umm, yes we do. Her voice faltered. "Sammy, I'm sorry to have to show you this. I'd hoped to protect you from Lucas."

"Lucas? He can be a swine but he's harmless."

The film scrolled across the main screen behind Swanson. A room, dimly-lit, the walls plastered with photographs of women. Samantha watched in growing fear as the camera zoomed in on several of the pictures. Every photograph was her—many as she slept, some in various state of undress, and several of her during the summoning rituals. All the photographs seemed focussed on her neck, her breasts.

"I'm sorry, Samantha," her mother said. "I'll never let you suffer that again."

"You won't have time to worry, Eva," said a calm, egotistical male voice from the screen. There were overtones of triumph in the words that followed. "You'll be too busy chasing your own tail."

Chapter Five

The voice meant nothing to Samantha. *Were they being watched?* She wondered. She looked around the room and noticed two distinct reactions. Her mother had gone pale, her eyes wide, as she stared across at Swanson. He appeared the same. Gila Byron, Forrest Kyle, and oddly, John Wolverton wore similar expressions. They knew who the voice belonged to, or at least suspected. The rest of the council varied from intrigue to mild confusion.

"Aren't you going to welcome back an old comrade?" the voice asked. "Surely it's not been so long you've forgotten?"

Nina spoke first. "Why don't you show yourself and refresh our memories?"

Amused, the voice said, "Ah yes, why don't I indeed, little princess? Put you all out of your misery, so to speak."

The screen flickered, static becoming a camera lens with a body filling the view as they set the camera in place. The man stepped back. Eva gasped.

"It can't be," Swanson whispered.

John Wolverton frowned at the screen. "Is this some sort of joke?"

The man stared in his direction. Piercing eyes, like a hawk watching prey, were framed by grey hair streaked with white hung loosely down his chest. A nest of a beard was a similar mix of colours. He wore a white t-shirt bearing the word 'Prophecy'. "No joke, oh mighty Mir-Shikar."

Samantha knew enough about her father figure to recall that term. It was the name bestowed on the head of the Shikari, an elite force employed by ARC to undertake only the most dangerous of tasks. And she knew enough to now be worried, as the room around her volleyed with cryptic whispers. She stared at the screen with the rest of them.

"Let me introduce myself to those of you that do not know me. I was called Porter Rockwell. I died so that you might live, Nina Scott."

"You can't be here," Eva said. "We saw you taken from the transport. We saw your body, ripped apart by Bel…" Eva paused, as all attention fell on her. "We saw you die."

"Yes, you did," Rockwell purred. "And now you see me made anew. You abandoned me in Hell, the plaything of Belphegor. Now you will soon know what that will cost you."

"We didn't leave you," argued Gila. "That was a one-way ticket. We all knew that, accepted that. You were no different. Save Nina. Prevent an apocalypse. It was that simple."

Eva turned a laptop toward the rest of the council. On it was one word. Hacked.

Rockwell glanced in Eva's direction. "Hacked like you wouldn't believe, Director Scott."

The screen fizzed as the word Eva had typed disintegrated. Colour came back as it was replaced with one of the Aeon Fall propaganda posters, three modern spires reaching for the sky with the words 'Find your Salvation' floating above them.

"Find out how he's doing this," Swanson's raised voice revealed panic. They'd never been caught like this. Ever.

A satisfied smile spread across Rockwell's face. "Reap what you sow, ladies and gentlemen. Consider this a courtesy call. You all have front row seats to what's coming next."

The screen blurred, Rockwell's eyes the last image to fade before being replaced by the Aeon Fall logo. A triumphant theme began to play, as if angels had descended blowing holy trumpets and announced with fanfare the coming of a greater being.

Samantha watched as these oh-so-cocksure board members crumbled in confusion, anger, and helplessness.

"What's going on here, people?" Swanson demanded, thumping the lectern with a clenched fist.

In an instant, everybody was speaking, trying to be heard above everybody else. Wolverton was up and away from the table, on his cell, her mother trying without much success to reboot her laptop.

"We're locked out," Gila cried as she tried without success to alter the conference screen.

Swanson pounced on the tabletop control console, screaming, "Hollie, Hollie get in here. Hollie?" He mashed the speaker button with his thumb. Nobody answered.

A moment later Hollie burst in through the conference room door. "I'm sorry, Council."

"It's okay, Hollie. We're locked out."

"I know."

"Can you … what do you mean, you know? I only just called you."

"I never received any message, sir. You aren't the only ones locked out. Somebody's disabled the entire facility. Hunter's Ridge is dead in the water."

The room fell silent. Nobody knew what to do.

"Work the problem, people. Who are we?"

John Wolverton was the first to respond to Swanson. "Phone's aren't down. There's just no signal out of the base."

"You've got power everywhere though," Samantha said.

"What good is power if you can't use it?" Swanson replied.

"Yes, but if you have power, then surely you have somebody in this nest of geniuses clever enough to figure out why there is no signal. Is it blocked? Is there a satellite being diverted?"

Swanson turned. "What did you say?"

"Is the signal blocked?"

His face fell. "It couldn't be."

Her mother closed her eyes, taking several slow breaths.

"What?" Samantha asked. "What did I say?"

"You might have hit the nail right on the head, Sammy. It could be him."

Samantha looked about the room. "It could be what? Him who? Mom, what's going on here?"

"A month back there was a falling out in my department. One of my more gifted experts decided that for his own reasons he had had enough of ARC's development strategy. He was working on security here at Hunter's Ridge and then nothing. Just gone. When we searched his quarters we found a two-word note: 'Going Home'. Surveillance picked him up in Split, but after that we lost track of him."

"Who was he? Did you check his home? Wasn't he tagged? I mean you keep track of me pretty well."

"Security checked all of his known contacts and came up with nothing. You're correct. He was indeed tagged, and the signal failed in Split. The other possibilities—someone is either hiding him, or has abducted him."

"Someone like Porter Rockwell?"

A slow smile of satisfaction spread across Eva's face. "Told you she doesn't miss a trick."

What would you do, Sammy?

Across the room Nina stared at her.

"Look. This guy, who is he?"

"His name's John Myhill," her mother provided.

"This Myhill, if he is with them, this is planned. Look at what you have and focus on that. You have power. You have communications. Start there. Do you have redundancies for the satellite?"

"We do," Eva confirmed. "Isolate those routines and work on getting them in action. Maybe if that small piece fits in place it'll be easier going for the rest. One problem at a time."

"Already on it," Swanson replied as the rest of the Council moved into action with a purpose. A flow of section heads scurried in and out of the room.

"That was good going, kid," Charlotte Benson approved. "You might be of some use yet."

"Panicking helps nobody," Samantha replied.

A few minutes later a pale-skinned, frightened looking woman in a white lab coat stepped in and announced, "This signal, it's everywhere."

"Everywhere?" Swanson sounded incredulous.

The lab woman held up a portable television. The same picture was on the screen. "Yes sir."

The music changed, becoming a stronger fanfare.

"Welcome to the grand debut of the New World Order," Thorsten Guyomard wryly commented.

Those in the room stopped as the Aeon Fall logo began to glow, first yellow, then white.

"How dramatic," Samantha said.

"Come on, people," urged Swanson. "This is gonna happen unless we prevent it."

Spurred back into action by their new leader, everybody resumed their frenetic pace, running in and out of the room as ideas took root and became actions.

All the while the screen became more animated, images of religious significance, grails, angels, passed across the screen around the Aeon Fall logo.

And then it disappeared, fading to reveal a group of people. In the center stood a now-suited Porter Rockwell dressed in black surrounded by a group of equally dour, black-clad comrades.

"Now we see what card we've been dealt," Swanson muttered. Eva joined him, Nina coming to stand beside her sister.

A man with short-cropped, dark hair took a step forward. Hands folded in front of him, he smiled at the screen.

The smile sent a shiver down Samantha's back.

"My name is Tommy Baxter. I speak for Aeon Fall. You will have heard of our organisation by now. We're here today to call humanity to account. For you are alone. Your God is dead. We have watched over mankind for the past twenty years while you have, unknowingly or otherwise, suffered one of many fates."

Baxter took a couple of steps toward the screen and it divided. Behind him, several people were revealed.

"There he is," her mother said, pointing. "The sonofabitch. There was nothing to indicate this."

"Someone knew," Swanson accused. "Someone recruited him."

The person identified as Myhill seemed nothing special to Samantha. Aside from the fanatic eyes shared by everybody on the screen, he was unassuming, a young man balding early with a cocky expression. She had seen dozens like him.

On screen, Baxter turned toward the center, holding out his hand. A picture appeared of people walking through a busy city centre. "The first of you get on with life, a practical approach. You weren't religious to begin with, not recognising a higher power. Despite all of the demon incursions that clearly proved there was something more."

The right-hand screen flicked to people praying. At pews in church, lined in rows inside mosques, individuals grasping rosaries in St Peters square, outside the papal residence in Vatican City. The imagery went on and on. "The second group of you carry on believing. The core knot of you that believe in a higher power. Your enlightened level of understanding means you will never give up, stubbornly hanging onto broken dogma. Your God is dead."

The picture faded, replaced by shots of a running street battle. Masked combatants went toe-to-toe with armed forces, casualties dropping in sprays of blood on both sides. In a doorway behind the violence, a small girl sat on the step cradling a toy dog. Blood dripped down her face and onto the toy as she stared blankly from behind the mental buffer of her trauma.

"The third of you have given up in the most glorious of ways, and descended to the joys of base instinct: wrath, pride, lust, and envy. You are the new minions of Hell in human form. Bereft of hope, ignorant of your future, you lash out. Commendable, if fatalistic. The final group embrace the teachings of a new church. Science. Technology. You have forsaken religion because it offers you nothing."

The screen blurred to show Hunters Ridge as the sky sling took off, the twin jets powering the cradled rocket into low orbit. Now Samantha watched the technological marvel she had tried so hard to avoid.

"This can't be good," Swanson said. He turned to a small group nearby. "Have you worked out what Myhill did to this facility?"

"I'm sorry Director," said one, "the systems have been encrypted. It operates like a virus, but there is an unusual arm to it, something we have never encountered before. It's taking our very best just to keep up with the code. Every time we find a potential means of access, the encryption slams down on us like we were base-level programmers. For the moment, they have total control over us."

Swanson frowned. "Over what, exactly?"

"This facility and through it, the global ARC network. Director, they could spill every secret ARC has filed away should they so choose."

As if watching them from on screen, Tommy Baxter said, "Yes, Director Swanson Guyomard and your vaunted ARC Council, now you know what it is to truly lose control. No more will you be the chalice of technological superiority, hidden behind benevolence and scientific progress. To those of you around the globe, a small lesson about the recent history of our world. We were not alone. Not always. The world had purpose, direction. This woman ended that hope. Eva Scott—the Devil's whore."

Eva put her hand to her mouth as footage flashed up on the screen showing her on a mountain.

Samantha had never seen it before. Her mother was strung up on a platform as a tall figure cloaked in black carved at her arm with a knife not unlike that which Samantha had used to raise her father. Behind them an angry red portal swirled.

"How?" Eva whispered.

"They have it all now," Swanson said, his voice barely suppressing his frustration.

"Who is that?" Samantha asked.

"Iuvart," Eva replied. "A demon Prince. He masqueraded as my boss at Worcester State Hospital. You, of all people, would understand such beings are real."

Baxter continued, "What Eva and those like her don't want you to know is that they are responsible for closing the path to the divine. This happened."

Images of demons rampaging across a desert in battle with countless armed forces followed.

"This happened. The voice you all heard in the night sky was this man. Madden Scott."

An image filled the screen of a good-looking man with stubble and a brown ponytail, a cheeky grin on his face.

"He is for all intents and purposes, the Devil. This man walked into Hell, and killed God by doing so. The purpose has been taken from humanity, and you don't know why. Aeon Fall is here to explain why. Your technological saviour, calling themselves Angels of the Knight's Resurrection, seek a way into Hell, to open the gate permanently. They've had a glimpse of Pandora's Box and they want a taste of more. The satellite they launched moments ago is not a global defence mechanism as they have claimed. It is designed to open a portal to Hell. Your saviours want their King back. Your only hope lies with us. Death is waiting for you. By their means, or ours. To the governments of this world, you can still stop them. To the directors of this organisation, I issue this declaration. Shut your satellite down. Allow it to fall from the sky, and we will do nothing. Persist with your efforts to ruin this world and…" Baxter smiled. "Well, there are many facilities in this world that, if not properly maintained, could spread a lot of damage to a great many people. It would all be on your head."

All images disappeared, the screen focussing on Tommy Baxter and those around him. "Heaven has forsaken you. There's no respite. Except us. You put your salvation, or your decimation in Aeon Fall. Expect the sky to light up with the answer of those that would rule in silence."

The screen went black, except for a web address.

"Really?" Swanson scoffed. "Aeon Fall dot com? A website?"

"It's all rather clever," Jeanette Gibson said, one ear pressed into a cell that clearly wasn't working despite repeated attempts at speed dial. "It gets the common man thinking, especially if we have no way to answer."

"Having fun?" Porter Rockwell's voice echoed around the room. The screen flicked on. He gazed at them, his piercing eyes causing more than one person to look away.

Samantha met that gaze, whether he could see her or not.

"You would really hold the world to ransom like that? I can give you our answer right now if it will save lives."

"Oh it won't," Rockwell purred. "There are no lives to save." John Myhill was shoved trembling into view. Rockwell grabbed him by his shoulder. "This one has nothing left to tell us, Eva. He was most cooperative. I want you to remember this moment for the rest of your lives, as short as they'll be. The moment ARC was rendered helpless, beginning with this."

Rockwell lunged, his fist erupting through Myhill's chest. Blood shot everywhere.

Samantha and her mother gasped as one. Others screamed.

Rockwell let the body slide out of view. "In five days, and for every five days after, we shall disable a nuclear facility. You will watch your world burn. When there's been enough damage, enough chaos, then the world will look to Aeon Fall for survival. They will rip you apart."

"But if you don't care about the answer—" Swanson's comment was cut short as a siren began to wail. Red lights flashed on a panel beside the monitor.

"Someone's activated the satellite," Gila gasped.

"To do what?" Samantha asked, worried.

On the screen, Porter Rockwell smiled.

Chapter Six

Whatever its purpose, ARC's jewel had come into being, and not by their design.

"Control room. Now." Swanson's order was followed by a rush of bodies as two thirds of the room's occupants exited.

Samantha remained where she was, staring back at Porter Rockwell, transfixed.

"It won't take long," Rockwell said from wherever he was hidden. "You will all see what has been wrought in the name of humanity."

A thought struck Samantha. She waved in front of the camera that pointed into the room. Rockwell didn't notice.

Nina had remained with her and gave her a quizzical look.

"Maybe it's a good thing," Samantha said aloud. The room had cooled somewhat with nearly everybody now gone. She wrapped her arms across her body to try and ward off the suddenly efficient aircon.

Rockwell tilted his head, his eyes making no sign of conscious movement. "Quick but not pleasant."

Samantha pointed at her eyes and shook her head.

He can't see? Nina's thought invaded her mind. *That's very perceptive of you. If that's the case, we have an advantage.*

"Clever, making it look like ARC's response to your threat is to plough on, regardless," Samantha said loud enough for Rockwell to hear. "Now we're the bad guys and you're the saviour." On a pad she scrawled the words 'signal in, no signal out' and showed it to Nina.

"I'd not have it any other way," Rockwell purred. "Let me tell you of an experience I would care to share with you. I took a trip with your mother once. We went to Hell."

"Well that's pretty blunt," was Nina's wry comment.

On a screen to the left of Rockwell, an image of a satellite appeared, what looked to be solar panels deploying.

"Not long now," Rockwell continued. "Hell was an awe-inspiring place, full of beauty, full of technology. There were majestic structures, spiralling towers dwarfing anything on Earth. I really didn't realise how insignificant we are until I saw it. I was cast asunder in that place, dragged from safety by Hell's minions, and presented to one of their captains, Leviathan. I was offered a choice: Serve, or suffer eternal damnation. Your father was a Hellbounce, an abomination in the eyes of Heaven and Hell. I was born anew on the plains of the Elysian Fields. I wandered there as souls floated down from the mortal plane soon attached to their own personal purgatory. I watched the sins of others as they were cleansed, touching spirit after spirit during their torment. Some were dirty, haggard, destined to remain forever. I beheld myself as one of them, the crimes committed while I was alive stacked up against me. After an eternity lost among others, he came to me."

Nina pointed at the door. *Let's test your theory.*

Being careful not to make any sound, Samantha led the way from the conference room. She pushed the automatic door open while Nina fought to keep it from opening automatically with its tell-tale noise. They crept out. It made no difference.

"Leviathan," Rockwell's voice echoed down the hallways of the control centre. He was speaking to them all. "He told me my penance was to travel on—further than any soul has ever been. To the source, to the very nexus at the centre of the Elysium Fields, wherein dwelt The Judges. They are Hell's sentinels, through which all souls must pass on their way to heaven, to demon rebirth, or the great beyond."

"This is Swanson Guyomard," a voice announced over the tannoy. Clearly they had regained control of that much. A message appeared on top of Rockwell's face. "All tech specialists to the situation room."

On a screen in the hallway, Rockwell continued talking. "...a choice. Hell had its chieftain once again. If a man sits on the throne of Hell, why cannot man take the place of the seat of Heaven? That's the judgment I decided upon: To deliver a message. Each man is asked to atone for his sins. We all face judgement."

Nina held Samantha to the side of the hallway, banging her ribs on the unyielding metal railing as several technicians in grey boiler suits dashed past.

Samantha glared at her sister. "Thanks."

"Panels deployed, satellite powering up," came Swanson's voice. "Everyone hold tight. We're going to cut the power to the facility."

"If they chose the lesser path their stay would be longer," Rockwell continued, "more painful. Many would never make it to Heaven. It's the question you will all have to ask of yourselves in the coming days. When the gateway is opened, how honest are you? Will you take the hard road?"

"Gateway?" Samantha stopped. "Do you understand what he means?"

Nina shrugged. "No idea. Come on, let's get to the control room."

Samantha took only a few steps when a silence descended over the station. All internal lighting went off, Porter Rockwell's monologue disappearing as all screens went blank. They were two doors from the control room. Nina tugged at the closed door. Only the early twilight gave her any sense of perspective. She remained still.

"Nothing."

Samantha shook her head. "What now?"

"Wait for them to bring the power back up, if it ever returns. For all our luck, Myhill catered for this."

Nina pushed the door open across from them. The room was dark, with all the blinds drawn, with only one occupant, a woman with archaic looking hair swept back either side of her face. Her hairstyle made her head looked strangely like a stingray. The woman paced the room, which had a row of computers on a desk in the middle of the room, facing out.

"Are you okay, Pamela?" Samantha asked, reading the nametag on the woman's lanyard. The stale reek of nervous sweat was strong in the room.

"I don't know," the woman replied, clearly agitated as she stared down at the floor. "I need to check with my supervisor." She continued to pace; the creeping movements made her look strangely gangrel.

Not a lot of thought in there... Nina nodded toward the woman.

A red glow burst from beyond the blinds. Samantha rushed across, pulling them back. "What the Hell?"

An intense beam shot across the sky from horizon to horizon, staining the clouds red. Pamela rushed to the blinds, pulling them shut. "Too much glare."

Samantha pulled the cord from the woman's hand, pulling the blind back open. "You can live with it. Nina, what is this?"

"The satellite was designed to tap into the energy they detected in Hell twenty years ago. It's been retro-engineered from the one piece of tech mom brought back with her. Everything uses that same energy. Soul energy."

Samantha waved at the window. "That? That's a detector? It looks more like a weapon firing."

Behind them, the woman Pamela shrunk to the floor in the glow of the nearly completely red sky. "Too ... much ... glare."

The lights began to glow, slowly and agonisingly returning to normal.

"Okay, time to move," Samantha decided.

"And her?" Nina asked.

"Leave her. There's more at risk here than one madwoman."

"You're all heart, you."

Samantha turned in the doorway. "Sis, I never wanted to be here in the first place."

In the hallway, the Rockwell monotone continued. "Does it all work now? Are you restored? You need to understand, none make it to heaven. Not anymore. The gates are shut. The blinds are drawn no matter how much you try to open them. Rewards and punishment: Both are false idols, to be sought after, but never attained. You mankind, are alone. Put your faith now in Aeon Fall, not in those that promised eternal glory with one hand, only to deny it with the other."

"Can someone please shut him up?" Swanson demanded as the sisters pushed into the back of the control room. It was crowded with countless ARC operatives gathered beneath three large screens. On them were displayed a schematic of the satellite, another of the earth, and on the third, real time footage of the red sky.

"I watched as souls were reborn. When my turn came, I was bidden to embrace my sin rather than atone. I would not forget my purpose, or my indiscretions…"

"What's this thing doing?" Swanson waved his arm at the satellite. "That's no detector."

"We've isolated the code, sir. Aeon Fall have altered not only the system encryption on the base, but also the satellite itself. Those aren't detectors in there. That's a laser. It's…" There was a pause. "It's firing, and at the terminus of the beam, there's an opening."

"An opening to what?"

"Sir, look! The magnetic field around the earth. It's altering."

The schematic of the earth showed the magnetic field surrounding the planet. Normally a neat figure eight, it was being distorted by a second source, far stronger than that of the earth.

The room shuddered. "Get that thing shut down," Swanson ordered. "That second field is far stronger than that of the Earth. This could tear the whole planet apart!"

It was too much for Samantha. The press of people was too great. She pushed her way through the tangled mass of humanity and out through the door. If she were to meet her maker it would be where she could see the sky, not in a crowded room.

It made no difference. She descended to the ground level of the control centre, and after a great deal of wandering, she was relieved to be outside the tropical haven of the foyer, although the screens still showed what was happening. More than that, while he had been silenced inside, Porter Rockwell's voice was still very clear on the edge of the runway.

"I opened my eyes to find myself lying on a beach in Jamaica. I was able to recall my memories of the afterlife. My return here was prophesised. I'm a herald of the end of days. Look about you, do I not speak the truth?"

The red glow intensified above the gloomy Adriatic.

"You're not kidding," Samantha gasped.

In several places, the cloud had begun to twist, spiralling into funnels of massive proportion. They were miles across in width, and as the vortices struck down, they drained the Adriatic and bore it aloft as waterspouts.

Samantha ran to the edge of the platform, leaning against the railing to witness the water disappear. The wind began to push against her as the air pressure battled to normalcy. Except there was none.

"Miss," shouted one of the ground staff in orange boiler suit and wind-goggles. "You've got to get inside."

Samantha shook her head. "Why? This is where all the action is."

"We're on lockdown. Everybody inside. Council's orders."

Samantha opened her mouth to argue and was hit by a blast of wind so intense it staggered her, knocking her from her feet and out under the protective barrier. She turned to see one of the mile-wide vortices bearing down, her feet hanging over the edge of the platform. The air reeked of fish where the seafloor had been sucked up and sprayed everywhere.

The deck-hand grappled with her as she struggled to regain her footing. The waterspout closed on them.

Above, where the red was most intense, a black hole was forming. Clouds spiralled up toward the darkness, the very air pulling at her. The base groaned in metallic agony as gravity from the hole threatened to tear them apart. Samantha felt her shoulders lighten as the feeling took hold.

"We're gonna get sucked up if we stay out here much longer," she shouted above the wind. "Sucked up…"

That was it! Battling against the atmosphere, she fought her way back into the base.

"You're crazy, Miss, if you don't mind me saying!" The deckhand shook his head as he secured the outer door.

"Let's hope so," Samantha agreed, hurrying back to the control room.

The entire base now shook as the waterspout continued to bear down on them, heading away from the control centre, but still aiming for the middle of the runway. More than once, Samantha fell as she climbed the stairs, banging her legs, elbows, and her forehead.

"Reap what you sow, Eva Scott," the voice of Porter Rockwell gloated. "You should never have messed with forces beyond your comprehension."

Mercifully, the voice cut out as the base shrieked once more. Was that the last they would hear of Porter Rockwell?

Samantha made back to the control room, now in a state of pandemonium. People had fallen to the floor as the base juddered, breaking limbs and opening wounds. Her mother cradled one arm with the other, wincing every time she moved. Swanson stood staring at the flickering screens.

"We can't break the code," he said aloud. "It's impossible. All this, for nothing."

"Blow it out of the sky," Samantha shouted above the noise, causing everybody to pause and stare at her. The base heaved, the lights and screens flickered. A few people screamed.

"You have access to weapons, yes?"

"That satellite is one of a kind. We lose everything if we destroy it."

"And if you don't? Hello? That machine is creating a black hole that's going to rip this planet apart, starting with us!" Samantha pulled one of the sealed windows open. The wind sucked at them, depressurising the room and drawing the breath from her lungs. The waterspout filled the view, twisting with agonising deliberateness as it began to brush the runway. A plane turned as the vortex began to consume it. "You're running out of time. Aeon Fall called you out, and your response is to allow it to threaten all life on earth? Whatever's up there is not your technology. End it before it ends us."

For once in his life, Swanson appeared indecisive. Samantha knew the hype. This was to be their big day; the beginning of a new Era for mankind and a jump of generations in power and technology. It had all gone wrong.

But why?

"Swanson, if we're gonna do this, do it now." John Wolverton held his hand over a panel, ready to take action.

"Is there any hope of the redundancies kicking in? Of self-destruct?"

"There is no self-destruct," Eva answered. "Once the probe hit its orbit, it became self-functioning. It's been rebuilt right under our noses."

"God help that this doesn't make it worse for us all." Swanson closed his eyes. "Do it."

Wolverton slammed the heel of his hand on to a button on the console on front. "Launch in three … two … one…"

A brief surge of flame from the distant launch pad was consumed in moments by the twisting waterspout. The sky darkened as the whirling natural forces assaulted Hunters Ridge; the noise was deafening. Samantha let go of the window, which slammed shut. The rattle continued as the waterspout veered toward them, the light growing dimmer as more of the horizon was taken up by the gargantuan waterspout.

Very quickly, the air pressure equalised. "Did it launch?" asked Swanson. "Did it go up?"

"There was something from the other end of the base," Samantha answered. "A burst of flame that was swallowed up in the water."

The panels of the control room blinked off, leaving the inhabitants in darkness. No one said a word, as debris hit the outside of their refuge and the building shuddered, threatening to tear apart.

"May the angels forgive us," Swanson prayed aloud.
Was Swanson ready to die?
Samantha vowed this wouldn't be her ending.

Chapter Seven

"Nina, what is it?" A twelve year old Samantha, bored of waiting on her mom to conclude another meeting, had gone wandering the grounds of the Château d'Yvoire, ARC's headquarters. She found her sister staring at an old photograph of their parents, tears running freely down her face. She sat down beside her, placed an arm around Nina's shoulder, and squeezed.

Nina reached up and gripped her hand in reply, not looking up. "I miss him. I only knew Madden briefly, and even then the memories are fleeting."

"I never knew him," Samantha mused. "I can't miss a photograph. But he's not gone, is he? Pop's just elsewhere. As long as that's the case, you're never truly alone. Besides, you've got me, and Mom."

Now Nina did lean into her. "Thanks, Sammy. It's good to have you around. We'll always have each other."

Samantha sighed. "If only there was a way to reach him, maybe we wouldn't feel so alone."

Nina lifted a bag from beside her, placing the photo inside and withdrawing a leather-bound book. Handing the book to Samantha she said, "Maybe this will help."

* * *

Samantha pushed forward, ignoring the nervous sweat of several crowded technicians as they cowered. The moisture on her arms was a distant second in importance compared to the need to survive. Why were these people so quick to give up?

Reaching the console at the front of the room, she leaned over the top of the woman who sat frozen, staring at the screen. Samantha recognised her—Tilly; Samantha couldn't remember her surname. She may or may not have helped her mother at some point in the past.

"What needs to happen here?" Samantha asked. "How do we get the monitors back online?"

Tilly just stared at the screen. Dark, shaking with the intensity of the imminent destruction of Hunters Ridge, the technician was unresponsive. The air was filled with the rank onion scent of nervous sweat. These people were terrified.

"Dammit." Samantha touched Tilly's arm. It was ice cold and shaking. She was going into shock. "Can we get a medic here? Anybody?"

There was no response. The room was dark, cold and icy air filled the space. Everybody was dead. Their bodies were just waiting to catch up. Why was she the only one with any spirit left in her?

"Come on!" she yelled, smacking the console. Tilly flinched. Maybe she wasn't dead yet.

Samantha pummelled the console, the sharp edges of switches catching on the skin of her hands. The pain was sharp and sudden. Blood smeared over the controls.

Calm yourself, Nina said as she crossed room. *Remember father.*

Samantha turned to her sister and their eyes met.

Breathe. Let the panic subside.

And the answer will present itself, Samantha agreed. She closed her eyes, drew a deep breath, and pressed the override button on the unit. At the same time, Nina leaned over, a hand placed on her shoulder, and keyed in a sequence on a number pad. The screen began to flicker. "Maybe this will help."

"What … What did you do?" Tilly turned toward Nina, eyes still glassy and uncomprehending.

"We never give up. Come on," she urged the screen, the power of the base, just beyond the level needed to self-sustain.

The screen flickered once more, then went dark. Samantha sighed, falling to the floor as a boom sounded outside, inside, everywhere at once. Many others fell as well, destabilised by the sound. Those who remained standing held their hands over their ears. Several had nosebleeds, but at least they were alive and moving.

What the hell was that? Nina's silent voice asked, *What did you do?*

Samantha turned to find her sister staring at her. She raised her hands, confused.

"Look!" Swanson shouted, pointing.

The screen flickered again, then filled from left to right with static, which quickly became the schematic of the earth with the magnetic field restored. The other two screens followed in quick succession. One-by-one, all systems were re-established. On one screen a radar pulsed, a dot speeding across the screen from left to right.

"Debris," called one of the technicians.

"Heading?" Swanson stepped up to the screen.

"It looks to be hitting Dubrovnik head on."

From outside came a crack and a boom as the unknown object roared past, high in the sky. The dot passed off the radar screen and the room went silent. After a few moments Hunters Ridge rumbled with the echoes of a distant impact, the vibrations running up through the floor into Samantha's legs.

"What just happened?" Swanson asked. He raised his head, struggling to listen. "Are we still under attack?"

One of the technicians opened the panel to the outside once more. A strange pink glow shone from outside, filling the room. "It's gone. It's all gone."

"What's that light?"

In an instant, the population of the control room began to pour out into the corridor beyond. Swept up by the curiosity, Samantha found herself buoyed along by the tide of humanity in this desperate need to escape from their would-be tomb.

The pink glow was everywhere, filling every small window without giving away its source. Samantha tripped, stumbled and had to grab hold of those around her to prevent being trampled. She was not alone. Others joined the council and technicians realising they had survived.

As they spilled out onto the flight deck of the base, Samantha heard the words 'heaven' and 'miracle' called out by people ahead of her. Struggling to see what had all of her companions mesmerised, she helped the throng push forward. When she finally made the doorway, she pushed through those stood still, gazing at the sky, until she found a small open space.

The air was warm, with a slight breeze. Samantha tasted the salt tang of stirred up ocean detritus. Hunters Ridge was a mess, planes strewn in the distance, wings broken off, many resting on their fuselage where wheels had been ripped asunder by the waterspout. The runway was covered in seaweed, flapping fish, and a thin layer of silt. It rippled where the remaining seawater poured off the surface to the muddy brown surface of the Adriatic below.

It was the source of the pink glow that held everybody captivated, and as Samantha looked up she could see why. In the same area of sky where the gravity anomaly had been focussed, she now witnessed a marvel. A series of concentric circles radiated out from a distant point, the cloud that formed them caught the setting rays of the sun. The centre of the circles glowed bright pink. Light sparkled among the cloud, making it appear as if it were a tunnel, a pathway to a higher plane.

"Red sky at night," Nina said, coming to stand behind her.

"Why does this not feel like I should be celebrating?"

"Give it time," her sister advised. "We're lucky to be alive." Nina turned to the runway. "So much for the great experiment, the mighty fortress."

"But alive we are, and this is ARC's mess to clean up."

"You're still not on board, Sammy? Aren't you willing to get the least bit dirty?"

Samantha turned to her sister and shrugged. "Why?"

* * *

The sisters headed back inside to a packed conference room. Swanson stood at the front with Eva, Jeanette Gibson, and John Wolverton. The lights flickered every few seconds but other than that, the room was habitable, sustaining only broken glass from the recent assault.

Swanson watched Samantha over the heads of his people, nodding to her as she slid in with other staff.

"Okay people. In brief, this is where we are. The good news: We're still alive and the earth hasn't been torn apart. Hunters Ridge still functions, what's left of it." Swanson paused as he was handed a document, shaking his head, knitting his brow as he read the content. "It seems that's just about all the good news there is. We've screwed up here, whatever our intentions. There are immediate calls for ARC to account for its actions by the United Nations, America, China, just about every sovereign state on the planet."

"But we didn't do this," Eva protested.

"No, we did not," Swanson agreed. "Yet, we are in this position because, for the good of the world, we keep secrets from the rest of humanity. To the nations of planet Earth we appear to be as much a terrorist threat as Aeon Fall and to our detriment, our response was to appear to say, 'To Hell with you. We would rather see the world burn than remain with you in it.'"

Swanson shifted uneasily from foot-to-foot.

"Now not only have we acted rashly," Swanson continued, "we have no evidentiary proof that someone other than us was directly responsible for what was launched in the sky sling. There are tasks enough for all of us. John— you, Eva, and Forrest are to look into what happened here. How did Aeon Fall amend the satellite for their purposes?

"Jeanette, together with Alexander and Gaspard, will lead the charm offensive. The world has to know that we were not responsible and when we know why, present this information."

Gaspard Antroobus raised a hand. "Even if it brings to the fore facts we would rather have not revealed?"

"I think it's a bit late for that," Swanson answered the elderly Belgian. "Thorsten, Mohammed, and Clare, see what you can do to clear up this mess about the world. Please! All of you! Use your departments where necessary. All facilities must now be geared to clean up. Gila, Tricia and I will co-ordinate."

"From here?" Samantha knew she spoke out of turn but she wasn't about to stop now.

"No, from Geneva. Once we can get the runway clear we're relocating. I don't want anybody looking at ARC and seeing Hunters Ridge as an example of our legacy. You, however, will be going in a different direction. I want you working with your aunt. Get your feet dirty that way."

Samantha started. "As if. I don't work for you."

"Like it or not, you *are* in with us. We need every pair of hands,. and you have more experience almost anybody."

Samantha laughed. The nerve. "I get you're panicking, Swanson. But me? You can't be so desperate that you're trusting the black sheep of the family with world-ending stuff like this?"

Swanson moved through the crowd and past the sisters. "Follow me, please." He led them into a side room, closing the door on the team outside. "It's because you're here that I'm using you for this. Rebel all you want, but you're not leaving us again unless I'm certain you're trustworthy. Through dumb luck you've never said a thing about what we do, who we are."

How did he know? "I—"

"We keep track of those who we consider noteworthy, Sammy. You will do this, or you'll never again leave this base. I'm offering you a choice here. Redemption, or confinement. We've had enough of your games."

"It looks like I have no choice then. What about you?" Samantha asked her sister.

Nina remained grim-faced and silent.

"Sammy," Swanson said purposefully, "Nina is attempting to infiltrate Aeon Fall."

"It's been part of my remit since I formally agreed to work for the organisation," Nina elaborated.

Samantha stared, uncomprehending. The words registered, yet there was a sense of finality about them. "You—"

"I leave immediately."

"That's crazy. It's suicide."

It is what it is, sister. I have to do this. They have to be stopped.

Nina took her face in both hands, "You're headstrong, little sister. We all have our parts to play, and right now, yours is to listen to Aunt Clare, and try not to be a thorn in mom's side. I suspect there's more to all this than she's letting on. You may end up being her only outlet for that. Listen to her. Please?"

Samantha felt cornered, the air pressing down on her. "Okay. I will."

Nina stepped back though the door into the press of people in the conference room.

"Nina—" Samantha shouted above the throng, but there was no answer. Samantha searched the swarm of faces for her sister, pushing aside notables as though they were random strangers, but Nina was gone.

"She's good at that, you know." There was pride in Swanson's voice. "Practically invisible. She can get in and out unseen if she wishes, another legacy of your father."

"Yeah, she's a princess all right. I can summon a demon's image and I'm a dab hand at reading bird portents in a field," Samantha replied, her face deadpan. "We all have our gifts. It seems hers don't lead to an inexhaustible energy source, right?"

Swanson blinked. "True. If only you'd stayed, maybe this would have happened differently."

"Don't you lay the blame for your failure at my feet. I live to summon the image of Satan, not destroy the world."

Swanson appeared unmoved. "The 'image' of Satan. I daresay you can do more than that. Blood doesn't summon images. At least you have your father's sense of humour. A dry wit goes a long way. I'll be taking my leave now, Samantha. Major world crisis and all that."

Looking awkward, as if he had no real escape from the difficult conversation, Swanson turned and shuffled off through the crowd with none of the grace of Nina.

"It gets easier," her aunt Clare whispered in her ear, startling Samantha.

"I didn't see you there, Aunt Clare."

Her aunt laughed. "The first time I spoke to him, he offered me a job with ARC. What could I do but give up my very meagre ambitions of becoming a detective? The problem was, becoming a detective had been my only goal for a decade. He was in control that day." Clare indicated around the bustling room with her open hand. "This is anything but control. It is, in fact, pure chaos. Let's get out of here. We have to get busy and quickly."

Clare pulled Samantha through the crowd, ignoring those they bumped into. Only once did Samantha make eye contact with her mother. If there was any emotion in those eyes, any feeling, she could not read it. Her conduct over the next few days would affect the outcome of her reluctant ARC career.

"Is it worth it?"

Clare looked over her shoulder. "The job?"

"All of it. The job, the lifestyle."

Clare shrugged. "Definitely. I only had my half-brother Jeff to grow up with. My mother and step-father weren't exactly model citizens." The way she spoke about her family, the slight pause, the catch in her voice, revealed barely-masked pain. "I never met my real father, your grandfather."

"He died before I was born," Samantha replied. "Grandma went not too long after. That was when I was very young."

"See? Your family's all here. I've spent the past decade hunting creatures that should not exist. It's an amazing job, all brought about by an organisation founded because of one immutable fact: Demons are real. You know this. Now you have to ask yourself where else would you really want to be?"

"Not Dubrovnik, that's for sure." Charlotte Benson appeared ahead of them, filling the corridor with the musical lilt of her voice.

She reminded Samantha of an Amazonian Warrior—six feet tall with an imposing frame and well-tanned skin, towering above them with coffee-coloured hair tied back, sunglasses resting atop her head like a fashionable tiara.

"Come on, boss. We need to brief you."

Inside the room, three people Samantha didn't recognise were seated, two men and a woman. Screens on one wall showed similar diagnostics to those in the conference room.

"So this is it, then?" asked a rotund man of middle age in a green boiler suit with a black beanie hat. "Five of us against the world?"

"Six," Clare corrected. "This is my niece, Samantha Scott."

"Ah," said boiler suit. "Okay."

Clare snorted, pointing at the beanie capped man, "Don't worry about Jim, here. Clever and inventive? Sure. Able to get you out of a tight spot? Always. Wary of outsiders, though."

"Especially rebels with your reputation." Jim watched her with suspicious eyes.

"Live with it," Samantha replied. "I haven't exactly covered myself in glory recently. Nobody here has. Besides, once you have a low self-opinion, it's much easier to perceive the faults of others." She patted Jim on the shoulder. "Nice to meet you, Jim."

Behind him, a man in his early thirties bellowed a laugh and slapped one hand on his thigh. "That's genius," he said, wiping a tear away from a face bedecked in a short blond beard. His hair was tied back in a bun. While not as large as Jim, he radiated strength.

"Sammy, meet Mitch Russell," Claire said. "We're not exactly sure what he does. Comic relief, mostly. Good in a tight spot."

"Though how he fits into a tight spot is beyond me," commented a small woman with long dark hair and a friendly smile around the English accent.

"Are we ready, Carrot?" Clare asked.

"Carrot?" Samantha repeated.

"Natalie Scarrot," the small woman explained. "I'm sure you can see how that one stuck very quickly. You can call me Nat." She glanced at Mitch who smiled back.

This wasn't lost on Samantha. The relationship was the core of the team.

"Carrot's our pilot," Charlotte explained. "She's got a knack of getting in and out of some very tight spaces. We might need that tonight."

"Tonight?"

"You think that injured people are going to wait until morning for us to rescue them?" Clare asked. "What's the situation?"

"We're out of here just as soon as the ground crew give us the green light on the bird," answered Jim. "As you can imagine, the world is in a bit of a state following the satellite malfunction."

Clare snorted. "They're really going with that?"

"What choice do they have? It's much more diplomatic than 'terrorists reprogrammed our technology to open a black hole'. That's the least of the problems, though. Look at the charts. Weather's all screwed. Jet stream's realigned south to north and as of now, it's ignoring the rotation of the earth." Jim pointed at one of the screens. "The earth's atmosphere looks like a peeled orange, segmented by weather patterns. Many of those leaders were caught in the attack. Aeon Fall pulled off a master stroke. The President of the U.S.A, the British Prime minister, Russian and Chinese premieres, just the tip of the iceberg. They were all caught in the storms, and so far, no news."

"What makes Dubrovnik so special?"

Jim pointed to a second screen, showing a coastal city from above. An ugly scar cut across from the inland, east to west near the sea.

"Two things. First, Tien Tran, the Secretary General of the United Nations was en route to Dubrovnik following the launch. He likes to see the sights. Second, it wasn't weather that hit the city. Whatever the radar picked up just now came down and smashed into the hills behind with such force that they crumbled halfway to the sea."

"The satellite?" Samantha guessed.

Jim frowned. "Or something else."

Chapter Eight

What else could cause an avalanche? Samantha struggled to consider this as she followed her aunt onto the runway. The sun failed to reappear following the waterspout; clouds streaked across the sky in a pattern of parallel lines more akin to jet trails than any normal formation. Everything had changed.

The few lights that hadn't been destroyed pierced the twilight, leaving the enormity of Hunter's Ridge shrouded in the darkness and foulsmelling silt. It filled Samantha's nostrils and muffled her footfalls. She took a moment to lament for Brusnik, which surely would have been swamped in the violent conditions. Her once peaceful and calm demeanour was overtaken with chaos.

Up ahead, the whunk-whunk noise of a helicopter powering up revealed their destination. Carrot was already in the pilot's seat, her face revealing a frown in the glow of the instrument panels.

Clare handed Samantha a headset and placed another over her own head. "How's it looking?"

"Jessica took a hell of a hammering, boss. The waterspout sideswiped her, leaving her in a heap of debris with muck everywhere but the ground staff did a stellar job."

"Jessica?" Samantha asked.

"My little sister," Carrot answered. "She's a redhead, and temperamental. Not unlike this bird. You'd have to see her in the daylight to understand."

"Who? Your sister?"

"Either.

They climbed in, Charlotte Benson up front, next to Carrot, Mitch and Samantha seated mid-row, and Aunt Clare and Jim at the rear. Clare pulled the door shut as Carrot announced take-off.

"Okay, here we go." The speed of the rotors now whined as the helicopter struggled to gain lift. The bird rolled skyward as its wheels pulled free from the suctioning silt. Samantha's stomach lurched sideways; she was thankful she hadn't eaten.

"How far to Dubrovnik?"

"About a hundred fifty miles," Jim answered. "This is a retrofitted Huey, so just over an hour at best speed."

The helicopter leaned over as they banked to the southeast. Samantha gasped when she saw the damage done. Half of Hunters Ridge had collapsed into the sea. Had that missile taken off any later there would be no one to rescue.

"Yeah," Mitch added as if reading her thoughts, "we were damned lucky."

Hunters Ridge disappeared into the twilight, the Huey staying true except for the occasional buffeting. After half an hour Samantha's curiosity got the better of her.

"Jim?"

"Huh?" The big man dropped a map and pen to the floor.

Samantha reached down to retrieve the lost items, looking at the map. "They're isolated."

"What's that?"

Samantha indicated the city of Dubrovnik with a finger. "If the rumbling we heard was the ridge collapsing, we will have to drop right into the city."

"Thanks," he grunted. "How'd you figure that?"

"I studied."

Jim appeared surprised. "That's not the reputation you bring." He spared a guilty glance for Clare.

"Just because you've heard something about me, doesn't mean it's *not* true." Samantha said while looking at her aunt. "I could fly this bird if I had the opportunity. I don't agree with much ARC does, or my assumed place in this organisation. There is too much that is hidden from the public; the very same secrets used to develop enhanced technology—a technology that ultimately failed."

"Yet," Jim countered, "you're the daughter of the Devil. Not only that, you're on this mission to rescue people who may be victims of that specific technology."

Samantha grinned. "Victims of circumstance, aren't we all? Now what do you want with Barbegazi?"

This appeared to catch Jim off guard. The big man looked down at his crossword, avoiding her gaze. "I dunno what you mean."

Samantha leaned back with a smug smile on her face, the leather of her jacket creaking against the seat. "You've written the word 'Barbegazi' on the map. We're on the way to a site of devastation and the exact word you've written names a creature that has a legendary reputation of bringing down mountains."

A slow smile crept across his face. "She's her mother's daughter, no doubt. It's just a theory, though. We don't discount much with what we've seen."

"Such as?"

Clare handed her over a tablet. On it was a picture of what looked like an emaciated man with glowing eyes. "Viruñas," she explained.

"The creature that started this twenty years back—right about when your mom was pregnant with Nina, it was chasing me and those like me around Massachusetts. It killed my mother and stepfather. But for my cat Steve, it would've killed me too. That creature and others like it exist. As time went on and my ARC career unfolded, I was exposed to many more of these mysteries. Every single one of these creatures has some sort of foothold in reality. It's almost as if, what happened…"

Clare looked out at the sea, "…down there affected everything up here. All the bad things we were told as kids: the boogieman, the dark creatures in tales, all stepped it up a notch while your father was being a hero."

"You're right," Samantha agreed, "he was a hero." Finally, someone saw the world the same way as her.

"And yet, there were unintended consequences. There always are. Look at your little tribe. Did you foresee Lucas Rossi using you the way he did? Or the reactions of the crowd on Brusnik? They fished the body of one out of the Adriatic just before Aeon Fall hit us, in case you were interested. Most of the others had already been sent ahead to Dubrovnik's airport. You should understand sometimes consequences can be good. Just look around you. I picked up this lot and others over the years while on the trail of such creatures. As it stands, not one of us on this mission now would be anywhere else."

"Unless it was lying on the beach in Cancun sipping on a Margarita," Mitch piped up. "That'd be quite good."

"Sorry buddy," Jim countered, "Cancun got wiped from the map in the storms. Tidal wave."

"Oh." Mitch looked crestfallen. "I'm sorry to hear it. Still, plenty of places to drink Tequila."

"The latest search we were undertaking was that of the Voydanoy," Jim continued, glaring at Mitch.

Mitch winked back.

Jim smirked and went on, "Froglike humanoids that break dams, abduct people, and drown them. We have the remains of one back at the lab. We were en route to the Czech Republic to look for more when we were diverted—you know, so Boss could be invested in the special club. As soon as we heard about Dubrovnik, we went straight to the most unusual of sources."

"Folklore?"

"Exactly. Witches, pixies, creeping bodysnatchers. They all have myth but behind them is fact. Have you heard of Krampus? Found him in Vienna. The legend is he turned families into dolls. Turned out, what he really did was abduct and eviscerate them. The myth feeds the legend. People accept what they think is truth, no matter how far-fetched."

"He's right," agreed Clare. "I was so fixated on my parents' murderer being one person it almost cost me my life. Never the obvious. That's our motto."

"So, you think Dubrovnik is Barbegazi?"

"Until we can prove otherwise, yes. It's a place to start."

"What about the assertion that it's part of the satellite? Surely that's a much more reasonable explanation?"

Jim inclined his head, conceding her point. "I think when you've had as much experience as—"

"Land ho!" cheered Carrot. "Now maybe you boys can do something useful rather than try and induct poor Sammy into your X-Files club."

Charlotte Benson turned and gave a mock-scary face, eyes wide, mouth 'O-ed'. "It's all a conspiracy… "

Carrot flew the team in close over the city, just above sea level. In the darkness, there wasn't much Samantha could see.

"It doesn't look bad from here," she observed. High walls stood atop cliffs a hundred feet above the roiling sea.

"The coastal side of the city isn't the problem," Clare reminded them, "though I wouldn't make a point of walking the walls with what's happened behind them."

Carrot pulled the Huey higher above the city. In the dark all Samantha could see was a scar in the distant mountain and a stain that spread across the metropolis a couple miles wide. Houses that once stood on the lower slopes were obliterated.

Silence filled the cabin as darkness masked a thousand unseen horrors. Broken limbs, parents crushed under debris, orphaned infants lost with no understanding of what befell them.

"I don't know if we should go down there." Samantha found it hard to admit, but she was scared.

"There's no choice, sorry." Mitch's voice was full of genuine sympathy. He'd seen her moment of vulnerability.

"Surely there's somebody else who—"

"There is no one else," Clare's tone was final. "Even if we didn't have an ulterior motive, we're the first to respond outside of the city and we're well-equipped."

"But we're ARC. The whole world just witnessed our response to Aeon Fall."

"There's nothing to indicate who we are or where we're from," Clare shot back. "You signed on, under my supervision. Well this is where our first mission takes us. You think these people are going to care where you're from, or if you can speak their language? You offer them food, water, first aid. You give comfort to those in need, those who have lost more than you probably ever will. At the end of this night, you'll see the bigger picture."

"And if I don't get the bigger picture?"

"Then I might just leave you until you do."

Samantha slumped back into her seat, avoiding all eye contact. This day was getting worse and worse.

* * *

Carrot hovered above the city. In the lights of the helicopter Samantha could see people waving at them, others shielding their eyes from the luminous assault. Dust billowed everywhere.

Mitch handed Samantha a large backpack. "Medical supplies. Water. Clothing. Emergency gear. Keep your headgear on or you'll end up alone."

Samantha took the gear, nearly dropping the pack. "It's heavy."

Mitch turned back from handing out other packs. "Maybe you'd like mine?" He indicated a pack on the floor.

She leaned over to lift the pack. It wouldn't budge.

"We all have burdens to bear." His tone showed he was not impressed. All trace of the joker was gone. These people took their job seriously.

"People are dying out there. I get it. I'm sorry." Afraid to look anybody in the eye, she opened her pack and stowed her own bag in the top, pulling the straps tight.

A glance showed Mitch still watching her. "There's no space for souvenirs."

"We all have burdens to bear," Samantha said, throwing the words back at him. "All I have of my sister is in there."

"Leave it, Mitch," Jim said. "She has to carry it."

"Okay, time to get busy," Carrot said. "This is as close as we can get without causing more damage. You're gonna have to jump."

Jim took the lead, launching himself into the darkness. Mitch then handed lights and supplies down to him; they were only four feet from the ground. Carrot's reputation was well deserved.

Once the supplies were out, Mitch followed. Charlotte Benson jumped out of the front and this left Samantha peering out over the ruined city.

"Jump," Clare urged from behind.

Swallowing and closing her eyes against the dust, Samantha jumped, Clare following. The landing was rough and uneven but hands caught her.

"Stay there, boss," Carrot instructed. "I'll find you when I ditch the bird."

The helicopter lifted, moving out of range in seconds. The dust began to settle on a very still Dubrovnik. In the dark it was difficult to see the devastation. Samantha expected to hear screams but the only noise aside from the team of rescuers was the occasional shift in rubble. A brick falling loose from a nearby overhang clattered to the paving beneath, making her jump. Jim solved the problem of darkness by powering up the lights. Bright white halogen beams shot into the darkness outward from their position.

They were in the middle of the walled city, on the leading edge of the rubble where paving cobbles crisscrossed diagonally underfoot. A bronze statue of a seated man was nearly covered by what remained of the hillside beyond. The statue appeared calm, accepting. It was what it was.

Behind them a church emerged from the darkness relatively unscathed.

"Dubrovnik Cathedral," Jim informed her. "If you get lost, just head for it. All avenues lead here.

"What do we do now?" she asked.

"We try to figure out if the Secretary General is actually here," Charlotte answered. "We try to help anybody we can or at least pinpoint them for the proper emergency services."

"Why here? Why not up there?" Samantha pointed at the slope beyond.

"There's nothing standing up there." Charlotte's tone was sympathetic. "Anybody who was in a house between the walled city and the origin of the avalanche has been wiped off the face of the earth. You don't move that much mountain and live. It's called triage. We help those who have a chance.

This happened when people were eating dinner in restaurants. I think the best idea is to concentrate on the wide-open spaces. The boys are going to do what they do best and solve this problem. You and I are gonna help the injured. But be careful, Sammy. You don't want to end up being one of them.

Like I have any chance of avoiding that fate. Samantha thought. *Nina, how about you come swap places with me?*

* * *

Samantha spent the night following Charlotte around like a tethered goat on a cliff, being led across rubble and into dark holes as they attempted to find those hadn't fled the city. It was hard going at first but soon she became attuned to the ruins Dubrovnik and people began to emerge.

Her aunt was dead-on. If they didn't speak English, or were too traumatised to try, an unspoken language emerged. She began to care for these dust-caked strangers with broken limbs, and cuts, tears streaking muddy rivulets down the coatings on their faces.

Her pack became lighter as the night wore on, the clothing and water soon exhausted as they aided victim and rescuer alike. They had not moved more than five hundred yards from the Cathedral. The restaurant district was extensive, and heavily populated.

"Water?" Charlotte asked, holding out a hand as she found a gap in rubble through which desperate hands clawed.

Samantha opened her pack. "I don't have any. It's all used up."

"Dammit," Charlotte cursed. "It'll be light soon. We can't stop." Charlotte looked at her, peering into her face. "You're exhausted kid. You've done well. I'll get another pack so we can carry on. We're not done yet. Sit tight and take five. Remember we're still the bad guys."

Samantha shouldered her pack and collapsed to her knees, seeking a way into the people behind the rubble. Alone, she would never move the broken masonry. All she could do was hold the nearest hand. A weak grip, it eventually dropped away. She collapsed back, oblivious to the effort that continued nearby. The ground was cold and unyielding, yet it was a blessing to rest. She closed her eyes, exhausted, thinking about what she could have done for Tracey. All the carnage around her and she could have prevented one small part of it.

Only a minute or two later, the crunch of debris underfoot alerted her. "You back so soon? Thought you'd be as tired as me."

The footsteps stopped. "I'm fine," said a familiar voice, one that chilled her to the bone.

Samantha looked up. "No."

Chapter Nine

Lucas stared down at her, his eyes wide, his brow furrowed. *Of all the bad pennies,* Samantha thought, *it had to be him. And how had he gotten here from the beach across from Hunters Ridge. Were Tamsyn and Donna here as well? And what about Tracey? Had her body been found? Did they bury her?* Samantha's mind scrambled to understand all of this, as he menaced above her.

In the near dark, with his hair hanging about his face, shielding his features from everyone but her she realized this was simply camouflage, He looked like another dust-covered refugee to anybody else, but reeked of the familiar stale sweat.

Samantha rose to stand.

"Stay still," Lucas hissed.

"What are you doing here?" Samantha hissed back, hoping Lucas did not realise how exhausted she was. *Stall for time*, she silently intoned. *Charlotte would be back any moment.*

"Your security goons shipped us here, that's what. They didn't even take us as far as the airport when the world went to hell. It's providence that I found you." Lucas grabbed her by the arm, tugging her to her feet. "Now you're mine. No more demon spells. I'll get what I deserve."

Her arm wrenched behind her back, Lucas forced Samantha along the street they had been searching and down an abandoned side alley from which survivors had already fled. Anyone nearby would miss her distant calls amid the outbursts of anguish already echoing the city and the distant wailing.

Lucas paused, searching for a suitable dark spot. A neon light flickered in the window of what appeared to be a tobacconist. He pushed her through the door.

On unsteady legs, Samantha collapsed to the floor amid the rubble of ruined cigarettes, tobacco leaves erupting from their paper wrappings as they absorbed moisture and swelled.

"I've been looking forward to this for years," Lucas growled. "Ever since the party where we met."

"The Star Wars party?" Every word, sentence, gesture, delayed the inevitable.

"You called me 'Han Duo' because of my size. That really pissed me off, Sammy. I've imagined saying this to you multiple times. Each time less angrily but you always set me off. I'm not in the mood to put up with your crap comments. You never thought it through before saying it."

Samantha climbed to her feet. "Lucas what sort of a moron are you? One with no sense of humor, that's what. I was joking and what did it matter? You were thousands of miles away in seven different time zones on a computer screen!"

"It was an online date," Lucas growled through clenched teeth.

"I was at a party and someone filmed it. You were watching me, as you always have. You know who watches people like that, Lucas? A stalker. That's all you are. A stalker, a bully and a coward."

Samantha instantly regretted her choice of words. Lucas turned away then lashed out, catching her full in the face with the back of his hand.

Knocked to the rubble-strewn floor, Samantha moaned in pain. Behind her, she heard Lucas unbuckle his belt. *My God, he was going to rape her.*

"This is what I am. I—"

Footsteps charged past her from darkness beyond the rubble, the sound of an impact overloading her already stressed senses, another ringing in her ears. Then someone picked up Lucas, physically lifting him off the ground. Samantha pushed at the rubble and turned, trying to make sense of what was going on.

A man stood above her holding Lucas up by the lapels of his jacket in one twisted fist. It seemed her pursuer was assaulted by a statue. The man didn't move or tremble.

"Who … who are you?" Lucas gibbered.

"Kinship and companionship are honorable and terrible things," the deep-throated stranger replied. "They are sacred, not to be abused." With only a slight shift in stance, the stranger hurled Lucas out through the doorway and against the opposite wall, crumpling to the ground.

The stranger turned back to Samantha and for the first time she clearly saw her savior. Standing in the neon light he looked beautiful, yet simultaneously alien. His skin was dark, almost completely black in the shadows. He was totally bald, but sported a full white beard. His upper torso was impressively muscled underneath the tattered grey shirt. His jeans were similarly ruined—all of him ripped, dusty, clearly a casualty of the avalanche, yet serene as if it hadn't affected him.

"Thank you," Samantha said, climbing to her feet. "I think he … well he was about to do something terrible to me. Are you okay?"

The stranger squinted at her. "Your speech returns me clearly home."

"Excuse me?"

He stumbled forward a step, breathing heavily. "Your speech and your appearance: Both alike." With that, he fell against her, nearly crushing her under his weight as he dropped unconscious to the floor and rolled onto his back.

Samantha checked his pulse and breath, much like she had been doing all night. She would never make a decent field nurse, but at least she knew the basics. He lay as if knocked senseless, his breath deep and even, his pulse strong. She looked out into the alleyway, suddenly fearful that she was again alone with Lucas.

There was no sign of the body, just a hole in the wall opposite where the stranger had thrown him. Where was he? Had he gotten up? Fear-ing for her life, Samantha began to panic. Her eyes on the hole, she stumbled over the rubble of the tobacco shop and back out into the alleyway. The darkness beyond the hole was absolute, the building looking as if it would collapse. She left it all behind.

"There you are," Charlotte said as Samantha emerged onto the boulevard, her voice relieved. "You were meant to stay here."

"I'm sorry. I heard voices." A wave of guilt and responsibility overcame her, "There's a man down back there."

"Show me," Clare, who was standing behind Charlotte commented, "You've certainly been busy."

Samantha turned and led them back down the alleyway, her eyes fixed on the hole where the guy had thrown Lucas through a wall! So why did she still feel uneasy?

"What, in there?" Charlotte asked, peering into the hole. Before Samantha could reply she shone a flashlight in the gap. "Nothing. It's empty."

"But that can't be. There was a body."

"You sure, Sammy?" Her aunt leaned in close, pulling her eyelids apart. "Bloodshot, dust filled. I'm surprised you can see anything, especially given you've been awake all night."

"There was … I saw … never mind. That's not who I found. In the shop opposite. He's in there. Be careful."

Charlotte shone her flashlight in through the window for a moment then pushed the door open, saying something in Croatian. Samantha picked up on the word 'help'. She'd heard it enough in the last ten hours.

She followed Charlotte through the doorway back into the shop. The stranger was no longer lying prone on the floor, instead sitting on rubble with his head in his hands.

Charlotte tried a myriad of different languages, the stranger responding to none.

"He was speaking English when I found him. He said my speech and appearance were both alike."

At those words the stranger perked up. "It's you," he said, his face relieved. "What happened to me?"

Samantha put a comforting hand on his arm. She couldn't help but notice that the muscles underneath were rock-hard. "You were in an avalanche. Something caused the mountainside behind the city to give way and collapse. What do you remember?"

"Falling. I fell a great distance. I was up high. Then this." He held his hands out. "I saw my body floating from above. Then I awoke."

His voice had the same rich, deep timbre, but was clearer this time, and he seemed much more aware.

"Do you remember anything else? Your name perhaps? Where you're from?"

He looked up at her. "I … oh. No, nothing comes to mind. I have no idea where I'm from. Something tells me quite far away."

Samantha smiled. "I-oh? That's it—Io. Io will do. It's better than John Doe, at least until you remember."

"Io, can you walk?" Clare asked.

Samantha gave Io a warning glance when he looked past her to the wall opposite.

"I should be fine," he replied. "Guess I must have been on the edge of the avalanche."

"You've no idea!" Charlotte said, turning to lead them out. "Fancy helping us? I assume Sammy here looked you over." She chuckled, viewing him slowly up and down.

"I'm fine," Io replied. "I don't appear to have suffered any major injury. Just lead the way and I'll help where I am able."

Samantha snickered. If Io noticed Charlotte's wanton stare, he didn't react.

Back on the boulevard, Mitch and Jim reached their location.

"Where's Carrot?" Clare asked.

Jim finished tying off a bandage on the arm of a teenage boy while a worried woman, likely his mother, watched. "I sent her off a while back for a few hours shuteye. No point having a pilot who's too exhausted to fly us out of here." He nodded at Io, who waited patiently beside Samantha. "What's his story?"

Samantha repeated Io's experience to Jim, who pursed his lips in thought, rubbing at his chin with one grimy hand. "Out of body experience, eh?"

"You don't believe him?" Samantha felt very protective toward the hulking man beside her, despite the fact he didn't appear to need it.

"They're well-documented," Jim replied, not rising to the bait. "The floating, the seeing of one's self. I highly doubt you were up there though, pal." Jim pointed at the ugly scar in the mountainside. "Not unless you're some sort of superhuman rock surfer. Besides, I know you've got a history of picking up strays, Samantha."

Samantha glared at Clare following the barb, mostly intended to refer to her recent activity. The only way they could have known was for her to have told them. Her aunt ignored her.

Io paid no attention to the conversation, staring instead at a pile of rubble. "There's someone in there."

"That's just a pile of rubble," Mitch said. "Swept up against that wall."

Io continued to stare, revealing the truth to all of them. Samantha crouched and began to shift the rubble, making sure each lump of ruined building and mountain rock was free to move before she tensed to lift.

Io watched, now stilled as if by will he could rescue whomever was buried. As Samantha struggled, Charlotte joined her, helping lift the more sizeable masonry. As a hole emerged in the wall behind, Io stepped forward.

"Give me a light," Samantha asked, holding her hand out behind. Someone passed her a flashlight to illuminate the gap. She saw movement. "There are people in here. Two or three."

"Help us," a weak Italian-accented voice cried.

At the sound of the cry, the rest of the team realized Io was right, moving in to make light work of the rubble. Io's face was animated, his eyes widened and his head tipped to one side as he struggled to listen amid the cries of despair in the Dubrovnik dawn. Finally, he too joined in, removing the largest pieces of rubble. Samantha watched furtively, admiring the way the muscles of his shoulders bunched under his t-shirt.

When a sufficient gap had been cleared, Io dived in. Not waiting for permission, Samantha followed in a crouch, meeting heartbreak within. An old lady, legs crushed under a collapsed wall, lay watching them, her head on a rolled-up blanket. The rest of the room had a gap no more than the height of her shoulders. A cot was up against one wall. There was no doorway. Shards of wood stuck out of the rubble. Presumably this was the door.

Io's attention was focussed on a young woman with a baby. Samantha joined him. The baby mewled weakly, clutched in the dead arms of a young woman with blood running out of her ear. A young woman no more.

Io plucked the baby up with immense care.

"It's my granddaughter, Evangelina," the old woman said.

"Is that your daughter?" Samantha moved over to her. Io followed with the baby.

The old woman nodded, her movement barely a gesture.

Samantha put two fingers to the old woman's jugular. Her pulse fluttered. "She doesn't have long."

Io passed the baby back out of the hole to a waiting Charlotte, then turned his attention to the old lady. "What is your name?"

She smiled up at him, her face peaceful. "Chiara. I can see you; are you here to help me on?"

"We're here to get you out," Samantha said as she threw a questioning glance at Io, but his gaze was fixed on the old lady. "Just hold still and we'll get this rubble off. There's a team waiting to get you to hospital."

"It's too late. My time has passed. But thank you for rescuing my Evangelina. Please, we were her only family. See she is looked after. She is precious."

"Your grandaughter will lead a long and fruitful life," Io assured her. "You will see her again."

Chiara turned her head back, facing the ceiling. "Who are you girl, to be present in the company of angels?"

"My name's Samantha. I'm gonna get you out."

Chiara reached into a sewn pouch on her dress, just above where the rubble ended, withdrawing a thin length of what appeared to be twine. "I have a gift for you. To remind you that you're special. Hold out your hand."

Samantha did as bidden, expecting the old lady hand her the twine.

Instead, in what seemed a final effort, Chiara grabbed her wrist in an iron grip, pulling Samantha closer. Chiara then began to hum, a soothing melody like waves lapping at the shore. She wrapped the cord three times, four times about Samantha's wrist, tying it off in such a way that only cutting the cord would remove it.

Samantha pulled back, staring at the material. It was dark, and appeared to have no weight at all. Golden flecks shone in the light from outside. Raising it close, Samantha smelled lemon and spices on the cord.

"It's beautiful."

"It is Byssus. The soul of the sea. I give it to people that need my help. It brings good fortune to outcasts, people in need. You are such. I pray that you find your fortune, so that all humankind can benefit."

"I need help. We're here rescuing people."

Chiara took a shallow breath, her eyes remaining closed. For a moment she didn't move. Then her eyes opened a crack and in a whisper she said, "You need this. Before the end you will see the truth." Chiara turned her head to look at the body of her daughter. "No more will be spun."

"No more spun? What do you mean? Chiara?"

The old lady's face remained frozen in the stare, eyes unblinking.

"Samantha," Io said, turning her to him. "She's gone."

Chapter Ten

Samantha sat in silence, the noise of rubble a distant distraction as she held the hand of the old lady who had gifted her as the last gesture of her life. But what did it mean?

Out of respect, Samantha composed the body, closing Chiara's eyes and placing her hands folded across her lap.

"She's with her daughter," Io said. "There's nothing more to be done here."

"Who are you?" Samantha wondered aloud. "Those things she said about helping her on."

"I do not remember," Io replied. "Perhaps she just knew it to be her time and was glad not to be alone. To see her granddaughter safe was her last wish in life."

"Was it?" Samantha murmured, examining the twine on her wrist. It weighed nothing. The material was so smooth on her skin it nearly disappeared.

"Sammy," called Charlotte. "Can we get the injured out now?"

"There are no injured here. Just the dead. Head wounds and massive internal haemorrhaging if I were to guess." Sparing one tearful glance for the departed, Samantha wormed her way back through the gap in the rubble to the outside.

A few steps out, her legs turned to jelly. Samantha collapsed onto the ground, a cloud of dust billowing out either side of her. The sun was rising now, its rays turning the bracelet a radiant golden hue, the sparkles within holding her attention.

"You okay?" Clare asked.

About then, the rescue effort intensified, people swarming everywhere through the ruined Dubrovnik streets. Sirens wailed all around.

"She was ready to die," Samantha murmured. "She accepted it. But, what happened to the baby?"

"Local paramedics," Jim provided. "Look, people appreciate our efforts but they're starting to ask questions; in the daylight, we aren't faceless rescuers in the dark. There's nothing down here to indicate what happened. Be it mountain imps or the weather, we need to get to that mountainside."

"I said I'd make sure the baby was looked after," Samantha protested.

"And she will be."

"Her name is Evangelina."

Clare put her arm around Samantha's shoulders. "The little girl is safe. That's all that we can do for now. You've done so much good tonight. You're exhausted. One more stop then you can all get some rest."

On an impulse, Samantha said, "We will have an extra passenger." She pointed at Io, who stood gazing at the sun.

"I don't think that's a good idea. Who is he? Who is he, really?"

"I've no idea," Samantha replied, still mesmerised by the golden bracelet, "but I trust him. He saved my life and found those people by staring at a wall. Doesn't that intrigue you?"

"Unless you know something I don't, all I see is a man suffering from amnesia who found some people by luck. We can alert the local services to care for him."

Samantha folded her arms. "If he stays, I stay. I'm not that enamoured of ARC that I want to go back."

"Boss," Mitch warned, "we're starting to draw attention. It's time for a discreet exit." He pointed along the boulevard where two men in brown military uniform were talking to some of the survivors.

"Well, that's gonna get no answers if we're all in jail."

"Maybe they will thank you."

"Once they find out who we are it's only a matter of time. We move, now. Sammy your stray can come but we drop him off at the first medical that's not filled with military."

The team wormed their way through the destroyed city to the pickup point. Carrot was already in the air, unnoticed; the Huey was one of many helicopters circling Dubrovnik. As they gathered, more and more people began to watch them, some pointing, faces angry bordering on hostile. A group of military began to approach as the wind whipped up under the force of a descending helicopter.

The Huey dropped to a metre above the rubble, hovering as Carrot masterfully played the controls. The growing crowd started to press in.

Samantha pulled Io up behind her, straining at his weight. 'Sit' she mouthed at him indicating the seat opposite her.

The rest of the team piled aboard behind Io, Mitch giving the thumbs up to Carrot, who pulled the Huey out of danger and into the morning sky.

"What's all that about?" Clare asked as they all donned headsets. "Those people weren't just responding to your landing. They looked like they knew something by the looks on their faces. Something about us."

"It's Rockwell. Aeon Fall have been releasing information about ARC and not being shy about it. Their media guy, the crazy looking one with the black hair. He's doing interviews! The Council are all over the internet and you're now part of that, Clare. Here people might be in a disaster but they still have cell phones. Like it or not, this little team's the face of the rescue effort, or the public face of those responsible depending on what you want to believe. Who's our new companion?"

"Nobody knows."

"And you thought bringing a guy on board without knowing anything about him is a wise decision? Boss, I might be tempted to question your judgment."

"If it wasn't for the fact that I extended you the same courtesy all those years back," Clare answered. "Sammy trusts him and has·a rapport. He saved a baby girl by pure luck. I don't feel he's a threat. The moment that feeling changes, he's off the boat."

"Get us up within range of the scar in the mountainside. Circle around it. There's nothing else in that city for us but trouble. We've done all that we can through the night."

Samantha watched Io as the team flew into the sky, studying his face. His hair and beard were silver before their time. It was as if he had undergone a sudden shock. His face still held the slightest vestige of youth. No wrinkles marred his face or his forehead. She feared to have a conversation with him since the whole team could hear, yet she couldn't help herself.

"Anything? Any memories?"

Io blinked, frowning as he concentrated. His face fell. "Nothing. Only those fractions of my name. Io. It's familiar."

Samantha listened, saying nothing. Fully aware that once she opened up to someone it was full-on information disclosure, she feared to say any more in front of a team she barely knew, despite enduring a harrowing night together. Io's apparent innocence was alluring to Samantha. There weren't many innocents in her life.

"There," Io pointed as the helicopter circled into view of the massive scar where once a mountainside had been.

"Bang on," Jim agreed. "Look at that spot near the top. It's circular."

"That's not regular," Charlotte countered. "How can you have a circular impact imprinted in the rock face after a mountainside falls away?"

"Unless whatever hit did so with such impact it pierced the surface and lodged in the rock beneath. We need to get down there. Carrot, can you set us down on the top?"

"You got it, Jim."

Carrot found what was to Samantha a suitably precarious perch for the Huey, a surface of rubble midway between a white stone building and a small knoll with a cross atop a remote shrine. Behind them, the land fell on a shallow slope, the stunted bushes providing a carpet of green all the way up to the distant mountains. It was a huge contrast to the ruination below and to the south, the city crushed by fallen rocks.

"It's just unusual," Jim said, peering over the edge. "From up here you can see the spread of the rock fall. It's as if the mountainside liquefied and took everything with it."

"What should it look like?" Samantha stood next to him, as Jim threw his arm in front of her for protection. "It just looks like a rockslide."

"Well, that's the thing. It might look like that." Jim shook his head. "Boss, I wouldn't want to be here when this happened. The mountainside erupted outward and at a speed that covered the city. A simple avalanche would have been caught up in the first few buildings, and not continued nearly to the sea. Something propelled this rock much, much faster."

Clare looked confused. "How?"

Jim continued to study the destruction below. "There's a fault line in the Adriatic but that's what created those islands; it wouldn't cause this sort of damage. It's not like the Pacific Northwest, yet just look at it. The rock's levelled everything as if it behaved exactly that way. Those people caught in this didn't stand a chance. The impact caused this rock to liquefy, to become superheated. Something big hit this mountainside and set it off."

"Sammy, I want you to take Io and get back away from the edge. Go wait up by that building. Helping the injured is one thing. You can't help here."

Nonplussed, Samantha answered, "Clearly. Come on." She turned and grabbed Io, pulling him along with her.

"Just don't go too far," Clare cautioned.

Trudging along the limestone path, Samantha shifted the strap of her rucksack. Nearing the building, which judging by all the chairs and tables appeared to be a restaurant, Samantha stopped to view the city below. The Adriatic stretched out to the horizon beyond. Ruined Hunters Ridge was out there somewhere.

She pulled a Bramley apple from her bag and offered it to Io, who stood docile beside her. "Want one?"

Taking the apple, Io turned it in his hands, examining the dark-green skin. "What do I do with it now?"

The simple question took Samantha aback. "That rockfall really scrambled your brain, didn't it? How come you have a perfect grasp of the English language to the point of making super-profound statements yet you don't retain enough knowledge to know what an apple is or that you're supposed to eat it?"

"I. . ." Io examined the apple once again, looking at her as if unsure.

Samantha took another apple out of her bag and bit into it, the flesh firm and the sharp tang, refreshing after the hard night. It rejuvenated her.

Watching her do this, Io copied her actions. He sighed with pleasure as he chewed the apple.

Samantha giggled. "It's as if you've never eaten anything before."

Io finished the apple in several greedy bites, juice spilling into the white of his beard. "It's not a sensation I can recall."

Samantha smiled. "That must be amazing, feeling all these impressions for the first time and being able to process them."

"This is not how it happens?"

"Of course not. Have you got memory loss, or been on a different planet?" *Why didn't he know this?* Samantha wondered. A little in awe, she said, "That must be amazing. Feeling all those positive sensations again as if for the first time."

Io held up the apple core. "This is a positive sensation?"

He opened his mouth to eat the core and Samantha grabbed the arm. "Not that bit. More of those will grow from that part if you bury it. The core isn't good for you."

"Oh." Io reached back and instead hurled the core up and over the restaurant. A collection of outraged squawks arose from where the core landed.

"Follow me," she said.

Io looked back watching Charlotte winch Jim lower over the scarred slope. "What about your companions?"

"They have their methods to find the answers. I have my own. Come on."

Samantha led Io around the building and down a limestone scree slope onto a lower access road. In the fresh breeze of the morning, distant herbs, thyme, rosemary, wafted in from the hillside. Nearby a radio antenna tilted at a precarious angle toward the city. Beyond them, on a shallow slope of scraggly birch and half-dead bushes, a flock of twenty-plus crows gathered—the source of the squawking.

Samantha turned, looking back from where they had come. "You threw that apple quite a distance," she observed.

"My apologies," Io replied. "Was that wrong of me?"

"No, it was just unexpected. A good throw." Samantha opened her bag, pulling out a brown leather-bound book. She opened it to reveal a series of geometrical patterns. "Let's see what the birds have to say to us."

Io stood close. Samantha could feel the warmth from his body as he leaned over her shoulder to examine the pages. "You're a very spiritual person. You have faith."

The statement could have been a question. Samantha didn't know how to take it. "Not in religion. Not in God. Certainly not in my family. I love Nina but Mom always doted on her. The shining star, the *special* one." Samantha flicked to the next page. "Mom never gave me the time of day. It taught me faith in myself."

"Who's Nina?"

The question stopped her dead. It had been years since she'd been asked that. Everybody knew whose daughter and younger sister Samantha Scott was. The sensation was refreshing. She smiled. "My sister. Far less of an inconvenience than I. Hold this please." She handed Io the book, withdrawing two rusted metal pegs from her bag, unwinding the string most of the way before tying it off. At Io's questioning look she explained, "The circle varies in size depending on the time of day and the number of birds."

"You have faith in nature then?"

Samantha paused. By the intent look on Io's face, this question was very important to him.

"Yes, I do. It's never steered me wrong. Step back please."

Io complied and Samantha inserted the first peg into the limestone soil. The ground was well-drained and loose. The outer peg carved a large circle as she moved it around. When she had finished, Samantha wrapped her tools back up and stored them.

"Now what?" Io asked.

"Now whoever wants to read the signs holds the book and casts an object into the midst of the flock. If you're lucky the flock will settle and you'll be able to pick out shapes. It's a method of divination. Like reading tea leaves with birds. But you have to believe."

"That should not be a problem for me," Io replied as he stepped into the circle and kneeled to pick up a fist-sized chunk of green-stained limestone. "I can't remember anything about myself so I don't know if I believe or not. I'm a blank parchment."

"That's good enough for me," Samantha conceded. "Now is it good enough for them? Just throw the rock into their midst and try not to hit them. Let's see if they make a shape we can recognise."

Still watching her with those big, dark eyes, Io hurled the rock out into the field.

The flock of crows rose in unison, squawking with alarm, and flying in randomly across the field.

"It's working," Samantha called out, feeling exultant.

"Then why do I feel nervous?" Io called back.

The crows, shrieking now, flew about them, some getting so close that Samantha instinctively ducked as they tore over her head.

"Is this supposed to happen?" Io asked, head lowered, shoulders hunched.

"It's unpredictable," she replied. "They'll land once they calm down."

But the crows weren't done. As the flock surged back and past the perplexed Io, they flew up into the air, forming a cone, the birds spiralling tighter and tighter as they neared the peak. When it seemed they could get no tighter, the flock dived straight toward Io, an arrow of black fury directly at the heart of the circle.

Chapter Eleven

"Get down!" Io shouted, moving toward Samantha.

"No! Stay in the circle! You'll ruin it." Samantha could do nothing more than duck behind Io as the crows screamed past, the circle with Io in it bisecting the shooting crows as they flew to either side. The birds regrouped as soon as they had passed, flocking over the field once more. Instead of massing for another attack, the flock settled to the ground in two arrow-shaped patterns, one inside the other. The crows watched Io with what Samantha could only describe as expectation. It was as if this was not yet over.

"Is this a sign?" Io asked, clearly startled by the turn of events.

Samantha stood beside him in the circle. As one, the crows turned to regard her before looking back at Io.

"More than I've ever seen. That pattern. It's the Thornfalcon." Samantha turned a couple of pages in the book and pointed midway down the page to a drawing where two arrows were slightly offset. The words *spina vulturem* were scrawled in Latin underneath.

"There's a problem with this pattern though, Io. It's the only pattern with no explanation. The casting rarely works at all and then it's more guesswork than interpretation. There were several other signs, easier to read." She pointed at the floor to where three feathers had settled to the ground as the last bird had passed. "Three feathers falling from one crow means you'll be forced to leave something precious behind. Your memories perhaps?"

Io laughed. "I certainly hope not. I'd like to know who I am and where I came from before this is all over. What else do you have?"

Samantha flicked through the pages. "Two arrows of crows in two different directions is a symbol for two dangerous fronts coming. And here." She pointed at a drawing of a circle. "A circle of screaming crows means protection."

"They were spiralling and could have been screaming," Io sounded dubious. "But protection from what?"

Samantha closed the book. "There is one other possibility with what happened. The spiral could have been a cone of power in the sky, I've just never seen one before. It's one of the most potent tools used in magick. It focuses power upward so that your spell can be released to the universe."

"But you're just reading signs."

"Yes, but in a way, that's a spell. We are entreating nature to reveal the future to us through a specific set of events. The circle for protection. The rock. The crows. It's what I believe. Whoever you are, I would say the crows recognise you as a kindred spirit."

Io moved to the edge of the circle and the pattern of crows shifted to follow him.

"Definitely," Samantha confirmed.

"Hey guys, we're just about done here," Mitch shouted from up by the restaurant. "You finished playing?"

Samantha broke the line of the circle and the crows scattered, cawing as they swirled in a low cloud to then settle into a random pattern on the ground. Their message had been erased. "We need to find the meaning of that," she said as she led Io from the rock field.

"You think it's important?"

"Yeah. Doesn't it appear somehow convenient that the one pattern with no explanation forms when we most need answers? I have a feeling. I think we need to work out where this book came from."

* * *

The two figures walked off over the hill to where their fellows waited. Karael watched. Nebulous, without any discernible form and invisible to the eyes of the mortals who had unwittingly called him, he felt a sense of satisfaction. But which of them was it? The signal indicated the male. Sure, powerful, yet somehow lacking presence. The female appeared to be leading. Dominance was a trait he could associate with. After all, he was a Power, one of their strongest. All was not as it should be, though it didn't matter to Karael. If the fallen one was not aware of his or her power and importance, so much the easier for that one to be contained and eventually dispatched. Fallen was fallen. None of their order was allowed on this plane. Not since He descended and took many of their brethren with them so long ago. He decided to follow, but at a distance. A vessel would present itself to him in time. *The hunt was on.*

"So. Crow divination, eh?" Mitch had a knowing smile on his face as if he were a party to some secret or joke only he could understand. "How's that working out for you?"

They walked back toward Jessica. The Huey was, as Carrot had implied, painted red. Bright on top with a darker hue on the underbelly. Not a vehicle to be missed.

"It has its uses," Samantha replied. "What about you guys?"

"We're done here," Charlotte said as she hefted a pack before sliding it across the floor inside the Huey with the rasp of metal scraping metal. Jim grabbed the pack and stowed it up against a bulkhead.

"There's an impact point in the side of the mountain," Clare added. "It's best seen from the air unless you fancy climbing down."

Samantha walked to the edge of the cliff and looked over. The ruined city lay beneath, houses flattened by the rockslide. Like ants, people scoured the surface debris looking for any signs of survivors. From this distance it was all so detached.

A hand grabbed her shoulder, pulling her back. "Don't stand there too long," Clare warned. "The entire rockface is a spiderweb of fractures. It could go at any time."

"And you're up here with a helicopter?"

"We don't have the luxury of time and safety, not if we expect to get any answers," her aunt tersely replied. "We're packing up and heading back to the city. We need to take a look at the rock fall on the upper slopes."

"Why?"

"For remains."

"Of what."

"Let's get airborne and we'll show you."

Clare waited for Io to climb aboard and offered a hand to Samantha before climbing in the cockpit next to Carrot.

In moments they were airborne, the Huey circling out into the air above the scarred mountain.

"Here." Charlotte offered her a pair of electronic binoculars.

"We not getting that close?"

"I think this one's best explained with a bit of perspective," she answered mysteriously.

Samantha waited until Carrot indicated with a wave of her hand that they were in a stable hover. Jim pulled the hatch open and despite being strapped in, Samantha leaned back.

"What do you see?" Jim asked over the headset.

"Rock," she replied. "Lots and lots of rock. Like a mountain's worth."

"Funny. Look again, about three quarters of the way up the bare face."

Using the binoculars, Samantha zoomed in on the rock face, moving the field of vision around until she spotted a dark circular area. "Well that's odd."

"What you're seeing is marble, formed under intense heat and pressure."

"What's so significant about that?"

"This is a limestone ridge. It's sedimentary in nature. The pressure and heat needed to turn it into marble is found at convergent plate boundaries. Basically you need two continental plates to make that stuff. Zoom out."

Samantha did so. "Radial fractures in concentric circles around your marble. Also fractures in different directions but all perpendicular to that central spot."

"Have you ever seen such a pattern before?"

Samantha looked at Io.

"I haven't," he shrugged.

Jim pulled out a tablet computer and flipped the screen in his hands so that she could see it. On the screen was a fracture pattern almost exactly the same as the mountainside.

"Bullet fired into a Plexiglas sheet," he elaborated.

Samantha looked back at the rock face. "You're saying someone started this disaster by firing something at the mountain?"

"I'm saying something hit the mountain with such force that the heat and pressure at impact caused the rock to melt and reform in a process that normally takes millions of years."

"Well what could do that? No conventional weapon could have such an effect."

"We don't know," Jim admitted. "I couldn't find a single scrap of debris."

"Could it have been destroyed and melted in that central area?"

"No. Anything man-made would have resulted in residual material. If it were nuclear in nature, we'd all be seriously ill. Even an underground nuclear test wouldn't have such a defined effect. Do you understand me? Nothing on earth could do this."

Samantha nodded. She understood. She'd learned enough ARC lore to get what Jim meant. In front of Io, whoever he was, it was not the place or time to discuss the fact that ARC was formed to monitor and if possible prevent demon incursions onto earth.

"Carrot take her down," Clare ordered.

Samantha's stomach lurched as the Huey tilted away from the rock face. A pilot herself, she made a mediocre passenger at best. She had learned to manage, but preferred to concentrate on the instruments and controls to cope. If she were honest, she would admit she hated the lack of control.

Io watched her, a slight smile on his face. "You'd rather be in control."

This surprised those around her. "You do fly?" asked Charlotte. "It just sounded like bravado when you made the claim before."

"I thought you lot would know that about me," Samantha replied, gripping the sides of her seat. "Smaller craft, fixed wing planes. Nothing like this." Finding everyone staring at her, disbelief written plain on their faces, she added, "I didn't spend my entire life rebelling and raising demons, you know."

Those around her chuckled—all except Io, who looked at her in horror. "Why would you do that? How can you do that?"

"You've fallen in with special people, friend," Mitch said with a grin. "This one especially."

"It's just an image, if it ever works at all," Samantha admitted.

"Who are your people?" Io asked, looking around at all of them.

"Probably your best chance at getting out of this city in one piece," Clare said. "Come help us, or stay in the bird, it makes no difference to me. Just don't have a panic attack while we're in the air and we'll see you safe. Time to land."

* * *

This time, instead of hovering, Carrot set the Huey down on a square of concrete that was not caught in the rubble. About them lay the remains of houses swept away by the landslide. Dust billowed everywhere as the Huey whipped up the remains of the slide. Samantha had to cover her mouth. There were fewer people in this part of the city. At the base of the mountainside, all trace of habitation had been swept away.

"Must've been the foundation of one of the buildings," Jim grunted, fingering a few slivers of stone.

"How is it so clear?" Samantha asked.

"The force of the impact, the speed of the falling rock, shoddy construction. Pick one, or all three. Pick others. This was a freak event. There's no precedent for this devastation. From here, the closest thing

I can compare it to is Mount St Helens. The volcano exploded sideways and took everything with it for miles. We don't have miles here, but as for the rest—" Jim shrugged. "Your guess is as good as mine regarding the events that followed, but the source is up there. Let's call it our heavenly bullet. If there are any remains, any sign at all, it'll be here."

Samantha looked up at the mountainside. It loomed above her, the scar fresh and angry, the edges jagged where the rock had been pulled away following the impact. Knowing what had happened left Samantha feeling edgy and small. The awesome destructive power of nature was a tonic to remind humanity their existence was merely temporary.

"Are you wondering how this could have been avoided?" Io asked. In the shadow of the mountain there was a chill. Samantha shivered and Io stood close, putting his arm around her shoulder.

"Bit forward, aren't you?" Io stepped away, but Samantha added, "No, stay where you are. You're warm." His heat reminded Samantha that she hadn't slept in a day and she began to feel drowsy.

"In answer to your question," Samantha added, "Yes. In part. I was thinking how brief our time is on this earth, to have it wiped away by something that could have been avoided. This is all Mom's fault. She sent that satellite into orbit. If it hadn't been there, Aeon Fall wouldn't have been able to override the systems. Humanity's great ideal and all we have is more chaos."

Io turned to her. "You don't think any good can come of this?"

Samantha stepped away from him, pointing downslope at the flattened buildings. "There is no good. Period. This is the nearest disaster to Hunters Ridge and they send us straight here. What else has happened around the world that we don't know about?"

"There's no conspiracy theory here," Jim said from nearby where he was examining more stone splinters. "Sometimes the path isn't clear to us and we have to take a leap in the dark."

Samantha fingered her tattered backpack, poking at one of the holes. The book within caught in her fingers. A leap of faith was needed.

"The symbol worries you," Io said.

Once again he had unintentionally read her thoughts. "It does," Samantha admitted.

"Maybe we're looking in the wrong place."

Samantha took the book out once more, opening it at the page with the Thornfalcon on it. "If you're causing such a prolific reaction maybe we need to research this symbol."

"Where does the book come from?"

Samantha flicked through the pages. "Nina gave it to me a few years back. She pulled it from the ARC library in Geneva, where we grew up. There're some names inscribed here."

The writing on the front page was spidery and faint. Samantha held the page out in the sunlight to better see.

"No, that's not what you wanna do," Jim said as he came over, dropping the stone chips he was examining. "Shine a light behind the script, then the writing is silhouetted rather than reflected with the rest of the page. But you want to do that out of the sunlight. Put your book away for now."

"No luck?" Samantha asked, indicating the remains of house and mountain.

Jim made a noise of disgust, somewhere between a growl and a curse. "There's nothing here. Whatever happened up on the mountain, it didn't translate down here with the rubble."

"How do you know?"

"I don't. My gut tells me this is fruitless. That and a frikkin' big landslide. Where do we start? The answers lie up there." Jim pointed up. He could have been pointing skyward or at the mountain.

A thought struck Samantha and she followed the skyline until she caught view of Io. He stared into the distance, fear on his face.

"What is it?"

Chapter Twelve

"I know him."

"Who?" Samantha turned to follow Io's gaze. In the distance, on a street littered with rubble, a man in a long black jacket stood watching them. She could only make out the coat and black hair but the way he carried himself was familiar. "It can't be."

"Friend of yours?" asked Jim as the figure began to walk toward them.

The features became more defined as the figure neared. "It's Lucas. My stalker. He led the group I summoned demons for."

Samantha looked to Io, who hadn't taken his eyes off Lucas strolling leisurely, as if enjoying the moment.

"He misled a lot of people. He's not a good person. He found me once before, last night."

"He what?" Clare asked. "Sammy, what did he do?"

"Io saved my life by throwing Lucas through a wall."

Jim and Clare both stepped back from their new companion, who kept the approaching Lucas in his sight.

"He should be dead. Don't you see? This is wrong." Samantha implored.

As Lucas neared, Mitch moved to bar his way. "That's close enough, pal. What do you want here?"

Lucas stopped, eyeing up the larger man for a second. "Move," he said in a low voice devoid of emotion. It didn't sound like Lucas. That one word demanded compliance.

Mitch was not intimidated. "Not till you answer my question. You look like a man on a mission. What's your business here?"

Lucas began to laugh, reaching out and laying a hand on Mitch's shoulder. "A mission indeed. Move aside."

Mitch folded his arms. "Not a chance."

Lucas shrugged and with the slightest shift in his stance, sent Mitch flying backwards through the air until he hit an undamaged wall.

Samantha cringed at the sound of the impact and watched in horror as his body slumped to the ground, a red stain on the wall where his head collided. He lay against the wall, unmoving.

"Mitch!" Carrot screamed, running to him. She knelt next to the prone Mitch, his arms splayed out and one leg folded underneath at the knee. Blood ran from his nose. "There's no pulse. You bastard. You've killed him." Carrot stood, tears streaming down her face, moving to confront Lucas. Clare moved quickly to keep Carrot where she was, holding her by the arms. "Don't. You want him to kill you, too?"

"He was dead the moment he barred my path," Lucas said in a calm voice, his eyes on Carrot. "Anybody who bars my path to you will suffer the same fate."

"Lucas, what the hell's wrong with you?" Samantha took a step back, bumping into Io. His body was rigid, unyielding.

"I've come for *you*."

"Can't you just leave it alone? I don't want any part of your sordid cult."

Lucas took a couple of steps closer. "Why did you do it, Brother? You know the consequences of falling. It was decreed you would be hunted and your existence forfeit, yet you fell. Why?"

For the first time, Samantha realised that Lucas wasn't looking at her but at Io directly behind her. She turned. "Io, what's he talking about?"

"I know him."

"Of course you do. That's Lucas. You saved me from him in the city. He was going to rape me." Her voice wavered, overwhelmed by the admission.

"The man you knew is gone. There's someone else inside. I can see him," Io's voice was questioning, as if he didn't believe his own sight.

He turned to Samantha, asking, "What does it mean?"

Samantha quickly focused, "I—"

The man she knew as Lucas interrupted, "It means you're a traitor, Ioviel. It means the instant you made the decision to forsake your brethren and join those who fell, you forfeited any rank you may have held. You are no better than the master of base treachery himself, the prince of darkness. It's my appointed task to hunt down and rid the heavens of your rebellious souls. But you know that."

"Maybe I should," Io answered, "but I'm telling you I don't remember how I came to be here. I can see you're not really the man who stands before me." Io stretched his hands out palms up, looking at them. "I don't recognise myself. I've no idea why."

"If that's the truth you want to cling to, so much the better. It makes my task easier." Lucas held a clawed hand out to one side. A sword blinked into existence as everyone took a step back. The hilt and cross-guard were golden, the blade of burnished silver that shone brighter than the day. Samantha held her hand in front of her eyes. The sword was in complete contrast to the black-clad goth who wielded it.

"That can't be real," Samantha whispered, dazzled by the sword. "Lucas, who are you?"

"Lucas is dead. I am Karael, here to redress the balance." Lucas's regarded her for a moment and then he hissed, "Abomination! I never considered for a moment Ioviel would consort with hellspawn. Thus is my journey twofold: To prevent the falling of my brother and to rid humanity of His progeny."

Lucas, or Karael, moved toward her with catlike steps, stalking her.

"I don't care who, or what you are," Io said. "You'll not raise a hand against her." He ran forward, one hand outstretched to grab, the other balled in a fist, ready to punch. Crossing the distance between them in only a few steps, Io launched himself at his sword-wielding opponent, only to be caught in mid-air by Karael's free hand.

"You think yourself in any way my equal?" Karael shouted, eyes blazing, lips peeled back. He threw Io in the same direction he had thrown Mitch. Io slammed into the wall, dropping to his knees as the stonework crumbled behind him. Strangely, Io appeared unharmed.

Samantha cowered, naked and alone in front of Karael's fury.

Karael turned away from her, his attention again on Io. "Even were you at full strength with all of your knowledge and experience, you don't have my virtues. He set me on His ordained path, to rid our ranks of dissenters. He imbued me with His essence, from His very hand. Do you not understand? This is the sword of Jophiel. I wield its righteous power." The sword glowed brighter and a flame wrapped around the blade, as Karael stalked after Io, the edge held low. As the sword burned, the eggy stench of sulfur filled the air.

"Even without this, I could end you with my bare hands, traitor. Were you at your full strength, with the Powers at your command, you would not prevail. If you remembered who you were, who I was, you would wish for my Divine mercy. As it is…" Karael raised his face skyward. "Let this be a lesson to those who would choose the path of the fallen over the service their creation demands!"

Io staggered to his feet, evidently unharmed. "I … won't … let … you…"

Karael hit Io with a series of punches and kicks, forcing him to drop to his knees, head bowed as he tried to support himself with his hands.

"What makes you think you have a choice?" Karael moved his sword arm across his chest so that the sword angled up behind his head, tensing for a backswing that would end in a killing strike.

But the blow never came. From behind, something tugged at Karael's hand, pulling it past his throat and back over his shoulder. A metallic cord wrapped his arms to his chest, two, three times. The cord tightened and one sharp tug jerked Karael from his feet, his body crashing face-first to the ground. The sword fell loose, dimming to a dull grey as it did so.

On the other end of the line, Charlotte Benson said, "Don't you wish everything was tech, like Helltech? Io pick up that sword."

Pushing himself to his feet, Io did as asked. The sword failed to respond when he touched it. He looked to Samantha and shrugged.

"Do with it what you will," Karael growled from the ground. "End me as I would have ended you. This will be your only chance, Ioviel."

Io raised the sword above his vanquished foe, trembling as he held it aloft.

Karael watched, waiting for the blow. "Do it."

"No," Io lowered the sword, letting the tip touch the ground as he leaned on it. "This isn't right. I would never do such a thing."

Karael began to laugh, a wheezing, guttural noise. "If you only knew who you are, what you are, you would have struck a killing blow. It's what you do best."

"That may be your truth but I will discover the reality on my own, without your poisonous words to taint me." He looked to Charlotte. "Will that hold him?"

"Hard to say. It's doing a good job of it so far. What do you reckon, boss?"

Clare took her phone away from her ear. "I'd say we've found a prettier prize than some Barbegazi. I need to stay here and help coordinate the search for Secretary-General Tran. He's still not been found. ARC are sending some people to pick this one up and take him to a facility." Clare looked from Benson to Io. "Him? I'm still not convinced, but Sammy you're doing a good job with him. See what else you can discover. I'm giving you Charlotte. I need Jim here. Carrot?" she called over to the pilot, "Can you fly?"

Her face stained with tears, Carrot looked up from the body of Mitch. "Whatever you want, boss."

"Get these guys to our Dubrovnik hangar and see them onto a plane. Then come back. We could use you here. We will move Mitch's body in the meantime, and see him given the respect he deserves."

"Gotcha." Carrot stood, walking over to Samantha. Looking her in the eye, Carrot turned, and with a few quick steps, kicked Karael in the face. "That was for Mitch. Come on, guys."

As Samantha walked off, Io followed, still trailing the sword in the dirt. "What does this mean?" he asked her.

"I don't know. Together we'll find out."

"It means I will escape this," Karael roared from between broken teeth. "Soon. This body is weak. I'll make it stronger. I will come for you, forsaken prey!"

Karael continued to bellow curses at them as they climbed into the Huey, his voice soon drowned out by the chop of the rotors.

"Something unhinged about that one," Charlotte commented as they took off.

"You think?" Carrot said over the headsets. Her voice was subdued. How she wasn't in shock was beyond Samantha's comprehension. This group was tough.

"I'm sorry, sweetie. I know you two were close. This is all happening so quickly."

Io sat staring at the sword. It gave off the faintest glimmer as he turned it in his hands. "It looks familiar." He hefted the sword in one hand. "It feels familiar."

"Maybe holding on to it will help you remember more?" Samantha suggested. "What was it he called you? Io Vel?"

"Something like that."

"Well it's something to go on. He called himself Karael. That's something else. First though, what was that rope you bound him with, Charlotte?"

"Helltech, reverse-engineered from what your mother brought back from her trip down below."

This made Io look up. "What did you call it?"

"Helltech. It's a pretty appropriate description."

Samantha asked, "May I fill him in?"

"If your stray dog is gonna stay to heel, you may as well," Charlotte agreed. "It's not like he doesn't have his own secrets."

Samantha flashed a grateful smile. "Twenty years ago, Mom went to Hell. Literally. It's in no way a figure of speech. Do you remember the disturbances across the Earth?"

Io shook his head.

"Demon incursion. They found a way to come to Earth to flee Hell. By all accounts something worse broke free and Hell was freezing over. They needed to balance the numbers on the mortal plane and this would have become a new Hell. One demon prince, Belphegor, kidnapped my sister Nina just after birth, and took her to Hell. They wanted Mom to follow. In time she did, with my father, and a small group to rescue Nina. I don't know every detail but in short, my father became the new Satan."

"Surely such a feat is not possible," Io said. "Satan was a fallen angel."

"And yet, happen it did. My mother was given a piece of technology while there. Armor that drew on an energy source and regenerated both her and itself. For a while she was nigh-on immortal. The armor came back with her."

"We can't make the armor work without the power source it drew on in Hell," Charlotte said, "yet using it we have been able to enhance our own tech. Armor, transport, weapons."

"And yet you fly in this machine?"

Charlotte laughed. "We've developed transport, though nowhere near perfected it. This however, might be useful." She reached beneath her seat and pulled out a shiny black case. Two locks opened with a clunk as Charlotte opened the lid. She turned the case so Samantha could see. "Take it."

Nestled in the foam-lined interior was a handgun. Samantha reached in and withdrew the weapon. "It's nearly weightless."

"It's as close as they could replicate to the material used in the armor. It's a polymer. The pin and a lot of the internals are still metal, but the bullets are made of the same material. It might be useful if he finds you again."

Samantha was dubious as she gripped the gun and turned it. "I hope that's not gonna be the case. Won't your rope hold him?"

"Maybe. But better to have every fighting chance if you're going to be looking over your shoulder the rest of your life. Let me tell you a little about your aunt. You know she's diabetic?"

Samantha nodded.

"Her first job was hunting down a creature that preyed on diabetics. She killed it, but in doing so, almost killed herself. Now that illness stalks her every day of her life. She accepts it and makes the best of what she has. I think she wants you to learn that you're more than the shadow of your mother, or your sister. Maybe it's time for Samantha Scott to embrace her responsibility to the world."

"Is that what we're doing here? It seems more like an escape."

"Whoever it was back there wanted Io here, and manifested a sword out of thin air. A flaming sword. If you don't agree you've been plunged deep into the mire with the rest of us, you're kidding yourself, Sammy. Now do you want to let us have a look at this book you've been carting about? Maybe I can help you make sense of it."

"Book?"

Charlotte gave her a knowing look. "You two weren't the only ones present at your demonstration with the crows. There's always someone watching. Show me the sign that perplexed you."

Confused, Samantha placed the gun in her bag, pulled her crow divination book out and opened it at the page with the Thornfalcon drawn on it.

Charlotte reached over and took the book. For a moment she stared, turning the book in different directions and frowning as she did so. "It says Thornfalcon but that's not what it means."

"You recognise it?" Samantha began to tense with expectation.

"Yeah. It's Hebrew. One word. The letters are basically drawn but nonetheless recognisable." She looked up at the both of them. "The word is Karael."

Chapter Thirteen

What had she done? "Io?"

"Are you an angel?" Charlotte asked.

Io's face darkened as he considered this. Confused as he was, he probably remembered nothing.

Samantha watched him struggle and felt for the man, if he were a man at all.

"I don't know. I can't remember."

"That excuse is gonna wear thin soon. Karael certainly seems to think you are," Charlotte pressed. She flipped the book so they could see the pages. "You carry a book around full of divination and prophecy. The one unexplainable glyph that forms out of wild birds, points at you. Five minutes later, a man Sammy expects to be dead is walking around throwing people through walls and manifesting glowing swords out of thin air, and he is looking for you. On top of that, a city lies destroyed from a landslide that should never have happened. We've got evidence that something impacted the surface and turned limestone to marble. You're at the centre of this, and you can't remember a thing? Or is it that you refuse to remember? Or tell?"

"Charlotte enough," Sammy intervened. "Can't you see he's distressed enough without this grilling? It's not his fault Mitch is dead. The blame for that lies ultimately at the doorstep of Aeon Fall. Without them we wouldn't be here."

Io shuddered at the mention of the name.

Samantha paused, "What is it?"

"That name. Aeon Fall, a thousand years of darkness. I feel it all around me, the apathy. Even from you. One can be blind to their own mind and still see that looking to demons for salvation is a bad choice."

"It got you out of Dubrovnik though, didn't it?" Charlotte countered. "Humanity will remember the big picture, not necessarily the events that brought us there. It's what we do best. Foreboding is another thing we do well. These weapons, that armor, the technology ARC is developing may one day mean the difference between survival and extinction. Mankind may never know what saved them, but we sure as hell will." Charlotte flicked through the book, pausing at the front cover and frowning. "Divine Mercy—where have I heard that before?"

"What do you see?" Samantha tried to get a better look but Charlotte had the book tilted up.

"It's a stamp on the inside of the cover." She ran her hands over the cover and along the spine of the book. "This feels off. Anyone got a knife?"

"No, you can't," Samantha protested.

"Never mind," Charlotte continued, pulling a penknife from her pack. "Have you never noticed how thick the cover is?"

Samantha shrugged. "I just figured it was an old book."

Charlotte snorted. "Kids today. Surprised you lot know what a book is!"

Before Samantha could cry out again, Charlotte ran the blade down the inside of the cover where it met the spine. As the blade cut through the material, the inside of the cover pushed up, revealing folded sheets almost the entire size of the cover. "Jackpot. We may get to the bottom of your strange crow antics yet. How far to the airport Carrot?"

"Ten miles or so. Not long. We'll be touching down soon."

Samantha looked out of the window, the Adriatic hurtling beneath her while she was lost in thought. The icon meant Karael and now he knew of them. Was Io's peril her doing? Would Karael be soon following them? Angels did have wings. She looked at the tormented Io. *Well they are supposed to. Most of the time.*

Supposed to what? Intervened a voice in her head.

Nina? How can you hear me so far away?

You're my little sis. I know what to listen out for.

Where are you?

There was a brief pause. *On my way to meet my contact. I won't be able to do this much after now. Just stay safe, and listen to Mom. Now what's up?*

Nina, there are angels on Earth and your book has a map in it. When there was no reply she continued. *Nina? You there?*

Nothing.

"Let's see if we can solve your conundrum before we do," Charlotte decided, not having been a party to the conversation in Samantha's head. As she unfolded the pages, she said, "Moresby? Who's Moresby? The author?"

"Where does it say that?"

Charlotte turned the book around again, holding the opened page flat against the cover. There was a map on it, along with rows of numbers. "A series of navigational jottings and one word. 'Moresby'. This is an island somewhere. This points here," she indicated the top of the page, "is where the map ends."

"Is that where we will find Divine mercy?" Io asked.

"Why don't we cross reference that?" Samantha suggested. "This is the age of technology, after all. Give me your tablet."

Still occupied with the new pages, Charlotte handed over the computer without looking up. It didn't take long for Samantha to bring up a search engine. She typed in 'Divine Mercy Publications in Port Moresby.' "This could be it."

"Or, a convenient combination of words," Charlotte replied. "That's a real leap of faith. Where's Port Moresby?"

"Papua New Guinea. It's the capital city."

"It's also on the other side of the world."

Samantha's face brightened. "Perfect! Aunt Clare said she wanted us far out of the way. No better reason than to visit this place and find out if they know anything. And besides, we could do with some sleep."

"If only she'd been through the special forces sleep deprivation training," Carrot muttered over the headset. "Then she'd know what tired is."

* * *

In a couple of minutes, the helicopter began to descend. The sun was high in the sky, an astounding contrast to the day before when the malfunctioning satellite set off bizarre weather systems on a global scale.

The bleached concrete of the airport glared at them annoyingly as they touched town at the warehouses constructed at the end of the runway—far from prying eyes and the airport main terminal at the other end of the complex.

Samantha squinted as she jumped down, not sure where to look. She raised her arm above her face against the blowing dust and tugged Io along with her free hand.

"This way," Charlotte shouted above the noise of the rotors and led them out of the daylight across a windswept pile of refuse, the mess still everywhere at ground level.

As they slipped into one of the hangars, Samantha asked, "Is this ARC?" It took a moment for her eyes to adjust to the looming shapes of two small airliners above her.

"Of course. The organisation has a hangar at every airport. It began with main airports decades back and now they maintain a presence at pretty much everything bigger than an airfield."

"Hello?" A voice called from an office at the rear of the hangar.

"Captain Novak?" Charlotte asked.

"Ah, Miss Benson."

The voice continued in the dark; the monotonous accent was familiar to Samantha after a night in Dubrovnik.

"Your boss, Director Rosser, called ahead of you. Give us thirty minutes to complete fuelling and pre-flight checks and we will have a plane worthy of you. Where is your destination?"

"Port Moresby, Papua New Guinea," Samantha spoke before Charlotte could answer. "As soon as you can, Captain."

"We have a change of plane. The ARC jet was damaged during the fun yesterday. We have borrowed this passenger jet from Croatia Airlines for your journey."

The discussion went on, but Samantha found her eyes drooping now that there wasn't an immediate need to do anything. The lack of sleep had finally caught up with her. Strong hands caught her by the shoulders. "Time for some rest," Io said in a low voice, guiding her toward stairs that led onto the plane.

Samantha let herself be guided. She had fallen into the middle of this mess, and the one person she wanted to look out for was now her guardian. Angel or not, she trusted him and the feeling comforted her.

Five days until Aeon Fall carries out their first threat, she thought as she watched the earth fly by.

Sleep meant Samantha missed most of the first leg of their journey, as the pilot flew across the middle-east and India before refuelling at Mumbai. Through sleepy eyes, she looked out at the Java Sea, the mass of water that formed the heart of the Indonesian archipelago. Daylight had caught them up, the surface of the water below glistened in shades of silver around the green specks of islands dotted in the sea.

"I needed that," Samantha said as she stretched, breathing in the scent of a clean, empty plane, devoid of the usual crowds. "Did you get any sleep, Io?"

Her companion tilted his head as he looked at her from the row in front. "Was I meant to?"

"Well it helps."

"With what?"

The innocence in his face, as Io parried her comments with simple questions was unnerving. To take for granted such basic fundamentals in life and have them queried in the manner Io responded made her want to question them too. "With feeling better, with having the energy to take on the next day—Io don't you remember any of this?"

"You keep asking me that question as if it will all come back to me, Samantha. In truth, I have been examining this weapon." He tilted forward the sword, its hilt rested against the seat next to him. "It responds to me, in its own way—a glint, a feel of warmth. You claim I'm an angel? Perhaps I am. Perhaps this indicates such facts. I can tell you that closing my eyes would not help me discover the answers. Looking inward might provide more insight."

"And? What did looking inward give you?"

Io sighed. "No solace. It is as if I am an empty vessel, lacking that vital ingredient or that piece of information that would bring forth my essence and make me whole again."

"If you ask me, that so-called angel Karael let go of his sword a little too easily," Charlotte said from the row of seats behind them. "It's almost as if he wanted you to have it."

"None of this seems to leave you overawed," Io said. It was the closest he had come to an accusation since he had rescued Samantha in the Dubrovnik store.

Samantha turned to regard her companion.

Charlotte shrugged. "Angel. Demon. All the same thing when you reduce it to the lowest common denominator."

"And that is?"

"Supernatural creatures that think they're better than us. What I've seen in my life makes me think the human race is no more than a meat feast for any higher power that decides to come to snack. Demons from below try to make the earth their own. When we go there, as I'm led to believe is inevitable, our souls," Charlotte tapped the side of her head, "are used as a power source. God alone knows what you use us for up there."

"And you have decided that if I am indeed what you believe me to be, that I should answer to you for Heaven?" Io retorted, nostrils flaring. It was as close as Samantha had seen him come to being riled. The warmth he normally exuded radiated off him in waves.

"Io, I've decided if that transpires, if you're more than the amnesiac you currently appear to be, that you should look around you. Consider what you see is not what you would expect to see. Nothing more. Eyes wide open, Io. While you don't remember who, or what you are. Eyes wide open."

Taking her literally, Io began to look around the plane. His eyes trained on the window and he moved to the row in front so he could get a better look. "It's so peaceful from up here. It's beautiful."

"It's detached from the painful reality that is human existence," Samantha said. "Down there, every day is a fight for life. Up here with a different perspective you have to remember that being alive is about more than just breathing."

"And what does your detached reality tell you, Samantha?"

Io looked at her from between the headrests of the seats in front.

"That we got hold of that sword a little too easily. That Karael wants you to remember everything before he finds you again. That I think my sister is walking into a trap. That she could be anywhere and there's nothing I can do about it."

"Nina knows what she's doing. Focus on what you're doing here rather than events you can't control," Charlotte advised. "We aren't flying halfway across the world for nothing. That crazy guy down there wants Io for something important but not in his present state. He wants you to remember."

"What do you suggest?" Samantha asked.

Charlotte smiled. "Don't remember a thing. Ignorance is bliss."

* * *

Another hour saw them crossing the coast of West Papua, the end of Indonesia and the beginning of Papua New Guinea. Turbulence shook the plane as they crossed a mountain range. Up ahead, the sky was shrouded in darkness. A cloudbank hung in front of them. She could see it being pulled along by a strong breeze. The plane shuddered as a strong crosswind hit it. Samantha, used to flying small aircraft, held on to her seat with a grim determination. It was hard to ride the air while not at the controls.

Io was having a much more difficult experience. His eyes wide with uncertainty, he said, "Does this usually happen?"

"Only when a global organisation with ultra-secret plans aims a satellite into space and fires off a beam of God only knows what. When the resulting shift in the earth's magnetic field then tries to stabilize, dragging all weather on earth with it? Yes, in short, this usually happens."

"I don't like it." Io looked very sorry for himself.

"An angel afraid of flying?" Charlotte said, barely concealing an amused smile. "Whatever next? Demons with an aversion to fire?"

Samantha gave her a warning glance. If Io was an angel, even one with amnesia, every tale she had been told about the two species' interaction ended violent, gory, wrathful and bloody. It was no wonder, if Io had done what Karael accused him of, that the reaction was so vitriolic. And here she was with a ticking time bomb at her side.

"Just try to hold on, we'll be down soon enough." Samantha hoped her reassurance was enough. The plane bucked in the turbulence, the window losing the view as they entered a band of rain. It was as if night fell outside and all the lights in the cabin blinked on in an instant. The plane lurched again.

Charlotte grabbed the intercom, crashing into the door to the galley as she did so. "Novak, what's going on?"

"Buckle up back there," came the voice of their Croatian pilot. "We've got a jet stream coming down across the island and on to the coast of Australia. It's too low and we're hitting it sideways. It's dragging us South. I'm going to lose some altitude and it's not gonna be an easy ride. Stay in your seats."

Charlotte took a step back toward her seat when the plane lurched again, making her lose her footing. She crashed headfirst into the bulkhead, landing in a heap on the floor.

"Charlotte!" Samantha tried to unbuckle her belt but Io reached out and took her hand in an iron grip. His hand shook; he was terrified.

"It'll be fine," Samantha reassured him.

"How do you know?"

"Because Aeon Fall is going to start blowing up nuclear power stations and we have to do our part in stopping them. I'll not leave my sister alone on this planet to see that through. We will survive, because we have to."

"Brace!"

The plane leaned forward into a steep dive. Samantha closed her eyes and squeezed Io's hand tight, praying Charlotte was okay.

Chapter Fourteen

"Are we safe?"

Samantha opened her eyes, her hand still clasped in Io's. He was leaning forward in the brace position, his arm jammed through the seats. He sat up, watching her. Strangely, he did not look the least bit afraid. The tang of nervous sweat assaulting her nostrils was a reminder that she hadn't showered in days.

Outside the window was streaked with water. They had levelled out and while it was raining, there were glimpses of clear sky. Behind them the trail of dark clouds hurtled above. There was no juddering. The turbulence ended. The high-pitched whine of the engines was the only outside noise.

"I guess we are," she replied, not letting go of his hand. Then what had happened hit her. "Charlotte?"

Unconscious on the floor, Charlotte lay where she had fallen by the bulkhead, one arm twisted beneath her, face down.

"Io, help me." Unbuckling her seatbelt, she pushed him ahead of her into the aisle. "Roll her gently, careful with her arm."

Io did as asked, and soon Charlotte was resting comfortably on her back, a folded green blanket beneath her head.

"Is she well?" Io asked.

Samantha pulled Charlottes eyelids back, one at a time. "Pupils are the same size, so hopefully no concussion. Just an enormous bump to the head, I think. It's probably best to leave her still until she has to be moved." Samantha reached for the intercom, the line coming alive with a click. "Captain Novak?" Her voice echoed throughout the plane. Clearly the wrong channel. "We have injured back here."

"On my way."

In moments, the small, thin man in spectacles, white shirt and creased black trousers appeared. "Miss Scott?" he queried in a melodic accent reminiscent of Dubrovnik, overlaid with a concerned tone. "Miss Benson was caught in the dive. How unfortunate." He checked her over, feeling round Charlottes head and neck, checking her eyes as Samantha had done. "There doesn't appear to be anything broken but she's going to have quite the headache when she wakes. You've taken the correct action. I'll call ahead and get her looked at by a doctor when we land. It should be under an hour, assuming we're done with the jet stream. Aeon Fall really broke the world with that satellite."

"You're abreast of the situation?"

He smiled. "Of course. You don't think Director Scott would allow you to take this flight without ensuring the pilots knew all the risks?"

"You're not alone up there?"

Novak looked for a second in the direction of the cockpit. "No. I have a new guy up there. He came with the plane. Doesn't talk much, but knows his stuff. He's signed off by the organisation. Your mother said something about an adventure she once took that changed her life. She hoped this might be the same for you."

"It's been all kittens and flowers so far," Samantha replied, her sarcastic tone not lost on the pilot as he smiled. Io didn't react. "Thank you for coming back here."

Novak nodded and returned to the cockpit.

* * *

As predicted, in less than an hour, they descended from the scuddy-gray sky to the airport in the city of Port Moresby, the capital of Papua New Guinea. Green mountains filled the view as Samantha watched the descent by Charlotte's side; the terror of the cloud-filled jet stream five hundred miles back was a distant memory. Refusing the safety of a seat belt, she rode the bumpy landing on her backside. The stunning view disappeared as buildings closed in. They entered another dark hangar. *ARC.* She thought. *Perpetually in the shadows.*

"Where do we go without her?" Io asked, his face full of concern as he came to kneel beside them.

"We go exactly where we were supposed to go. We take this book and these notes to this shop. Maybe we'll learn something about it." She frowned. "I'm not happy about leaving Charlotte here but what choice do we have?"

"The clock is ticking, so I would agree."

Io's dour demeanour dampened Samantha's enthusiasm somewhat, but the sense of urgency was too great. "Who knows? These charts might even prove the solution to your missing memory. You never know, we might even find a sense of humor for you too."

"There's a vehicle waiting for you outside the hangar, Miss Scott," Captain Novak said as he entered the cabin.

Samantha glanced down at Charlotte.

She's injured Nina. Nina? Samantha strained to feel for her sister.

Who?

Charlotte. Knocked herself cold. The pilots are going to look after her.

There was a pause. *Then let them. Sammy, I can't keep doing this, or they'll notice and that spells trouble for everybody. Trust the people around you to do their jobs. Who is the pilot?*

Novak.

Who? Never heard of him. Sammy, be very careful. The contact broke.

"Don't worry about Miss Benson," Novak said, not giving any sign he had noticed her distraction. "We have basic medical facilities here and if she needs anything more, we can have her moved. We will be flying back tomorrow so you have until then to find whatever it is that you seek."

Samantha folded the loose pages into the book and closed it. She noticed that the book drew Novak's eye as she pocketed it in her bag. "Who's the driver?"

Novak shrugged. "Not my business to know. Check the credentials if you like. They will be on the ARC database."

"And how do I find that out?"

Novak gave a knowing smile, as if he was the keeper of some secret to which Samantha wasn't privy. "If you need me to tell you then you don't belong in ARC."

* * *

A frustrated Samantha and smiling Io left Captain Novak to his plane, finding, as promised, a nondescript black sedan waiting outside in the heat. While still cloudy, the humidity was overwhelming, intensified by the heat reflected from the tarmac; Samantha broke into an instant sweat. After the chill of midnight in the ruins of Dubrovnik, the New Guinean climate was an assault on the senses.

Not waiting for Io to open the door, she pulled on the handle and almost dove into the car where a wave of cold greeted her.

"Air con," she sighed, shivering with pleasure.

Io climbed in behind her, inspecting the interior. "What manner of vehicle is this?"

"I'm not sure what you mean? The car? Or everything herein?"

"It's a standard ARC transport mate," the driver said in an accent that sounded broadly Australian, his tone friendly but formal. "Like this all over the world. Genesis Koto. I'll be your guide."

Samantha pulled her cell from her bag, contacting her mother and typed in the name, "Genesis Koto?" Within seconds the reply "ARC Operative, Australasia. Can be trusted," popped up in a text message. Samantha put her cell back in her bag. "How'd you come by a name like that?"

Skin as dark as Io's split into a grin beneath black hair with blond highlights. Dressed in khaki shorts and a short-sleeved shirt, Koto looked more like a taxi driver. With a little envy, Samantha realised his attire would be a lot more suitable in this heat than her own.

"Just unlucky, I guess. There's some clothes back at the hotel for you, Miss. I'll bet you'll be wanting to get to your bookshop as quick as you can?"

"Immediately. This can't wait. One of my companions is injured and I want to get back to her as soon as possible."

"Okay then." Koto gunned the throttle and they took off at a pace. Soon the airport roads became a highway that split a large area of scrubland to either side as they rounded the end of one runway. The road angled up into a series of low hills. In the distance houses were visible in amongst the foliage, dense and green.

"You seem to know where we're going," Io observed.

Koto grinned again. "Fella, you're after a book, yes?"

Io turned to Samantha, who nodded. "Yes, we are," he said.

"Then with all the different languages they speak in this crazy place, you want to go to a book shop. Everybody knows there's only one decent bookstore in the whole of Port Moresby, probably the whole country. That's up in the hills at the University that used to be run by those Pacific Adventists."

"Used to?"

"You know the story as well as anyone, Miss. It's not what it once was. All religion's suffered in the wake of the demons twenty years back. It's like everyone's just given up. The university goes through the motions. Kids come in and learn. Life goes on. It's just that the religious agenda has all but fizzled out. You'll see what I mean when you get up there."

Samantha continued to probe Koto about local lore as they made their way up into the hills behind Port Moresby. Off to their right, the land fell away into a huge quarry pit. Their guide informed them that the mining company built most of the roads in the country.

Beyond the quarry was an enormous cemetery stretching to the horizon where the hills fell off.

"That seems very close to the quarry," Io observed, his voice troubled.

"Yeah mate," was Koto's jovial agreement. "Nine Mile Cemetery, they call it. You can see why. It goes on forever. They expect to start digging up bodies any day with the blasting. The company doesn't care. Rock's more important than bones."

No respect for the dead, Samantha thought, agreeing silently that Io was correct to be troubled. If he was an angel, this lack of concern for the dead could become damning were he righteous.

The cemetery disappeared as they rounded a hill and entered the jungle where soon after a road to the right appeared.

"Pacific Adventist University," Io read the grubby unkempt sign aloud. "Educate to serve." He sighed, "There used to be a great body of religion here." He closed his eyes, as if seeking an answer from within. He raised his chin. "It was enormous. But cut off. Nobody heard their pleas."

"How can you tell?"

Io opened his eyes and turned to her. "I don't know. I just can. The apathy, it's like a poison creeping through the ground. It's strong here."

"Welcome to our world, mate," Genesis Koto added, all traces of humor gone from his voice.

* * *

Their driver parked in front of a series of low, white buildings at one end of the university compound, and waited while Samantha took Io on a walk through the grounds. They encountered a couple of men who could have been students or teachers; it was hard to tell. They directed Samantha and Io onto the path for the bookshop. Io looked more and more distressed the further they walked.

"Is it really that bad?" Samantha asked as Io looked at one particular building and winced.

"That's a place of worship. Abandoned." He opened his eyes. They were filled with tears. "Samantha, I can't rid myself of this sensation. It is as if prayers, long unanswered, are now focussed at me. But I don't know what to do with this information."

"Io, I'm sorry. I wish I could help."

"I think I am what you consider me to be. It feels as if in this place, I stand alone, accused of these people's abandonment. But without my memories it is impossible to process." He raised his hands. "This is what a thousand years of darkness looks like in its infancy."

The campus opened up into a series of lush green lawns interspersed with single story buildings amidst a scattering of tall palm trees. "It doesn't seem all that bad," Samantha countered. "It's a bit warm, granted. And this looks more like a military base than a university, yet life goes on."

"Imagine this abandoned, decaying. These sweet-smelling borders will become unkempt and wild. That lake ends up foetid and filled with the skeletons of creatures that once called it home. That is all I see of this place—a future shrouded in death."

Was this memory coming from this most unique man she had dragged halfway around the world on a whim, or was it from outer forces? "Io, how could you know that for certain?"

He turned to her, his eyes fierce. She could see the belief, the utter conviction as he held her shoulders in gentle hands she was sure could have crushed her. "Because I can feel it. I don't know why, nor how, but you have set me on the right path. I don't belong here. This place, its future haunts me. These people. These so-called pious innocents. All shall die. The earth shall be wiped clean of their flesh."

Io pointed past her at the side of a building. Groups of brightly dressed students walked past a small area of graffiti on the side of a building, paying it no mind. Samantha recognised the logo, running forward as if waiting any longer could worsen the situation.

"Your God is Dead," she read aloud. Underneath, three vertical lines not unlike the towers of the logo she had seen at Hunter's Ridge were painted in black. "Aeon Fall have reached here too."

"Their curse is not death," Io said in a low voice so that only Samantha could hear. "It is apathy. Your people don't care because they are being conditioned that way, slowly, subtly, and to think their conclusions are their own ideas."

Samantha turned from the graffiti to her companion. "Mom always said that something life altering happened when she was down there. I don't understand what Hell has to do with humanity forsaking Heaven. We aren't suddenly a bunch of devil worshippers." She paused, recalling her own skill and the damage it must have caused. "Well, we didn't mean to be."

"What is, is. This group must be stopped. They will ruin you all."

The profound change Samantha now felt in her companion was noticed by other passers-by. Io's repeated gesticulation at the graffiti had drawn a crowd of men, students probably, who watched him from a dozen steps away with hostile expressions.

"I think we should move," Samantha suggested. "We aren't here for a confrontation."

The righteousness had clearly turned to belligerence as Io said, "You think a few of them are enough to stop me?"

"It's not *us* I'm worried about," she replied. "Come on. We aren't here to start a fight. This pattern could be what sets you free. Let's see if they can help and then go from there."

"And if it doesn't?"

"Then let's hope we get you back before Aeon Fall start blowing up nuclear power plants. Or before Karael finds you once again."

* * *

The bookshop turned out to be in one of the single story buildings on the campus, in woodland furthest from the main road, where the land fell away in a series of cultivated crop fields. The hostile looks directed at them continued, though the students kept their distance.

Samantha pushed the door open, the almond scent of mouldy literature washing over them as they walked in.

"You can just smell the education," she said as they passed down a narrow aisle crammed from floor to ceiling with texts.

"I smell the concentration of decay," Io replied, his clipped tones revealing his obvious distaste. "It is like the feeling on the campus compounded. This education is ignored. Wasted by those that have forsaken prayer."

"The sooner we get you away from here, the better," Samantha decided.

At the back of the shop was a simple table with a cash register. The cashier, an old man in a white shirt, watched them approach.

Samantha greeting him in English, hoping the man understood. "Hello," she said, "I have a book bearing a print mark from this store. I wonder if you could tell me anything about it?"

The man stared at her for a second, chewing on the inside of his mouth. "A book," he said in a very thick accent. Clearly, he wasn't used to speaking English.

Samantha nodded, opened her bag, retrieving the crow predictions. "I got this from my sister a long time back, and it's sort of a conundrum that I'm attempting to solve. Maybe if you have a look?" Samantha's words tailed off into silence. The second she had revealed the book, the old man's eyes had widened in horror.

"Where did you get that?" he gasped.

"From my sister. I wondered. Do you know anything?" She pushed the book forward and the man recoiled. "No. No, I don't want any part of it. That shouldn't be here. I don't know anything."

"Sir, please. We've travelled a long way."

The old man shoved his seat back, standing and taking a step back. "No! You take that and get out of here now! You hear? Get out!"

Chapter Fifteen

In a panic, the old man rose from behind the table, revealing his considerable bulk to push them back. "Out!" he cried moving around the table.

Samantha grabbed the book, clutching it tightly to prevent the now loose extra pages from falling to the floor. Io glanced back, his face questioning, but a moment later they were outside, the door locked behind them. The metallic rattle of lowering shutters followed quickly.

Io stared at the door. The lights inside winked out "He's leaving. Maybe we can find him out back."

Samantha opened the book, securing the loose pages. "I don't think it would do any good. Did you see the look on his face?"

"He was terrified," Io agreed. "Beyond the capacity for rational thought."

"He knows something but we're never getting any answers out of him—not with this in my hand."

"Can I help you?" A small woman, not much taller than Samantha's shoulder peeked her head around the corner of the building. Long black hair past her shoulders framed a pretty face.

"I don't know," Samantha replied, hugging the book close. "Can you?"

The young woman approached. "My name's Adreana." She spoke in an Australian accent. "Adreana Black. I work in the bookstore for Mr. Vaitai. What just happened in there?"

"We've travelled a long way seeking answers about a book marked with the Divine Mercy Publications stamp. I must admit, I didn't expect the reaction I got."

"Mr. Vaitai is a very superstitious man. May I ask what book you showed him? I was out back at the time and only caught the tail-end of it."

"Where did he go?" Io asked.

"Oh, he's well gone by now. He lives off campus. He tore past me telling me to close the shop. I've a free day today and have far less hang-ups about looking at a book, if you care to share. Though I must admit things have been a bit strange around here recently."

"How so?"

Adreana furrowed her brow. "Well take that mural over there."

Samantha looked back to where they had come from. "The graffiti? Aeon Fall?"

"Yeah. This is the last place you'd expect that. Since the broadcast, people have stood there, denouncing God. Here—in a place built around worship!"

"Religion has failed." Io announced, his voice booming with conviction.

"Shhh! You want to get us lynched? Look if there's anything I can do to help, I will. It's the least I can do after Mr. Vaitai's reaction. Just not here. You've drawn far too much attention already."

Samantha turned to Io. "What do you think? Can she be trusted?"

"You believe I can tell this?"

Samantha smiled. "You had a very solid reaction to certain people in Dubrovnik. I trust your instincts, Io."

He stared at Adreana, who stood waiting, confused by their conversation. "I believe this one has a pure heart. She wants to help."

"Who are you?" Adreana asked.

"Trust me. You'd laugh if you heard some of the theories offered about my friend. Just not here. We've got a car. Do you fancy a road trip?"

Adreana shrugged. Why not? I've no more lessons this week and Mr. Vaitai won't likely be back today."

* * *

Samantha led her companions back to the ARC car and the waiting Genesis Koto. Without much comment he drove them off the campus, sparing only a glance for Adreana.

Io would have known if Adreana were false. He had clocked Lucas in a second on pure instinct. As it was, they all breathed a little easier once back on the highway.

"Could you sense it?" Io asked. "The unease, the buried malevolence? Something was at work there. It's at work everywhere but there more than most places."

"I know I didn't like being there one bit," Samantha admitted. "The way people looked at us. It wasn't hatred as such, more the slow building of anger. It festered there. Adreana, did you ever notice this?"

Adreana's face had a serious demeanour as she said, "I know that the campus is not what it was. Religion doesn't drive the establishment like it once did. The church is seldom used and when it is, the numbers aren't great. But the student numbers have been consistent over the past few years. I saw how people looked at you, Io. It was as if you embodied everything they resent."

"Perhaps they fear my belief," Io said.

"That, or your righteous nature," Samantha added.

Genesis Koto took the small group to a hotel called The Raintree Lodge, a white stone building surrounded by tropical ferns and clad with so much bamboo it looked like part of the jungle. With promises to pick them up in the morning, Koto insisted that anonymity would serve better than armed protection. The three of them were led into a white-tiled suite full of the crisp scent of clean linen on two beds by a smiling old man whose grin never went beyond his mouth. His eyes betrayed signs of alarm every time he looked at Io. For his part, her companion never even noticed the man, lost in the wonder of the suite.

"What is that?" he asked, pointing to the far side of the room as the old man backed out door, closing it with a barely-audible click.

"It's a bed, mate," Adreana said, her voice incredulous. "You sleep on it. Seriously? You can't remember beds?"

"I can't remember anything of comfort." He sat on the edge of the bed, pushing his hands down on the mattress as if testing it for the first time. "It's an alien feeling."

Adreana stood opposite him. Despite Io being seated, she was barely above the top of his head. "What's going on in there?"

"You've found him in the middle of a massive case of amnesia," Samantha provided. "We're hoping this little trip might jog his memory."

Adreana stared into Io's eyes, touching his face with her fingertips and tilting it up toward her. "No, that's not just it. There's something in there. Something blocked."

"How do you know?" Io asked.

"I was always told by my mother that I was empathic. I could sense the nature of others." She turned away. "Do you want to show me what brought you to the bookshop? I don't need empathy to know you came a very long way for an answer. Add in the fact that you show up within hours of the earth being dragged halfway to hell and that you clearly recognise graffiti denoting Aeon Fall, then mention Dubrovnik—this tells me you're tied up in this. Your guy Io here is somehow the key. Try denying it."

"I can't," Samantha admitted. "We don't even know much more about him than his name. Io Vel."

"Io. Well that could be anything. The name is used all over. A moon of Jupiter, a name from Greek mythology, the incorrect chemical symbol of Thorium."

"Thorium?"

"Yeah. It's used in those new-gen nuclear reactors."

Samantha looked at Io for a second. It couldn't be that there was such a profound link and she'd never seen it. She removed the book from her bag and passed it to Adreana.

"I've had this in my possession for years."

"Crow divination?" Adreana asked, flicking through the pages.

Samantha laughed. "Is there anything you don't know about?"

"Not a lot. I was brought up outside of the standard education system. It was more tribal than formal. A lot of irregular beliefs and strange takes on humanity."

"And yet you wanted to come to a university run by Pacific Adventists?"

Adreana looked up from the book. "I wanted a place that would allow me to study why pre-religious tenets—pagan beliefs—would outlast mass religion. This book is an ideal example. Have you tried it?"

"I have, with varied results. The most recent is what led us here."

Adreana shook her head just a touch as she pursed her lips. "I don't follow."

Samantha turned the pages until the unmarked glyph showed. "The crows formed this in Dubrovnik."

"And there's no writing. Any idea what it means?"

Io stood. "Karael," he said in a booming voice. "It is his mark."

Adreana shrugged. "I don't know what that means."

Samantha withdrew the loose pages from the back of the book. "I hope you're prepared to have your belief tested, Adreana. Karael is an angel."

"Yeah, of course."

"It's true," Samantha insisted, unfolding the pages. "He was wearing the body of a man I knew to be dead, mostly because Io threw him through a wall. He, in turn, did the same thing to a man who was part of our rescue team in the city. We escaped purely by blind luck. He was after Io."

"Why?"

"Isn't it obvious?" Samantha locked eyes with Io. The gaze that met her was so knowing, so agelessly wise that she couldn't deny what she saw. "Io is an angel too."

"You are?"

"I know not what I am," he admitted. "I have no memory. I woke up in this." He stretched out his arms, turning his palms upward. "I am that I am."

"We're here because Io is in danger. We all are. We need to jump start his memory. All we have so far are fragments of information and impressions."

Adreana took a step back, giving Samantha the impression they were losing her co-operation. Her voice cautious, she said, "Suppose I do help you, all these crazy pronouncements aside. What do you want from me?"

"The book was stamped with the name of the shop where you work. We found these inside the book, sealed in the cover." Samantha handed over the pages. "Be careful, they're very delicate."

Adreana took the pages and placed them on a nearby table. "These figures look like lunar distance navigation."

The term flummoxed Samantha. "What?"

"It's a way of working out where you're going based on the night sky and the use of a sextant, and a nautical almanac with tables of lunar distances." She looked up from the numbers. "These haven't been used since the nineteenth century. It was before chronometers and clocks were readily available."

"And you just happen to know this? It all sounds very random."

Adreana shrugged. "You asked."

"Can you make anything meaningful out of it?"

"I can't, but I know a guy who might be able to. These all point to some sort of a trail. Maybe we can map them and get GPS points or something? You're gonna have to let me take this, though."

The book felt suddenly heavy in her hands. Samantha looked to Io, who nodded encouragement. "Everything?"

"No, only these pages. I don't see anything in there that will help work out co-ordinates. I can tell you this though, that book has a twin. You see the stamp? The number underneath the name? Mr. Vaitai's family have been running a bookshop of sorts for decades. Their book stamps are like a badge of office. There are three. One with the common stamp and two with numbers on, for rare books when they come across them."

"How bizarre. What if the set is more than two books?"

"They put a mark through the stamp. This one has a two in the print, with no other markings. Somewhere it has a sibling. I'll be back in a couple of hours. Just sit tight."

Another book? Samantha considered this as she sat next to Io on the bed. She remembered when Nina gave her the crow book; she had not mentioned any other book. Perhaps the copies were already separated much earlier—they were, after all, more than a hundred years old.

"What's wrong?" Io didn't sound concerned but clearly he detected her unease.

"I'm just thinking about stuff. The book. Nina. You know, Io, time is running out. Aeon Fall said just a few days until they hit a nuclear facility and we're currently on the far side of the world. My sister could be in terrible danger and I'm doing nothing. I'm out of the way."

"You're helping this ... me," Io countered. "You're helping me."

"Can you contain a nuclear reactor meltdown?"

Io's face rose in an approximation of a smile as he shrugged. At least an approximation from a man, a being who had never knowingly smiled before. "I don't know. Maybe?"

Sighing, Samantha said, "Well maybe we should try to get some rest. You take this bed, I'll have the other."

"What do I do?"

"Lie down, close your eyes. You haven't slept since you found me. Your body must be exhausted. I know I could do with the rest."

Io lay on the bed, smiling with amusement.

Samantha watched him for a moment as robotically he shut his eyes. She stretched out, turning away. It was still light outside and there was nothing to do but wait.

* * *

Samantha woke to a sound in the room now shrouded in darkness. *Where was Adreana?* She wondered. It must have been hours. Samantha sat up, listening as the breeze from the open window wafted the sound of crickets through the net curtains in gentle eddies. Maybe that was it, the movement of the curtain. Something nagged at Samantha, an itch, a premonition. She wasn't alone.

"Io?"

"I'm here," he said in a voice not much above a whisper. "Stay where you are. Don't move or they might come back."

"What?" She turned to see the outline of her companion facing her on the next bed. Lit by the glances of streetlight that made it through the trees, she saw that his arms were bound behind his back.

She jumped to her feet beside him. His wrists were bound in cuffs of an alloy that wasn't metal, though it was as cold.

"Can't you break them? Io, you're strong. Ridiculously so. Just snap the cuffs."

Io flexed his arms. "I can't."

Samantha tugged at the cuffs. "Why not?"

"Because they aren't meant for mortal man," a deep voice said from the hallway.

Samantha looked up. The tallest man she had ever seen filled the room nearly to the ceiling. Dressed mostly in black, he was bald, what light there was gleaming off his scalp. She felt his face glowering at her in the darkness. This was trouble, plain and simple.

"Who the hell are you?"

The man stepped into the room, filling it with menace. He held up what she presumed to be a gun. "I'm the guy with his finger on the trigger," he said in a clipped and precise South African accent. "You want your fallen angel here to live? Then you'll do as I say and come with us. Now."

They knew who Io was.

Chapter Sixteen

How was Io so unaware of the danger they faced? He sat across from her in the back of a van as it swerved round corners, perfectly balanced, not moving a muscle as she was thrown all over the place. Separated from the driver by a sealed interior, she had no idea where they were going, nor why.

Nina, contact Mom. We've been kidnapped. Nina?

There was no reply from her sister.

"Why did you let them cuff you, Io?"

Her accusation melted off him. It appeared that he didn't recognise the risk without an existing physical confrontation with which to react.

"He had a weapon to your head. I had no choice. Even I cannot move that fast."

Caught short, Samantha found no initial reply. "I'm sorry. I didn't know."

"You didn't wake because no words were spoken. I could see the intent in the man above you. He wanted nothing more than chaos and death. He ordered me to move, taunting. I knew if I did he would strike you a fatal blow. I held back and here we are."

Their conversation was caught short as the van came to an abrupt halt, both of them slamming forward. Pain lanced across Samantha's back as she hit the metal divide.

Almost immediately the van's back doors opened, revealing the concrete interior of a warehouse. Puddles appeared between the rubbish filled floor, an accumulation from years of disuse. The walls were patchy and decayed with concrete cancer; rusted steel cables laid bare to the humid environment. A rattle shook the building, as flocks of birds took flight, escaping through the one open window. The remaining windows were black with the night beyond.

"Out," ordered the bald man, his eyes piercing in the light. He looked at them with barely contained fury, as if it were their fault he had been robbed of sport that night.

Samantha stayed where she was. In moments two stocky Papuans dressed in jeans and polo shirts jumped up into the van, one grabbing her, the other Io. Without anything resembling care they were thrown out onto the floor, Samantha barely retaining her balance, while Io hit face first. He grunted as he lay there.

"Hey, what's wrong with you?" Samantha yelled.

The two Papuans shared a smirk and climbed back into the van, turning the ignition in a cloud of stinking diesel smoke. In seconds they were gone; a corrugated steel door dropped shut behind them.

"They don't understand your words, ya little bint. It's me you want to worry about. This is my domain. Here I am God."

"I doubt that," Io muttered, earning him a kick to the ribs.

"Got you pegged back pretty tight, haven't we, little man?" the bald man taunted. "I'd say those cuffs were meant to hold you. Special metal. We know who you are, mate. Even if you don't."

"Christopher!" an eerily familiar voice shouted from a shadowed doorway, "let's not give the game away just yet."

Samantha faced the doorway. Her stomach tightened as the owner of the voice stepped into view. A grey scraggly beard with white touches at the corners. Long, dishevelled hair reached down past his shoulders. His condition meant nothing; it was the eyes that held her. The whites were large, and so luminous they appeared to glow from a fire within. The darkness contained in those orbs was endless. If there was a soul it was well hidden.

"Porter Rockwell," she said, finding the words difficult to utter. He had a presence on the screen, but in person it was nearly unbearable. Yet, his gaze was magnetic. She couldn't look away.

"In the flesh. And you are young Samantha Scott, the girl who can raise demons. Daughter of Eva and Sa—, uh, Madden."

He stepped close and leaned forward. In a country full of heat and humidity there was no warmth from his skin. He made Samantha's flesh crawl.

"I was there, you know. When your father did the dirty little deed and you came into being. I was in the very next room." He looked at her, wiggling his eyebrows a couple of times.

"What do you want," she spat, "a medal?"

Rockwell smiled and stood back, raising his hands to either side of him in a grandiose gesture. "What do I want? I want the world. The whole world. I want Heaven and I want Hell all wrapped up in a nice little package. And I want you to get it for me. Take your cell out of your bag and call dearest Eva."

"I will not."

Rockwell turned to his colleague. "Christopher?"

The bald South African walked over to a table groaning under the weight of countless guns. He picked up the gun Charlotte Benson had given her and held it to Io's head. "If ya think the cuffs'll hold him, what do ya think this'll do? Made of the same stuff, I'll bet."

"Mr Lanier's moral compass doesn't exactly point North. If you want your angel-in-waiting to carry on breathing I suggest you do as I ask. You might want to consider the health of your friend from the plane. She's not in hospital and if the people she is with do not hear from me within the next thirty minutes, she won't need one."

Samantha's breath caught. She prayed Rockwell hadn't noticed her concern. "She's no friend of mine," Samantha shrugged, trying to appear nonchalant. Inside, she began to panic, images and scenarios playing out in a simultaneous cacophony, all ending badly. There was no way to win this. Rockwell was holding all the aces. Samantha opened her bag and withdrew her cell. A quick series of numbers and the phone began to ring.

"Put it on speaker," Rockwell instructed.

"Samantha?" Eva's voice was filled with anxiety. "Sammy? Are you okay?"

"I'm fine, mom," she said in a tone so neutral that she knew her mum would be on instant alert. "I'm not alone."

"Are you still with your travelling companion?"

"Not exactly," Rockwell said, taking the phone from her. "She's made some new friends." Rockwell gazed at Samantha as he added, "Some very good friends."

"Porter." There was a pause.

"I don't expect you to start with the 'why' and 'how' questions, Director. You're far too clever for that and I'm already three steps ahead of you. I propose, instead, a trade."

"If you harm her."

Rockwell grinned, and this time the smile held genuine glee; his eyes were wide and mad. "Them, Eva. If I harm them. Even if I were on my own, as a former Shikari, you know what I'm capable of. And I have resources to rival yours as you'll find out in oh, let's say five days' time. Your world is going to burn, Eva. I have one of your daughters. Soon I will have both of them. I'm willing to give them to you."

They were on to Nina. All other thoughts vanished from Samantha's mind. Had their contact cost her sister? Is that why she hadn't replied? Was she in danger? Samantha remained still, rolling her eyes, as if the whole situation bored her.

Rockwell smirked. Her act was succeeding.

Her mother continued. "You seem to be holding all the cards, Porter. What can I possibly have that you want so much?"

"Metatron's ashes. I want you to give me the remains of the angel that fell defending you from the demon Belphegor, emissary of Crustallos. Give me what you gathered, and I will return your children to you, more or less intact. Refuse, and the only way you see them again will be the same way you see that fallen angel. A fading memory, and a pot of ash."

At the mention of Metatron, Io perked up. There was more than an empty gaze there now. A flicker of recognition. He glanced at her and shook his head, not much more than a frown and a shiver.

"Why would you want that?"

"It doesn't really concern you. Suffice it to say your fallen angel here is broken."

"My what?"

Rockwell reached out and turned Samantha's face toward him with forefinger and thumb. "You see, Sammy? This is what ARC does to people. It turns the honest into liars and takes the faith away from the believers. Eva, why don't you tell your daughter exactly what that satellite was intended to do?"

"Porter, don't." Eva's tone was grave.

"What do you remember of your father, Sammy?"

Intrigued by whatever Rockwell had over her mother, she answered. "Nothing. I never knew him."

"That's not strictly true, now is it? You've seen him many times during your summoning. Eva, you are aware, no doubt, that your daughter is capable of bringing forth an image of the Devil, the man you know as Madden?"

There was a frosty silence on the other end of the line.

Samantha's stomach tightened. Her mother had never known. Only Nina, who had sworn to never spill that secret. She cut her question short. He knew, and there was no point denying it.

Rockwell winked. "Demon," he added as if that one word was all the explanation required. "You see how this works, Madame Director? You could say, arrange the transport and anonymous deposit of Metatron's ashes and we leave your dirty secret where it is. Except of course that dear Samantha here knows that there's something she is unaware of, but is so close to—"

"Tell her what you like, Porter. You're not getting Metatron."

There was a sense of betrayal in those words. Samantha heard the deep hurt in her mother's voice.

"As cold as ice. Well Samantha, it appears that the satellite sent aloft for the grand energy scheme was not an exploration satellite at all. Your mother was trying to reach your father. These last twenty years that's all she's been working toward. That satellite was designed to open a portal to Hell. How delicious that despite all her efforts, you've been able to talk to him at will? Obsessive doesn't begin to cover it."

"After everything that happened, you would risk the Earth?" Despite her façade, Samantha couldn't believe what she was hearing. "That makes a mockery of his sacrifice."

"You're one to talk about a mockery," Eva retorted. "You can bring Madden here and you never told me?"

Rockwell grinned. "And so the seeds of sedition are sewn from your very own family. When the rest of your organisation learns of this, things will get interesting. As it stands, it didn't take much of a tweak to turn the technology to Aeon Falls' use. Mr. Myhill was more than willing. So that you know, Eva, that satellite wasn't pointing at Hell, but at Heaven. We went angel fishing but what we got was a dud."

"Tell that to the population of Dubrovnik," Samantha growled. "You're responsible for countless deaths."

"Collateral damage. You want to blame someone? Try the person that created the weapon in the first place. The weapon, I may add, that's still up there. It's only a matter of time until we regain control."

Samantha wondered why Porter Rockwell wanted the ashes of an angel when he had one at hand—unless he wasn't holding all the cards. "Mom, don't give him anything. We will find a way to—"

Samantha found herself suddenly in mid-air, crashing to the ground several metres away from where she had been standing, the side of her face completely numb.

Io strained at his cuffs but was unable to break loose, the rage on his face scary to behold. "When I get free."

Ignoring him, Rockwell went on, "Nice act, Sammy. Almost convincing. Eva, you have five days to deliver Metatron's remains, or both of your daughters will be standing atop a nuclear reactor when it malfunctions."

"It won't take that long," Eva replied before the line went dead.

Rockwell considered the cell for a moment as he turned it over and over. "Get her a seat," he said to the big South African Lanier and winked at Samantha. "Waste not, eh?"

Lanier brought a heavy wooden chair into the centre of the warehouse and pushed her down on it. Rockwell pulled out a rope, bound her hands together at the wrist and then yanked her backward to secure her on a rib underneath the chair. Her shoulders screamed in protest.

Whistling a happy tune, the demon who had, while mortal, been tasked with her mothers' safety, left them in the warehouse under the watch of Lanier.

Samantha, moments later, heard the noise of a car leaving in a rush, tires screaming and the engine over revved, as if driven by someone who had been behind the wheel for a very long time.

"What did he mean by that?" Io asked as Lanier waved the alloy gun in Io's direction.

Samantha stared in turn at their captor as Lanier ogled her. The way her arms were tied back accentuated the curves of her body. She recognised the look on his face. Covetousness. Underneath the shaven head and beady eyes, Christopher Lanier was no different than Lucas. "He means that one way or another, the fun isn't over yet."

"It is for you," Lanier purred, pulling a cloth hood over her head. Hands trailed down her body, squeezing her breasts and lingering between her legs. With no other recourse, she lashed out with a foot, striking a soft area somewhere in his middle.

Lanier grunted. A moment later something hard hit her in the face, knocking her over onto her shoulder. Pain erupted down her arm and she tasted the iron tang of blood in her mouth. "You'll regret that, missy."

It was a small victory, but it showed defiance. Shortly she felt her legs being tied at the ankle to the legs of the seat. Lanier moved to Io, presumably to hood and bind him too before footsteps led away from them. A door slammed, echoing around the warehouse.

They were alone.

"Samantha, did he hurt you?" Io's voice was full of concern.

"No more than any coward would hurt a tied-up woman." She forced herself to calmness, taking deep, slow breaths. The hood was rancid, yellow stains riddled the otherwise white material. She tried to ignore the acrid stench, breathing through her mouth and concentrating on her throbbing cheek. "Can you see anything?"

"They covered my head the same way they did yours. It's not very pleasant."

"What was all that when they mentioned Metatron, Io? I saw your face."

"That's not a conversation to have here. If we get out then we can talk." His voice trailed off. It was a big if.

"Did you see all those guns?" she asked, feeling the need to talk about something. Anything. "It looks as though they're ready to wage war."

"Or defend a prize."

The heat of a Papuan night only got worse as morning crept in. Samantha could tell as the colour of her hood changed, along with out-side noises. The infrequent rattles began to gain a pattern over time. "At least we know where we are," she said. "If I'm not mistaken those rattles are the result of planes taking off. We're at the airport."

"How does that help?" Io asked.

"I have a plan," she replied, not willing to say aloud that she could fly a small aircraft, if she could find one. Anybody could be watching in silence.

"You realise that this also means they could move us out of here at any moment. If you want anybody to find us, now is our best chance of being located."

The sound of feet running stopped any further conversation. Three or four people burst into the warehouse, heading in the direction of the weapons.

"Get out front," Lanier ordered. "In the office. Cover positions. Let 'em see you before you take 'em down." He moved close to Samantha. She could sense his nearness, the warmth of his breath stirred in the heat of the room. "When we've dealt with this lot, nobody'll come for you. Then, I'm gonna have me some fun."

Chapter Seventeen

Gunfire sounded from somewhere close by, glass smashing to fragments under a hail of bullets. Had Lanier forced the others out to where they would be seen? This wasn't a standoff. It was murder.

Samantha pulled at the ropes that bound her. This only tightened them, cutting through her skin. Warm fluid oozed down her fingers.

"You thought this might happen," Io said.

"Not exactly. I knew by phoning mom ARC would be able to track us. Rockwell knew we were coming to Port Moresby and had people in place. But, how did he know? She said we could trust the driver, Genesis Koto. Did she know anything about the pilot? Does she know what condition Charlotte is in? What if this is all a set up, too?"

"A set up for what?" When the gunfire became intermittent, she could hear Io straining against his bonds. "It's no good," he gasped. "Whatever these are, they aren't coming loose."

A distant door creaked.

"Hello?" Samantha called but there was no answer. Footsteps, as gentle as a breath of wind on eyelashes, gave away the fact that somebody was in the warehouse with them.

"Don't move," a voice whispered nearby, only loud enough for Samantha to hear. "They're close and we don't have much time."

A click was followed by movement. "You." Io said in a low voice. "I'm glad there's more to you than I suspected."

"Hurry," the voice replied, "they might come back at any moment."

Urgent hands attacked the ropes binding Samantha to her chair. Her shoulders throbbed with pain and she let out a small groan.

"Sorry," the voice said.

Samantha immediately recognized the voice. "Thank God you're here."

"I've got to pull this rope tight in order to gain some slack. Just give me a sec."

Samantha bit her lip as the pain increased. Then only a moment later, it ebbed as her arms were released.

When the hood came off, Io stood in front of her. She blinked, and turned. Adreana knelt on the ground, loosening the remaining ropes from her ankles. "Welcome back. Not a moment too soon."

"It's like a war zone out there," the diminutive Australian replied. "Come on, we've got to skedaddle before they find their boss missing."

Dodging puddles, Adreana led them toward a door Samantha assumed Lanier had also used. The sound of the gunfire increased as they neared.

"You sure this is the safest way?"

"It's the only way, mate. Side entrance. Move quickly, or let them kill you." Adreana pushed the door open, shoving against a blockage on the other side.

Samantha followed, stepping over a body for her trouble. A man with no hair lay unconscious in the hallway. "Lanier? But how?"

Adreana knelt and retrieved a wooden post. "He was going past and I clocked him with this, right on the back of the head."

"Is he dead?"

"I don't know. You want to hang around to find out? You got those guys out the front who want to kill you. You also have militia outside, heavily armed and firing into the building, who also want to kill you. Let's go. I've got a car."

* * *

Would a car be enough to get them to safety and to the source of the patterns in the book? Samantha doubted it. She followed as Adreana led them out the side of the warehouse. They emerged midway along the building between a set of dumpsters filled with rubbish and stinking with age. The gunfire was louder outside but shielded from the battle by the bulk of the warehouse.

"Strange that they would only try a frontal assault when there's a door to the side," Samantha mused aloud.

"You want to go discuss tactics with them? I can get you to safety now, or you can wait around for a stray bullet to hit you."

"We have to rescue Charlotte. Rockwell has her." Samantha pulled in the opposite direction.

Adreana refused to let go. "Get a grip, girl. You can't help her from a jail cell, or worse off, dead. She'd want you to do what you came here to do first. Get free of this first, then rescue her second."

Sirens in the distance indicated the imminent arrival of the authorities. Samantha saw no choice but to get in the waiting car, a beaten-up yellow affair that was patched all over with brown rust. "Io, come on, unless you fancy flying us out of here."

"Flying wouldn't be my first choice," he replied. "I don't appear to have wings." Io climbed in next to her.

Adreana took the driver's seat, and with a grinding noise that made Samantha and Io both wince, set off along the side of the runway.

Samantha looked back through the rear window's clouded glass. Nobody followed them.

Adreana floored the gas, whizzing past a series of hangars and planes alike, swerving around baggage carts without slowing.

The bright morning coupled with disturbed sleep meant Samantha was a little disoriented. "Adreana, did you get the co-ordinates?"

"In a nutshell, yeah. It's another part of the island, a few hundred miles away. If you want to visit it, you're gonna have to find another way there."

"Do you know exactly where we need to go?"

Adreana nodded. "I've got a mobile GPS. I can put you right on top of the final co-ordinates."

Samantha spotted a white plane, propeller spinning on the nose, cockpit hatch open. She pointed. "There. Take us to that plane."

Adreana changed direction. "What're you gonna do? Kidnap the pilot?"

Samantha grinned. "Better. Just pull up next to the plane, grab your stuff and follow my lead."

The car had barely come to a stop when Samantha jumped out and climbed onto the wing. She peered into the hangar. The pilot was at the back of the building, his back turned, arguing with someone at the counter.

Perfect, Samantha thought. She waved at Adreana and Io to follow her, "Hurry!" she said, settling into one of the two leather pilots' seats.

Io sat down beside her, Adreana behind them.

"Pull the hatches shut," she instructed. "It's not just angels who can fly."

"This is foolish," Io warned her. "Only bad will come of this."

Samantha turned to find Adreana grinning.

"Will a plane so small get us there?" she asked as she pulled the rear hatch with a yank. It clicked shut.

"How far are we going?"

Adreana opened a map and studied it. "Three hundred miles directly north. Can we make it?"

Samantha studied the instruments in the mahogany panel. This was a rich man's toy. "Fuel gauge is at maximum. Barring any major course corrections and with some good flying conditions we should make it there and back in one piece. You'd better be right about Charlotte. Hang on."

As she taxied into position, the pilot, a silver haired New Guinean in a far-too-youthful jumpsuit came charging out, waving his arms. Samantha checked the fuel mix and pushed the throttle forward. The plane jumped into life, leaving him in their wake.

"You sure you can do this?" Adreana sounded worried.

"We're about to find out," Samantha replied and turned the plane on to the lone, clear runway.

A voice blared over the radio, issuing a warning in a language she didn't recognise. "They don't sound pleased."

"A warning from the tower," Adreana provided. "You aren't authorised for take-off."

"Not going to stop us," Samantha lowered the flaps on the wings, pushed the fuel mixture knob in, and upped the throttle. The plane surged forward, veering toward some warehouses as it did so. An easy correction on the rudder pedals and they were straight.

The plane gained speed with ease, hurtling along the runway.

"What are those?" Io said, pointing ahead.

Three black objects had appeared and were closing on their position. "Looks like cars. Someone doesn't want us leaving. One guess who."

It was a game of chicken. The plane closed in on the cars at a frightening pace. Samantha's heart was in her mouth as she watched the needle on the air-speed dial creep toward sixty knots. The cars loomed larger and larger. Hands waved out the side of the foremost vehicle.

"They aren't stopping this flight," Samantha growled, pulling back on the column between her legs.

Io copied her effort and the plane began to tilt skyward, resisting at first, then lifting as the take-off speed was reached. She felt the cars pass underneath, one clipping the landing gear, the plane juddering. Immediately, Samantha began to bank the plane until they were pointing due North. They were free.

In the distance, a column of caustic black smoke rose from the jungle just outside the city. "I wouldn't want to be there," Samantha hollered above the engine din.

"I was there," Adreana replied. "It's the university. The bookshop and several other buildings were set alight—it looks like arson. I tried to confirm the GPS coordinates with a colleague but we the roads were barricaded. We could see the flames above the treeline, all the way back on the road."

"You still can," Io added.

Samantha levelled the plane off with a tender correction of her stick, adjusting the rudder to compensate with the pedals at her feet. She stole a glance at the campus as it passed by below. Borne aloft by the intense column of heat, the smoke rose far above them until it moved off to the East as it finally hit a strong breeze.

She adjusted the flaps and looked ahead. "I'm gonna have to fly low. If they pick me up on radar, they'll track us all the way to … where are we going?"

"I don't know," Adreana admitted. "I've never been up past Lae, which is south of the King William coast and the mountain ridge that cuts across it. There's not a lot of civilization in the region. Come to think of it, there's not a lot of anything up there except trees and mountains."

"Like this?" Ahead of them a jungle-covered mountain ridge thrust up behind Port Moresby. Shrouded in morning mist, it reflected the sun's rays upward into the thermosphere. Samantha found the effect dazzling. "It's beautiful," she breathed. "So peaceful."

"You'd better hope the mist burns off, otherwise, you'll have to land in that," Adreana warned.

This brought Samantha's mind back from wandering. "So these GPS coordinates, let's have them. The pages we found in the book, too. Give them to Io, please."

Adreana passed several pages in a plastic cover to Io, who looked at them with a blank expression on his face. "Numbers. What do I do?"

Samantha reached out and pressed a switch, bringing a screen in front of Io to life. After a few seconds a satellite image of the island filled the screen, the yellows and greens of the landmass surrounded by a deep blue ocean.

"What you've got there are decimal latitude and longitude readings, indicating points on a map. You can search and store waypoints on the plane's GPS by touching the search box and just entering the numbers."

With a little help from Adreana behind him, Io managed to master the GPS system and in a short while they had a series of coordinates in a line on the map.

"What does that look like to you?" Samantha asked Adreana.

"One end of the line is on the coast, the other up in the mountains. It looks like someone was on a mission, a trek that ended there." She pointed at the nearest waypoint and pulled out a map. "Just like on here. If those lunar navigation points are accurate, they were taken every night. Your explorer sailed to the coast and then walked a week into the wilderness for his crows."

"And we're flying to the southernmost point. The end of the trek. It's a good place to start. Is that what kept you? If so, you have my thanks."

Adreana smiled. "When we saw the fire, Chase, my friend who studies navigation, wanted to get out and help. So I left him and came looking for you. When I was pulling up to the hotel I saw you both being led away with bags over your heads. I followed the van, at a distance, until it reached the warehouse. After that I had no plan. I drove around the building in darkness until I happened across the side entrance. When the shooting started, I ran in, my only thought being to find you. That guy got in the way and I just grabbed what was near and hit him on the head. He had the keys on him. The rest you know."

* * *

Having grown up on a diet of ARC adventures, Samantha was unable to avoid becoming mixed up in her mother's schemes. For them both, it seemed peril led to peril. Fortunately, the plane, a DA40 Diamond Star according to the details on the instrument panel, was easy to handle. It skipped over the surface of the foggy hills like a flat stone thrown across a calm lake.

"One could suspect you're actually enjoying this," Io said after an hour or so.

"I am," Samantha admitted, smiling. She took a deep breath. "Whatever else is going on in the world, at this moment I'm in control. It's me and the plane keeping the adventure going."

"Don't suppose you want to keep the adventure going a little smoother?" Adreana asked.

Samantha glanced over her shoulder. The diminutive Australian looked a little green around the edges. "It depends whose watching.

We need to stay below radar so this was never going to be straightforward. Besides, if we're looking for a place to land we need to be close. Fly too high and we might miss."

Io looked dubious. "Have you seen the landscape below? Virgin jungle, dense and angry, never before touched. You have to consider the possibility we might get to your coordinates and find no place to land."

"We can fly back, if need be," Samantha countered. "I'll land in a field if I have to. Where are we?"

"Just passed over Lae," Adreana provided. "There's sea off to our right. According to this map, there's a mountain ridge we have to clear, and the first coordinate is on the lower slope on the North side. If you want a runway, the closest strip is down there. You might want to give thought to finding a helicopter and a pilot."

"Aeon Fall could also be down there waiting for us, if they're as prevalent as ARC. Let's have a look first. I'd rather avoid humanity if I can."

The mountain ridge emerged on the horizon and before long Samantha followed the contours up, crossing the rock strewn crest by only a few metres. More patchy forest met them on the north of the ridge. Samantha pushed the plane into a descent so sudden it was more like a dive. "Hold on."

"The first coordinate is below us," said Adreana as she gripped the map in one hand and the seat back in her other.

"I don't see anything," Io said.

Samantha's heart sank. "I guess it was too much to ask for just a little luck. On to the next point."

"Wait," Adreana shouted, pressing her face against the window. "There's an airstrip down there."

Chapter Eighteen

A runway cut into the middle of the jungle on the side of a mountain?
"It can't be. There's no settlement down there. Why would you set a plane down in such a place?"

"Why would you hide lists of numbers in the cover of a book a hundred years old?" Adreana countered. "There's a clear defined airstrip down there, meaning we aren't the first to come looking. If there's a settlement maybe its inhabitants live under the canopy. Papua New Guinea is full of tribes who have barely any contact with the outside world. You won't know unless you land and we have a look."

"We've come this far," Samantha agreed. "Strap yourselves in. The landing could be rough. I'll circle around and land up the slope, if I can land at all."

Samantha tugged on her straps, making sure they were as tight as could be. She heard Io and Adreana doing the same. The lower slopes of the ridge stretched out below her, an ocean of cloud-swathed green ready to swallow her whole. She banked the plane into a slow curve, dropping down almost to the tops of the trees. A bead of sweat ran down the side of her face. She ignored the tickling sensation. She had to be responsible. There was nobody to turn to. The landing strip, not much more than a narrow cut in the trees, approached with alarming speed.

"Flaps down, speed dropping but above stalling," she spoke aloud. "Don't forget the slope." She pulled back on the yoke, lifting the nose of the plane so it was parallel to the approaching slope, praying silently that their collision with the car on take-off resulted in no permanent damage. There was no point worrying her passengers.

"Did you want me to do something?" Io asked.

"Just hold your stick. Let me do the work. It helps me sometimes to say everything aloud. Keeps me calm. It used to drive my instructors crazy. When we land I'll need your strength."

"If we land," Io replied.

Samantha considered a retort. She concentrated instead on the strip ahead, keeping the plane from shearing sideways with the rudder pedals. The plane began to resist her mastery. Trees rushed past. She was committed to the landing.

The plane hit the ground with a jolt reverberating up her spine.

Io grunted and Adreana yelped.

The stick shook with such violence it threatened to loosen her grip. "Io, now."

The muscles in Io's forearms tensed, tendons sticking out as he clenched the stick, his efforts synchronised with Samantha's own. The plane bucked and bumped as Samantha applied the brakes.

"End of the airstrip coming real fast," Adreana warned.

Samantha kept one eye on the instruments, the other on the trees. The slope helped and soon the plane taxied around under the overhanging canopy to point back down the slope. She turned to Io. "Thanks. I actually think we got down without breaking the landing gear."

Popping the catch on the roof, she powered down the engine. The propeller slowed to a halt, leaving them with a jungle full of distant birds, but nothing close by. The air was warm and damp with the mists on the mountainside. She felt less than comfortable, but it was better than being tied to a chair.

"Think we disturbed the animals," Adreana said.

For a moment none of them moved. In the distance, sounds of the jungle wildlife began to grow closer as the planes' disturbance dissipated. The chirping of birds was interrupted the occasional hoot of a nameless animal across the mountainside, answered moments later by another of its kind.

Content to watch for any signs of being followed through the mist above, Samantha settled back into her seat. After a few minutes of normality and absolutely no air traffic, she began to climb out of her seat.

She paused. "We aren't the first ones here."

Adreana followed her gaze and laughed. "Looks like it could be crowded."

"What's wrong?" Io asked. "Who's here?"

"Come have a look," Samantha invited him, and climbed out onto the wing of their plane.

Farther back under the canopy sat another plane. Unlike their pristine white Diamond Star, this was green with extensive patches of algae and detritus from being stored under the jungle canopy. More importantly the plane was lacking a nose cone, windows, and the two engines had nothing resembling propellers.

"I don't think this plane will be leaving any time soon," Adreana noted, walking up to the relic. She climbed onto the wing, the corroded metal straining under her weight. "It's been stripped, barely a component in here."

"So a plane with no parts that hasn't been used in years, yet there's an airstrip in good enough condition to land on. This doesn't add up."

"It does if someone else has been using it to fly in and out," Io said, kneeling at the edge of the runway, running the back of his hand across a fern, the plant springing back up with the elasticity of youth. "These plants are young. Maybe a year in age, maybe younger. This strip is being maintained if not used." He turned to Samantha. "They're waiting for someone."

How did he know? "Who are?"

"The watchers in the jungle." Io took a couple of steps out into the daylight, his eyes fixed on a point above them, somewhere near the top of the ridge. "They're out there, waiting. They knew we were coming."

"How?" Adreana asked, her eyes strangely bright. "What's their intent? Are they hostile?"

Io turned away from the ridge, a slight smile on his face. "How did they know we were coming? Look at the book we carry and what you can learn from it. Are they hostile?" He closed his eyes, lifting his head as if seeking a scent. "Mmmm, I don't think even they know that yet. Our actions will determine our safety. Be forthright. Respect the jungle."

A guilty look on her face, Adreana picked up a candy wrapper she had discarded moments before.

Samantha turned away, smiling inwardly. Io missed nothing. "What do we do now?" she asked, attempting to keep the amusement from her voice. "If this is the last GPS point on the map, one would hope we would find a reason for landing."

"Unless this was just the last reading your mysterious map maker took before he became distracted by the real reason for being here." Adreana pointed. "Look. There's a trail going off into the jungle past the plane. How about we follow it?"

The trail was not much more than a slight flattening of the surrounding foliage, a drying of the compressed earth underfoot. Samantha led the way, Adreana in the middle with Io at the rear of their little group. The going was slow; more often than not she found herself slipping down muddy scars in the mountainside and before long her hands were stained red with the iron-rich clay.

"Let's hope we aren't too far from the end of the track," she said as they pulled themselves up a steep incline using vines that hung loose from the branches above. "I'm not cut out for a jungle trek."

"You have to hope the goal is worth it," Io replied. "Under here." He ducked and then dropped out of sight beneath the rotting horizontal trunk of a fallen tree wrapped in more vines. "Come on, the path is this way."

Adreana shrugged, not looking up at him, and hopped down into the darkness. "Watch out, Sammy, the rocks down here are slippery. Make sure to duck."

"Like I can't see for myself," she muttered. Alone for the moment, she felt the isolation and oppression of the giant jungle trees above her. It would not bode well to be alone, lost with no point of reference. Movement caught her eye. A large head, too large to belong to a person, shifted in the foliage back up the path. They really weren't alone. "Io," she hissed, "we aren't alone out here." Not waiting a moment more, Samantha climbed under the fallen trunk.

"What did you see," Io said, turning to her.

"Just a large head. The body was obscured by the foliage. It was following our trail. We need to hurry."

Io indicated their path ahead. "I hope you have a light. It will mean we move faster."

"You're kidding me," Samantha groaned.

Ahead of them lay the entrance to a tunnel. The bulk of the fallen tree had hidden an approaching a rock face from view. The forest grew overhead and there was no way to climb around it; the slope dropped to a precipice.

Samantha turned on the light of her cell, shining it into the depths of blackness beyond. The ceiling was well above even Io's height, the chisel marks clear and concentrated. The tunnel had been carved from hard rock. "Well at least we don't have to duck," she said and stepped in to the darkness.

Holding her cell aloft, she led the way. The tunnel curved left making it impossible to see more than three feet ahead. The damp earth underfoot smelled loamy and organic. "We definitely aren't alone," she said, her voice muted by the mass of rock above her head. Probably a good thing if her follower was close.

"Tell me more about our friend back there," Io whispered.

"It was checking the trail we used, like it was tracking us. It looked to have a massive head, disproportional to its body. The eyes stuck out at funny angles. It was grotesque."

"Could be the jungle playing with your senses," Adreana said from behind, pulling a silver object from her pack. Another light came on with a click. "Flashlight," she added. "Save your phone."

Samantha laughed. "Thanks. Let's lead with the flashlight next time." More light failed to give rise to an exit. The one saving grace was that the tunnel was cool, the heat failing to penetrate this far under the earth.

They might have been in the tunnel for seconds, or an hour. Samantha found it difficult to keep track of time. "So what might our follower have been?" She asked in an effort to keep the silence broken, turning round with the light pointing along the floor.

"Who knows?" Adreana replied, her hand held out to prevent the glare of the light from dazzling her. "He could be a man in a mask or somebody with a genetic deformity. There are many myths and legends around the island. I'd need to see our distant companion in order to work out if he conforms to any of the known stories. Round here, science and myth are intertwined. Just look at Io here. Angel? I mean, really?"

"There are demons," Samantha countered. "The whole world saw what happened twenty years ago. They were going to overrun the planet."

"So you say," Adreana replied. "I wasn't there. In fact neither were you, mate. So we rely on stories, pictures. The evidence may be overwhelming but it's not first hand. What often happens, especially in isolated communities, will be an event that is interpreted by an elder or a wise man, written down and passed along to the next generation. A volcano blows its top and within five generations it's a titanic battle between a giant and a god, the land laid to waste as they fought. The information is wrong but the cultural memory is preserved. Fact becomes story becomes legend. If your angel here does something holy." Adreana paused and turned to Io. "You *can* do holy things, can't you?"

"I have no idea," Io admitted. "Apparently I can lay waste to a mountainside and destroy half a city with nothing more than my own body, if you call such an act holy."

Adreana smirked. "Sounds more like a twisted case of divine retribution. But the point stands. In the past, people have turned to the supernatural as a means of explanation. Atlantis may have been an island sinking in an earthquake, sea level rise or a volcano blowing itself to pieces. Like Krakatau, only a couple thousand miles away from here."

Samantha stopped. "That argument's fine for isolated people, living in the jungle, divorced from the rest of mankind. Yet we come from a world where technology captures everything. You can't put a demon incursion down to supernatural battles when it's on CNN. Science is replacing religion. That's the core of the problem faced in places like your university."

"I agree," Adreana said. "Well stated. People want to believe but they are finding nothing in which to put faith into." She turned to Io. "You, mate, are the answer humanity seeks."

Samantha snorted. "And if Aeon Fall get hold of you they'll make sure nobody believes in anything ever again. What's contained in this book is itself a measure of belief. Ask yourself this, Adreana. Do people record crow patterns because there's an actual fact, proven and absolute, that crows in a certain formation will lead directly to a change in their circumstance? Or do they accept the sign given and find ways to make their fate come about for good or bad?"

"You're talking about self-fulfilling configurations." Adreana resumed their slow shuffle through the tunnel, holding her free hand out for balance. "The pattern makes the event much more likely because the believer wills it so. This in turn reinforces the pattern as prophecy."

Samantha repeated Adreana's comment, "Fact becomes story becomes legend, just mixed around a bit. Everything is self-fulfilling."

"I have to admit you both sound confused," Io said.

The girls quieted, waiting for him to continue.

"Science replaces religion, prophecies become self-fulfilling. You're grasping at concepts, the fundamentals of which have been laid down since the very start of existence."

"And that is?" Samantha was intrigued. Was this the angel speaking or the memories of the man risen to the surface?

"It's simple. Everything is connected. All life is one."

The phrase set off alarm bells in Samantha's head. "Someone said that to Mom once, when they wanted to take her into a cult, for her own safety."

"Maybe they were right," Io suggested.

"You wouldn't make that assertion if you had met them," she shot back.

"All life is one," Adreana pondered. "You talking about Gaia theory, mate?"

"If your theory refers to all life being part of a connected organism, then yes. The ant is insignificant but the hive can enact miracles. Do you see?"

"And where do demons fit in?" Samantha asked. "How does their invasion make our organism function any better?"

"It causes mankind to react," Io replied. "Much like you do to my comments. Your minds become broadened, your consciousness expanded."

"Making greater acts possible because I believe them to be within my grasp." Samantha said, her voice filled with wonder. "Io, you're a genius."

"Self-belief is one of the most powerful tools granted to mankind. When applied correctly, the results seem like miracles. Miracles become stories become legend."

Up ahead, natural light began to turn the tunnel from black to shades of grey. "Look! We're nearly there," Adreana pointed, her voice eager.

Samantha could appreciate such a feeling. The dark, clammy tunnel to who-knew-where was oppressive and she was feeling the weight of so much rock over her head. "Can we pick up the pace?"

The three of them moved toward the light, like a sapling in the jungle around them. More than once she stumbled on uneven rock from underfoot. The pace picked up as the light increased. Soon, Adreana switched off her flashlight.

"Careful when we get outside," Adreana warned. "The light will be harsh on our eyes and if this is the end of the trail, anything could greet us."

The tunnel twisted suddenly, sunlight kissing the tunnel wall. Samantha pushed forward, leaving her two companions in her wake. With the exit so close to hand, her need for space became overwhelming. Only the faintest need for caution kept her from breaking into a run and when she turned into the sunlight she was glad she hadn't done so. "Guys, we're not going anywhere."

Chapter Nineteen

"Where's the path?" Adreana asked, sounding baffled.

Samantha didn't turn, her eyes transfixed by the vista spreading out below her like a map on the internet, while her hands clawed for a grip at the edge of the aperture. The lowlands beyond the ridge they traversed were scrubby and filled with patches of trees. They stretched across a shallow slope until the distant edge of the formation was once again engulfed by jungle. Daring to glance down, she regretted the decision immediately. "That's got to be a hundred metres, maybe two. Io, fancy producing one of your self-fulfilling miracles? We could really do with a pair of wings, or at the very least another tunnel out of here."

"Is there a ledge to either side?" Adreana continued. "A path along the cliff?"

Io put a hand on her shoulder, startling Samantha, who jumped on reflex. "Let me," he offered, leaning out. "There is nothing, Adreana. This is a vertical rock face."

"So where's this bloody book taking us?" she yelled into the expanse.

Samantha took a deep breath, enjoying the fresh air. A breeze played with her hair. At least there was one benefit to being up here. Calmer, she said, "We go back. It's not like there's a choice."

"And our friend back there?"

Samantha shrugged. "One of him, three of us. We take the plane and work out how to stop a nuclear plant going critical."

"Or we hide," Adreana countered.

"No, we don't do that. Adreana, you've helped us more than I could ever repay. Porter Rockwell was there to kidnap me. His presence makes it personal. If I can aid my mother in any manner, it's now my duty to her, to everybody, to do what I can." Samantha took a couple of steps back into the tunnel, space enough to find her cell. The ARC private network, fuelled by satellites around the globe, shone bright and full in the top left corner of the screen. She pressed the quick-dial and raised the phone, stopping halfway to her mouth. "Guys, we're not alone."

"Hello?" a voice from the phone queried. "Samantha? Sammy?"

"Mom, it's me," she whispered, watching the tunnel and not making a move. Rockwell had us. We escaped into the jungle with a little help. We've got a situation. You need to find Charlotte. Rockwell's goons have her. I'll call you back. I'm fine, just find her. She's in danger."

"Samantha? Where are—"

Samantha cut off the call, replacing the phone in her bag as slowly as possible. She had heard his low intake of breath.

In the dark, a figure waited, watching them, a homemade spear held low. The head was distended, the skull wide and flat, reminding her of pictures of the grossly-distorted demons her mom had once fled from.

"It's okay," she said, her voice as calm and reassuring as she could make it. Samantha slipped the strap of her pack back over one shoulder. "It's okay," she repeated.

Behind the figure, more of its' kind appeared, attired in a similar way, naked but for loincloths barely concealing genitalia. All were armed with spears. All had oversized heads of varying dimensions, eyes pointing up to the roof of the tunnel, out sideways at odd angles.

"I know them," Adreana said.

"You do?" Io replied from behind Samantha.

"Well, I know of them. They look like members of the Honihin mountain tribe. The masks are to frighten intruders."

"I'm surprised anybody's gotten close enough to study them given the impossible route in," Samantha whispered out of the side of her mouth.

The foremost of the tribe raised his spear and bellowed words in a language Samantha didn't recognise.

"I don't think he's best pleased to see us in this tunnel."

"What gives you that impression? The waving spear or the threatening tone of his voice."

The tribesman took a sharp step forward, thrusting his spear at them.

Samantha stood her ground. "I don't care what you do with your stick, little man. You're not pushing us off the cliff." She spoke with such authority the tribe paused for a moment, looking at each other.

"Let me forward," Io asked. "I can't do any good from back here." Shifting in the small space at the end of the tunnel, Io made his way to the front. "Listen," he said, his hands raised in a gesture of placation. "We aren't here to hurt you. We're friends."

"Yeah, nice one mate," scoffed Adreana from the back of their trio. "Try the five year old's approach to diplomacy."

However, with Io now in view the tribe collectively took a step back, turning to discuss something in frantic whispers. Their pursuer pointed at them repeatedly with his spear. A bead of sweat ran down Samantha's neck disappearing into the material of her top. The heat of the day filled the tunnel from behind them. She could feel the sun's rays starting to burn her skin as they stood, immobile. They needed to move.

It appeared the tribe had reached a decision. Two of their number stood, spears planted vertically in front of them, while one disappeared into the darkness behind. The remaining two took a couple of steps forward, looking up at Io.

"Friends," he repeated, as if the word was part of a universal language.

Placing their spears on the ground, the two looked up at Io from bended knee. One uttered a word, the same word, several times.

"Agela", he seemed to say. Then the pair knelt fully, bending forward at the waist, raising their hands palm up in a gesture of supplication. The pair began chanting.

"What did you do?" Samantha asked.

"You saw as much as me," Io turned. "Adreana, do you know why these people might decide to fall down and worship me?"

"Maybe they saw the footage of you falling out of the sky and destroying a city."

Moments later, the fifth tribesman returned, an elderly man hurrying in his wake. The elder had a face painted red with white around the mouth, and a crest of feathers arranged across the top of his head. The masked man dropped to the floor with his two fellows, again proclaiming the word 'Agela' from behind the grotesque mask he wore.

The elder remained where he was, assessing both the reaction of his warriors, and the three strangers stood in his midst.

"What do I do now?" Io asked. "Am I supposed to respond?"

He began to kneel but the elder jumped forward in an instant, preventing him from getting any closer to the ground. "No, you do no belong in the earth." His face showed concern.

"You speak our language?" Samantha caught the old man's attention. "What's going on here? This word these men keep using: Agela. What does it mean?"

The elder stared at her for a moment before looking back to Io. "Angel."

* * *

Samantha had a lot to think over as the small group of tribesmen led them back through the tunnel, initially taking a turn into a fork the three of them had missed in the dark. The tunnel stretched on forever and they walked for hours. The torches the Honihin held spit and crackled, bundles of rags tied to sticks and likely dipped in something Samantha preferred not to know. Several times they had to be replaced. In the sooty darkness, Samantha had a long time to consider what she had witnessed. To a man, the Honihin had recognised Io for what he was, a fact everybody who had seen him up to until now had missed, with Aeon Fall the only exception. How did they know?

"Can you see him for what he truly is?" She asked the warrior closest to her, getting no response as the man stayed stiff as a board, staring straight ahead.

"They may not choose to answer you," Adreana advised. "Don't assume they all know English. Of course, they might not answer because you're a woman. Papua New Guinea has a history of gender inequality; it's way behind the developed world, especially in the isolated parts."

The Honihin elder stopped and turned to Adreana. "Not true," he said before resuming his march. The tunnel began to dip and at length they once again saw the faint glow of daylight ahead. Without prompting each Honihin warrior doused his torch at a sooty spot on the tunnel wall, depositing the brand in a crude basket woven from leaves.

"How did you know who they were?" Samantha asked Adreana.

"There are four groups of people in Madang, which is the region we're in. They are the islanders, coastal people, river people, and these, the mountain people. There are stories about entire tribes going missing that Mr. Vaitai used to tell me. One was a story about a tribe on the Bismarck Range, which is the ridge we flew over. They lived in the shadow of the peak later called Mount Willhelm and were the owners of the weirdest, most gross hunting masks."

"Isolation does a lot for one's perceptions of the outside world," Samantha tried to agree but Adreana shook her head.

"I think they prefer to be left alone and the masks are part of their efforts to remain isolated."

"Hasn't worked though, has it? Somebody hacked an airstrip right out of the jungle. They can't have flown in and then done so. They must have trekked in here first."

Further thoughts on the origins of the airstrip evaporated into thin air as they reached the end of the tunnel and a vision of spectacular beauty hit Samantha. She stopped, as did Io and Adreana, while the tribesmen continued on ahead.

"I never thought I'd see the like," Adreana breathed.

Samantha craned her neck to follow the ridge that rose to a peak almost directly behind them. The jungle grew high and dense up the steep slopes to either side, large trees leaning out to frame a patch of grass which was the only area directly exposed to the sunlight above.

Underneath the shade of the trees to either side squatted a series of wide straw-covered huts, the entrances of which were now filled with women staring. The sounds of children playing filtered through from beyond the huts.

Io trotted ahead, crossing the grassy glade in a quick few dozen steps. "Come look," he called.

Samantha followed him, Adreana close on her heels.

"That's Mount Willhelm directly above us," she said. "No wonder all traces of the Honihin disappeared. Nobody would think to look up here. Planes don't even fly over here because of the peak and even if they did, they'd only see a patch of grass in the trees."

"There is more," Io said, beckoning them forward. "Just watch your step."

Samantha came to a stop beside him. "I see what you mean."

"Great," Adreana added, "More cliffs."

The trees still above, the grass ended in a sudden drop of at least twenty metres, the cliff angling back beneath the rock upon which they were standing. Feeling less safe in this knowledge, Samantha stepped back.

Turning to the village, she said, "So what now? What have moon readings and crow predictions got to do with a lost tribe on a mountainside? How does all of what we've seen help you, Io?"

Ever mercurial, Io replied, "This is your trek, young Samantha. I am but a companion and witness."

"Well, you're a lot of help. Okay, we have a lost tribe, some of which have seen you for what we believe you truly are, an angel. We have a sigil in a fortune-telling book that has no explanation, but forms precisely when you step into the summoning circle. And we have measurements taken from a hidden compartment in the same book, a book with a twin, pointing us to the lost tribe."

"Sounds like you were meant to be here," said Adreana. "It all adds up, mate."

"But what to do with this?" Samantha found herself watching the trees. Small shapes fluttered about in the canopy, cawing to each other. Not small shapes, she corrected herself. Birds in the trees. "What are those birds?"

Adreana followed her gaze. "That's the Gray crow."

"A crow," Samantha wondered aloud. "Where's the elder? I want to know what they use this open space for."

Adreana and Io both turned to scan the huts where several Honihin still watched them. A few children emerged, took one look at them and disappeared with a squeal into the treeline, unmindful of the intruders.

Samantha approached a young woman in the doorway of the nearest hut, trying her best to ignore the semi-nakedness of her appearance. Clothing was clearly not top of the Honihin's priorities. With the heat of the New Guinean jungle, she could appreciate why.

Smiling at the woman, she said, "Do you speak my language? Can you tell me where to find your elder?"

The young woman smiled back, revealing teeth stained brown, and said something to her in the Honihin dialect, pointing in the direction of another hut.

Samantha turned to Adreana, who shrugged. "Sorry mate. I can make do with several of the languages but nobody in Port Moresby speaks Honihin. I reckon nobody in the world speaks Honihin, other than these guys."

"She say your hair is very beautiful, and the women's hut is that way, if you want to dress like her." A feeble voice mumbled from across the grass.

"My hair?" self-conscious all of a sudden, Samantha touched a hand to her hair, bound in a loose tangle since the night before.

The young woman beamed a smile and pointed once more. Samantha couldn't help but smile back. She turned. A wizened old man was shuffling toward her, the elder warrior she had met before at his side.

A couple of dozen Honihin followed in their wake, the warriors who had led them here, women, and curious older children.

Io and Adreana joined Samantha as the strange procession stopped. The old man, a beard hanging down his chest, stood chewing, his eyes unusually bright. He looked to Io and gasped.

"Agela!"

The entire following dropped to their knees, heads bowed, all murmuring the same word and refusing to look up, as if they were not worthy.

For his part, Io appeared confused by the entire affair, an awkward look on his face. "Please," he said when he could clearly stand it no longer. "Please, all of you, stand up."

The elder ceased chanting, looking up at him.

Io nodded encouragement, holding his hand out.

The elder's eyes widened, and he reached out to touch Io's hand. "You are not this man."

His words were slow, and slurred, presumably on account of whatever he was chewing, but they showed his understanding of language to be clear.

"I'm beginning to understand that," Io replied, and the elder looked at him in confusion. Io nodded. "I am not this man."

The elder climbed to his feet, leaning on a gnarled stick for support. Once up, he waved his arms to either side, mimicking wings. "You are an angel. I see you."

"How do you know this language?" Io pressed.

The elder smiled and turned to a young man behind him, saying something in Honihin.

"We came here using notes from this book," Samantha said, stepping forward and pulling the book from her bag.

The elder glanced at her book and looked away, then took a second longer look. He gasped. "How have you that? How?"

"My sister gave it to me."

The young man returned with a package wrapped in cloth, handing it to the elder.

Dropping his stick to the ground, the elder unwrapped the cloth. Inside was a book, the cover of which was identical to her copy.

Chapter Twenty

"There's your book," Io held his hands out. "May I take a look?"

The elder looked at Samantha with suspicion. "You may. But first your name. Tell me."

"Io Vel."

"Io … Vel?"

Io shrugged. "I don't remember it all. I'm not quite myself."

"I am Turatup. I am…" he struggled to find the word. "I am wise man."

"Like a shaman?" Samantha asked.

Turatup considered this, narrowing his eyes at her interruption. "What means Shaman?"

"A wise man. A healer. He can see things others can't. Like Agela." Samantha indicated Io with her free hand.

"Yes. I am shaman to the Honihin. I see you, Io Vel." He turned, indicating the elder warrior. "This is Banar. A great hunter. This his men you meet. Soki, Suara, Pila, Yokiba."

Upon hearing their names, the warriors looked up from their reverence of Io, who nodded in response. "How is it you understand us?"

Turatap smiled. "My father teach me your language. He tell story of man come to mountain on walk quest."

"Expedition?" Samantha supplied.

"Yes. Expedition. He came looking for birds." Turatup raised his hands to the trees. "We worship the spirits of our ancestors in the birds. He taught my fathers' fathers' father your words. He built our village. He brought the book."

"He brought us a book, too." Samantha held up her book of the crow patterns, opening it to one of the pages of formations.

Turatup leaned in to look at the pattern, one telling of making a choice for good or for ill. He gasped. "This is new. The crows make this pattern two day past. I send Soki to watch the cut jungle."

"The cut jungle? You mean the airstrip?" Samantha was eager for more information and this man had the answers. It was clear by the shaman's reactions to her—mainly frowns and sidelong glances as he tried to refer to his *angel*—he wasn't used to women being in charge.

Despite Io's amnesia, he understood this too, and he knew where she was going. "Turatup, who cut the jungle where Soki found us?"

"More men come later. They bring Areca nut and tell my father to watch for Agela."

"Areca nut?"

Turatup grinned, chewing and spitting a wad of leaf pulp into his hand. "It gives me power. Let's me see spirits. We all see spirits."

"Do men still bring you Areca nuts?"

"Yes. They bring the nut, maybe once season. They ask what we see in the birds. Which patterns." He signed. "We do not know all the patterns."

"Maybe this will help?" Samantha offered the Shaman her book. "If we can look at your book, you can have our book."

Turatup's eyes narrowed. "Trade?"

"No. Gift. We just want to look at your book."

The Shaman's eyes lit up. "My home. Come there. You can look at the book of Honihin." He turned and shuffled off, beckoning them to follow.

Samantha looked at Io and shrugged, trailing in the old man's wake. He headed to the largest of the huts under the trees to their right and entered without stopping. Samantha followed him in and had to hold back a laugh when she saw the interior.

A mat that probably served as a bed lay along the back of the hut. The rest of the room was taken up by seats removed from the aircraft. In various stages of decay, the seats were cracked leather, and looked well worn. A stump with a metal panel covered in skins served as a table in the middle. Light came in from the windows, but not enough to make reading a book easy.

Io placed the Honihin book on the table and opened it with the protesting creak of very old leather. As if anticipating their needs, Turatup lit a candle in a rusting lantern and placed it near them. Once done, he sat opposite, cradling Samantha's book of crow patterns as if it were a newborn.

"I never expected this," Io said.

Standing in back of them, Adreana asked, "What do you see?" Her face was eager.

"A few of the pattern drawings but," he leafed through the book, the pages delicate and threatening to crack, "it's mostly a diary. A log of the author's journey." He looked up. "The date of these entries. These were logged in eighteen eighty-three."

"The year Papua New Guinea was colonized by the Germans and the British," Adreana said. "What else is there?"

"A picture of a church, partially completed. The text is too faded for me to read. Except the year. Eighteen eighty-two. But look at this." Io held the book so that both Samantha and Adreana could see the pattern on the ground by the church.

"What is it? Adreana asked.

"The Thornfalcon," Samantha replied. "Exactly how we witnessed it formed in Dubrovnik. These books are without a doubt related." She turned her cell on. "No signal in the middle of the jungle. This thing's never been so quiet." Selecting the camera app she photographed the church drawing. "What else is there?"

Io leafed through the pages. "Mostly dates of log entries and drawings, presumably of the crew and landmarks he saw on his trip. Took a few months, it seems. Nice drawing of the ship here. After, some lists of numbers and then more of your crow drawings. This gentleman was quite the ornithologist."

"That can't be everything," Samantha's voice rose as frustration threatened to overwhelm.

"I'm sorry," Io shrugged. "The writing's too faint. This hasn't been kept in an airtight library like your specimen. We're lucky to be able to read as much as we did. Hang on. There's a page stuck." Io reached for a thin stick with a black end on the table, presumably a rudimentary writing implement. Inserting it with care, he pried the two pages apart. The pages protested as they separated, small sections of the lower page remaining stuck and ripping from the surface to remain on the upper page. What they saw caused a gasp in all three of them.

"Thornfalcon," Io began to read. "Only in the correct place may the mark be revealed and contact made. Look at the picture. It's an angel in a circle."

Samantha gazed in wonder. The picture was beautifully crafted, detailed down to the detail of individual feathers on the angel's wings. Both terrible and majestic at the same time, the angel did not belong in the realm of mortals. Its face was manlike but the eyes held such ferocity Samantha couldn't look at the picture for more than a couple of seconds. She felt it was watching her.

"So you stand in the circle and make contact." Adreana said, pointing at the page. "Io, you could get your memories back."

"The picture certainly indicates such an approach," Samantha agreed. "But what about the church? What does that say underneath?"

Io squinted. "Philippe LeClerq. Means nothing to me."

The name sounded familiar to Samantha. "LeClerq? I swear I know the name."

"Maybe the writer met a man called Philippe LeClerq from France on his journey to Papua New Guinea. He drew the church and signed it."

Samantha nodded in Adreana's direction. "You make a good case. Keep looking. You might find something else. Io, can I speak to you outside?"

Io stood, leading the way. Adreana stood watching as Samantha followed him out into the glade.

"The sigil means Karael," he said in a low voice when they were alone. "She doesn't know that. When it formed before, Karael found me. What if the sigil is some kind of tracker to allow him to locate me?"

"It doesn't explain why it's by a ruined church in that book. Who was Karael hunting then? And why you?"

Io appeared distressed, walking in a small circle as he tried to think his way through the problem. "Karael said I was a fallen one. Am I really evil? If I remember who I am, do I become what I once was? Samantha, I don't want to bear the burden of such possibility."

"What are you proposing?"

"I want to know what's going on. Why I'm here. Karael no longer has possession of his sword. He can't be any stronger than me. Maybe I can get answers from him if I let him know where I am."

"That's a dreadful risk to take."

"What choice do I have? We can't go jumping all over the world trying to jog my memory with ancient books and expect to have anything meaningful inside. Not if your Aeon Fall is going to destroy the planet. We are taking risks anyway. Ask yourself: Who benefits from keeping an isolated tribe drugged on hallucinogenic nuts? If you're determined to help, let's at least be direct about our efforts." A pensive look crossed Io's face. "Just don't tell Adreana what's going to happen," he said in hushed tones. "And keep that gun you were given by your friend on the plane."

Charlotte Benson, supposed to be her protector and guide, now injured and missing. A wave of guilt washed over Samantha. How would Charlotte feel at having lost them all? Would her mother be talking to her? Samantha shook her head, looking down at the grass. "Let's hope this works out, Io. I have the feeling I'm gonna be in a whole heap of trouble before the end."

* * *

In the hut, Adreana was still poring over the Honihin book under the watchful gaze of Turatup.

Samantha nodded at Io.

He nodded back. "Elder Turatup," he asked, "when do you read the crow patterns?"

"At all times," the shaman replied. "The spirits speak to us when they will. Morning, day, night." He looked a little sheepish as he added, "We bring them out of the trees to feed."

"Could we try to bring the crows to the ground now? We could test your book for patterns." Samantha indicated the book she had given him.

Turatup stood. "Two days ago the birds predicted strangers among us. I sent Soki to watch. It is wise to ask the spirits for guidance once again. Follow me. Bring the other book." Shuffling out, Turatup yelled something in Honihin.

At his call, the tribe gathered together; children, naked but for wooden jewellery, materialised from the jungle around the village. Some watched from the safety of their huts. One of the hunters placed a circle constructed of branches bent and bound with vines in the middle of the glade, facing the cliff. Everything was ready.

"What do we do now?" Samantha asked.

Turatup held out a hand, indicating the circle. "You stand in the circle. We call the spirits."

"Not how I'd do it," she said to Io as she passed.

He grinned back. "What's normal about any of your adventure?"

Careful to avoid standing on the wooden frame, Samantha stepped into the circle. Two blindfolded women emerged on either side from huts and randomly threw chunks of red fruit onto the grass. The women backed off and in their place two men appeared. Naked, they were painted with white to make them look like living skeletons.

"Death dancers," Adreana said from behind the circle. "Many tribes have them here. They are not uncommon among the aboriginal people back home."

"Won't they scare the crows?"

The two men began chanting, a warbling ululation mixed with the occasional high-pitched shriek.

"They are praying for intervention with the dead," Io said in a quiet voice.

"How do you know?" Samantha replied without turning. Both men had begun to gyrate in a series of spasmodic steps, each taking them closer and closer to the cliff edge.

"I can feel it. There's more to their prayer than just words. They call to the spirits for intervention and they dance to ward themselves from being taken."

Samantha turned. Io's gaze was fixed on the cliff edge. Behind him Adreana's eyes were bright as she watched him. Not the event before them, but Io himself.

Ahead, the dancers' prayer reached a crescendo and simultaneously, both men stopped, dropping to their knees, arms stretched in front and foreheads touching the ground.

"They have called the spirits and link them to the earth, if they come," said Turatup. "We shall see."

Above them, the flock of crows became more active, first cawing in excitement at the fruit being strewn about the grass and then, as if an invisible net had been removed, launching into the sky to swirl above Samantha's head. The noise grew to a deafening level as the excited murder of crows continued to swirl, descending toward the circle and her head. Samantha ducked on instinct, raising her hands to protect herself. As she did so, the crows split in two, landing on the grass to peck at the fruit.

Her heart thudding in her chest, Samantha drew in several gasping breaths, leaning forward with her hands on her knees. She looked up at Io. "What. The?"

"Dramatic," Io observed.

"There is a sign," Turatup announced. Turning to his people he shouted in Honihin and the gathered tribe cheered.

"Those women encouraged the crows down with food," Samantha countered, the doubt growing in her.

"No." The shaman's voice was sharp the cheering tribe immediately stopped. "The fruit women cannot see. They were born blind. You want to know the reading, yes?"

"I do," Samantha hoped her scepticism wouldn't cost her.

His face twitching in irritation, Turatup consulted the book she had given him, turned it around and handed it to her without a word.

"Return home. Seek the answer from someone close," she read aloud.

"Sounds like a fortune cookie," quipped Adreana.

His face now serious, the shaman took possession of the book once again. "These omens are not to be ignored. Your gift of the book is beyond treasure, but even spirits say it's time for you to leave."

Samantha stepped out of the circle, nodding her thanks at the old man.

Io turned to follow her as she moved off but Turatup placed a hand on his shoulder. "You stand."

"I shouldn't," Io replied with a grateful smile, intending to walk away.

Samantha's heart missed a beat as she remembered his warning. Karael, the name a distant memory in this sweaty jungle, had found them after the crows had formed the Thornfalcon, the Hebrew glyph for his very name.

Turatup's hand did not move, keeping Io in place. "You stand," he insisted, his voice commanding.

If Samantha had learned anything about Io the man, it was that he had a gentle nature. He didn't want to fight a people who didn't know better.

"Be ready," he warned her. "I don't know what my actions will precipitate." To Turatup he said, "I will stand in your circle. I apologise."

Samantha could see his meaning. Io didn't apologise for his refusal to stand in the circle, but for what might happen if he did. They had information now. They needed to get it to where it would be of use.

Io turned from them, stepping over the wooden frame into the circle. Once there, he stood head bowed, repeating a phrase under his breath. "Please don't."

The crows ceased their feeding and raised their heads, watching him. For a moment nothing happened. Then one by one the crows cawed, hopping and flapping as they were compelled to move.

Samantha winced as each bird fell into place, the puzzle complete in moments. The Honihin gasped as one.

"Agela has been given guidance," Turatup muttered, then raised his voice and shouted the same phrase in Honihin. The tribe moved from awe to celebration, whooping and cheering around the glade.

Io turned to Samantha. "I'm sorry, Sammy. I couldn't fight them. They know not what they do."

From above there was an ear-splitting boom as an object hurtled out of the sky, at a speed faster than sound. There was no time to move as it plummeted to the ground, impacting with such force the rock deep beneath cracked and split. Dirt flew up into the air causing the entire tribe to duck. Samantha fought to stay standing as the very earth recoiled from this alien intrusion. As the displaced dirt fell to the ground, a pair of eyes looked up at her from within the impact crater.

"Karael."

Chapter Twenty-One

Samantha reeled, falling over her feet as she stepped back, only to be caught by Io. How had it been so quick? How could they ever escape?

Karael stood, the rock beneath the weight of his presence groaning in pain as the folds of his long black leather jacket draped around him. He wore the body of Lucas well, giving him intensity, a purpose that, while alive, had seldom been expressed. Eyes, wise beyond imagination, hard without mercy, assessed the situation. "Brother," he said, addressing Io, who had remained in the wooden circle. "Why are you doing this to yourself? Calling my attention down upon you in the ruined city was unfortunate on your part. Yet you escape just to run halfway around the planet and call me down once again? One might suggest you're a glutton for punishment."

The crows that hadn't been wiped out of existence by Karael's thunderous entrance began to caw at him, clearly rattled by what had happened. He nodded at the birds and in an instant they flew back to the trees and were silent.

"How did you?" Samantha realised even as she asked the question. "The Thornfalcon?"

"*My sigil,*" Karael corrected her. "If it calls to me, I come."

"But they had you bound."

"Only until I was called on again. Your bonds mean nothing in comparison to the power of Heaven's chosen. My sole purpose, you know, is Eradication of Heaven's rabid fallen." Karael stepped up out of the impact crater. The rock shuddered beneath his feet, as if recoiling from him.

Samantha touched Io's shoulder to steady herself. His muscles were rock hard with tension. "What is it, Io?"

"I feel this is a bad idea but I do not understand why. Again, I recognise him, Samantha. Not this mortal form but the presence contained within. I feel a kinship, but nothing more."

The lack of recognition enraged Karael. He threw his head back and roared in anguish. "Where are you, Ioviel? Why do you persist in masking your presence with this mortal affliction, this amnesia? We were brothers, you and I. Forces among the Powers, the Order of Angels and Heavens' protection, guardians of the very gates, you were foremost among us, the greatest of our kind. Does leaving the sanctity of our domain for your own selfish purposes mean nothing to you? Ours is a life of servitude, Ioviel. Ever since He formed us out of nothingness, pulling us from the void, we have served. Your wishes do not come above obedience, and for that, you must be destroyed."

Karael took another menacing step toward them, only for Turatup to step in the way, flanked on either side by Suara and Yakiba. The shaman raised his hands, speaking in Honihin,

'Agela' was the only word Samantha recognised.

Together, the three men walked toward the angel, their faces reverent, eyes wide.

Karael was clearly aware of their approach but his eyes remained on Io. "Is your choice to remain behind mortal men, brother? Would you cower so? A mighty captain such as yourself reduced to a whimpering cur?"

Karael stepped forward and Turatup reached out to touch him. With a sneer, Karael balled his hand and rammed it through the shaman's chest and out between the ribs of his back. The hand remained closed, blood dripping to the grass below with a series of loud spatters.

"Turatup!" Samantha screamed, her voice joining those of the tribe around the glade.

The limp body of the shaman continued to hang off of Karael's arm, the lifeless head tipping forward onto his shoulder.

The weight of the man was inconsequential for the angel. "These, Ioviel, these men—they're a means to an end—power. Surround yourself with man and I'll remove them no matter how pure their souls."

"Karael, please don't." Io remained in the circle.

Karael took another step forward. The two warriors were unsure how to react, holding their spears low.

"Suara, Yakiba, get back," called Samantha.

"Hearken to the words of the spawn of Satan," Karael mocked her, addressing the tribesmen. "She would save you despite her impotence."

They didn't move.

"Don't then," Karael continued. In a flash, he withdrew his hand from Turatups body and grabbed each by the throat. "I'll take them from you one by one." With a jerk of his hands, he tore their throats out, leaving them both on their knees, gasping for air as blood choked them from within.

"No!" roared Io, running forward.

"At last!" Karael rejoiced, dropping fistfuls of skin and cartilage to the glade. He moved forward to meet Io's charge, knocking him from his feet with a sidestep and a straight arm to the chest. "This will be a day long remembered. The day one of our mightiest ends his desecration. Get up, Ioviel. Give me the satisfaction of a clean kill."

Karael stepped back, allowing Io to regain his footing. "You don't have to do this," Io gasped as he attempted to draw deep breaths.

Karael grabbed Io by the front of his shirt and twisted, pulling him close. "You've fallen less than two mortal days and already you think to tell me what I can and cannot do? This soul sack you cower in, it's affecting your judgement. There is no do, or don't do. There is obedience. When you disobey, you're punished. When you disobey, you fall. When you involve mortals in our affairs, they pay the price."

Karael shifted his foot, readying a hard punch, and in that moment Io ducked, tackling his opponent and sending him sprawling across the broken ground. Attempting to press his advantage, Io launched himself after Karael, aiming to land atop him. Karael pulled his feet in, lashing out as Io descended and flipping him over and into one of the huts. The delicate building burst apart in a shower of sticks and straw, sending several of the Honihin screaming into the forest.

"Sammy, you gotta do something, mate." Adreana urged her.

"Like what? I don't exactly have a good angel up my sleeve."

"Think of something. Io's fighting half-cocked. He needs to remember who he is and he'll be okay."

One of the warriors attempted to halt Karael in his pursuit of Io. Without pausing, the avenging angel thrust a hand in through his ribcage and began to use the body as a club, swinging it at Io. Blood spattered everywhere. Getting to his feet, Io shielded his face from the blood until Karael landed a blow, sending him flying back into the glade.

This was more than enough for the majority of the tribe, who melted into the jungle. Samantha felt for them. She'd brought this fate upon the innocent Honihin. She fingered the gun in her bag, realizing a firearm would be an ineffectual tool. "Adreana, I need a distraction."

Her face pale with fright, Adreana replied, "You want me to go over there and talk to him?"

There was only one distraction within her power enough for an angel. "Just watch them. I need a moment."

From the other end of the glade she heard Io cry out in pain. "Brother, stop,"

Karael hissed. "You have no power over me, Ioviel. You're no longer my captain, only my target, unworthy of a place in our ranks."

Io continued to appeal to Karael even as they fought. Samantha stepped down into the depression caused by the angel's dramatic entrance, the only clear area of dirt. Beneath her feet she felt the dirt shift. The cliff didn't have long. Closing her eyes and taking a deep breath she began to draw glyphs.

The practice was so familiar to her. It had only been a matter of days since she summoned her father's image yet so much had changed. She glanced up once. Karael had pummelled Io to near insensibility. The fact that the angel Karael wore Lucas' body was not lost on her.

"This is what it means to defy His word, brother. Your fall will be a tale told forever." He threw Io to the ground, standing above him. Holding his bloody hand out to one side, he smiled as it now filled with a glowing sword. Holy. Righteous. A weapon of divine execution "You didn't think I only had one?"

Scratching at the earth in desperation, Samantha completed the circle of glyphs. "It's gonna have to do. Dad I hope you've got your ears on."

Clenching her fist, she sliced at the skin of her forearm with the jagged edge of a rock. The pain, so familiar and so instant surged through her, and blood began to seep from the wound. Holding her arm away from the glyphs until she judged there was enough blood, Samantha proceeded to let her life fill the patterns with power.

Karael stopped, sword raised aloft, turning toward her. "What are you doing?"

"Bringing my own angel to the fight." Samantha turned back to the pattern at her feet. "Come on."

At first the blood did nothing, spattering on the dirt. Then, as the liquid sank into the glyphs, a red glow appeared along the lines she had drawn. The glow increased, the glyphs coming alive and dancing within the confines of the enclosing circle.

"That is forbidden!" Karael bellowed, his attention now on her. Behind him Io stirred in the grass.

"Not from me," she shot back. "Adreana, step back."

The glyphs began to swirl, coalescing into a glowing circle of deepest red. Adreana took a few steps away from the crater, standing near the edge of the cliff. A tremble reverberated beneath. The cliff reacting to Karael's landing? No, this was a different vibration. A deep-seated, otherworldly growl she had heard before.

The red circle began to spin. As it increased in speed, the deep red glowed brighter, stronger, passing into shades of pink. As the circle reached white, it began to emit a keening noise.

Samantha grinned at Karael. "He comes!" she proclaimed. *Get up, Io. Get up!*

Karael let loose a terrible roar, striding with righteous fury toward the portal, Io forgotten, his sword blazing. Simultaneously, a blurry form rose out of the light, coalescing into the shape of a man. Adreana looked up, letting loose a scream of such horror Samantha suspected she would never regain her sanity. Karael stopped in his tracks, also looking above where Samantha stood.

She had long known that whoever beheld the Devil saw what they chose to see. For Samantha, Madden Scott stood a little taller than her, brown hair tied back, a twinkle in his eye and a half-smile. Dressed in black, the Lord of Hell's figure was imposing. Just for a moment, Samantha felt safe and in that instant, the mortal beheld Satan and they were father and daughter once more.

The moment gone, Samantha swivelled, hearing a noise behind her. Karael stood there, sword in one hand and a grin of triumph on his face. He grabbed her with his free hand and tossed her over his shoulder, as she clung to her bag.

"This day will be rejoiced," Karael crowed. "The day the most accursed of my brothers was brought before me and slain. Fallen one, prepare to meet oblivion at my hands!"

Sammy love, fire!

The words rumbled in her head as Madden spoke through her mind. She soon realised the din was not just her father. The entire cliff was about to give way.

"Adreana!"

The tiny Australian still screamed, her eyes fixed above Madden's head.

Karael pulled his arm back, ready to end Satan. His arm flashed round, sparks striking off displaced rocks as the sword passed harmlessly through the summoned image of her father. Instead, the blade struck a fatal blow to the cliff.

The image of her father wavered and disappeared with a bang as the glyphs were ruined. The surface dropped a step as the rocks began to crumble.

Karael turned. "What is this, defiler? Mortal weapons cannot harm me."

Samantha held the ARC pistol, arm steady, pointed at the angel. "You said that once before. For a heavenly being, you're awfully dense." She fired one shot, the bullet taking him in the shoulder and knocking him from his feet. The cliff could stand no more and gave way with a deafening roar, the ground around her subsided as she tried to jump back.

Adreana was gone, Karael too. It all seemed in slow motion to Samantha as the cliff began to rise above her. She was done for. Reaching for the edge of the cliff seemed futile, but in a desperate last action, she had to try. She closed her eyes. In her mind she heard a voice say *Time to show your mother. Show Eva!*

Something grabbed her. Io was there, leaning over the edge of the new cliff at an impossible angle, his hand clasped about her wrist.

"Gotcha. Hold on."

As Karael had done only moments before, Io hurled her up and over the cliff edge to safety where she landed on the springy turf with a bump. He followed a moment later.

"I'm out of it for a second and you're ending the world! Come on, we need to get out of here before Karael finds a way up this cliff."

Samantha glanced down at the rubble beneath them. A big scar had opened up the forest, rubble flattening the jungle on the side of the mountain. Somewhere down slope an angel and a girl who had only tried to help were buried alive in the avalanche. "The Honihin won't remain isolated and undiscovered after this." Was that movement she spied? Samantha turned back. "Where are they?"

"Gone," Io replied. "Like you said, their world ended. I doubt you'll see them here again. Come."

The sound of rubble shifting spurred Samantha into action, but not where Io tried to direct her.

"What are you doing?" He called as she dashed off into Turatup's hut.

"The books. If they aren't coming back, they won't need them." The first of the twin volumes was still in the hut. Samantha stowed it in her backpack. Returning to the ruined glade she found Io holding the other book, its cover stained red with blood. Turatup's blood. With regret she placed it next to the first book. "Let's go."

* * *

She didn't look back as they reached the tunnel and using the flashlight, hurried along through the oppressive darkness. "I keep thinking he's there," she said, jumping at yet another imagined noise.

"It's just your mind playing tricks," Io replied, not pausing to turn and look. "If he *is* back there, us stopping and staring into the darkness isn't going to be an advantage. All we can do is get to the plane. And then—"

"We get some place safe, without flocks of birds," Samantha finished the sentence for him.

In the darkness behind, the rattle of dislodged stone echoed up the tunnel.

"Run," Samantha hissed. "Run now!"

The flight through the tunnel was one of the most terrifying moments of Samantha's life. Io at her side, flashlight only giving them a sphere of guidance, they ran. The darkness swallowed the light behind them, an ever-yawning chasm chasing them. Heart thumping, she made a mental note of what she would have to do with the plane. Footsteps closed behind her, or were those echoes of her own feet? Of Io?

Praying for the light, she ran until she thought her chest would burst. Ten minutes may have passed, or thirty. She couldn't tell. A hand reached out of the darkness to grab at her. She screamed and stumbled.

"It's just me," said Io. "Watch or you'll hit your head here."

Near blind in her frenzy, Samantha nodded and ran on, the flashlight casting wild shadows around the tunnel. She stumbled into the light of the airstrip, eyes closed, lungs protesting.

"I'll hold the tunnel. You get the plane started."

Panting, Samantha nodded even as Io turned away. Forgetting all her pre-flight checks, she climbed into the cockpit and started the engine. The propeller whirred into life and she released the brake. "Get in!"

Io turned and leaped, landing soft as a feather on the wing. He climbed in and closed the hatch. "Go."

Chapter Twenty-Two

With the advantage of the slope, Samantha swiftly had the plane airborne. Flying north she circled around to come back past Mount Willhelm.

"Do you see the avalanche?" she asked, tilting the plane as they flew to try for a better view. The sun hung low in the western sky, mimicking the vivid crimson orb from which her father had arisen.

"There's a disturbance in the distant jungle but most of this side of the mountain is in shadow now. You can circle around, have more of a look and let my brother throw things at you until he hits the plane, and he *will* hit the plane."

"Your brother? Did your memory return just now?"

Io pursed his lips as he considered her question. "Not entirely. However the proximity to another of my kind added to taking such a beating couldn't help but knock some sense into me. And memories."

"Well, who are you?"

"My name is indeed Ioviel, first among the Powers, the Order of Angels dedicated to maintaining and enforcing heaven's purity. I was on patrol. Ensuring the sanctity of Heaven is our most sacred task and we have had to be vigilant in the recent past. My problem arose when I was knocked from my patrol by a beam of energy. When I came to, I was in a ruined city, obliterated by my own descent." Io's face crumbled, his eyes brimming.

"Angels land, and the earth crumbles under the weight. Adreana found that out and we lost a companion. The Honihin lost a home." Samantha sighed. "Calling Karael was my fault. We have to end this."

Io cleared his throat, "I fell," he said, "Karael landed. The actions were the same. I know it was never my intent; we stay off the mortal plane unless given absolutely no other choice. We're just too dangerous. Karael embraces his role with unmatched zeal. He is an enforcer, one given the authority to despatch other angels. He's less concerned with the consequences."

"By who?"

Io turned. "By the Most High. The Creator himself. Were we to descend here at a whim, it would mean easier access for those from the lower realm."

"You mean Hell?"

Io frowned. "We do not speak that name. Not since our greatest champion chose to fall and enter the domain of the damned. He presides there for eternity."

"Satan was your greatest champion? Well I'm sorry to break it to you now that you've got most of your marbles back, Io, but that particular angel no longer exists. He was destroyed. My father now rules under his name."

"Your father?"

Samantha shrugged. "So the story goes. My sister was abducted by a demon named Belphegor, taken to Hell to lure my mother there. Pop went along and it turned out he had an affiliation for the place and satisfied certain requirements. In order to keep everybody from harm, he chose to remain there. It all happened before I was born. They said what was down there was worse than Hell and they had to keep it sealed. Didn't you see what I did to distract Karael?"

"No. I was out of it for a moment back there. Karael hits hard."

"Okay." Samantha pulled the plane up to a safe cruising height and levelled out. "Let's just say that my father and I share a certain link. It's probably best you didn't see or you might have reacted the way your brother did."

"Intriguing. Maybe I'll get to see one day. No, all I remember is catching a glimpse of you and Adreana by the cliff. When I came to, I knew you were in danger, much like I did in Dubrovnik. The rest you know."

"Pop said to show my mother," Samantha said, remembering her father's voice. "Io, didn't Adreana's behaviour strike you as odd at times?"

"I don't follow."

She pulled out the sat phone. "She seemed particularly eager for you to step into the summoning circle. Go with me on this."

Samantha pressed the speed dial button once again.

"Sammy, where in Hell's name did you go?" Her mother was never one for pleasantries.

"I'm sorry, Mom. We were in kind of a tight situation. I had to move quickly, without distraction."

There was a strained pause on the phone. "You fled as we were attempting a rescue. Aeon Fall had you in a warehouse."

"That was you?" Samantha nodded at Io. "Adreana's actions make sense. Mom where are you now? Where's Charlotte?"

"She's at the airport in Port Moresby with a large bump on her head and a temper to match. She was rescued from the hangar. They never moved her. I'm in Geneva, at the Chateau. And you?"

"Flying south over the jungle with more questions than answers. We'll be at the airport in a couple of hours. Then we're coming to you. Mom, Porter Rockwell was here. In the flesh. He seemed to know we were coming out here which means he was here before us."

"Or somewhere between the Adriatic and your current location."

Samantha groaned. "Which only leaves us with half the world to look around. I take it he wasn't at the warehouse?"

"No, just a few hired thugs. Locals out to make a buck."

Hesitantly, Samantha asked, "Was there a white guy? Bald? Tall?"

"Not according to Charlotte's report. Was he important?"

"Dangerous would be closer to the truth. His name's Lanier. Christopher Lanier. We think he's South African."

"We'll do a search."

"While you're at it, could you look up the name Adreana Black? Cross reference it with Aeon Fall."

"Certainly. Sammy, it's good to hear your voice. We'll see you soon."

"I've a few more surprises for you too, but that will have to wait. I've got to get back to the job of flying this plane." She hung up, her mind still busy putting all the pieces together.

"What do you mean, connecting Adreana with Aeon Fall?" Io asked. "She was nothing but helpful to us. She saved our lives more than once."

"And yet I have this nagging itch between my shoulder blades," Samantha replied.

* * *

The remaining hour and a half of their return flight was to the backdrop of a glorious sunset and an angry red dusk. The redirected jet streams had done their damage, causing what Samantha expected to low level disturbances all over the world. At least the winds to the West had stayed where they were. In darkness, they touched down at Port Moresby, parked the plane outside the hangar, and were about to exit the cockpit when three armored black sedans pulled up beside them.

"Not taking any chances this time?" she said as Charlotte Benson opened the hatch, the warm, humid air flooding in.

Charlotte's face was a mask of repressed fury. "In the car."

Feeling like a naughty schoolgirl, Samantha climbed out onto the wing.

"Put him in the second car," Charlotte ordered one of the people behind her.

"Glad to see you're feeling better, Charlotte, but he stays with me." Samantha jumped down from the wing and stood staring up at her guide in defiance.

Io smiled as he climbed out past Charlotte, saying "There's not really a lot you can do to stop that."

"Got your mojo back, have you Ioviel?" Charlotte seemed unsurprised.

"Something like that, but she's the one in charge." Io pointed to Samantha.

A vote of confidence from an angel and Samantha's heart swelled.

"Careful," Io said, his voice quiet as he passed. "Pride is one of the seven deadly sins."

Samantha followed him into the car. Charlotte behind them.

"Go," Charlotte said as she shut the door.

"Yes, lady," said a familiar voice.

"Genesis Koto? Is that you?" Samantha felt relieved to see a familiar face.

"Yes, Miss," he caught her reflection in the rear-view mirror as he pulled away from the plane. "I see you managed to lose your third wheel, eh?"

"I want to feel badly about that," Samantha paused, remembering all that Adreana had done for them. "But I get the feeling we've been led around by her. It's so unfortunate we'll never know. She was caught in an avalanche."

"Mebbe not quite as unfortunate as you think, Miss. We had word from Director Scott. Did a little digging. There was no student at the Pacific Adventist University called Adreana Black. Nobody with that name who worked at the bookshop, either. When we tracked the owner down to ask him about this he was unable to talk."

"Too scared?"

"Too dead. Someone had ripped his heart out and skewered it to the wall of his bedroom. Painted the words 'Your God did this' on the wall with his own blood. Must have happened sometime last night."

"And we're one day closer to a nuclear meltdown with not a lot to show for it, Samantha added. "Charlotte, I'm convinced what we saw in the jungle we were meant to see." She opened her bag, passing the papers taken from the hidden compartment of her crow book as well as Adreana's GPS calculations. "Could you have someone take a look at those numbers?"

"Did you find their meaning?"

"Maybe. The first are lunar calculations from the late nineteenth century. Adreana, who swore blind they were GPS calculations taken from the first set of figures, gave the second to us. They led us to a long-lost tribe, the Honihin, who just happened to have been stoned for their entire existence and told to wait for an angel."

"What do you hope to find?"

"Trust. If those figures match, we know Adreana was genuine. I'm having a hard time believing in coincidence lately. You know, she sat here in a car in Papua New Guinea with an angel and the world on the edge of war with very well-equipped terrorists. It's all a bit crazy."

"Is there anything else you need?"

Samantha nodded. "I need my mom." The panic and chaos of the last few days hit her all at once. She wanted to be reassured that her family was safe, that Nina was okay—as unscathed as any of them could be under the circumstances.

The thirteen-hour flight back to Geneva gave Samantha time for some much-needed rest. One definite advantage of working for ARC was a well-fuelled plane and a lack of airport red tape. She let down her guard, once she was sure they wouldn't be riding random jet streams, and fell into a deep sleep. When hours later, she opened her eyes, the sky outside was still dark. She looked carefully from the cabin window to see a glimmer on the eastern horizon.

Samantha stretched, pulling off a blanket someone had draped over her.

"Morning, sunshine," said a cheery-sounding Io.

"Wha—how long was I out? Where are we?"

"Somewhere over eastern Europe," Charlotte answered. "Give it an hour or so and we'll be touching down at Geneva airport. Before we do, you want to tell me what you think you've learned from this?"

The question, and the edge of incrimination in Charlotte's voice were immediately off putting. "Well, Samantha answered cautiously, "I can tell you when Io stands in the summoning circle, he calls down a vengeful angel hell-bent on his destruction. They treat him as some sort of rebel because he's here and not up there. And I can tell you it all sounds very absolute."

"Absolute?"

Samantha turned to Io. "Tell me Io, is there any free will in Heaven?"

"We obey," he replied.

"And having been down here, and having seen what free will is like, does it not appeal to you?"

Io smiled. "It does. But it's not my place to exercise my judgement as I see fit among you. I cannot dispense justice. I am not God."

"Well aren't there routes back in to Heaven? Surely someone somewhere would be sympathetic to your cause. You aren't here by choice."

Io frowned at Samantha's comment. "There should be. There are back doors only the Powers, the Order of Angels know about. Karael was said to have used one the last time he was sent to dispatch a fallen angel. Beelzebub was on earth. Karael fought a mighty battle and was wounded. He would never say how he entered Heaven, only that his task was complete. Besides," Io reached one hand over and pointed at his back. "You see a distinct lack of feathers."

"That's a host body, isn't it?"

Io looked down at his body. "If it helps you to know this, the soul had departed before I took possession. I was granted permission as he departed."

"So you're no parasite then," Charlotte judged.

"He was a good man. His life cut short by tragic happenstance. It would not matter if I wanted you to see my true self and was able to reveal it. The fallen lose their wings. What your weapon caused, trapped me in a mortal shell, albeit with some of my skills. In truth, it was felt amongst the angelic host that preserving mortals was less important than seeing to our own borders. We watched the abhorrent underbelly of your domain try to erupt. While your efforts were valiant and ultimately successful, not a prayer has been spoken since that time. The words dried up. Where once Heaven was an audible delight, full of humanity's voice, now it lies still. We hear nothing."

"The prayers stopped? When?"

Io thought for a moment. "This may be hard to understand, but your prayer doesn't reach heaven the instant you give thought or voice to the words. It flows with the souls into the Gates of Heaven. Hitches a ride, you might say, much like we are doing on this plane. The souls kept coming, but the voices stopped. I would say the last prayer was heard no later than the day you were brought into this world."

Samantha was silent for a moment while she decided what say next. "Do you hear them now?"

Io's eyebrows raised. "I had never thought to listen until now." He raised his head, tipping it back as he sought for a sound only he could hear. After a moment he looked at her, his eyes full of unshed tears. "The prayers are there. Not many, but I hear them."

"And were I to pray directly to you, by name, would you hear that?"

"I would," he replied.

Without speaking, Samantha rose from her seat and walked to the rear of the cabin where she took a seat and leaned forward, hands clasped together. "Ioviel, this prayer is for you and you alone. When my mother went to Hell she was saved from death by an angel. His name was Metatron. I believe he was your prayer conduit. He died from injuries sustained in combat with a creature that had once been the demon Lord Belphegor. That happened a few months before my birth."

When she returned to her seat, Io sat ashen faced and silent. "It worked then."

His response was not immediate. "How could you know such things?" he whispered, his voice one of devastation.

In some way she had broken his world.

"I'm Satan's daughter, Io. I know many things, most of which we really need my mother to speak of. I don't know who outside of the Council knows much of my history, of those dark days. I'm sorry, Charlotte."

Charlotte nodded her approval. "Following protocol isn't to be discouraged. Your aunt will be at the Chateau, along with many of the

ARC Council. They will be best placed to decide the way forward, including who needs to know what." The pointed way she said this left Samantha in no uncertainty; revealing certain secrets would not be tolerated.

She turned to Io, his face screwed up as he strained, for what she couldn't guess. He had grown hot, the heat coming off of him in waves. His hands were balled into fists which shook, banging on the seat arms.

"Io, what's wrong?"

He looked to her, his eyes popping open. "I feel them: the prayers."

Samantha jumped back, startled. "Your eyes, they're glowing."

Io smiled. "I can feel the prayers of the devout. They are few, but there are those who haven't yet forsaken Heaven. I have answered them. 'There is still hope,' I said. 'Trust in the Lord God Almighty for He will not lead you astray.' "

"Did they hear you?" Charlotte asked, her face sceptical. She sounded a woman who needed a lot of convincing. Odd, given the work she'd accomplished with Aunt Clare.

Io's face radiated heat, and contentment. "They heard me. They will spread the word. I am the only angel listening for their words. Now I'm tapped in, and my memories have been fully restored."

"Great. What do we do now, Io?" Samantha ticked the items off on her fingers: "We have a terrorist uprising to quash, an angel after your neck to hobble, not to mention you have no wings, and the entire planet is ripping itself apart because the weather's gone nuts."

"I need to get home, Samantha Scott. My brethren need to know you still worship, that mankind is still looking heavenward for its answers. Tell me, have any of you heard of the Phaethon Stone?"

Chapter Twenty-Three

Samantha was speechless seeing the view of Geneva enlarge in the small window as the plane began to descend. They had flown higher than usual in order to avoid the unpredictable weather; she now watched the curve of the earth above the clouds, the deep blue of the fading atmosphere bordering on the emptiness of space. It was profound.

"Sammy, are you okay?" Io asked from beside her.

Io. Ioviel. The angel made to fall by the actions of mankind. They had so much to answer for. "It's something spiritual, seeing our planet from this height. It's so clean, so pure, undiluted by hate, politics, selfish ambition. It's as close as mankind gets to touching Heaven, I imagine."

Io smiled. "It strikes me we've had this conversation before. I feel your outlook on life has changed in only a couple of days."

"Has it really been so short a time?"

"It only takes a moment to open your eyes to the world and yet a lifetime to appreciate what you have."

Samantha sighed. "A lifetime is not enough."

"It's never enough. We watch mortals try to extend what they have, curing ailments, eating healthy. You all end up in the same place. When you touch Heaven, actually pass through the gates with the other souls, with the prayers, you will know a peace unlike any calm you've experienced. Your troubles will be over."

"Is Heaven truly the end of the journey?"

Io's smile turned mysterious. "That I cannot reveal. We, all of us, are on a journey together. We all play our part."

"Then Adreana's assertion about Gaia theory was not so wide of the mark."

"You cannot balance the scales from only one side. Just believe me when I say the view of your realm from the celestial vaults is beyond words." Io fell silent. It was clear he was pushing the boundaries of what he could say.

Charlotte returned from the front of the plane. "We're descending now. You might want to strap in. It could be choppy." She turned to Io. "What's a Phaethon Stone?"

Io buckled himself in, pulling the strap tight.

Samantha glanced at Charlotte and they both watched in silence.

Io looked up. "This is for your safety, not mine. My host was a big man and an angel's spirit gives the body, shall we say, a certain density. A Phaethon Stone, *the* Phaethon stone, is an object of unspeakable power. It can open a portal to Hell, to Heaven. I think it could open a doorway to anywhere. I could fashion one had I the ingredients. It's the only way a fallen angel can regain their place in Heaven."

"What is this stone made of? Can we help you find the ingredients?"

"It is unlikely you will ever locate what I need. The ashes of an angel died in self-sacrifice, a source of unspeakable power, and the grave of a demon. It is clear I cannot sacrifice myself and allow you to carry my remains to heaven. The power required to open the door would obliterate any mortal."

"What about Karael?" Charlotte asked.

The plane began to buck as they hit the top of the cloud that covered Switzerland. The cloud tops were being pulled into the shapes of waves by high-level winds. Samantha felt her stomach lurch and was thankful she'd had no food.

"I do not think it likely Karael will lay down his life in defence of any of us, least of all his target. He is an arrow fired on high and his only mission is at the end of his arc."

"My mom can help you there, Io," Samantha assured him. "But you're gonna have to convince her first."

"To do what?"

"To part with her most precious gift."

* * *

The remainder of the flight couldn't pass quickly enough for Samantha. The wind shear, coupled with the geography of Geneva, the great lake and surrounding mountains, meant that on a good day the best pilot still needed their wits about them. Today was not a good day. When they finally broke through the cloud bank, it was raining, the sky dark and threatening above them. Still, Geneva airport was a welcome sight; Samantha breathed one word in relief. "Home".

"You live in the airport?" Io asked.

Samantha grinned at her friend. Despite his strength, his otherworldly knowledge, all that marked him as a celestial being, he still took her words literally. "No, doofus. I learned to fly here. I may not have wings, but I was born to be in the air."

Io gave her an odd look for a moment. "Yes, I do believe you were. One day, Samantha Scott, you shall soar."

"What's that supposed to mean?"

But the moment had passed. The plane tilted to the right as they touched down, the pilot correcting just enough to get all wheels on the runway. Instead of the normal route back to the terminal the plane moved to a large hangar at the far end of the runway.

"Perks of the ARC family," she said as they descended the steps into the hangar. There was a chill in the air, the cold of massive concrete and metal with the added tang of aircraft fuel.

"Welcome back." Her aunt Clare stepped forward, Jim behind her. Clare embraced her for a moment as if it were a miracle they were going to see each other again, then stepped back. "Idiot. Irresponsible, reckless idiot. What in God's name were you thinking?"

"Charlotte was injured—" she began.

"Yes. Charlotte was injured. Your guide, the person I sent specifically to watch over you was injured and you disappear into the jungle of Papua New Guinea and then don't tell anybody where you are?" Clare held up her own ARC sat phone. "We have these for a reason!"

"I know, but—"

"You were fleeing kidnappers," Clare cut in, her voice cracking like a whip. "You were tied to a chair, our friend here bound in ARC technology, and a *student* releases you both and guides you to a lost tribe?"

This was enough for Samantha. To have her judgement called into question was probably deserved. Not caring what her aunt was saying back she blurted, "Adreana Black is Aeon Fall."

Clare stopped, staring at her, mouth open.

Samantha realised they had just said the exact same words at the same time.

"Let's take this back to the house," Clare said, her tone instantly mollified. "You're gonna need these." She waved a hand and one of the ground staff produced a series of fur-lined parkas. "The weather's a trifle inclement today. A far cry from the tropics."

Samantha settled into her thick jacket with pleasure, feeling warmer. "Aren't you going to try one?" she asked Io, who eyed his garment with confusion.

"I am not cold," he replied. "I do not feel the weather like you."

Samantha was sure he was about to add the word, *mortals,* to the end of his sentence and was glad he didn't. Best keep his origins between as few people as possible.

Io smiled and nodded.

"But that wasn't a prayer," Samantha said.

"It does not matter. Your thoughts are like a beacon to me."

Samantha followed her aunt into a large black range rover parked in the hangar, which moved off the second they were inside. "Where are the others?"

"They'll be along. A lot has happened since Dubrovnik, Sammy. In truth, only a couple of days from the first of the promised attacks on nuclear facilities and we're no closer to finding the location. Add to that Nina has gone missing."

"Nina? I spoke to her a couple of times since Hunter's Ridge. She was getting pretty deep. I'd hoped Porter Rockwell was bluffing when he said he had her. How? Where?"

"We simply don't know. She was in regular contact for a day or so after Hunter's Ridge, but then all communication ceased. Nina is a resourceful young woman. You both are, which is why this is so worrying. Did she say anything about her location?"

"Nothing. Just that she was okay, surrounded by enemies, and wanted me to keep our conversations to a minimum."

They pulled out of the airport, driving only a half-mile or so until they turned into a walled complex marked with the words 'La Reserve Geneve'.

"I see why you refer to this as the house," Io said as he looked out at a two-story farmhouse that had been converted into a spa facility for the rich and shameless.

"No, this isn't our destination," Clare advised him. "Just a change of transport."

The car stopped and she got out. At the end of a pontoon sticking out into Lake Geneva rested a speedboat, rocking gently in the shallows.

Clare held out a hand, palm up, indicating the boat. "Sammy, if you would do the honors?"

Samantha grinned. "It's been a while." She crossed the pontoon in a few quick steps and hopped down onto the boat. She turned the keys already hanging from the instrument panel and the engine fired with a guttural rumble. "I've missed the lake," she admitted. "Hold on."

A quick turn of the boat and in no time, they were skipping across the surface of a strangely placid Lake Geneva.

"Your destination lies elsewhere?" Io asked.

"To the locals it's called Le Chateau d'Yvoire," Clare said from behind. "Geneva and especially the lake, have been intertwined with ARC's destiny for decades."

Her hands tight on the wheel, Samantha increased the throttle until they were skipping across the surface of the lake. The wind was cold on her knuckles but she relished the open air. "ARC used to have headquarters in the city," she said. "After certain events occurred before I was born, the decision was made to move. The official home of Anges de la Résurrection des Chevaliers is Hunter's Ridge, in the Adriatic. The true power has always and will always rest on Lake Geneva." Samantha glanced back.

Clare frowned at her.

"What? He's going down the rabbit hole in mere moments. He's gonna know everything soon anyway."

"True," her aunt conceded.

Io's face paled. "What is that?"

Samantha looked around. On either coast marinas were packed with yachts, the walls behind them built up with flood barriers. "I don't see anything, Io."

Io spread his hands wide, palms down. "In the water beneath us, all around us. It's dark, ancient and brooding." He looked into the clouds above. "I sense evil above us. This is worse than the darkness below. What happened here, Samantha? Something momentous, and yet terrible."

Samantha glanced at the murky waters. "This is where my parents were chased by a giant demon. Tall as houses, it stood—tall as several houses. My father was … They called him a Hellbounce."

"Abomination," Io hissed, then abruptly he appeared confused. "I don't know why I said that."

"It gets worse," Clare added. "Eva's blood was used to open a portal to Hell through which Leviathan was supposed to enter. They used her blood on a blade called 'The Well of Souls' to track her. This demon dropped out of the open air on top of a very pretty castle at the other end of the lake, at Chillon. It destroyed the castle and chased them across the lake to about this point where it was wounded. Whatever those demons were fleeing, it ripped through the veil and tore it to shreds. It died here, but not before causing a great deal of damage. It sent a giant wave into the city, killing thousands and destroying buildings, artwork, and architecture—hundreds of years of history lost. Innumerable lives lost. Families torn apart. A world on the brink of becoming a new Hell. You're an angel; why you don't know what happened here?"

"It is not in me to disobey," Io replied, his voice still shaky from the brush with the shadow of ancient evil. "My orders are to maintain the sanctity of Heaven. There are those whose orders are to watch."

"Okay, then why didn't they act?"

"Because Heaven was not threatened."

"Are you sure about that, Ioviel?" Clare asked. "Where do you think the demons would have looked next had Madden not sacrificed himself and Hell had been overrun? If you wish for Eva's help, you might want to be a little more diplomatic with your choice of words."

"I understand your choice of words, and the pain they carry," Io answered, pleading with her. "I have now walked among you for a time far longer than any of my brethren, save one. My experience, however brief, has benefitted me greatly. Was I still in Heaven, I would continue my mission, guarding against all threat, not seeing the peril that awaits the mortals below. Down here, I have learned one fact above all others: No matter who you are, life is a struggle. To live is to fight off a thousand different perils both interior and exterior, only to die. Angels do not understand struggle. They do not understand choice. They are beings of power, brought into existence by a Father who instilled into them the concept of obedience above all."

Clare began to laugh.

"Something funny?" Samantha asked, keeping her eyes on the lake. The coastline was becoming very familiar as they neared Yvoire, the silhouette of the medieval castle appearing through the distant mist. A tree she had sat under when Nina stole her out from under the nose of their mother stuck out on the bank, naked without any leaves. When no answer was forthcoming, she risked a glance back at her aunt.

"Why would someone who creates an army of such majesty give them something as precious as choice? Io, by grasping the idea that we are free to choose, you may well truly be a fallen angel. It may well be that your kind is the failed experiment He perfected in man."

Io considered this. "To err is human. To succeed out of the ashes of failure is true victory." Io appeared a bit coy as he added, "I would not like to return home with that statement foremost in my mind. Such revolutionary thinking might precipitate a negative response from my kind. They've never lost a battle. They are not known for their flexibility."

"What kind of negative response?" Samantha asked.

"The entire Host descending to Earth to purge mankind of those who corrupted one of its own. They have no point of reference. Each mortal would be the same in their eyes, responsible for Metatron's corruption and equally capable of accepting judgement. Imagine thousands upon thousands of Karael obliterating all that is known, all that is loved. We existed before mankind. We will be here after you are gone. It is my role now to make sure my brothers and sisters know that mankind can still call to us, to Him. Metatron needs replacing as the conduit. A decision needs to be made. The Highest decision."

"Do you think they'll listen to you?" Clare asked.

"I have to try." Io smiled, bringing warmth to the cold and dreary day. "A little struggle brings out my human side."

Chapter Twenty-Four

Samantha considered the dilemma of what would happen to mankind as she piloted the speedboat out into Lake Geneva, ready for a head on run at the cliffs.

Send him home with the appropriate message, and cure the problem of religion, in which I don't hold any store and yet has been immutably proven. We go back to zealots and religious terrorism. Send him home with a single wrong word and we're all wiped out.

Above them the Chateau d'Yvoire dominated the headland separating the two main areas of Lake Geneva, the *petit lac* and the *grand lac*. It was a magnificent sight, the main house buttressed by walls seeming sprung from the lake itself topped by small towers on each corner of the roof.

"That's beautiful," Io said as he stared up at the chateau.

"It's been standing for over five hundred years," Clare replied. "The walls around the base were added after the tidal wave. It might not have had quite the same effect this far out but everybody was struck by the surge. Hold on."

Io lurched as Samantha gunned the throttle, sending their small craft leaping over the water directly at the castle.

"Hadn't you better slow down?" Io asked, bracing himself with his hands on the back of the seat next to Samantha.

She grinned at him in response, not saying a word.

"Some kids just can't behave," Clare grumbled from behind, her voice resigned.

Samantha wiggled her eyebrows at Io and then winked. "Time to go down the rabbit hole," she said, pushing the boat faster.

His face now pensive, Io reached out to take the wheel.

Faster, Samantha leaned forward and pressed a button on the console in front of them, knocking his hand out of the way. "Watch."

Ahead of them, the rock parted revealing two cleverly concealed doors. They opened to a man-made tunnel. Not slowing at all, Samantha held her course steady and pressed the button again. The doors began to close.

"We're still outside," Io said.

"True," she answered.

"Give it up, Io," said Clare. "She's been like this from the moment she was able to pilot a speedboat. You're not gonna change her just because you're an angel."

The speedboat shot through the doorway, missing the closing doors by inches. As they moved down the tunnel, banks of lights blinked on, the doors closing with a boom behind them. Samantha pulled back on the throttle as the tunnel swung left. This was familiar territory. She felt as though every flickering light over the pathways to either side of the water knew her, welcomed her home. It had been a year or more.

"Deceptive," Io said.

"We like to think of this as well camouflaged," Clare countered.

The tunnel opened out into a wide circular cavern with a shallow domed roof. A heavy bank of lighting illuminated the ceiling. A small group of people waited at the end of a jetty stretching into the middle of the lake.

Io shuddered. "Bad memories," he said in response to Samantha's unspoken question. "I visited a place in Heaven once. It helps to have my memories returning except perhaps this." There was a haunted look in his eyes. "It wasn't a pleasant place. Those there revelled in dealing out pain. It was a place of fear, where those who were to be made an example, those who had disobeyed beyond falling at the end of Karael's blade, were housed. We were shown these dissenters as a warning for what might happen if we disobeyed. It was the Fearvent—Heaven's prison, the only dark place in Heaven."

"Yvoire isn't a prison," Samantha countered in an attempt to lighten the mood. "It's a place of light, of beauty. It just happens to have a very useful and extensive network of tunnels, which ARC have acquired and adapted. Let me show you, Io."

"That is not my full name," he said, his mood not yet entirely lifted.

"And yet, I'll continue to use it," Samantha smirked, hopping onto the pier and tying off the front of the speedboat. "Welcome to the retreat. Welcome home."

Waiting for Io and her aunt, Samantha walked along the jetty, her steps adjusting to compensate for the soft movement of the wood floating on the water. Quickly the makeup of the small group became clear. Dominating them through sheer size, John Wolverton stepped forward to crush her in a bear hug. "I'm so glad you're safe," he said, his voice gruff. "When you disappeared from the warehouse we feared the worst."

"I never really felt in that much danger, Uncle. There was just too much to do."

Io stepped into the ring of light and John extended his hand. "We've got you to thank for bringing Sammy safely home, I believe."

Unfamiliar with the custom of shaking hands, Io looked down at John's open palm and copied him, not shaking the proffered hand but holding his own out about two inches away. Taking this as a jest, John grinned and shook Io's hand vigorously.

Understanding now, Io shook back, squeezing as he did so.

John's eyes widened as his face quickly registered pain. Pulling his hand back, he shook it to regain blood flow. "Damn, that's one hell of a handshake you have there, sir."

"Did I do it wrong?"

Not understanding the source of Io's confusion, John burst out laughing. "Not in the least. I have a rule. Always trust a man with a strong handshake. You, my friend can fly with my Sammy any day."

"What if I am not a man?"

"We'll get to that," Samantha said, cutting off John's obvious question. She stepped past her uncle and embraced the ruby-haired Tricia Pelirrojo.

"So good to see you alive and well, darling girl," the treasury head breathed in her English accent. She stepped back and let loose one of her ever-present smiles, the radiance lighting up the room. "Your mother is upstairs with Director Byron and Director Guyomard." Her smile faded.

"Something's happened?"

"It's best if we let your mother explain it to you," Tricia turned, leading the way past the ever-present ARC black-ops and into the elevator.

A brief ride up and Samantha found herself being ushered outside into the gardens of the castle. "Are we not going to the council chambers?"

"Your mother's out there, Samantha, in the cottage at the end of the gardens," Tricia indicated a small building partly hidden by the many trees that grew around the castle. "When you're ready, bring her back to the council chambers." Tricia turned away, disappearing into the castle.

Samantha waved to Io, but he was already walking off in a different direction with John. Now alone, she wandered through the gardens, picking her way randomly toward the cottage. She tried to enjoy the gardens she had always loved, but the lead-colored skies and the misty cold threatened to penetrate even her thick parka. She missed the scent of the flowerbeds. She hurried instead to find her mother.

Opening the heavy wooden door with a grunt, she called out, "Mom?"

"In here," came the reply from the kitchen.

Quickly Samantha shed her coat. The living room had a roaring fire burning in the hearth that leant a flickering glow to the interior of the cottage. "It's hot as hell in here, Mom."

"I don't like the cold."

Samantha found her way through to the kitchen where her mother was rolling out pastry. Her hair was tied back to keep it from falling over her face. Her eyes lit up when she set them upon her daughter. "Cookies? They won't be long in the oven. I can make you a coffee while you wait. Want to help cut them?" Eva held up a round cookie cutter.

"Okay … sure, Mom. Isn't it a bit late to start with the mother and daughter routine? We could have made cookies when I was a child."

Samantha immediately regretted her words, reopening old wounds as she caught the flash of pain in her mother's face.

"Let's get this done and then we can talk," Eva answered crisply.

The two women finished preparing and baking the batch of cookies in silence and when they were done, Samantha sat opposite her mother. Two steaming mugs of chocolate and a plate of cookies hot from the oven filled the room with the aromas of cinnamon and chocolate—and the awkwardness between them.

"It's good to see you," Eva began.

"And you, Mom. Look, I've got to ask. Is this the point where you dress me down without the rest of your colleagues present, or are you just preparing me for some kind of formal inquisition?"

Eva took a sip of the chocolate, indicating Samantha should do the same. The drink was delicious. A slight tang of orange mixed with vanilla lingered in her mouth.

Eva closed her eyes, taking a few slow breaths. "Sammy, there's no other way to put this. I screwed up. I'm sorry."

How was this not about my own conduct? Samantha wondered. Confused, she replied, "How have you screwed up? You're not the one who has been all over the world, breaking protocols at will."

"Oh, I've been breaking them. Just not in the way you think. Since before you were born, in fact from the very second your father sent me back to that beach in Jamaica, I've been trying to find a way back to Hell. When Swanson offered me a chance to head up the Technological Research division of ARC, I saw it as nothing more than a way to further my plans. They had tech that we had recovered from Hell, and reverse-engineering…"

Eva sighed, pausing. "Well," she went on, "in truth, we've advanced our understanding of materials, of power and engineering by decades. The culmination of all this was the sky sling and the satellite we put in orbit. I had a team working to use Hell's own technology to open a portal, using my blood, and that of yours and your sisters. Sammy, it was supposed to open on Hunter's Ridge. I was supposed to see your father again. I can't bear to be apart from him any longer. I'm no better than my predecessor."

"So what happens now, Mom?"

Eva shrugged. "Not a lot of this is a surprise to me. I met Porter Rockwell. He doesn't like you very much. I got the feeling he was quite proud of turning John Myhill away from the ARC cause, from my goals. John knew the satellite inside out, and he had the help of a demon. In my selfishness, I handed Aeon Fall the capability to touch what nobody should touch. Sammy, I nearly ended the world."

"So what is all this? Punishment?"

Eva took one of the cookies, breaking it in two, passing half across. "I think they want me where they can keep an eye on me, but don't feel up to placing me in a dungeon. Swanson and Gila are my closest friends. I don't blame them for being angry. I've become another Benedict."

"Benedict Garias? Mom, everybody knows his history. The guy was a monster. He worked with the demon Rosier, turned that Larter woman into a predator. You're nothing like him."

Eva stared into her mug. "I've placed my own daughters at risk to further my ambitions. I've nearly destroyed the world to get back to my husband and you know what, Sammy? I felt the effort was worth it."

"Was?"

Eva sipped her drink. "Yes. I've come to my senses but not before a lot of damage was done. They'll throw the book at me, if they have any brains. Look around the world, at the weather damage, at the countless dead."

"You think Dad would approve? You behaving like this? If he was standing here now, do you think he would want you to continue down such a path of self-flagellation? There's already a kingdom of loathing out there. Most of humanity suffers because of what happened the last time you were in Hell."

"We rescued Nina," Eva protested. "We sealed off the gateway to a realm of nightmare."

"That's not all you did. I'm going to do something now I should have done a long time ago." *You'd better have your ears on, Pop,* she thought.

Samantha stood. "Come with me."

Leading her mother outside, Samantha chose a spot of cleared ground where once there had been a kitchen garden. Kneeling, she carved the glyphs that would summon her father.

"Who are you, and what have you done with my daughter?" Eva sounded worried. "I've seen those markings before."

"It's fine. I'm fine, and what you're seeing was requested of me. Now stand back." Samantha sliced across the palm of her hand, an act she hoped, like always she would never repeat.

"Sammy!" Eva shrieked.

"It doesn't hurt, Mom. If you'd taken any notice of what I could do growing up, you would know that." Blood flowed from the cut, dripping as she held her hand directly into the central pattern.

The glyphs began to move, the portal began to glow, while Samantha held on to her mother to prevent her from bolting.

"This is forbidden," Eva hissed.

"Some might say bearing two daughters to Satan is forbidden," Samantha countered, "but look how that turned out."

The spinning portal glowed white and with a shudder a form began to coalesce. Samantha could feel him before she could see him. She watched her mother's face, now white with fear.

"They'll never forgive you for…" Eva's words trailed off as the misty form became more solid, the features more defined. Around them the breeze stilled. Birds slowed in the sky above. "Madden?"

Samantha watched as black-shirted and ponytailed, Madden Scott, Hell's master, beheld his mortal bride. He grinned.

Despite herself, Eva grinned back. "Sammy, what is this trickery?" Eva asked.

Although Madden's lips formed words, he spoke directly into Samantha's mind: *This is no trickery. Hey gorgeous.*

Tears poured down Eva's face; Samantha could see her mother was hearing the same words.

Eva turned to her. "Samantha, how long have you been doing this?"

All of her life. Eva, it's time to stop seeking me, love. I'm here, watching over you, missing you and yet praying you don't do something stupid enough to end up down here. Let me tell you, your card has a good chance of being marked long term after this last event. The bill always comes due.

"But it's not fair. I didn't ask to fall in love with you, or to lose you." Eva dropped to her knees, looking up at the shade of her husband. "You're my hero, Madden. I only want to be with you."

Not this way you don't. Remember, sacrifice is the key.

"But I've sacrificed everything to find a way—"

The image of Madden grew redder. *No, Eva. Self-sacrifice. Not using others for gain. Benedict Garias. Remember Benedict Garias. His purgatory will last forever. He will sit in the Elysian Fields for eternity. Don't follow him down that path. Find a better way, my love. Seek redemption. Help my brother find a way home. That will go a long way to restoring the natural order. I love you, Eva. We will meet again. Let it be on our own terms. Do what your heart tells you.*

The image of Madden wavered. For a second he held his hand out. Eva reached, her own hand brushing through air where there was no substance. With a smile, Madden faded into the grey mist, only a lingering trace of the red surrounding him remained.

Eva remained on her knees, watching the empty space where her husband had been, as if he would reappear. After a moment she collapsed, her head in her lap, her shoulders shaking as she sobbed uncontrollably.

Samantha knelt, putting her arm awkwardly about her mother. The contact felt alien.

"What have I done, Sammy?"

"You've wandered off the beaten track, Mom. We both have. You just needed to find your way back. That way starts now. They need your help. They need *our* help."

Helping her mother stand, Samantha brushed the tears from her face.

"He said he had a brother," Eva said. "He had no brother. Sammy, who did you bring here?"

"An angel."

Chapter Twenty-Five

"An angel? Samantha, You've brought an angel to Chateau d'Yvoire?"

When Samantha had said the words 'An Angel', she had no idea what response to expect. Shock? Disbelief? Certainly not intrigue. She steadied her mother as she struggled to understand. "Yes. Your satellite shot him out of the sky. You need to help him now."

"What can I do?"

"You can get cleaned up, then come to Council and listen to his story. Once you've heard Io speak you'll know what to do."

Eva took hold of Samantha's shoulders with muddy hands. "It's only been a couple of days, yet the girl I knew has become a woman. I'll need to hear your story too."

"You will, Mom. Just tidy yourself up first." She pushed her mother's hair back from her face and smiled. "I'll walk you in and grab my jacket."

Back outside, donned in her warm outerwear, Samantha wandered across the walled garden between the cottage and the castle. The heavy mist made everything damp, soaking through her shoes, chilling her to the bone.

"Was that who I believe it was?" Io said from beneath the cover of a vine-draped portico.

"My mom?"

"No Samantha. You summoned Satan."

Samantha laughed. "You make it all sound so matter-of-fact, Io. Not even a hint of righteous indignation? Of Holy Rage?"

"Against an image?" he shrugged. "Not a lot I could do if he were there beside you. Without the Phaethon stone I have strength, but not much more. I know now how you distracted Karael. You performed another summoning, did you not?"

"Io," Samantha pleaded, "I had to do something. Karael was winning. He was killing you."

"Perhaps that was for the best." His words had no emotion. "Too much death in my name already."

"I don't believe that. Anybody who has been wronged deserves a chance to be set right. Anyone who has aggrieved another should be given a shot at redemption."

Io smiled. "I think you're too good for this world."

Samantha grabbed his arm. "Come on, let's go tell our story and see what they have to say."

* * *

The entire ARC Council, both the six sitting members, always required by the ARC statutes, and the six non-sitting members, who had the freedom to execute their roles wherever they saw fit, were seated and ready to hear Io's story, with only Eva's chair yet to be filled. They gathered around the ever-present oval table, the original that was rescued from the tidal wave disaster before Samantha was born. The Council were arranged around Swanson Guyomard, with only one seat empty, that of her mother's. Others were gathered around the room. Charlotte Benson spoke in hushed tones with Jim, and the helicopter pilot Carrot close behind where her aunt Clare now sat. Other groups of people, special ops or scientists of some description, stood across the room from the door. More than a few heads were turned toward Io.

"Word's spread," he said.

"Not surprising," Samantha agreed. "Outside of the Guyomards, it seems the Scott family are those making the biggest waves around here."

As if to emphasise the point, Eva came in after them, slamming the door and striding across the room, sparing a glance and a nod for her half-sister. She stood in front of her chair and began to speak.

"I know all of this is my fault. I fought for the sky sling project from its very inception with no other goal than to find a way to enter Hell and re-join Madden. There, I have confessed. I'm not going to apologise because quite frankly, words are no compensation to any of you, or to the countless numbers made homeless, childless, lifeless by the weather that resulted from the satellite being fired.

"Do I have regrets? More than it's possible to atone for in a lifetime, but I have to start somewhere. My sector knew what they were building, to a point. Only a handful of us knew the true goal, and that was my responsibility and mine alone.

"John Myhill was one of those who knew the truth, but this was all my doing." She slowly sat. "Do with me what you will. I'll accept all consequences."

"What's changed, Eva?"

Samantha eyed Mohammed El Rafi, one of her mother's oldest friends, head of Grail, the artefact research division, who spoke up.

"Why are you saying this now," he continued, "after days of silence?"

"She has had a visitation," Io spoke up.

Samantha watched Mohammed turn first to regard Io, and then study her as well.

"Dear Visitor … young Samantha's guest, please, introduce yourself."

Io stepped forward. "My name is Ioviel, First among Powers, Heaven's guardians. I am an angel."

The pronouncement caused a stir, especially between Mohammed, the elderly Gaspard Antroobus, and Alexander Steadman, son of the previous ARC curator and head of biblical interpretation.

"An angel?" Steadman repeated, half up from his chair.

"Powers?" Jeanette Gibson asked. The longtime media face of ARC turned to her colleagues. "Does that make any sense?"

"Angels have ranks, not unlike the demons," Steadman replied. "According to medieval texts the highest circle consists of Seraphim, Cherubim, Thrones, Dominions, Virtues, Powers, Principalities, Archangels and Angels, in that order."

"The author was not wrong," Io agreed.

Again, Samantha watched as all eyes trained on Io.

"But," he went on, "not entirely correct. Your list sounds as though the rankings are listed in an order of importance. All are angels. The rankings are more names of service than a rank of ascension. My mission as a Power is to protect heaven. Seraphim and Cherubim serve Him directly at the heart of Heaven. We do not mix."

"And Archangels?" Steadman asked, his face animated. "Are they Heaven's fiercest warriors?"

"They are foremost among the army. Great captains, all. Not always the fiercest, but the most canny." He turned to Samantha. "Unlike Karael."

"Who is Karael?" Swanson asked. "The one who appeared at Dubrovnik?"

"He's Heaven's pitbull," Samantha explained. "Released to hunt down and despatch the fallen."

"The fallen? Like Satan?"

"Yes," Io replied, forestalling Samantha from leaping to the defence of her father. "His role was created as a response to the princes who forsook Heaven. I believe, however, that events surrounding my fallen brother have taken a complicated turn."

"What do you know about what lies beyond Hell?" Swanson leaned forward, eager for an answer.

"I have no knowledge," Io admitted. "It was not my mission to hunt fallen, nor comprehend the meaning of their choice and destination."

"And yet, you're here," Swanson threw back at him.

"I was shot out of Heaven by a beam of energy from your creation. When that happened, I fell, though not by choice. To Karael, I am a fallen angel and his mission is to end me. I have been saved twice by technology you have developed."

Swanson looked to Eva. "Helltech? It was supposed to be on lockdown."

"My fault again," Eva interjected. "I allowed Clare and her team to trial the tech. I stand by that decision only because without it, my younger daughter wouldn't be standing here with us today."

"Eva the hero," Thorsten Guyomard said, his tone deeply cynical. "Not exactly the villain Benedict Garias was, but you don't appear to have covered yourself in glory taking on his role. And what about your daughter, here?"

"What about me?" Samantha took a step forward. "I came here seeking answers."

"And here you shall get them," John Wolverton intervened, preventing Thorsten from unleashing more invective. "But please, Samantha, tell us of your story first."

"Briefly?"

John smiled. "Succinctly."

Here goes, Samantha thought.

"After Hunter's Ridge, I went to the devastation of Dubrovnik against my will to help, and was almost assaulted by the man who ran the cult in which I participated. I was saved by Io.

"We then found that an ancient method of divination that worked a little too well on Io, bringing down the angel Karael on our position.

"After finding secret notes in the book of divination, we travelled to Papua New Guinea to find the origin of the book. We were captured by Aeon Fall, met Porter Rockwell and were saved by a student who had some ancient navigations translated into GPS coordinates.

"We escaped Aeon Fall and using the directions, found a lost tribe in the jungle who had the companion book to my own. We called down crows as a method of divination and Karael appeared again. I summoned my dad to distract Karael and the angel fell in an avalanche, as did the girl who helped us. And then we came here." She took a deep breath. "I think that covers everything."

"Except that massive parts of your story were a set-up." Swanson shuffled through some papers. "The girl you knew as Adreana Black was no student at the Pacific Adventist University." He slid a photo across the table.

Samantha stepped forward. 'Adreana' stood proudly at the right hand of none other than Porter Rockwell himself. "I thought she was an imposter," Samantha stated. "Adreana was just a little bit too mysterious to be genuine. Not at first, mind you. She was nothing but helpful. Later on, her behaviour appeared a bit forced. I started to have doubts when she insisted upon Io having his fortune deciphered by the crows."

"And yet, you allowed this to happen?" The question came from Clare.

"What was I supposed to do? We were in the middle of the jungle surrounded by hunters, many of who appeared less than cordial toward us. How were we to know what we were walking into?"

"That's a child's answer," Swanson spat. "Take responsibility for your actions."

The jungle felt a million miles away at this moment. "Okay. I should have refused point blank to even try. Io and I thought that between his strength and the ARC gun I carried, we could deal with Karael. Adreana appeared to know nothing about the gun. Her only familiarity with the technology was undoing the lock on Io's cuffs with a key."

"Would it surprise you to learn the coordinates she had you follow were entirely fictitious?"

The question caught Samantha off guard. "You know this how?"

Swanson pressed a button on a control in front of him; the wooden panelling behind him, split apart, revealing a screen. A map appeared, pale brown land on the blue sea, like a weather map. A series of red dots connected over the United Kingdom. "We got to work checking the lunar navigation as soon as you sent the numbers through. They don't relate to anywhere in the Pacific."

"But we were there. The second book? The hidden numbers?

"The book may be real, but Adreana Black translated no navigation entries. These numbers point to an area in the south-west of the United Kingdom, near a town called Taunton. We also have records of repeated flights into the region where you were led. Someone was flying in supplies to that area monthly. The name we found logged at the airport was Vaitai. Does this name mean anything to you?"

Samantha stepped back, deflated. "That was the name of the bookshop owner at the university. Adreana said his store was set on fire by anarchists."

"More likely she was covering her own tracks."

"The tribal elder said they were given supplies of a narcotic bean that helped them expand their consciousness and read the signs. The bean didn't grow in the highlands but could have been sourced from just about anywhere else in the country." It all clicked. Samantha gasped and turned to Io. "It's you. This wasn't about a simple kidnap. It was about you."

"Explain," Swanson requested.

"If Adreana Black is Aeon Fall, and they are hell bent on exposing and bringing down ARC, why did they let us go? They had perfect leverage in keeping us locked away, hidden. Yet they hold us in a building that's an obvious target, send in one of their own to release us, and aid in our escape. They keep us away from a rescue by masking it as a perceived threat to our safety. And I fell for it, *book* line, and sinker."

A few people chuckled.

Samantha struggled, as well, not to laugh at her pun. She continued, stone-faced, "When I first met Io, he was confused, had no idea who he was. Karael confirmed this. He was actually a little disappointed Io wasn't at full strength. He voiced the same opinion when we met the second time. He wanted Io at full-strength so he could do something to him. But what?"

"He did appear to go down a little easily in Dubrovnik," Clare admitted. "He was well armed, ridiculously strong. He seemed to want you to escape. As if you weren't quite ready. Ioviel, what weren't you quite ready for?"

"Do you have the sword taken from Karael in the ruined city?" Io asked.

"Mark, if you please?" Swanson turned to one of the lab-coated scientists, Mark Sellick, a bearded man Samantha knew, who stood behind Eva.

Mark nodded, placing a locked security case, a metre or so in length, on the table. Two twists of a key and the case flipped open. Inside, resting on a cushion of sponge fashioned exactly for this weapon, was the sword.

Io leaned forward.

Mark snapped the case closed, watching Io.

"The question you have to ask yourself, Swanson Guyomard, descendent of Jerome, is 'Do I trust this man with this sword?' "

"I thought you were an angel, Io" Swanson replied.

"To you, until I pick up this blade, I am a man who may make bold claims, who has luckily survived encounters with a real angel. Do you trust me?"

"It's not for me to say. Samantha, it's your decision to make. He's your charge. Prove to us that we are right to give you this responsibility."

Samantha felt a swell of pride. Despite everything, the admission of guilt by her mother, the crazy antics, the wild goose chase, they were still capable of allowing her the space to grow. She could taste the cynicism in the room. Io needed his chance. She stroked Io's rock-solid shoulder. "Io, take up the blade. I believe in you. I have faith in you."

Io reached out, his hand hesitant.

"Take it," she urged.

His hand hovered above the blade for a second. A hum began to sound on the table. The case vibrated, twisting slowly clockwise as the hilt moved closer to him. It seemed to Samantha as though the sword wanted to be taken. Waiting just a moment longer, Io reached into the case and grabbed the sword by the hilt, raising it aloft.

The hum grew in intensity and Samantha and others had to cover their ears. Shimmering at first, the blade was now a blinding white. Samantha turned her head, closed her eyes, and with hands over her ears, she could nonetheless feel the presence of another being in the room—one beyond the ability of mortal comprehension. Yet she turned to behold him. Ioviel. Angel, floating in the air on wings of purest white that glowed with a radiance that spoke of a purity mankind had never known. His true form finally unveiled.

He stared back at her, and then at the sword glowing in his hand, saying "This should not be possible."

Chapter Twenty-Six

The glow faded. Io stood as before, wingless, human, dressed in a torn tee shirt and the slacks he had been wearing the day he had found her.

"You want to tell us what the little light show there was?" John Wolverton was on his feet, ready to pounce, although not as quickly as he was in his younger years.

Samantha stepped to Io's side, placing a hand on his arm. She would lead here. "It's okay Io. You're safe here.""

Io gave her a quizzical look and turned to the council. "I believe the metaphysical change I just underwent belies any rational explanation. Wasn't it obvious that my powers were restored? The sword is a conduit to the power of souls. I drew on that energy and regained abilities beyond those you would consider explainable."

"You're saying that you are now you a match for this Karael?"

"Almost." Io laid the sword back in the security box. "I believe you will want to keep that."

Swanson chuckled. "It hardly seems we would be capable of stopping you should you decide to claim it permanently."

Io grinned back. "True. But there is an item in this castle that I desire more." He looked around the table of ARC heads. "You were there," he said as he pointed at John, "as were you, and you." Forrest Kyle and Gila Byron were singled out in quick succession. Io turned to Eva. "You were closest to my brother as he fell. Tell me of Metatron's fall."

"We decided long ago to keep such matters in the past," Eva warned.

Samantha arched her back, immediately wanting to jump across the table and throttle her mother. How could she remain so obtuse despite her recent admission of fault? She settled for glaring at her instead, and for a moment she caught her mother's eye.

"That being said, Swanson, my fellow directors, you all have a record of our time spent with the man known as Janus. His exploits saved my life several times. His last intervention cost him his life and allowed us to rescue Nina. We were atop the citadel in a great mountain city called Forente-Lautus. A false signal tracing Nina led us there. We were trapped and he placed himself between a being known as Exerrocks and us, formerly the demon Belphegor, taken by the ice and reborn. We escaped, losing several of our team. As we were about to leave the city, a light shot out from the citadel above. It arced downwards, plummeting at incredible speed until—"

"Until it hit the ground, doing incredible damage," Samantha completed for her mother. "Io, what does that mean to you?"

"This entity wasn't trying to kill Metatron. It was trying to convert him, to make him fall. He was part of the way there. What happened after?"

"We rescued him from the impact crater. He was impossibly heavy. Dense might seem a better word. There was a lot more than a human body to him. Once we took off he whispered a few words. He told me he was my friend and that his name was really Metatron. Then he turned to ash." Eva was now teary, her voice thickened as she added, "He just disintegrated there in my arms."

"The ashes of a righteous angel, killed defending others," Io said. "What did you do with them?"

"I gathered as much as I could and took them with me. I had one feather from his wings."

Io's face grew intent. "Was it black?"

Eva nodded, afraid to speak.

"Is that significant?" Samantha asked.

"It is the key to his divinity, his essence. Father placed a black feather in each of us. It is the source from which our abilities stem."

"Father? You mean God?" Tricia Pelirrojo was clearly very caught up in the story.

"I do. Eva Scott, you still have those ashes, do you not?"

"How do you know?" Her mother turned to her, ready to accuse.

"I felt them when I touched the sword. It's hard to not notice another angel nearby when I held onto such power."

"Karael?"

Io shook his head. "Bound into a host, he will only come when summoned. I believe my death at his hands is the intent of others, and the ultimate outcome of their goals. They would not need me if they had Metatron's ashes, for they are one of the two ingredients of a Phaethon stone."

"What's a Phaethon stone?" asked Swanson.

"A way back into heaven," Samantha replied.

"Well can't you just ... you know ... whoosh?" Swanson spread his arms, imitating a bird's wings.

"Alas I have no wings," Io turned his head to look over his shoulder.

"But this black feather?"

"I wish it were as simple as inserting a feather, Swanson Guyomard. There is a place in Heaven where angels are born made by our Father in the Angelforge. One cannot do such a thing alone. Your beam caused me to fall but I can't regain my wings on earth without considerable power. The only way back is through the use of the Phaethon stone. It makes a doorway, one, which I believe others want to exploit. Tell me, what do you know of the angel Metatron?"

"The scribe," Alexander Steadman said. "The voice of God, communicating His will because Gods voice is too much for lesser beings to hear."

"The scribe part is true," Io admitted. "The second part is more of a metaphor. Metatron was a conduit for prayers, and prayers being answered. When his spark was extinguished, the conduit vanished. Heaven ceased receiving prayer, and those worthy of reply were never heard."

"Your God is dead." Jeanette Gibson, normally a vocal force at Council meetings, spoke up. She grabbed Swanson's control and pointed to the screen. A series of Aeon Fall propaganda posters began to cycle across the screen. "You're saying Aeon Fall know this as well? Are you saying this is all a set up?"

"Porter was there when Metatron died. He saw what happened, knew I took the feather and ashes." All turned to Eva. "What was it Karael said, Io? That you weren't ready?"

"Those were indeed his words."

Eva stood. "Swanson, Gila, John, Forrest. Would the four of you please join my daughter, Ioviel, and me in my quarters? The rest of you will have to beg my indulgence. I'll fill you in when we're done."

Without waiting, Eva left the room.

Samantha followed, Io on her tail. "What are you doing, Mom?"

"The honourable thing, sweetie. I'm no better than Benedict Garias, whatever my intent. I wanted a portal to reach your father. John Myhill wanted to tap the soul energy that powers everything in Hell. When we found out his intent, I had him thrown off the team, and he walked straight into the arms of Aeon Fall. I made a promise to my friend Janus, whoever he really was. If this is restitution to any degree, then it's a start. Heaven needs to know of his fall. He asked if ever I had the chance to pass on word of his fate that I should do so. I never thought the opportunity would present itself."

They passed along stone hallways carved from the bedrock beneath the headland, made habitable with underfloor heating and atmospheric lighting that emitted a permanent soft glow. The musty smell was suppressed by air conditioning, but it was never quite gone, a reminder they were essentially living in a hole.

After the brief walk, Eva stopped. "I make no excuse for anything you may see." She turned back and opened the door to her chamber. "Please, won't you come in?"

The room was dark, the lighting muted by an excess of art all over the walls. The wall above her mother's bed was covered from end to end with a giant mural depicting the earth surrounded by a double helix of blue gas.

"You didn't know about this?" Io asked in hushed tones.

"Mom always came to us, stayed with us," Samantha answered. "I've never been in here before."

"The view of earth from Hell," John Wolverton said, admiring the mural. "Eva, that's stunning. Now I know what you spent all those hours doing apart from everybody else. I never knew you could paint."

"I've had a lot of time to learn. Ioviel, do you recognise this view?"

"I do," Io replied. "In what you have painted as a nebulous gas around the earth, I see as the countless souls on their way to Heaven. Your representation is nevertheless accurate. How did you come to see this?"

"It is what you see when looking up from Hell," Forrest Kyle, who until now had been content to observe, spoke up. "I understood it to be part of their perpetual torment, an eternity of being able to see the earth, yet never within reach."

Samantha noted the haunted look on his face.

John placed his hand on Forrest's shoulder. "We all lost someone close to us on that mission, Son."

"That was the inspiration for the sky sling," Eva said, her eyes lost in the picture. "Were it not for my girls, I'd have found a more permanent solution to finding Madden. It might have been Hell but there was a beauty there to be found beyond anything on Earth."

Samantha crossed the room to a frame containing a t-shirt. "Daddy rules," she read aloud.

"Your t-shirt from New York, Sammy. It was only a few years after the mission and Nina wanted to see the Manhattan Henge, where the sun sets exactly in the middle of the East-West streets of New York. She always had a proclivity for seeing the unusual in the mundane. It probably never occurred to most people what occurred around them. Most people reacted to us with amusement, a few older citizens with scorn. The rest ignored us. People have all sorts of weird slogans on shirts nowadays."

"Do you think they have her, Mom?"

Eva shook her head. "No." Her voice was adamant. "If there's one thing I know about you girls, it's that you always find a way. If Aeon Fall knew about Nina, they would have paraded her by now."

Io moved past Samantha to a closet. "I sense the aura in here. Guarded by your husband?"

Samantha smiled as she looked over Io's shoulder, seeing countless representations of her father: carvings, drawings, paintings, and one small porcelain figure, all on a series of shallow shelves. "They all look like him, Mom. You haven't missed a thing. They even have that spark of amusement he's always carried. A twinkle in his eye, or the set of his jaw with a grin."

Eva softly smiled as she looked over the art, but it was a look or regret, of profound loss. Samantha had seen it many times before. "Let's get to it, Mom." She wanted to move on, to push back at the hole that gnawed her.

Eva pressed a hidden button behind the statuette. The whole shelf dropped back with a clunk and slid sideways, revealing what could only be called a shrine. Small, framed photos of hard-looking capable individuals were set in the alcove around a box. Several fat white candles stood atop chunky silver stands, the wicks untainted; they had never been lit. A light dust coated the contents; the alcove hadn't been touched in quite a while. Eva took a box of matches and struck one, lighting the candles.

"The Shikari," John said, his voice thick with emotion. "Eva, you remembered them all."

"Someone had to," she replied.

"Kris Elliot, Emdy Sengupta, Matt Tanzer, Jenn Day, Ellen Covlioni, Jawara Shelton, Porter Rockwell, Wolfgang Stufflebeam, Scope, Rachelle Bishop … Luke Wolverton." John and Forrest said the names simultaneously. "Those are names never to be forgotten."

"One portrait is missing." Swanson pointed out.

"Porter Rockwell," John grumbled. "He was a good man when he was alive. Somewhat obsessed with his outlaw ancestor, but when it came to it, he was as solid as the next man—understandable that you perhaps removed him. His current incarnation is a poor legacy of the man he once was. Something's taken the man who died in Hell and molded a twisted version."

"And he's after Nina," Eva said, no emotion in her voice. "He'll have half the proof Madden ever existed."

Nina, hear me, Samantha thought, imagining her thoughts cast far and wide. In the past her sister would have responded. Now there was nothing.

Swanson shuffled on the spot. "Eva, if there was anything…"

"Don't give me excuses, Swanson. Give me my daughter. You sent her into the lion's den and now she's disappeared. Do we even know where?" Eva reached into the shrine, retrieving a gold box. Opening it, she handed it to Io. His eyes lit up as he gazed upon the velvet pouch within.

Samantha felt a strange feeling wash over her, as if the presence of a strong force had suddenly registered—the same sort of sensation she felt when Io showed up in Dubrovnik, and the two times Karael appeared. Io looked up from his contemplation of the box and their eyes connected. He knew. Whatever she was feeling, he knew.

Eva continued to speak. "We swore an oath to never reveal what happened in Hell beyond the ARC Council. Now you know both what happened and the treasure I have preserved. Is this enough for you to make your door to heaven?"

"Not quite." Io removed the bag from the box, handing it back to Eva. "A fallen angel has to perform the opening. That's me. I have to use the ashes of a righteous brother—these ashes of Metatron. The final ingredient is a corrupted source of unspeakable power. Consider this. The Phaethon is nicknamed 'The Icarus Stone' in Heaven."

"Because of the obvious reason?" Samantha asked. "Icarus did, after all, fly too close to the sun. Is your source of power nuclear? A radioactive element, perhaps? Plutonium? Uranium?"

"You said corrupted," Gila said, walking around as she considered the riddle. Nuclear fuels are elements. They are pure, despite their rate of decay being so dangerous." She stopped, facing Io. "What exactly do you mean by corrupted? Do you mean altered, say something man-made?"

Io thought for a moment. "Yes. You have a good point. When we say 'corrupted', the word can be misconstrued. In Heaven everything is pure. Souls come to us pure. Prayers are pure."

"Sounds like one giant clean room up there," Forrest observed.

"Heaven is no clean room," Io contradicted him. "There are factions and conflict. Maintaining an angel's mission can often be a matter of perspective. Just ask Karael. Many would argue that the brutal force, which he employs, might be excessive. He sees nothing wrong with the execution of his orders."

"I'll bet you're on the other side now that you've had a beating or two," Swanson commented, his wit as dry as ever.

"True," Io conceded. "Yet Forrest Kyle's point stands. Corrupted could mean 'corrupted by man'. You are, after all, a very corrupt species. From the very day Eve gave in to temptation, mankind has been walking a fine line, and in many cases, crossing over it."

"I don't believe anybody's totally pure," Eva said.

"I've got it," Gila burst out. "Go with me on this, Ioviel. The source of energy for your Phaethon Stone hasn't always been available, has it?"

"No, in fact it is only recently that such a source is recognised. We have never seen it because we no longer walk among you. The energy is not available in Heaven because of its impurity. Were it so, every fallen angel would have the source and Heaven would be a battlefield. It wouldn't matter because they would need ashes." He paused, looking around the room at all of them, his fist tightening on the velvet pouch. "This is a set up indeed."

Chapter Twenty-Seven

What had Io come to realise? He stood like a statue in front of her mother's shrine, his face concerned.

"But why now?" Samantha asked.

"Because Io isn't the only one trying to get into heaven," Gila answered. "There's a demon walking the face of the earth, the only one in the last twenty years—the very same demon who threatened nuclear meltdown in a matter of days. Io, what if you're the only one who can reach the power source?"

"I'm not. Karael is on Earth. He has the power."

"But he is not fallen. And he doesn't have any ashes."

"What about Porter Rockwell?" John asked. "Is he not a demon by its very definition—fallen?"

"No. A demon such as he, is different than a fallen angel. I have been in his presence. The evil in him is ancient, filled with malice for my kind and humanity as well. There is nothing in him that would allow him to create a doorway."

"He wants you," Eva said. "He wants you at the forthcoming nuclear incident." She nodded to Gila. "Now, I understand now. The power source is corium."

Samantha thought hard. 'Corium' wasn't a word she recognised. She stepped closer to Io, holding onto his upper arm and leaning into him. His rock-solidness was a reassurance. "Is it from a nuclear reactor? Just what is it?"

"Corium forms when a nuclear reactor melts down." Gila's one sentence hit Samantha like a sledgehammer. Suddenly the grand plan made sense.

"It's a hybrid material," Gila explained. "Corium only forms in the worst nuclear reactor disasters, when the core goes critical and melts because it can no longer be cooled. You get a mix of everything: nuclear fuel, cooling rods, concrete, oxides formed from the reaction of superheated fuel and water. It looks like a lava and can melt through just about anything. Corrupt is the most appropriate word to use. Nothing of this earth could get close without becoming massively irradiated. There are only a few examples in recent history: the disasters at Chernobyl, Fukushima in Japan, and Three Mile Island all produced corium. To get to any of those, you'd have to punch your way in through dozens of feet of concrete."

"Better to have someone immune to most normal forms of damage walk into a fresh disaster and return with a glowing ball of rock." Swanson said, the tone of his voice flat. "Aeon Fall could leave millions dead and dying to accomplish their goal, if indeed that is their aim. They don't care if God is dead or not. It's all a front."

"There's one way to find out," Io said. "Summon Karael."

"He's almost killed you twice," Samantha warned. "What if this time he decides you're really worth finishing off?"

Io smiled. "You misunderstand me, Samantha. I don't mean using your method of divination. My memory is now clear. In my realm, we summon each other by means of *sigils*. Any angel can summon another by the glyph bearing their mark. It enables us to move great distances in an instant, and Heaven, too, as you might expect, is very, very vast. There is no reason to suspect that the same will not work on the mortal plane. However, I have been to the Fearvent. I know a little secret to my brother's glyph. It can be worked inside an angel trap, such as those used in the Fearvent to keep the prisoners in place."

"Heaven has a prison?" Swanson shook his head. "Can't believe that."

"Pray that you never see it. Fearvent is not a pleasant place. However, I am confident that an angel can be bound within the trap."

"For how long?" John Wolverton asked. "I like the idea of trapping the monster whose been doing so much damage, but under the Chateau? In ARC headquarters? May I remind you all what happened the time a creature from another realm arrived in this region?"

"We have to take the chance. What if this Karael knows about the Phaethon Stone and Io's intent?"

"I can assure you, he *is* aware. We all are. My concern is this: Not only does he know, but I also get the feeling he is actively encouraging my rehabilitation. He wants me to make the attempt."

"If you believe that," Eva said, "what makes you in any way certain he will come?"

"Her." Io pointed to Samantha.

Confused, she looked around the room. All eyes were pointed in her direction. "Me? What makes me the center of the plot, all of a sudden?"

"Karael knows now that I will defend you, even if it means my own demise. All he wishes is to complete his mission. Once I am done for, he will return home."

"Except this time when he shows, he will be in a prison of our making."

"I know a place we can use," Samantha said, turning to the door, not waiting to see if anybody aside from Io would follow her.

* * *

In the hallway Samantha heard several sets of footsteps as she led the way toward the underbelly of Chateau d'Yvoire. Down numerous sets of uncomfortably narrow, spiral staircases, she entered a hallway where only the furthest reaches of the false light shone. A flashlight was passed forward.

"Thanks," she said to Io, who stared at the flashlight for a moment, and then handed it to her. "This should do, don't you think?" She switched it on, illuminating a circular room, which was a few metres inside an outer wall with a dirt floor and a ring of stone columns hewn from bedrock.

"This chamber was used for torture." Io's voice was clipped and judgmental. "Karael would probably approve. You might desire more light for yourselves. I shall make the necessary preparations." He moved into the centre of the room and picked up what looked like a thick stick, but could just have easily been a human bone. Everybody but Samantha's mother took this as a cue to leave.

Samantha decided not to examine his implement too closely. "So what happens if this goes wrong?"

"I die, Karael returns to Heaven, and your religion ends."

"Is it all that final?" Eva asked.

"Heaven is a place of absolutes. They believe mankind has abandoned them and pretty soon they won't open the gates to anybody for fear of an impurity. Religion has failed here, almost completely. Souls will continue to travel to Heaven but they will back up. Getting Heaven to listen is the only way to prevent this. I must try."

"Madden said something very similar when it became clear Crustallos was on the threshold of breaking through to Hell."

"Heaven is different," Io protested, "almost organic in nature. The angels maintain its purity, as they do the spirits that come from Earth."

"They come through Hell," Eva challenged him. "I was there. I saw what happens. Everything comes through Hell."

"Be that as it may, your version of events is not how we understand the source of souls to be. We have belief too. Belief that spirits come from earth. Belief that there is purity and goodness in everyone."

"Do you still believe that, even now?" Samantha asked, leaning against one of the stone posts as Io carved an intricate pattern in the dirt.

"I must admit I have come to reconsider my belief with only a few days in this host. It is clear while everybody is born an innocent, the corruption has spread and infects mortals very early on. I fear this revelation might truly make me fallen."

"Opening your eyes to reality is never a bad thing," Eva said.

"Others might not see it that way," Io replied. "The First Sphere, the Cherubim, Seraphim and the Thrones would close the gates permanently on a whim. While my order is steadfast to God, they are far more primal, almost elemental in nature. They surround Him and nurture Him. Their primary concern is to keep Him untainted even by us, his lesser creations. We are His caretakers, and are all about His glory. Some suggest that it is the First Sphere that caused Satan to choose the fall rather than serve under a master who has no mastery. I am sure my Father has no knowledge of Metatron's fall. I have to get back there. I have to try to make them understand."

Io finished carving the earth and stood up. "There. The trap is almost sealed. Any more carving and I will not be able to leave it. Samantha, will you finish the pattern for me?"

Two black-ops ARC operatives appeared at the bottom of the stairway, large spotlights on stands trailing power cables back up the stairs behind them. With a minimum of fuss they set up the spotlights at either end of the room, turning on the beams and focussing them at the pattern.

Now she could see what Io had carved, Samantha recognised the symbols. "It looks very similar to the pattern used to summon my … to summon the Devil."

"What you were doing was trapping his essence within an image projected by your mind," Io explained. "Anyone who beheld him otherwise would have seen his true form."

"That explains all the insane screaming," Samantha observed. "What do you need me to do?"

"Carve a circle in the middle. Link it by three lines at any point to the outer pattern. Then draw Karael's glyph in the centre of the circle. He will be compelled to come by this particular trap. Regardless of its potency, the temptation will be too great. A pure angel, a righteous soldier, will be trapped instantly."

Samantha did as bidden. Taking the implement from Io and trying her best not to look at what she held, Samantha carved the circle and three wavy lines joining it to the trap. As she finished, she felt a wave of discomfort wash over her. She grunted, taking a deep breath.

"Sammy, what's wrong? her mother asked.

"Nothing. I'm all right. Just need to catch my breath. This spell is powerful stuff." She looked up at Io, who appeared confused. "Just the glyph now? The Thornfalcon."

"Yes, do so."

His voice was uncertain, but Samantha had no idea why. She gripped the digging tool hard, feeling the sharp edge lacerate her palm where it was broken. Three swift strokes and the Thornfalcon was etched into the angel trap. She stood. "Now what?"

"Get out of there. The glyph works instantly when I summon Karael."

Samantha stepped in between the carvings of the trap, every step becoming more and more difficult as if a force sought to keep her inside. "What's going on?" she said as she pushed at an invisible wall.

"Unexpected consequences," Io replied, his voice mysterious. "Keep going."

Eva reached forward and tugged on Samantha's outstretched hand. The force was enough for her to move forward across the edge of the trap. Having done so, the oppressive sensation disappeared and she could breathe again. "I felt like the weight of the whole castle was literally on top of me."

"That shouldn't have happened," Io said. He raised his hand toward the glyph. "Let's see you again, brother." His palm began to glow, warmth pushing back the cold earthy damp of the underground room. In response, the glyph glowed a pale white and began to pulse. Yet nothing more happened. Io gritted his teeth and spread his fingers wide, the tendons sticking out on the back of his hand. After a moment, he let the glow fade. "He is not coming."

"How is that possible?" Eva asked. "I thought you said the pattern would compel him?"

"That pattern would compel any pure and righteous angel. I learned it from the one who created the original trap, which leads me to one of two conclusions. Either the trap never worked in the first place, or Karael is not as pure as he led us to believe."

"It felt pretty damned real to me," Samantha muttered. "Why don't you try standing in there and see for yourself? At least that way you know if I carved the trap correctly."

Io nodded. "If you did, you have but to erase any of the outer lines to break the trap and free me." He stepped across the outer edge of his construction. Once in the centre, he scuffed the glyph meant to call Karael. "No point having him appear now if this trap works."

"Does it?" Eva asked.

Io put his hands out to either side and pushed. An invisible barrier prevented him from stretching his arms straight. He snarled, pushing until the tendons stuck out on his neck, then stopped and dropped his head. "The trap is intact, leaving a single possibility. Karael has been corrupted. He has truly fallen."

"But wouldn't Heaven know? I mean surely an angel choosing to fall to earth is a pretty big deal."

"Karael has his skills for that exact reason. He is Heaven's enforcer."

"Well who enforces the enforcer? Everybody has to answer to someone." Samantha moved toward the trap. "Aren't you missing the obvious, Io? You're trapped. You said a pure angel would be summoned and held by the design. Granted you weren't the target, but you're in the trap."

"I'm not an angel without my wings. I can't just walk back into Heaven."

"Well somebody thinks you are, and whoever gave you this design must have done their job diligently. Maybe it's not what anybody else believes, but what you consider to be the truth that's most prevalent here. Let's get you out of there."

Io's voice was filed with doubt as he said, "If in his heart, he has forsaken Heaven we are in trouble. If Karael has fallen then this is all a set up. Aeon Fall wanted an angel who was able to create a doorway to heaven. They don't need me for that. However, if I'm in a convenient place, to be kept until needed..."

One of the black-ops guards moved to take position in front of the trap. Samantha stepped around him, but he blocked her way.

"What are you doing?" Eva said. "Stand aside."

"Sorry, Director. I cannot." The agent raised his rifle across his chest, a sign he was ready for action. "Please don't take another step toward the prisoner."

"The prisoner?" Samantha repeated. "He's no prisoner. He's my friend."

She took a quick step around the guard, intending to scuff the edge of the trap. There was a black blur and a flash of pain. Before she knew what was happening, Samantha tasted dirt, her vision full of the guards' boots.

"I'm sorry, Miss. I did warn you."

Not prepared to give up, she reached out to the trap. The guard's foot stamped down on her hand and she screamed in pain.

"Do that again and I break your fingers, Miss."

"What's wrong with you?" Eva shouted. Everything had happened so quickly. Her mother tried to approach.

The second guard appeared, rifle raised. "Don't, Ma'am. You take one more step and I'll be forced to fire."

"On whose say-so? You do realise I'm a director of ARC?"

"But you're not the only director," a voice said from the shadows of the stairwell.

Chapter Twenty-Eight

Who was it speaking? A man? Samantha strained to see from her position on the earth.

"Back," the guard indicated with the muzzle of his rifle. "Real slow. You'd look strange with a missing limb."

Climbing to her feet, she nursed her sore hand, sharing a look with Io. He seemed more concerned about her well-being than his current predicament, still pushing against the invisible wall that held him. Her eyes on Io, she backed away from the trap. "This isn't over." She turned to look past her mother. "You?"

Thorsten Guyomard stared back, his face beaming with triumph. "Well isn't this a bit of luck. We hook ourselves a nice fat fish and he has the good grace to jump into the boat."

"Thorsten, explain yourself. The council wouldn't want this."

"The council?" Thorsten spat back. "ARC. Just another family dictatorship with too much power. How is the name of Guyomard any better than the name of Kim in North Korea? Or indeed the name of Scott? In only twenty years your family has come to dominate hundreds of years of history. Dictatorships can be toppled. Will be toppled."

"You're them," Samantha realised aloud. The situation had suddenly turned from serious to grave. "A member of the council, a Guyomard, and you're Aeon Fall?"

"It's a philosophical choice, one made most poignant when standing in the presence of the Devil's whore and their degenerate offspring.

There's a new power rising, ladies." He turned to Io. "Tell me about the Godmissile."

Io looked stunned. "How could you possibly know about that?"

"Tell me. Tell me everything. How it fires, how to access it. Everything."

Samantha leaned in close to her mother. "Godmissile?" she whispered.

"I've no clue," Eva replied. "Ioviel, don't say a word. The council will come to find us."

"No, they won't," contradicted Thorsten. "The ARC Council has little regard for a director who has proven once again just how much of a poisoned chalice the Technology and Development wing can be. They have about as much concern for her wayward daughter as well as a junior member who is only present because he bears the name Guyomard. About now, they will be in session. With ten of the twelve present they will conveniently overlook our absence as they debate how to react to the revelation of the first nuclear facility to go critical."

"It's not been five days yet," Samantha replied.

Thorsten laughed. "Aeon Fall can strike any place, any time. We have no need to hide our plans and nor have we any need to stick to our threats. While they attempt to stave off a disaster, Porter Rockwell and his own tame angel are on the way to claim their prize. Until then…"

Thorsten placed a case similar to that which had carried the Helltech pistol on the ground, unlatching it with careful hands. "Now, Angel. Tell me all about the Godmissile."

Io stood resolute, his hands dropped to his sides. "I will do no such thing."

Thorsten detached an object from the inside of his case, holding it pointed at Io. "Sure?"

Io remained unmoved, saying nothing.

Thorsten smiled. "Let's see if we can't loosen your tongue a bit. I'm glad I finally have a chance to use this." He turned to Eva. "You didn't think you were the only one working on technology from your blessed body armor, did you Eva?"

While still watching her mother, Thorsten squeezed the trigger. Two projectiles shot into Io's chest, connected to the weapon by wires. A blue glow followed the instant the darts had hit their mark. Io threw his head back and screamed in pain, dropping to his knees and leaning up against the invisible barrier.

Samantha tried to move but her mother held her firm. "You take one step and they'll shoot," she said straight into Samantha's ear.

Neither of the guards had moved a muscle, both facing them, hands gripping their guns like claws.

After nearly thirty seconds of screaming, the blue glow faded. Io slumped to the floor, gasping.

"The only drawback with this weapon is the power source," he said conversationally, letting the weapon hang from one finger as he gesticulated. "Takes thirty seconds or so to recharge. However, despite the short bursts, it can go on forever. Great little gizmo, this. Ioviel, the Godmissile, if you please."

"No," Io muttered from between clenched teeth.

"Excellent!" Thorsten declared, setting the room blue once more with the glow of his torture device.

Io's screams this time drowned out anything Samantha's mother tried to say to her. She ended up putting her hands over her ears. When Io stopped screaming, she took a deep breath. Her throat hurt and she realised she had been screaming too.

"You bastard," she croaked.

"Possibly," he retorted. "I was never really convinced my father was really my father. Ioviel, dear chap, do you have anything to say on the Godmissile now?"

Io drooled onto the earth. "I am a warrior of Heaven. You're never leaving Hell."

"We shall see. You don't need to be alive when my master gets here, you know? You just need to die for your little girlfriend over here. And you *will* die for her. You and I are now going to have a nice long talk, Ioviel. And if you don't tell me everything I wish to know, when she returns, I'm going to use this weapon on her. If it can do this to you, a great and mighty angel, just imagine the damage it might inflict on a mere mortal."

He turned to the guard who had stamped on her hand. "Keep them nearby, but isolated. If either of them attempt to flee, or cause any sort of outcry, shoot the other."

"In the knee?"

"In the head."

* * *

Samantha said nothing initially as she followed her mother back up the stairs. The guard behind them felt perilously close with his rifle. She had to trust entirely on her mother remaining steadfast.

"You realise this isn't the winning side you've chosen?" Samantha queried aloud after they were well out of earshot of Thorsten Guyomard.

Eva stopped and turned, her face questioning.

Samantha indicated with a twist of her head she meant the guard.

"Keep moving," he growled, shoving the muzzle into her back.

Samantha jumped at the contact; the pain of metal being rammed into her spine was sharp and sudden. She continued her ascent.

In the hallway at the top of the stairs, their guard pulled the door as closed as was possible with thick black cable wedged in the doorway and shoved Samantha sideways. Eva caught her mid stumble and led the way, not even acknowledging the guard.

Behind them, another heart-rending scream echoed up into the hallway.

"Thorsten's working him hard," Samantha said. "I don't think he's gonna last." She stopped against a door and pretended to sob. "I don't think I can do this."

Eva leaned over to comfort her. "He's made of stern stuff."

Samantha dropped to the ground, still sobbing, looking like she would never stand again.

Frustrated by this odd turn of events, the guard poked at Eva with his gun. "Get her up."

"Can't you see she's distraught?" Eva shot back. "Give her a moment, for pity's sake."

The guard poked her again. "Get inside this room. It'll do for storing you."

Her mother made a grand show of hauling her up. "Open the door then."

With reluctance the guard did so one-handed, still pointing his rifle at them. "In."

Samantha shuffled through the doorway, dropping to the floor on the other side.

"I hope for your sake you win," Eva said to the guard, who smiled back.

"We will. If I see that handle even twitch I'll shoot through the door. So sit tight, like good little mice, till the boss comes calling." He slammed the door shut.

* * *

Once they were alone, Samantha looked up, all traces of hysterics gone. The room was dark and musty. It hadn't been used in a while. She turned one of the lights on, illuminating a room more like a library than somebody's personal chamber. A thin veneer of dust covered everything in the room.

"Good," she said.

"Nina's room," her mother said, her face solemn.

"I miss her too, and I worry, Mom."

"You've heard nothing more? Not a word?"

"Not since Port Moresby. She sounded like she was getting real deep." Samantha unshouldered her rucksack, pulling the twin crow books from the pocket within. She held up the book recovered from the jungle. "This we found in Papua New Guinea, where we were set up." She pulled out her first book. "This was given to me by my sister, here, in this room. It was part of the library recovered from Castle Chillon after the demon attack before I was born. It's a fake. The coordinates hidden in the book were fake. I'm sorry, but you have to accept the possibility that at the very least Aeon Fall have tampered with this information. I've had this book for years. They're playing the long game."

Her mother appeared worried. "Are you saying Nina might be a dupe?"

"That's what I hope. What if someone gave her the book in the hope of planting a seed ending in us going exactly where we went? What if they have been nurturing the tribe we found on a diet of drugs and false promises? There could be areas like that all over the world. Tell me, Mom. How well does anybody actually know Aeon Fall? They've got a former Shikari as their face. They've got one of our Council on their payroll. Maybe more."

"That's ludicrous, Sammy." Eva crossed the room to sit on the edge of the bed, being careful to not disturb the dust. "I know them well."

"Do you? Are you sure?"

"John, Gila, and Swanson are beyond reproach, as is Forrest and my sister."

"Half of the council," Samantha said, her voice flat, her words filled with cynicism. She began to explore the room, poking through the ancient texts that filled an entire wall of the room.

"Jeanette has looked out for me since day one. Mohammed is one of my oldest friends. Tricia is just about the sweetest person you could meet and Gaspard has been around since probably before I was born. He's earned the trust of everyone."

"If you call such bonds trust, you've still got two. Our friend downstairs, lest you forget, is a Guyomard. They have certain privileges when it comes to this council."

Her mother's face went pale. Samantha referred to the clause in the ARC charter that allowed a descendent of Jerome Guyomard to take direct control of the ARC council in certain situations, such as a nuclear incident. "He wouldn't."

"Put Swanson out of the picture, and he certainly could try. One assumes at this juncture he is meant to be the natural successor, the stopgap in case a fouler fate befalls his cousin. Remember it's not a few days since Daniel lost his life, and so much has happened since then. We can't let events overtake us without paying attention to the facts. Which leaves us with Alexander Steadman. A man in charge of books. He has unparalleled knowledge of both ARC and the unspoken history of the world."

"Sammy, just because he's the curator of our libraries, it doesn't implicate him in subverting your sister."

"Maybe. Maybe not." Samantha moved from the bookshelves to the writing desk her sister had installed, a solid piece of teak furniture with drawers down on one side. "It does give him plenty of access and through him the wrong person could do a lot of damage." The drawers weren't locked and Samantha began to leaf through the contents.

"Ah, here it is," Samantha said after a moment, picking up a key from the second drawer and holding it up for her mother to see. "This might come in useful."

"What does it open?"

Samantha crossed the room past her mother to an area of blank wall. "Scream. Curse. Throw some books around," she whispered.

Eva looked at her like she was mad for a moment and then nodded. "A distraction." She began to shriek, grabbing book after book and hurling them at the door.

Samantha ran her hands over the surface of the wall, the wooden panelling rough against her skin. Undeterred by the stabs of pain from small splinters, she kept moving until she found a spot different from the rest—softer, more pliant. She pushed and a small section of the panel dropped back, revealing a keyhole. "Jackpot!" Sliding the key in, she opened a panel in the wall two metres high.

Eva stopped, staring at what was revealed behind.

From the other side of the door came a dark chuckle from their guard, "Scream all you want, ladies. This part of the castle is secure. Pretty soon we'll have the entire compound locked down, so you're wasting your breath."

Samantha nodded at her mother and whispered, "Recognise this?"

"I thought these were lost," Eva replied, her voice a little choked up. What she referred to were combat suits. Black ops, figure hugging and most importantly woven from a material that made them as good as bulletproof.

"Not lost, just re-appropriated. Nina thought that storage in wooden crates in the archives wasn't the right place for such history. From what I understand the second suit was Gila's."

"Are they still intact?"

"Yes, Mom. And they come with most of their original kit, including new night vision apparatus that replaces what you lost. Now put it on."

Eva smiled. "Sammy, those days have long since gone."

"You'll need it. Gila's suit fits me, Mom. I've worn it before. Put yours on. It's gonna get dark real soon and we're ending this little insurrection before it starts."

Now clearly intrigued by her daughters' intent, Eva began to quietly slip into the black-ops suit. The change in dynamic between mother and daughter was absolute. Samantha was the one with the plan. Taking mere moments to slip out of her worn and dirty clothes and into the snug and surprisingly warm combat gear, she turned to look at the desk once again. "Something doesn't ring true about those drawers." Closing the hidden closet, she opened the drawer that had contained the key, pulling it all of the way out. Look. There's nothing in here, yet it's really heavy."

"It's teak, dear. Teak's heavy."

"Yeah but look at the depth of the inside. The base is shallower by a good inch or more than the outside of the drawer. Start screaming again."

Eva grinned, letting loose with invective enough to turn anybody's cheeks to flaming. As she began to hurl books, Samantha raised the drawer and dashed it to the stone floor. The drawer remained mainly intact and for a moment Samantha's heart sank. Then she noticed the inside had come loose.

"A false bottom." She pried at the wood with an energy born of desperation. "There's something inside." Her hands were frenetic as she furiously pulled at the wood until it finally came away.

"A book?" Eva said, looking over her shoulder.

"Yeah, a book. Like these," Samantha pulled the matching set from her bag and replaced them with the book from the compartment, "except this one is real. We'll look at it later. For now, put your headgear on. The wiring down here was only meant to be temporary. It's about to get real dark. Fill the sink." Samantha grabbed the wiring on the nearest wall and yanked hard, pulling it free. With a snap she pulled the plug from one end, exposing the naked wires.

Eva turned the tap on full and let it run. "Ready."

Samantha grinned. "Here goes nothing." She dropped the wires into the pooling water. Blue sparks of electricity flared up for a moment. In the distance there was an explosion.

The room went dark.

Chapter Twenty-Nine

The door clicked as their captor unlocked the gate to their prison. On the far side, in the pitch black of Nina's chamber, Samantha watched in silence.

"I know you're in here," the guard growled.

Samantha could just feel the words 'Oh *please.*' coming from her mother. She smiled. With the Shikari headgear on, the room was an eerie shade of green but the guard was totally blind.

"You come out now, identify yourselves and I'll make sure no harm comes to you."

Idiot.

In the moments between the darkness coming and the guard's hesitant response, Samantha and her mother had hatched a simple plan. Push one of the freestanding bookshelves on top of him. Knock him out. They waited, barely breathing as he moved into the room.

Rifle held in front of him, almost at arms' length, he took step after creeping step. Their luck held when he reached their chosen trap and turned away, so his back was to them. One thumb from Eva and they pushed, the combat suits making the task easy. The shelf, with so many heavy old books on it, crushed him underneath, a series of cracks indicating broken bones. As a bonus, his arm, gun still intact, stuck out to one side.

"I think he's dead," Eva said. "My gear can't detect any sign of a heartbeat. Take the gun."

"Eva?" Said a familiar voice over Samantha's radio. "Are you well? Not hurt?"

"John? You've got one of these too? Who else can hear us?"

"Never leave Hell without it," Wolverton quipped.

"Who else can hear us?"

"Private radio network between the suits will keep us off the air-waves. What's your situation?"

"Thorsten Guyomard's a traitor," Samantha said. "Chateau d'Yvoire is under attack from Aeon Fall. He's got Io trapped down in the cellar we took him to. John, Thorsten's torturing him with Helltech. He's gonna kill him. They locked us in Nina's room and we blew the power. Can you help?"

"Unfortunately not. Your trick blew everything and we're sealed in the council chamber. Most everything up here is powered by electronic locks. You're gonna have to reset the circuit breakers and come get us out."

"Well, we have a gun at least," Eva replied. "John, other than the Council, we don't know who to trust, if anybody we find is loyal to ARC or not. Porter Rockwell is on his way here, now. He's bringing the angel Karael with him."

"Then hurry, ladies. And shoot first, or better, hide."

"One more thing," added Samantha. "Keep an eye on Alexander Steadman. He might not be all he seems."

"Got it. I'll keep the channel open. Shout if you want moral support. I'll be listening. Chances are all the guards are locked away too. The only way into ARC will be through the tunnel and that takes them past the circuit breakers in the stairwell. Hurry!"

* * *

Samantha was first out into the hallway. There was no sign of the other guard. "Must be still down in the cellar," she assumed.

"Then hurry, Sammy. This place could already be crawling with Aeon Fall agents and they may well have the same gear we do, or better."

In moments they were at the doorway. Silence met them from below. Samantha leaned down and pulled out the plugs that had powered the lights in the cellar. "Better to be certain," she whispered.

Eva merely nodded. "Can you use one of those?"

"We'll find out soon enough. Stay behind me, a quarter turn on the steps. One of us is enough of a target." Hoping her mother listened to her advice, Samantha started down the stairs, her padded footwear falling silent on the stone, the rifle held tight to her core. She took slow, even breaths, willing herself to remain calm. Each step brought her closer to the potential reality that Io was already gone. She wasn't ready to accept such a fate and began to move faster down the spiral. Ahead of her, the blue glow of the Helltech Taser shone up the passageway for a moment before it moved away and left her in darkness with only the distant echoes of footsteps for company. The taser was being used as a light source. She became cautious.

A whimpering echoed up from below. They were almost at the room. Io was still with them.

"The glyphs," a very frustrated Thorsten Guyomard demanded. "Give me the glyphs of all of your brethren. I'll take them all."

"N … no," Io grunted.

The blue light started once more. Far past screaming, Io merely groaned, his body twitching as he lay in the angel trap.

Samantha scanned the room. The remaining fake guard moved into place beside Thorsten, perhaps attracted by the light from the Helltech. His rifle hung from his shoulder as he watched.

She moved across the room behind them, waiting for the light to fade.

When it did, the guard asked, "Shouldn't they be here by now?"

"They are," Thorsten replied. "They'll secure the grounds first, then the castle. The Council aren't going anywhere, and will spend all the time it takes The Master to get here trying to barter for the lives of the women."

Samantha heard enough. The muzzle flashed as she squeezed the trigger, dropping the guard in an instant.

In no time Eva was on top of the fallen guard, removing his rifle.

"What the?" Thorsten moved but Samantha was quicker, knocking the Taser from his hand with a violent swing of her weapon.

Thorsten screamed in pain, holding his damaged hand. "You've broken my goddamned wrist. Who—?"

Samantha shoved the muzzle of the rifle in his face, pushing into his cheek. "Be glad it's your wrist and not a bullet between your eyes, you traitorous son of a bitch." Reversing the rifle, she clubbed Thorsten in the face as hard as she could manage with the butt. "Pull some of that lighting cable loose. Let's leave them here for John to deal with."

Eva yanked several metres of cable free and rolled Thorsten onto his front, winding the cable around his wrists. Samantha turned to Io. She pulled the Taser darts from his chest and threw them aside. "Io, can you hear me?"

"That is not a pleasant man," Io groaned, trying to sit up. "Can you get me out of here?"

Samantha scuffed at the edge of the trap with the butt of the rifle until the outer lines had been completely erased on one segment of the circle. "Enough?"

"Help me up," Io asked, reaching out.

Samantha took his hand and attempted to pull him up. Nothing happened. "Dear God, Io. It's like trying to lift a mountain."

Eventually he managed to stand on his own, leaning on her for support. Samantha had read the schematics of the combat suits. She'd never expected to be using one in such a desperate situation.

"Lucky these suits can take a lot of weight," said Eva, as if echoing her very thoughts. "I never thought we'd be carrying angels."

"We're going to have to move quickly, Io," Samantha said. "How long do you need to rest?"

"Not long. Most of the damage was done by the trap itself. It's about keeping the prisoner weak as much as it is keeping them bound. His weapon didn't improve matters. But more importantly, what's happening here? Is the takeover systemic?"

"Aeon Fall are coming. Karael is on his way, too. They might already be here. The Council are trapped in the castle. We've got to free them."

"Lead the way," Eva urged. "I'll be close behind you."

Io gave her a warning look. "Be careful, Eva Scott. Intent can be as damning as action."

Samantha led the way back into the corridor above, Eva catching them up by the time they had ascended the stairs, rifle in hand.

"Try not to use those unless you absolutely have to," Io said.

"Murder is the greatest sin of all," Eva replied. "Yeah, I know."

"True," Io agreed. "However, if you keep firing a gun down here and there are terrorists about, don't you suppose it will draw them to you? Allow me to help."

They moved through the absolute darkness of the tunnels, Io had no problem seeing in the dark now he was in full control of his faculties. Every step took them closer to a confrontation Samantha wasn't truly ready for. All of her life she had played the rebel, using attack as her only form of defence. If they only knew how scared she was, her family might look upon her differently. The kidnappings, the glancing confrontations with Karael, had all been reactions. Now she was making a proactive choice to take a stand and it terrified her. She held on to Io with a firm grip. She would do it for him.

They had to double back when presented with locked doors. Fortunately not every tunnel was carved from the rock and as they passed under the castle there were more alternatives.

"The stairwell to the dock is through that door," Eva said, her voice quiet but perfectly audible over the headset. "The circuit breakers are about halfway down, through a door."

"Won't they be locked too?"

"It would be somewhat self-defeating if the solution to our problem was trapped the same way. No, that door is key locked. It just needs a good swift kick."

"There's somebody out there," said Io. "He's armed."

"Can you do anything from here?" Eva asked. "You know, sort of reach out?"

"It doesn't work like that," he replied.

"I've got an idea," Samantha volunteered. She leaned past Io and gave the door three gentle taps with her gloved hand. Stepping back, she waited.

The door creaked as it was opened from the other side. Predictably, an automatic rifle poked through as the door widened. Samantha crouched and Eva followed suit.

Taking this as a cue, Io grabbed the gun and slammed its owner against the wall. He reached out and clamped one hand over the mouth of their would-be opponent holding him firm. In seconds, the man's eyes began to smoke and then glow. He tried to scream but the sound was muffled by Io's hand. With a hiss of burning flesh it was over. The smoking body dropped to the floor, the mouth still agape.

"Io, what did you do?" Samantha asked. "His eyes have burned out."

"In the instant I held the man, I touched his soul and perceived his intent. Sometimes this happens when there's an evil festering deep down. Many can't bear to face the truth from within. He was damned and the force of my touch was too much."

"How can you know the truth about a man from a touch?"

Io sounded strangely sarcastic as he answered, "Hello? Warrior angel from God?"

Eva began to laugh. "You *have* definitely been spending too much time with my daughter. What else did you see?"

"This is a small force, more of a patrol. The main force is on the lake, waiting for a signal to enter the tunnel."

"We've got to get the power back up so our own guys can get down here," Samantha said. Urgency was needed. "Let's move."

"There is more," Io added, unmoving. "There are those in the council allied to Aeon Fall. This man is a pawn. He did not know who the moles are, but he suspects there is someone, or something, beyond those controlling them. The force on the lake is carrying a weapon, a gas. They intend to unleash it in the castle and end everybody here."

"Did he tell you what the signal was?" Eva asked.

"No. He did not know."

"You're crazy, Mom," Samantha said, already guessing what her mother had planned.

"Am I missing something?" Io asked.

"I've heard tales from several of the council regarding the crazy escapades of Eva Scott as I grew up, Io. I never thought I'd be in one. What mom's suggesting is that if you found someone who knew the signal, we could turn the tables on Aeon Fall, invite them in and trap them."

"You got all that from one sentence?"

Samantha shrugged, the suit sticking like a second skin with the movement. "Look at what you got from one touch."

"Is she correct?" Io turned to Eva.

"Of course she is," Eva replied. "She's my daughter."

Samantha's heart glowed.

* * *

Io led the way down the stairwell, his feet silent. He hardly even registered on the night vision but Samantha could feel him without looking. The closer she was, the safer she felt. Samantha found herself wishing she could replicate that particular camouflage. She followed close behind, her mother watching the rear with rifle raised.

"John, you getting all this?" Eva whispered. "We're caught in the middle of them."

"Get that power back on and all Hell will break loose," he promised. "I want you to flip the switches and hole up in there, you hear me? Stay safe."

There was no response from her mother. Samantha turned. Eva stood still, frozen to the spot with her rifle aimed down the stairs. At the limit of her vision were two figures taking hesitant steps toward them, dressed in similar attire but waving flashlights about as if expecting to get jumped any second. It appeared by the way they crept, they were just as afraid as she was. In front of the two was the door they sought; they stopped.

"This it?" one asked,

"Yeah. The Man said wait by the door, hold the passage until the rest come. Should be on their way, according to schedule."

Samantha decided it was time for some crazy tactics of her own. She pushed past Io, marching straight at the two intruders. She felt her mother's hand slip off of her shoulder, reaching to pull her back, but she was committed. She pressed a button on the pad on her arm that linked to the headset. Voice modulation.

"You two are supposed to be in the pool room," she barked, her voice sounding alpha male as it was cast into the darkness. "New orders from The Master until the light comes back on."

The intruders looked at each other in confusion. "The Master doesn't issue the orders," one challenged, shining his flashlight at her face. "Who are you? What's that gear?"

Both men began to raise their weapons, as did Samantha.

Io dodged in front of her, taking a bullet in the chest as the speaker fired. He held both hands up, one to each of their faces and his palms glowed. "She's a crazy person, that's who she is," Io growled as both men screamed, their arms slack as they were judged. "Just like your mother. Don't do that again!" he warned her over his shoulder.

"Io, look," Eva commanded.

Io turned. One of the pair, the man who fired a shot, dropped to the ground, eyes black and smoking. The other remained standing, staring at Io with wide, worried eyes.

Samantha seized the opportunity to open the door and pull her mother into the circuit breaker room. A series of large breakers were on a panel above a sturdy metal table. "Which one?" she asked as Io followed. Strangely, the intruder who hadn't burned up came into the room, staring at Io. "Are you God?"

"Sammy, why do you sound like a man?" Her mother had stopped in the hall behind them. Her voice was cautious, low. "What's happened to you?"

"It's the headset, Mom. It has all sorts of tricks. Which breaker is it?" Samantha nodded toward the panel.

"All of them. Make sure they're all flipped up, then the master switch at the bottom. Flip that one up too."

Samantha flipped the breakers, pausing before the last switch and offering a silent prayer. "I hope this works." She flipped the master switch and prayed.

Chapter Thirty

For a few seconds, nothing happened. Samantha's heart sank. "This was all for—" The lights blinked on, cutting her sentence short.

"John, you still there?" she asked.

"He's got Swanson," John yelled above the sounds of a struggle, screams drowning out many of the words. "—little bastard. Hold tight Sammy. We can't tell if Aeon Fall have breached the pool door yet. Agents are on their way. Barricade yourselves if you can. I—" The signal went dead.

"John? John?"

Samantha pulled her headset off. "The line's dead at his end. Mom, stop shouting." She turned to the captured terrorist, pointing her rifle at him. "You!" she said, "how did you get in here?"

His gaze switched between her and Io as Io lowered her weapon, pushing it firmly down. "You do not need it. Oliver here has undergone somewhat of a transformation. His companion Benjamin was not so fortunate."

"I've seen the light, been shown is more to the point. We swam in through a conduit that feeds water into your dock. It's at the base of the pool. We were supposed to take the castle once the angel—" he stared at Io again, "was secured but the power was cut, leaving the outer doors locked down."

"And the signal?" Eva asked.

"Red flares." Oliver reached to his belt, touching two rods with plastic caps.

"How many are there?"

Oliver looked confused. "Flares? We each have two."

"How many in your squad?"

"Twelve. Ben and myself, four more in the pool, and six on ahead."

"That means three in the castle then, with those we took out," said Samantha. "Okay we play it safe. Wedge this table under the handle. That at least will give us a few moments delay."

Oliver and Io picked up the table, wedging it tight to the door with considerable force, then moved to the far end of the room. As an afterthought Io switched the light off.

The minutes ticked by with no movement outside.

"What are they waiting for?" Eva growled. "The response team should be down here by now."

Io moved to the door, holding his hand against the panel. After a few moments he said, "Nothing. Wait here."

Before anybody could protest, Io shifted the table and was through the door.

"Great," Samantha muttered. "Our smoking gun decides to get creative." Replacing the table with Oliver's help, she settled next to her mother. Their recent convert hunkered down next to them, rifle raised at the door. In the dark, uncertainty gnawed at Samantha's resolve. To find some small measure of comfort, she replaced the blue tinge of her headset's screen with red. In the corner of the screen a word lit up, a word only someone with access to the Shikari armor would understand.

"Mom," she said quietly. "Turn your screen red."

The door burst open with a spray of splinters and Io dashed in. The table, a seemingly ineffective blockade, shot past them and smashed to pieces on the far wall. "This is a trap! There's nobody down at the underground passage. The castle is full of Aeon Fall and they're all upstairs! They came from the town. They appear to have known every way in."

Samantha turned to Oliver. "But you said…"

Oliver's beatific smile turned up at the edges, his face now a mask of pure hatred. He bared teeth like a wild dog in an inhuman approximation of a grin, his lips twitching with suppressed rage. "Enough to keep you here. For myself. Rockwell can have the scraps. I'll take the Devil's whore for Crustallos. She whose blood locked Him out, whose blade rendered Him sightless will make a trophy, indeed." Oliver spat on the floor. "Angels. Demons. Usurpers and degenerates. Your touch cannot taint me."

Oliver's body swelled as something snakelike writhed under his skin. Samantha shuddered.

Eva screamed. "No. Not again!"

Oliver laughed, a cold sound devoid of mirth. "You considered yourself safe! Ha!" His voice dropped several octaves until it grated like stone on stone. Guttural. Alien.

"Io," Samantha shouted above her mother's screaming, "Push him back!"

Io jumped at Oliver, shoving him across the room, hitting the circuit breaker panel.

Please work, Samantha prayed, and squeezed the trigger. Bullets spat out, the recoil surprisingly ferocious, the gun threatening to buck loose. Two bullets passed through Oliver's body and into the panel which exploded in a burst of pyrotechnics. Oliver twitched violently, electricity coursing through his body until he slumped to the floor.

Samantha turned away. "Come on, we've got a council to rescue."

Angry at being duped, Samantha stormed into the hallway, her rifle raised to her shoulder, ready to fire.

"Sammy, don't," Io warned, but she had the bit between her teeth.

Her mother followed close behind. "Be careful, Love. Don't let the crazy take over."

"There's no crazy here, Mom." Samantha felt energised, focussed, as she tore through the passageways, following the sight of her rifle. Was it the combat suit doing this to her? In moments they were at the outside of the council chamber. She was fearless, trying the handle.

It wouldn't budge. She stepped back, fired several rounds at the handle. The lock shattered. She kicked the door, jumped in behind it, and slipped on something wet. Pulling her mask up, she smelled a strange iron tang on the floor. She moved. The liquid was tacky and warm.

"Samantha," Io called from the doorway. "Listen carefully. Stand up and back out of the room."

"Why?" She pulled her mask the rest of the way off. "It's only—" She stopped, assaulted by a scene of absolute horror.

"Gila!" Eva dove to the floor and now Samantha understood Io's attempts to keep her from the chamber. At her feet lay the body of Gila Byron, one of her mothers' dearest and oldest friends, her face cold and lifeless.

"Nooooo. Nooooo," Eva moaned, holding Gila's body and rocking it.

Samantha stepped away, closing her eyes, trying to comprehend what had occurred. She looked up, gasped, covering her face with her hands. "There are more." She stepped around the room, tears streaming down her face. "Jeanette, Mohammed, Gaspard. Over there, John, Forrest, Swanson. Hang on."

There was movement. Swanson tried to cough.

Samantha quickly knelt by him. "Swanson, what happened here?"

The Council Head tried to draw breath, bubbles of red frothing from his mouth, blood gushing from deep wounds in his chest. He didn't have long. Samantha could see he knew he was lost. "Tho … thors…" he whispered.

"Thorsten?"

Swanson coughed.

Samantha waited for the spasm to subside.

He nodded. "Traitor. He came for me. John fought. Got me first. Brave, brave man. Rest had no chance. Alexander … aid him. Clare, Tricia, taken. Thorsten. It was Thorsten. He took her orders."

"Swanson!" Eva saw them from across the room and came hurtling toward them.

"Careful Mom," Samantha warned. "He's not long, now."

"What do I do?" she asked.

Swanson closed his eyes. "Protocols. Use protocols. You are ARC." He coughed, flecks of blood landed on his face and forehead. "Protect the world," he whispered. "Angels. Knights. Resurrection." He opened his eyes once more. "I'll tell Madden you said hi."

"Swanson, that's not funny," Eva said, her eyes closed, tears streaming down her face. When she opened them he was still staring at her.

Eva began to shake.

"Mom, he's gone. Step back." She leaned across. "Step back, Mom." Samantha closed his eyes with the palm of her hand. His skin was still warm, but limp. It was an odd sensation.

"The rest of them passed before we got here," Io said. "It is as this man said. The large one over there, he put up an effective struggle until he was defeated. The rest of the Council were not so lucky. It looks like someone had some fun before killing them."

"Who is 'her'?" Samantha said aloud. "Swanson said 'they took her orders'. And Aunt Clare's missing. Where's Jim?"

"Here," Jim said as he pushed the door to the chamber open and stopped. "Dear God, who did this?"

"Thorsten Guyomard and Alexander Steadman," Samantha replied. "There's a message."

The table was painted with blood. Messy, and clearly in a hurry, one of the attackers painted the words, 'A thousand years of darkness'.

"A thousand years of darkness?" Jim asked.

"Aeon of falling," Samantha replied. "They should have written, 'We did it'. Jim, do you know where Charlotte is?"

"She's securing the boat. We've been together since we came back, well, until just now."

"Oh," Samantha and Io shared a glance. She instantly felt guilty for suspecting a woman who had shepherded her through the last few days. "We have to get out of here."

"Not yet," Jim countered. "We need answers. Is anybody missing?"

"Thorsten was in the cellar, torturing Io. He and Alexander did this, and they took Tricia and Clare."

Jim sighed at the fate of his boss. "Why was the Council reconvened?"

"Thorsten reported that the location of the nuclear targets was released," Eva said, standing up. "We need to find out where they are." She wiped the tears from her eyes. "There's technology here too," she added. "It needs to be locked down." Eva booted up her computer; the screen opened at the front of the room, blood-spattered panels emerging from the wall. Two locations blinked on a map: Forsmarck in Sweden and Almaraz in Spain. "Really?" Eva complained.

"That doesn't make any sense," Samantha said. "If Aeon Fall wanted to maximise damage, they could choose any number of stations closer to populated areas."

"Protocol first," Eva said aloud, hitting a key. "Okay, this place is secured. The organisation is aware of what's happened."

She paused watching Samantha zoning out, staring into space. "Your father wouldn't want me moping. I was put in this position because I act regardless of circumstances. It's so very hard, Sammy, but we'll have to mourn them later. We have bigger concerns." She switched views on the screen. A red warning light showed up around the words 'Proximity Alert'. On screen they could see several boats landing at the waters' edge, men with guns climbing ashore. "The gas bomb. We're surrounded."

"Go," Jim ordered. "We can worry about this mess remotely. Our forces are on the way."

"How do you know so much?" Eva asked, her voice suspicious.

"Because your sister breaks even more rules than you do, Director. She trusts her team and disseminates information she thinks may be of use. I'd very much like to get her back."

Eva secured the console, then turned to the bodies of her colleagues. "We should do something for them."

"You are," Jim replied. "You're honouring their memory by staying alive and bringing those responsible to justice. Mourn them when it's all over. Until then we have to find Directors Rosser and Pellirojo. Let's get back what remnants of the ARC Council we still can. Go."

Avenge them, Samantha prayed as she passed Io.

"I will," Io promised.

"Go, go, go," urged Jim.

Eva chucked him her rifle, which he caught one handed. "I daresay you can use this better than me."

"Director, from what I hear there's not much beyond your abilities." Jim checked the rifle over. "Workable. I'll take the rear. Sammy, you take our friend and your mom. Head back downstairs."

Samantha nodded and pushed forward, relieved to get away. "Watch out for Mom," she warned Io, slipping her mask down and leaving the remains of her extended family. The musty smelling tunnels were welcome after all the blood. She eagerly sought their depths, hoping to find another Aeon Fall terrorist on her way. Her rifle remained cold and unused. No enemies were there.

"So much for Karael coming to claim you," she sniped.

"They never expected resistance," Io replied. "We might understand the extent of their plans if we find the remaining directors, though it could be retaliation to your opposition."

"Nice way to make someone feel guilty."

"If there is one thing I have learned, it is desperate people take desperate measures. This is far from over."

As if to emphasise his point, there was a loud explosion from far behind them.

"Whoo! That went off with a bang!" Jim shouted as he came running up behind them. He took the lead.

"What did you do?"

"Thermite explosion," he grinned. "Jerry-rigged to blow when someone disturbed the door to the council chamber."

"That's awful," Eva said.

Io's frowned, shaking his head. "Did you have —"

"Enough," Samantha intervened. Not like we can do much beyond vengeance anyway."

"My thoughts exactly," Jim agreed. "They've had a cremation of sorts. Plus it will give them pause and us more time."

They moved briskly into the bowels of Chateau d'Yvoire, passing room after room including the fuse room. Samantha stole a glance as they passed. The remains of Oliver still smoked against one wall, what looked like tentacles hanging limp from his middle. Samantha shuddered and moved on.

The passageway opened into the underground dock where an agitated Charlotte Benson waited for them, a speedboat idling. "About time," she said. "Were you followed?"

"Not with the flesh still on their bones," Jim grinned. "We've got to go now."

"Where?" Charlotte asked. "Where are Aeon Fall's targets?"

"Spain and Sweden," Jim replied. "It didn't make any sense."

That was the key. It *didn't* make any sense. On a hunch Samantha retrieved the new crow book from her bag, along with a torch. She climbed into the boat while everybody discussed Aeon Fall and their strange plans. Using the flashlight she read, and gasped at a page she had never seen before. "It wasn't there in the other copy," she whispered.

"Do you have something?" Io asked.

"I have everything," Samantha replied. "This isn't about ARC. It's just posturing. It's about you, Ioviel."

His eyes widened. It was the first time she had ever used his full name.

The others stared at her. "Is there a nuclear power station in South Western England?"

"Hinkley Point C," Jim replied. "But the area's no more populated than the other two sites."

"It's near a point of massive significance to us though," Samantha replied, turning the book and shining the flashlight on the page. "Thornfalcon. It's a place, not an object."

Chapter Thirty-One

The journey across the lake was a quick one, surprisingly free of incident. The fire in Chateau d'Yvoire drew a response from the surrounding village, the inhabitants gathering outside the walls. Aeon Fall wouldn't have it all their way, that is if any of the ARC council survived. Above Samantha, Charlotte, Io, and Jim, the helicopters flew past, descending to an area around the headland.

"Response team," Charlotte shouted above the noise of the engine.

"Responding to what?" Samantha shouted back. "It's all over."

Gunfire erupted behind them, sparks flashing off the descending helicopter, as bullets bounced off the exterior.

"It's never over. There's more to ARC than the obvious, Sammy. You know our secrets have secrets."

Samantha snapped around at Charlotte's voice. It was a low growl. "Yeah, she said, "and so does Porter Rockwell. We aren't being chased, now. We're playing catch up, being squeezed between Rockwell and his hound. Let's get on a plane, catch our breath. There's too much coincidence here for them not to be going to England."

* * *

They landed at the Bellevue jetty and Jim hustled them all into one of the ARC vehicles. In minutes they were in a smaller ARC jet where Carrot waited for them.

"Captain, has anybody been through here recently?" Eva asked.

"Yes, Director. Directors Steadman and the young Guyomard took a larger plane." The pilot frowned. "They neither logged a flight plan nor mentioned their destination. It was most irregular."

"Did they have anybody else with them?"

"There were several others. I couldn't tell who, but a couple looked like women. They were in a rush."

"Well it is dark," Jim said, reminding them it was now the middle of the night. "You're all aware of the protocols, yes?"

"Director Scott is acting Head of the Council until all department heads can be convened to ratify her appointment or replace her," Carrot answered, her face hard. "What happened over there?"

"Thorsten Guyomard and Alexander Steadman are renegades," Sammy said, her voice trembling. "They killed most of the Council and took Clare and Tricia. We're going to get them back. Get us airborne, Captain. Head for England."

"Bristol airport," Jim added. "There are hangars at smaller airports like Exeter but Bristol has better storage facilities and I've the feeling we'll need supplies on this journey. Plus, if Sammy's right, perhaps we don't want them to see us coming."

Jim sat opposite Samantha, flipping open a laptop. "Power grids and the Nuclear Regulatory Commission," he said without looking up. "I can keep an eye on all three sites from here. If anything happens, we'll know who guessed correctly, and who looks foolish."

"I didn't hear any of you disagreeing to my assertion," she replied.

"That's because you've got good judgment, girl. Now why don't you tell us what prompted you to be so certain about a previously unmentioned power station—one with the latest technology and safeguards?"

"Porter Rockwell knows this is Io's way home. Io, tell Jim what you need for the Phaethon Stone," Samantha prompted.

"The ashes of a righteous angel," he replied, hefting the small velvet pouch Eva had given him in the castle. "A corrupt source of power untouchable by man."

"And we're looking at nuclear power. That's pretty clean." Jim blinked. "Unless there's a reactor overload."

"And a full-on meltdown," Samantha finished for him. "Corium."

"I need to be a fallen angel. My situation is good enough for Karael so, like it or not, I must accept the truth of my condition. Finally I need the grave of a fallen demon. Leviathan."

"And with that, I give you Thornfalcon, in Somerset, England." Samantha turned the book around, showing the sketching of a church. "There's an account here of a battle between two mighty beings, one cutting the other down amidst the ruin of the church."

"But that can't be Leviathan?" Eva questioned.

"It is," Io replied. "Karael returned and reported the battle and the fallen one's identity."

"I'm telling you, that can't be," Eva pressed. "I've been to Hell. I've seen Leviathan's army, even been chased by his own floating citadel."

"But did you see Leviathan himself?"

Eva blinked. "I saw many things down there. What did he look like?"

"He was young by angel standards, one of the last formed by our Father."

"You mean He's not up there, churning out angels?" Charlotte said.

"Not for a very long time. The Cherubim and Seraphim, who surround Him at all times, succour him. Some think the relationship different, that they are drawing from Him. It's been aeons since a new angel was born. Leviathan took the form of a serpent mostly. He followed Satan and descended. However unlike my other brethren, he became distracted on Earth and dwelled there for a time. Karael was sent to despatch Leviathan. When he returned, he had a fire in his eyes. He was filled with fervor. Leviathan vanquished, he said. We decided Karael's purpose was such. The hound of God, some called him."

"Yeah but leashed to which master?" Jim asked. "Either way, if Thornfalcon's your target, and they blow Hinkley C, it will likely destroy the entire region."

"Or they want to get him there because it's close by, and the threat of so much devastation makes it too hard to avoid," Samantha said. "Remember, he's an angel. If he can carry corium, he can walk through irradiated fields. But he's also been exposed to humans—our frailties, our complicated nature."

"Is that how you see it, Io?" asked Charlotte. "Are you one of us now?"

"To know humanity is to love it," Io replied, his eyes sad. "By placing myself in this position, by saving Samantha and coming to know her, and you, I have come to terms with a truth. Heaven should be there for mankind, not keep itself separate, aloof. There should be symbiosis, but all I see is the parasitic nature of our existence, feeding off pure souls as they ascend."

"Is that what you do?" Eva asked. "I thought you were the guardians of those who experienced the rapture and ascended?"

"Everybody has their place in Heaven. But by being there, they emit a force."

"The same as Hell then," Eva decided. "They tap souls too. The only difference is sometimes the souls go rotten there. Do you have corrupted souls in Heaven?"

Io looked down. "They are called Pariah. I'd rather not speak about them."

"Okay well, what would you speak about? The Godmissile? Thorsten was pretty set on getting answers out of you. What is it? A weapon to destroy earth?"

"Aeon Fall want access to Heaven to set the Godmissile in motion. It is not a weapon as you would understand it. Not directly. It's a permanent gateway through which all realms become one. It's Heaven's final strike against Hell where all of the Heavenly Host is unleashed."

"This gateway, it doesn't happen to draw its power from a dark planet, does it?" Eva asked.

Io jumped at the question. "There is no way you could know that."

She smiled. "Unless I've stood on the edge of a trap designed to keep it out of this realm and watched as an angel sealed the breach. That's what Tartarus is, the Hell end of the Godmissile. And twenty years ago they nearly opened it by breaching the gateway from beyond. If the Godmissile opened from that end, would it have the same effect?"

Io was silent for a moment, as if there were no words for the gravity of the situation. He breathed in deeply, answering, "Yes."

Eva shook her head. "This isn't a beginning. The threat never ended. Don't you see? They just changed their line of attack. Crustallos knows this."

When her mother received blank looks, Samantha elaborated. "The thing beyond the deepest pit of Hell. The inhabitant of planet Nibiru."

Io stared. "You know its name."

"And I'm not the first, am I Mom?"

"Nibiru was the name used by the leader of the cult we found in Finland, on Lake Bodom," Eva continued. "They wanted to take me away, hide me somewhere safe so I could give birth to Nina ... Nina." Eva looked at her phone. "We could do with everybody we have now. I'd like my family together once more."

"Can't you call her back in?" Carrot asked, returning from the cockpit, she sat beside Samantha. "There are protocols, yes?"

"Nina agreed to go deep cover," Eva replied. "And now Rockwell has her. We just have to keep going."

* * *

Samantha watched the mountains pass below, the peaks stabbing through the cloud line. Disrupted weather meant several detours, and most of their company chose to catch up on sleep. She was weary but not enough to close her eyes and forget the magnitude of what they were flying into.

Io sat across from her, watching the views pass by. "It's strange, knowing I have to rely on mankind to allow me to do what should come naturally."

Samantha had no answer. She gave a sympathetic smile, her lips thin.

"Is there any more in that book?" he asked.

Samantha opened the crow book to the new pages. "Just history. Nothing of use. Thornefalcon was an Anglo-Saxon village from the twelfth century. The church was rebuilt in eighteen eighty-two by an architect, Benjamin Edmund Ferrey. The book doesn't say why it was rebuilt. Shortly after that Ferrey embarked on his journey, but not until he carved a map of the church's location into the church walls."

"That doesn't make sense," Jim said. "Why carve a map of the church in the church?"

"I guess we'll find out. He goes on to describe his journey to Darwin, Australia and how he met a Russian Anthropologist named Nicholai Miklukho-Maklai, who took a great interest in his theories on bird divination. He also met…" She paused, looking at her mother. "He also met a man called LeClerc. Edmund named one of the patterns after his home, which intrigued LeClerc. The Aussie also wanted to know why Ferrey had gone abroad after becoming such a distinguished gentleman as an architect."

"…LeClerc? The co-founder of ARC?" Charlotte asked, sounding surprised. "I thought they were abroad in Africa back then? You sure it's the same guy?"

Samantha nodded. "We're in a plane with an angel headed toward a site where a demon supposedly died. Yeah, I believe this is the real guy. You know why?"

"Because following these clues is a not-so-subtle method of finding our way into danger?" Jim asked.

"And because, Samantha added, "it's the only way to save Tricia and Aunt Clare. You think they've been taken on a whim? They're bait. Thorsten and Alexander are working with Aeon Fall and they're working for a demon. We're all so used to ARC pulling the strings here, nobody's able to react when control is removed. Nobody except us. I'm gonna miss them all. Even stuffy Swanson. But we do their memory a disservice if we don't finish this."

They all gazed at Samantha in silence.

Incensed, Samantha said, "That's the ARC way isn't it? Get the job done, worry about the casualties once it's finished. Well that's horse crap. Burying your emotions is bad for you." She looked pointedly at her mother as she spoke. "It can fester and cause crazy decisions if left too long."

"A rational head—" began Jim.

"A rational head?" Samantha interrupted. "You lot aren't rational. You're frikkin' robots! If Aunt Clare were here, she'd tell you all that logic may be good, but instinct can be better."

"And what does your instinct tell you at this very moment?" Charlotte asked.

Samantha slammed the book shut. "That we're walking into an Aeon Fall inspired trap."

"Any suggestions?" There was a strong tone of approval in Charlotte's voice.

"We do what they least expect. Armed with this knowledge we spring it."

"That could cost many innocent lives," Io cautioned.

"Yeah, were any rational person to attempt what we're about to undertake. But we're not going to play their game; we'll walk right in and assume control of the power station."

"You think you can stop this?" Io didn't look convinced.

"No," Samantha answered, "but you can. And they're counting on you to do it. They're also counting on Karael to defeat you. But we aren't going to let that happen."

"Why not?"

"Because apparently Charlotte's been stashing all manner of Hell-tech in caches over the world and we're about to land next to one."

Charlotte's mouth dropped open. "How did you know?"

Samantha grinned. "It's logical. You happen to have several pieces of developmental technology just at the time when they're needed most. You ask to land at an airport other than the strip closest to your boss, who is suspected of being kidnapped, and for whom you should be tearing apart the world. And worst, you're in no way panicking about her absence. It's as if you wanted her to be taken."

"She's your daughter no doubt," Charlotte said to Eva.

Eva inclined her head. "Told you. Sammy, don't think that we don't care. You're very perceptive. We're torn up inside. Devastated. Swanson, Gila, John, all the others. Losses beyond incalculable. But we can't stop focussing. That's where you come in. It's your role to be our emotional lightning rod. It took me a decade to understand, but I used to be that lightening rod to the Council before you were born. It's not a fun role, being constantly exposed like a raw nerve. Yet, you give us perspective. Just keep doing what you're doing."

"What are you doing?" Io asked her. Being an angel, it was clear he was detached from the conversation and unable to keep up.

"I'm winging it, Io," she replied. "Mostly I'm trying to work out a way to save us, my aunt, Tricia, you, Nina, and basically the whole world. Tell me if I'm wrong, here. If a demon sets foot in Heaven, that's bad?"

"Heaven would become corrupted and the natural order would cease to exist. Heaven would become Hell, and the reverse. There would be no purgatory, no sorting and cleansing of the damned and the worthy. Souls would become lost."

"Who would benefit most from that?"

"Something not from this realm," Eva said. "Something banished. Sammy that's brilliant."

"And if the Godmissile were forced from the other end?" She continued to ask Io.

"Retaliation. The Heavenly Host would pour into hell for one massive strike against Satan."

"Putting all of Heaven and Hell within touching distance of Tartarus," she concluded. "Somebody's preparing to finish the work Iuvart started before I was born."

"Porter Rockwell—" began Charlotte.

"Is a dupe, Samantha finished. "He's making noise, but what's he really done? Shown up exactly where someone sent him because we were there? Made a few broadcasts on television? That Aeon Fall soldier said a woman was in charge. He said 'her'. This is a bigger job than a distraction and I kind of like my reality." Samantha smiled at Io as she spoke. "We're gonna find the answer and put a stop to this."

"And how exactly are you going to walk into the middle of a heavily guarded nuclear facility such as Hinkley C?" Jim asked. "If you know, would you mind telling us?"

Samantha pulled three passes from her bag, the words 'AIEA' in bold down one side. "With these. You're now all members of the Agence Internationale de L'Énergie Atomique."

Chapter Thirty-Two

Every step was a gamble, Samantha thought as she gazed out the small window. She long ago admitted to herself that she didn't have a clue what she was doing. The city of Bristol shone with a million yellow lights in the night sky to the north. These people depended on her success, although they surely didn't know it.

The plane passed over a ribbon of traffic winding south, and then touched down with a bump in the darkness. "One angel and five people against the world," she said as the plane taxied to a stop.

"Sorry guys, the runway's blocked," Carrot called from the cockpit. "We're gonna have to walk through the terminal."

A hand took Samantha's as she strained to see out the window. Warm, firm, reassuring, Io held her. "It will be enough."

Samantha snorted. "Forgive me if I don't have your confidence." She turned to Charlotte, Io still holding her hand. "Can we get over to the hangar without drawing too much attention?"

"Of course," Charlotte's tone indicated this wasn't an issue. "We're just another group of tourists."

Samantha looked around the cabin. "You might want to take a second look. Our equipment and mannerisms scream 'Look at me, I'm up to something'. Try at least to look casual."

Charlotte nodded. "Will do."

Surprised by the meek acceptance of her request, Samantha looked back at Io.

"You're special," he said. "A leader. Unique."

Saying nothing, she smiled and stood, relinquishing Io's hand with great reluctance.

The party of five disembarked; Charlotte and Jim lugging heavy suitcases until Io intervened carry them as if they were light as air. He grinned and laughed along with Jim's forced attempts at humor. The dynamic changed as a more relaxed group mingled with the tourist crowd, thinning out and eventually becoming an elongated line of individuals. Samantha decided it was probably better that way. Less conspicuous.

"Scotty," a man with a British accent called out. Samantha turned sharply, losing sight of her mother.

A tall man in a beanie hat and red plaid jacket hurried past her, waving at a boy in the distance. "Scott! Keep hold of Jay. Don't move from there!"

A sweet-faced girl with long red hair waved to the boy, who was maybe thirteen years old. He hustled the girl to seats at the side of the walkway. Evidently satisfied, the man turned back. "I'll go back that way. You wait here and watch for Sammy."

"Excuse me?" Samantha said, presuming he was talking to her.

The stranger focussed on her for a moment, confused. Then he broke out into a smile. "I'm sorry, love. Not you. My wife over there."

Samantha turned to see a petite redhead, a slightly taller version of the little girl with the boy, frowning up and down the walkway, a long black coat folded over her arm. As she turned a collection of keyrings jingled on the bag she wore. "Well I don't know where she went. She was there one second. I turned around and that's it. Gone."

"Keep an eye on the other two. I'll retrace our steps."

"Don't get lost yourself," the redhead called.

The man glared back at her.

"Can I help?" Samantha asked.

With the resigned look of a woman used to chaos, she said, "Just desserts if they get lost. I tell them time and again to stay close, but they just have to mess about."

"What does your daughter look like?" Samantha asked.

"Denim jacket, no sleeves, red white and blue skirt like the USA flag, and worn black cowboy boots. She's got curly strawberry blonde hair, just like yours. She's eleven."

"And she's called Sammy?"

"Yes. You don't have to do this, you know."

"Anything for a fellow Sammy," Samantha said, her voice jovial. Plus, she thought, it would help disguise her true mission.

"Wait here. I'll see if I can spot your daughter."

Samantha moved through the crowd, looking for a small cowgirl type. Travellers bustled past, knocking Samantha about as she tried to focus. A flash of red, white and blue by a door caught her attention across the walkway and Samantha followed. Pushing through the door, Samantha found a girl, tall enough to almost be a teenager, searching around on the floor, worn black boots sticking out from under a stars and stripes skirt.

"You okay, love?" Samantha asked.

The girl looked up, her face a mask of panic. "My earring came out and I'm looking for it. Dad gave it to me as a present."

"The man in the red coat? You're Sammy?"

The girl looked pleased and suspicious at the same time. "Yeah."

"My name's Samantha, just like you. Your mom with the red hair's out there worried about you. I think they'd be happier to see you safe than worry about an earring." She reached out and took Sammy's hand.

As she did, the girl's eyes grew dark and focussed. Sammy stopped and stared up at her, holding her gaze, hands dropping to her sides. "Don't be afraid."

"I'm sorry?"

But the girl seemed to not hear her response. "They will find out who you really are. Sooner or later; it does not matter when they find out, nor how. They will fear you no matter your intent. What matters is what you do with your power. Your fate is balanced on a knife edge. You will use it for good at first. Beware of the day you can no longer distinguish. Good and evil are the same beast. When you're clouded remember the earring." The girl opened her hand, a crystal teardrop earring resting on her palm.

"Sammy!" A man's voice shouted from out on the walkway.

Samantha turned to the door, pulling it open. She turned back to gather up her namesake and found herself alone. The hallway was empty. She opened the door wide to see a young girl engulfed in the arms of her relieved but still angry father in red plaid.

"You found her then?" Samantha said, emerging onto the walkway.

"Just came running down the hall, like the dopey little thing doesn't have a care in the world," the father replied.

His daughter gave him a sarcastic smirk. "Your face is the only thing that's dopey."

He rolled his eyes. "That's what I have to live with. I'm doomed I tell you, doomed. Miss, thanks for your help."

"Nice to have met you, Sammy," Samantha called after the retreating family.

The girl turned her head, with an uncertain smile.

"Crystal earrings … I really *am* losing it."

* * *

Dodging the crowded departure lounge, A strong hand grabbed Samantha, spinning her around.

"You really do have a tendency to wander," Jim said, watching the crowds behind her. "No one's following you though, so that's good. This way." He showed her to a side door where the others waited.

"I swear we could lose you in an open field," her mother said.

"I thought you'd be at the hangar by now," Samantha replied.

"Io made us wait for you." Eva smiled at the angel, who continued watching past them, oblivious to Eva's approval.

"I can feel a wrongness in the air. A disturbance. Samantha, what just happened to you?"

They will find out who you really are. The words of the girl came back to her.

"I was helping a family look for their lost daughter. It's a nightmare out there."

"You are closer to the truth than you think," Io warned. "All of those people outside are scared. They can't wait to get as far away from here as possible, but they don't know why."

"I know why," said Jim, letting the door go. "Because they're fifty miles away from a potential nuclear disaster. They're sensible."

"No, they feel a more profound loss. Their connection to God is fading. Humanity is becoming truly alone. We need to show them there is something bigger in their world."

"Io, you can't force belief on people." Samantha urged him forward. "It's a decision they come to on their own—the core of what belief is."

"You believe," Io countered.

"It's safe to say we have a somewhat unique perspective on the situation," Eva replied, flashing her credentials at a guard. He frowned for a second, then opened a door onto the runway. A plane taxied by, huge twin jet engines whining as it was propelled into take-off position. She led them along a path marked with diagonal yellow lines.

"Mom's right," Samantha said. "If you were to go in there, show off your strength, and pronounce the existence of God, most people would look at you as if you were crazy. You could push people further away—doing Aeon Fall's job for them."

* * *

A Light rain began as Eva led them away from the main terminal to a hangar on the edge of the complex. The countryside was obscured where the runway ended and the hill on which they stood dropped away. A glimmer of daylight on the horizon reminded Samantha she had gone another night without sleep, but the rain was welcome—refreshing and cool on her face. She closed her eyes, savoring the sensation as a warm hand took hers, leading into the hangar. Samantha knew it was Io, and that he would guide and protect her wherever they went.

The inside space was typical ARC—large and dark, with the faint taste of chemical cleaner in the air. Charlotte went straight to a locked door, keying in the combination on the sensor. "Time to choose your poison," she announced, opening the door.

One door became two, sliding forward and out to the sides. Lights blinked on, revealing an arsenal: guns, knives with oddly wired hilts, belts of grenades, rockets and a launcher.

"Ready for the end of the world much?" Samantha murmured.

"Absolutely," Charlotte agreed, reaching to unhook a coil of the same rope she had used to bind Karael. "This is militarised stuff. ARC's been developing new materials, *and* a new power source that might one day replace nuclear energy. Eva's armour is amazing. The advances in retro-engineering have doubled, possibly even tripled in the last twenty years."

"But you've got no armor here," Samantha countered.

"What do you think you're wearing?" Jim ran a finger down the sleeve of Samantha's combat suit. "It may not be self-regenerating, but this suit was one of the most complex adaptions produced from your mom's armor. Nina was trialling one for us before she disappeared. This will deflect most of your more mundane weapons, and has the potential to keep you clean if exposed to radioactivity."

"The potential?"

"The suit was never exposed to high levels before, but it absorbed the levels we tested, making it more resistant. We all have them."

"Well we aren't going to be walking away from this because of a suit. What do you have in the way of a layout for Hinkley C?"

In the center of the hanger was a large black table where Jim touched the surface. It began to glow blue, resolving into lines and words. "Blueprints! What do you want to know?"

"First and foremost, any weaknesses?"

One press of a button and the blueprints rose into a three-dimensional hologram of the nuclear reactor from the inside. "What you're looking at is the core of Hinkley C. The reactor is designed to be efficient and well-protected, with multiple redundancies in case of any system failure. That being said, nothing's perfect—materials can have flaws, construction can be hasty. In earlier reactors, precursors to this one, the concrete base under the core was found to have cracks, and the steel reinforcement within the base was incorrectly distributed. In a French reactor they found the containment liner had warped at the edges leaving gaps."

"Is that enough to cause a disaster? How big a gap are we talking?"

"Millimetres," Jim said, leaning into the hologram. "Enough for a serious leak. However, if Aeon Fall doesn't care about finesse, they might go after the cooling pipes. If there's a failure in the primary coolent circuit, the reactors will become critical within an hour. Of course we might be overthinking this. Rockwell could just punch a hole in the shielding."

"With what?" Samantha crossed the room to the weapons closet, pulling out a small dagger. She approached the table once more, flipping the knife up in the air. "You don't exactly stab a hole in such comprehensive protection."

The knife spun, arcing down to the surface. Jim let out a yell and dived forward, just missing the knife, which buried itself hilt deep in the table. The projector went blank.

"Helltech," Jim growled, pulling at the hilt. The blade glowed blue as it came free. "You should be careful how you handle such a weapon. Imagine what it could do to flesh."

As surprised as she was shocked at the effectiveness of the blade, Samantha stepped back. "I'm sorry."

"Imagine how this would work on an angel," Jim added.

"Please don't," Io said. "I would very much like to avoid being a test subject again."

"You got everything you need from the toys?" Charlotte slid the doors of the weapon closet shut.

"I think it might be safer for everyone if I didn't carry weapons," Samantha decided. "I might do more damage than good. Words are the only weapon we have now. If Aeon Fall are already at Hinkley Point, we may be too late."

"If," her mother repeated. "You think they're gonna miss out once more on the opportunity to trap Ioviel?"

"I think their plan is one borne of desperation, Mom. We have Metatron's ashes. They still need them. If Karael has fallen, did he do it out of choice or was he forced like Io?"

"Karael was not forced," Io said, his voice thick with emotion. "My brother would not choose Hell over his brethren."

"And yet, he's the lapdog of a demon," Eva countered. "Ioviel, there's an element to this whole situation we haven't yet worked out."

"I think it's becoming clearer by the minute," Charlotte said, turning her laptop toward them.

On the screen Porter Rockwell appeared, standing by two women with hoods over their heads, their arms bound behind them. "The time has come to decide how you really want to play the game, Eva," he growled, pulling the hoods off of the two women, "or lose the remaining ARC Council." Both terrified, Tricia Pellirojo and Clare Rosser stared in helpless panic at the screen, their mouths gagged. "You know where to find us. Bring your angel, I'll bring mine."

The camera zoomed out, revealing a white panelled room with banks of instrumentation. Behind them most of the lights flashed red.

"Private transmission?" Eva asked, watching the now-frozen screen.

"No," Charlotte replied. "Aeon Fall broadcast that on every major channel in this country."

"We've got a problem," Jim added. "Hinkley C has just reported an emergency shutdown on its main reactor. The primary cooling system isn't responding."

"They've made the event public," Samantha said. "Time to go save the world, Io."

Chapter Thirty-Three

They will let me inside wearing a lab coat, a combat suit and a rucksack?
Samantha wondered. She looked herself over as she climbed into the
small black helicopter sitting outside the hangar. Her disguise didn't
exactly shout 'Office of Nuclear Regulation', but it would have to do.
Gaining access with her mother, Jim, and Io while Carrot and Charlotte
remained outside was the best she could do. Only four passes out of
the original five were in Nina's drawer.

"You should have faith in yourself," Io said as he climbed in beside
her. "You look fine."

"That wasn't a prayer," Sammy replied, her tone a warning. She
touched the sheathed blade Charlotte had insisted she wear despite
vociferous protests.

"It doesn't matter," he admitted. "I can choose to hear your
thoughts."

"Can you choose not to?"

Io inclined his head. "If you so wish." His tone was not offended but
it was clear he was nonplussed with the idea.

"What's this?" Jim asked as he squeezed in opposite. "Reading minds
now, Io?"

"If you pray to him, he can hear your thoughts," Samantha informed
the team.

"Could be useful," Carrot shouted as she brought the helicopter to life, the rotors above quickly blurred into the early morning. "Does it work the other way?"

"Yes," Samantha replied before Io could answer.

"Awesome," Carrot replied. "Sort of like two-way angel radio. How do I sign up?"

"Just offer me a prayer," he said. "It's that simple."

* * *

By the time they were airborne, rising over the hilly terrain south of Bristol, the five of them were all tuned into Io and testing the limits of his talents.

"So can I speak directly to Charlotte?" Jim asked. "Say if I pray to her through you, or include both names in the same prayer?"

"Possibly through an angel of exceptional power, a conduit such as Metatron. His great task was to listen to the pleas of mankind and to speak where it was deemed necessary. I am but a warrior."

Samantha zoned out from the chatter, watching the land flash by beneath them, the patchwork quilt of farmland interspersed with tiny villages. "There's too many," she said.

"People?" Her mother asked.

"Yeah. These small villages are everywhere. One person affected by a meltdown would be one person too many but those below us don't know what's about to happen. They live on the doorstep of potential tragedy."

"We all do, love. But it's not a tragedy if it doesn't happen. It's our job to stop this and protect these people from ever knowing."

"Too late for that, Director," said Jim, pointing. A ribbon of lights shone across the ground from a three-lane motorway, the vehicles not appearing to move. "Somebody's been putting two and two together."

"Carrot, get us there as fast as this bird'll take us," Eva commanded.

"I'm on it, Boss," Carrot replied indicating she was already doing all she could. "We've got to cross a bay to the South then we're at Hinkley. Maybe ten minutes."

"Bring us in from the seaward side," said Samantha. "Less likelihood of birds." She glanced at Io, who nodded.

"If we can avoid calling Karael's attention down on me, he's restricted to mundane travel."

"You're assuming of course that he's behind us," said Charlotte.

Samantha watched for the power station to appear. Just what exactly were they flying into?

* * *

The helicopter followed the line of the coast and soon a series of massive grey concrete buildings filled the immediate horizon.

"Hinkley Point," said Jim, pointing.

"That looks like more than the one reactor from the blueprints," Samantha observed. "I count at least three."

"The two on the right are the new EDF reactors, and our goal. To the left sit the remains of Hinkley B, the old magnox reactors. They're being slowly decommissioned."

"Which one do we land at?"

"Neither. There's a landing pad at the control building in the middle. That's our goal. The rest is up to you. ARC isn't exactly on the best of terms with the world currently, so you'd better be convincing."

The helicopter touched down in front of a horseshoe-shaped building and instantly Samantha slid open the door. Outside, a stream of people were hurrying away from the plant.

"You heard Jim," Io warned her. "You can't just walk in."

"That's exactly what I'm gonna do." She approached the security gate where two guards in brown uniform barred their way and held up her accreditation so they could read it. "International Atomic Energy Agency," she called across the intervening space. "Open up, you've got a problem."

"We know. Is this all of you?" The taller of the guards checked a small black meter and placed it in the pocket of his shirt.

Samantha wondered, *was he expecting them?*

"Four of us are coming in. Two more in the bird who will remain there."

"I'll take your word for it, Miss." The guard responded.

So far, the gates remain closed to them.

"As it is, the guard continued, "your colleague is already here and in the control center, overseeing the situation. If you would follow me, I'll take you to her."

The guard turned away and led Samantha and her mother past the gate into the control centre with Io and Jim trailing back a few steps. Samantha shared a confused glance with her mother. *Her? It wasn't supposed to be that easy,* she thought, turning her head.

Behind her, Io had a faint smile on his face. A moment later his expression was mirrored by Eva and Jim.

Your mother agrees with you and says to be wary. This is suspicious.

Samantha nodded without turning her head, remaining intent on following the guard into the complex.

Three sets of stairs and countless heavy reinforced doors later, the party entered a room with a half dozen large screens on the front wall above banks of computer desks full of studious looking technicians. Those who turned from their screens dotted heavily with red had one universal facial expression: Panic.

"Okay, talk." Her mother switched to boss-mode in an instant. "What's going on and what do you need to solve the problem?"

"Well, Director," said a very familiar female voice from amidst the technicians, "it seems we have an impending nuclear disaster on our hands, unless you can summon a miracle."

Samantha stopped, mid step. Her breath caught. "Nina?"

With a flash of platinum blond hair, one of the technicians stood, turning toward them. "Mom, Sammy. I'm glad you could make it. Do you have any ideas?"

Eva looked to Samantha. "It's your party."

A million questions popped into Samantha's head. Why was her sister here, now? Why the radio silence only for her to appear in front of them, unsurprised? Should she be relieved or panicking? Where was Rockwell?

"What's the current problem?" Samantha braved the intervening space to briefly clasp her sister in a hug. *This is a trap.*

"I see you remembered the badges."

Samantha regarded her accreditation for a moment. "Looks like we didn't need it with you here." She examined the nearest monitor. Vertical lines at the top of a reactor core schematic flashed red. "The control rods?"

"They're all locked out of position. The nuclear reaction is approaching its upper limit. The cooling generators are at maximum. Danger is imminent, not immediate. But if something were to happen to the pumps we go from dangerous to potentially catastrophic in minutes."

"How was this done?" Samantha led her sister away from the group of technicians. "You're supposed to be deep under cover. You're supposed to be imprisoned! Nobody's heard from you in days and now you're here?"

"It's Aeon Fall. They're everywhere. Porter Rockwell, sent me here to infiltrate and interrupt nuclear facilities. He wanted you to believe I was being held to make you desperate. We're all bargaining chips, Sis. Disrupting Hinkley Point was a challenge for them, but I was able to override any irregular commands they entered from a console nearby. There are so many redundancies and backups the place could run itself. It wasn't going well for them until Aunt Clare turned up with some of the ARC Council in tow."

"Clare was here?" Eva asked.

"Yeah, only a couple of hours ago. They had the whole place on lockdown, I mean an army of guys with guns throughout this building. Clare and Thorsten Guyomard went outside and attached a device to the exterior of the reactor shielding. Moments later the control rods were removed from the reactor core, and it went into overdrive. Rockwell blamed me for sabotaging their efforts and left me here with the facility staff. He's taken Aunt Clare and gone. We never saw them again." She pushed at a mouse on the desk. The arrow on the corresponding screen failed to move. "Everything's locked." Nina wiped the perspiration from her brow with the sleeve of her lab coat. "Whatever they did froze the entire facility. People are fleeing, but when this place goes, no amount of running will save anybody. I've stayed here to try and reverse this. It's not proving easy."

"Then we go outside," Eva decided. "We see what they've done and reverse it."

"No." It was Io speaking. "Going out to the reactor is too dangerous for you."

"The reactor's shielded by metres of concrete," Jim said. "You could walk across the roof and be fine."

"But not when someone's been outside tampering with the core and done all this." Samantha waved her hand in the direction of the screen. "Io, you know what this could mean?"

"I do," the angel replied. "I'm ready." He checked the pouch containing Metatron's ashes. "Director, please could I have my brother's feather? I need all of him, just to be certain. The Phaethon can be a fickle object. I will need my brother's sword, too."

Jim opened the case containing the silver blade, which glowed as Io picked it up. Eva pulled the feather from her bag and passed it over.

"Stay here," Io warned them as he sheathed the sword on his back. "No matter what happens."

"You'll be killed," Nina cautioned him. "No man can survive the radiation. Wait—" Nina turned to Samantha. "Sammy? Mom? Who is this guy? What's he doing with the sword?"

A section of the main screen began to flash red and yellow, an alarm coinciding with each red flash.

"The heat alarm!" One of the technicians shouted. "One, no make that two of the cooling pumps have failed. We need to get out of here. Now."

"Io, go," Samantha urged.

"Where?"

"I'll direct you." Samantha stared at him until he grasped her concept. Angel Radio.

Io nodded. "Let me back out," he said to one of the security guards, who looked to Nina.

"Do it," she said. "Sammy, what's that crazy guy think he's up to?"

"Saving everybody here. You just need to tell me where Clare planted the device."

Nina's eyes narrowed. "Up high. As best we can guess where the dome at the top of the reactor shielding meets the superstructure of the fuel building. There are ladders to get aloft. We think they met a helicopter up there."

Samantha communicated this to Io. By the looks on their faces, her companions were doing the same.

"There," Jim pointed at a screen and everybody crowded round. The stink of sweat from the nervous technicians was overwhelming. Strangely, Nina appeared serene, and happy to observe.

On the screen as if gravity was no restriction, Io scampered up a ladder. *Samantha, you need to get everybody away from this facility. What I must do here will put you all at risk. If the melding fails, you'll all be exposed.*

He reached the top of the ladder and began to traverse the rooftop of the fuel building. *Those people are terrified, and rightly so. I could sense the fear in every one of them. All except your sister. I can't read her.*

Samantha took a moment to assess her sister. Nina appeared the same as always. Beautiful, the centre of attention, and driven with it. She focussed on a screen showing Io making his way around the edge of the reactor shielding.

A second alarm sounded.

"Pump two's gone," announced one of the technicians. "Backups have failed. If we're getting out we go now."

"No!" Nina shouted. "He'll do it. He will." Her voice was animated to the point of excitement. What did she know?

Io, is everything all right up there? Nina's very insistent that you'll find the cause. She's swearing you'll do it.

And now I know why.

Samantha shouldered her way through to the screen. Ahead of Io a flock of birds gathered on the rooftop. "Crows," she gasped. "Oh no."

"Yes," Nina hissed in triumph. "Now he's ready."

"He's ready?" Eva repeated. "You know who he is?"

Nina turned to them, with a look of such malevolence on her face everybody took a step back.

"Clare didn't do any of this," accused Eva. "You did. You're not Nina. What have you done with my daughter? My sister?"

Nina tipped her head to one side. "Nina isn't home, whore of Satan." Her voiced was mocking, darkly sarcastic. "Nina's hidden safely away. Your sister is not long for this life."

On the screen, the birds began to form a familiar shape, a glyph.

Get out of there!

I cannot, Io replied. *The reactor is still going to explode. Get to safety. Get away from your sister.*

The glyph was complete, the birds unmoving.

Nina pressed a button on her console. "Porter, are you ready?"

"Yes, Mistress," came the reply. "We're in position."

"Mistress," Samantha hissed.

"Now it begins," Nina sang in triumph.

"What are you doing?" One of the technicians asked, attempting to access her workstation.

Nina grabbed the technician with one hand, sneered and hurled him across the room where he slammed into the wall with the crunch of broken bones. He slid to the floor, unmoving, eyes rolled up in his head and blood running freely from his nose. Several people screamed in alarm.

"Why?" Eva asked.

"Because you denied my Father his return and now I'm going to use your angel to open a door to Heaven."

Her mother's face paled. "But Madden is ... Oh my God."

"Your God is as good as dead," Nina taunted them. "Once we open the doorway, eternal Crustallos will return."

Many of the people in the room turned to her, their faces filled with fear.

"That's just theoretical," said one of the technicians. "The technology doesn't exist."

A slow smile crept across Nina's face. "Want to know how impotent you are, Sammy? Say hello to your sister."

Nina's face changed as Samantha watched. It sagged, becoming flaccid as another personality took residence. Hard eyes became fearful, a confidant demeanour shrank with the weight of imprisonment.

"Sammy? Mom?"

Eva took a step forward. "Nina?"

Nina began to cry. "He's got me trapped. I've been a prisoner in my own body."

"How long since they did this to you?"

A haunted look came over Nina. "Forever. He was always there. Everything I've done. Everything learned. All him. He taunts me endlessly."

"Nina," Samantha asked, "who is 'he'?"

"His name's Stektes. He's a minion of Crustallos." Nina appeared to panic. "He's coming back. Mom I can feel him. He knows what we are, Sammy. Help me. Get him out of me."

The frightened eyes hardened.

"Nina," Eva shouted into her face. "Nina, hold on!"

"She can see you. She can feel your frustration. I promise you will never hear her words again. Don't," Stektes said to Jim, who had moved to tackle her. "I don't want to kill you. My master has need of you. Of you all."

"We won't serve a demon," Jim spat back.

"Who said anything about servitude?" Stektes taunted. "He promises eternal glory. You just have to survive the imminent apocalypse."

What sounded like a jet closed in from outside, the vibration rumbling up through Samantha's feet, shaking the whole building.

Io!

I see him, Sammy. I'm ready.

Chapter Thirty-Four

The roaring intensified and Samantha found her screams drowned out as she tried to protect her ears. When she thought her head was ready to explode, the roaring turned into the boom of a colossal impact.

Thick, reinforced windows shattered, spraying those nearby with glass. Everybody was thrown to the floor by the force of the shockwave.

Samantha was the first to her feet, helping her mother up.

Eva mouthed some words and Samantha realised she had lost her hearing. She frowned, concentrating on her mother's mouth.

"What happened?"

She shrugged, then noticed one of the monitors was still functioning. Turning her mother toward the monitor she pointed.

On the screen was the last place Io had been standing before the impact. A hole about ten feet across was filled with billowing smoke.

Jim, now up on his feet, saw the screen. He looked up to the series of monitors above them. All were dark, many were cracked. He grabbed a keyboard and started typing. A reboot, Samantha figured.

The screens glowed red as they came back online. In the centre, a schematic of the reactor core flashed several shades of red. Many of the fuel rods glowed yellow within the diagram. Underneath the words 'Core Breach' flashed repeatedly.

Around them, people were stirring. As each rose, bleeding and broken, they caught sight of the screens. Many, in silence, put their hand to their mouth.

Samantha grabbed a pen and wrote the words 'Prevailing winds. Get them out. South.' as fast as she could manage.

He nodded and relayed the message to the screen.

The response was immediate. Those able to move did so, at first heading for the doorway, stopping and turning.

Samantha indicated those too injured to move and several of the group ahead of her nodded in agreement. Others began to hand out gas masks. Samantha took two, and heading to the back of the room, she tested the pulse of one unmoving technician. A steady beat gave her hope and she cleared him of debris, pulling the mask over his head. Her ministrations caused him to stir.

Thank God.

Get them clear, Samantha. Io's voice spoke inside her head.

Io, are you okay? There was no response.

A look from her mother and Jim indicated Io's message was not private. She mouthed 'Go' at them, pulling the now semi-conscious technician to his feet. He shook his head and focussed on the screen and then the slowly-moving group. It was only then Samantha realised Nina was nowhere to be seen. There were bigger concerns. The technician had a wounded leg and was leaving a trail of blood behind him. Each step was slower than the last, each moment passing making him a heavier burden despite the support of the combat suit.

Crustallos knows what we are.

Nina's fleeting thought was met with a feeling of wordless concern by Io.

A boom sounded from within the nearby building, the reverberation shaking the control room. The screens flickered and began to fail once more. The last word that flashed up was 'Critical'.

"Let's get you out of here," Samantha said, and realised that while still muffled, she could at least partially hear her own voice.

"Thank you," the technician replied, leaning on her.

Taking a deep breath, she hoisted him up, her shoulder bearing all of his weight. "We'll be fine." This time he seemed to weigh very little. Samantha moved quickly down the stairs and out past the security gate. Up ahead, the trail of struggling wounded stretched out ahead of her as everybody fleeing the site tried to make their way south. In the distance, their helicopter was landing to transport the worst of the wounded.

"How are you doing that?" Her mother asked, struggling to assist a woman with similar wounds.

Samantha looked down, realising she was carrying the technician, her arm wrapped around his waist.

"It must be the combat suit. You said it could carry great loads." While the mysterious girl in the airport had told her to be honest, she wasn't quite ready to admit the strength came from her and her alone.

"The smoke's worse," Jim shouted from up ahead. "We aren't gonna be able to get far enough away to escape this."

"The prevailing wind's carrying the smoke north-east," Eva shouted back. "As long as we keep walking south, we have a chance."

"What about all the people upwind?" Samantha asked. "There's villages, cities."

"Look around you, Sammy," her mum replied. "I'm sure everybody knows by now."

Samantha peered skyward. Several helicopters circled the power plant from a great distance, their noise drowned out by the harrowing wail of the alarm. "Why aren't they down here rescuing us?"

"To them, we're dead already. No sane person would risk a rescue. We've just got to make the best of it. Get whoever we can on our bird and get the hell out of here."

"We're not all fitting on that helicopter, Mom."

Around the helicopter, people had formed into an angry crowd. By the time Samantha reached them, they were restless, the tension threatening to teeter over into violence.

Jim and Charlotte lifted several of the more desperately wounded aboard, strapping them into the seats, while fending off those who were simply panicking. In the pilot seat, Carrot looked ready to pull away.

Samantha pushed through the small crowd, depositing her grateful passenger on the space in between two filled seats. "Take him, he can barely walk."

"Judging by your superhuman efforts he hasn't needed to," Charlotte observed.

"Adrenaline rush," Samantha lied, shrugging her shoulders. "Get these people to hospital."

"Hey, what about the rest of us?" shouted one angry woman. Several of the crowd bayed in agreement, pushing forward.

"The emergency services know about us. They're setting up checkpoints and a quarantine zone. Walk as fast as you can that way," Eva pointed south, "and pray the wind doesn't change. Go. We'll be back with help."

Several people ignored Eva's promise, trying to climb aboard the helicopter. Charlotte didn't hesitate for a second, pulling the Helltech pistol from a holster at her hip and pointing it at them. The crowd halted. "Back, all of you. Carrot, go. We'll return. Just make your way south."

Samantha kept eye contact with Charlotte as long as possible, reading an apology in her eyes. She turned away from the only viable means of escape, looking back toward the reactor. Another boom sounded from within, the vibration shaking the ground. The helicopter lifted off behind her and flew south.

"Not long now," said another technician, an elderly man with a few wisps of hair blowing in the wind. He saw Samantha watching him and continued. "You saw the sign go critical, yes?"

"I did."

"That means the fuel is ballooning and bursting, melting everything around it, steam explosions and a molten mass gathering at the bottom of the core."

"Corium," Samantha said.

"Correct. It also means radiation pouring out of that hole in the roof, flooding the entire region with air-borne poison. It means death beyond counting, cancer and a whole host of diseases for generations to come. Young lady, I saw a being drop out of the sky, hit shielding thick enough to withstand a direct impact by a plane and take your friend into the reactor core."

"How weren't you in agony like the rest of us?"

He popped a piece of plastic from his ear and held it up. "Hearing aid. When that awful noise started I just removed it. I'm a pure advocate of science, but what I witnessed was an act of God, just like I witnessed two decades ago during my days in the army. This will require a similar act of God for anybody to escape alive. The quarantine zone will be at least three kilometres out. Many of these people won't even make it that far, injured as they are."

"We have to try. We can't just give up."

"If your crazy friend returns with the helicopter it will be a good start. For most, her return is our only hope."

The old man turned away, trudging down the coastal path.

Samantha followed him, her mother by her side.

Samantha. Stay.

"Io," Samantha gasped aloud, turning back to the burning power station.

"Sammy, no," her mother urged. "He's dead already."

"No mom, he needs me. The corium. He knows what he's doing."

Fear and desperation were written all over Eva's pale face. Despite all her misguided intent, her mother was trying desperately to do the right thing. In that moment, Samantha saw herself through her mother's eyes, misunderstood, well-meaning. Caring. "Sammy, I've no idea what's become of Nina. Please. Don't let me lose another daughter within minutes of the first one."

He knows what we are... Samantha found herself caught up on Nina's words, regretting her past behaviour. *What are we?* Stektes lived off her sister her entire life. It had known from the very beginning, from the moment it had slipped through the portal in Tartarus.

"You won't, Mom. I'll survive." Samantha removed the gas mask, dropping it to the ground. "I'm stronger than this. Io knows. Nina knows. That thing inhabiting her knows. I think the problem I've had is accepting this. Mom, I love you. Io needs me, I can feel it. Maybe I can make a difference."

"Between an exploding nuclear power station and a psycho angel?" Eva tried to take her gas mask off.

Samantha reached out to stop her, realising now just how easy it was to hold her mothers' arm in place. "Don't, Mom. You're too important. When the helicopter returns, take your team to Thornfalcon. If Io fails here, you will be the only ones with a chance to stop Porter Rockwell from opening the doorway to Heaven."

"But how?"

Samantha smiled, embracing her mother. When she stood back, she said, "You'll think of something. I have faith. You closed them down before. And don't give up on Nina. She's still in there. One of us needs to be here to find a way to exorcise the demon in her. Whatever it is can never be allowed to make it to the doorway. Go."

"I love you, Sammy," Eva took a couple of steps backward before turning to follow the thin line of humanity fleeing south along the coast.

"I love you too, Mom," Samantha replied, turning back toward the power station, her fate now sealed.

* * *

Okay, Io. You've got me. What can I do?

There was triumph in Io's voice as he said, *I have Karael contained within the molten core. We fought and I prevailed. It's a mess in here and the whole building's melting.*

The smoke was billowing out of the hole now. *Can you do anything about the smoke? The radiation's gonna kill a lot of innocent people.*

No, but you can. You know you're strong, Sammy, but you don't realise the limits of your strength. If you will your strength and believe, you could call back all of that smoke with a thought.

Samantha watched the smoke for a second, then raised her hands. "Come back," she shouted at the smoke.

The only response was the continuing wail of the emergency siren. The site was free of humanity. She was alone.

Io, it's too much. If I can lift someone, fine. But move the winds? Suck back radiation? Hang on...

She began to pace. "Radiation is just a particular kind of particle—poisonous for sure, but still distinct.

I have to focus on the radioactive particles, not the smoke carrying them.

You've got it, Io's thoughts were awash with approval. *You're too new to your powers yet. Do you trust me?*

"I do," Samantha said aloud, forgetting the mental link.

"Then allow me in," said a voice from beside her. "Let me reside in you for a moment and your kind shall be saved."

Samantha turned. A fierce light radiated from where the voice emanated. "Io," she breathed, "you're beautiful."

"And short on time, choose quickly."

"I allow you in," Samantha said and in that instant she felt a surge of such power her knees threatened to buckle. The muscles in her shoulders tightened and she staggered, taking huge breaths. *Sammy ... what are you?*

She screamed. A wave of energy reached out from her, moving up through the cloud, enveloping the smoke. Further and further it reached. She could feel it gathering in all the radiation from miles away. There was no limit to the energy she expended and joyful, she erupted with radiance, her arms thrust wide. For a moment she even lifted off the ground, hovering an inch or two.

"Pull it back, Sammy. Suck it all into the reactor. Hold it there."

"I can do this," she said, confident in her newfound ability. The radiation was rushing back toward the plant. She was saving the world!

The elation turned to sickness within her. Samantha realised the feeling came not from herself but from Io within her. "Io, what is it?"

"My vessel's being ravaged without me. I must go. Also—no! Karael is breaking free! Samantha, I trust you to finish this."

With a rush of wind, Samantha found herself alone, her body suddenly hollow. The power she emitted began to falter.

"It wasn't him," she said. "This is me. If I can summon a demon I can finish this task. My God, this *is* me!" Guiding the stream of particles back into the core, she imagined a dome of pure energy atop the reactor chamber. No more smoke rose. She extended the dome down to encase the entire reactor building, her concentration the only requirement needed to hold herself mistress of this frightening ability.

"They're safe," she said aloud to the empty site. Realising she was growing very hot despite the overcast day, Samantha turned back to the reactor. Waves of heat pulsed up from the concrete casing with nowhere to go. Inside the shield the corrupted nuclear material was getting hotter and hotter.

Io.

There was no reply. The shield was too good. Samantha began to panic. Io was trapped inside with Karael inside a furnace thousands of degrees in temperature. Another boom and the ground shook with the nearby violence. Samantha had to save him. She poked at the shield, seeking to unravel her work. In the distance behind she could hear screams as people registered the smoke now pouring out of the superstructure. The occasional lick of flame could also be seen.

"You don't have to go through this alone," Samantha imagined her mother saying.

She turned. Eva stood a few paces behind her, no protective gear on. A Geiger counter in one hand. "Mom, why? You should be safe with the rest."

"I was always impetuous. I'm not leaving my daughter's side, Sammy. To Hell with the consequences. Is this you?"

"I think so. I had a bit of help from Io, but all the radioactivity is in that shell." As if mentioning his name was a reminder, Samantha turned back to the scene unfolding in front of them. The smoke from the fire had dwindled. The plumes that escaped were caught in the shield and now drawn back in. The hole in the roof began to glow a steady white. A keening emanated from the reactor, the same sound accompanying Karael's arrival.

"Oh, this can't be good," Eva said.

The roof of the reactor building exploded upward as the white light erupted forth, soaring into the sky. At its core Samantha saw a winged being arcing directly for them.

"Mom, its Karael," she tried to shout above the noise. He's beaten Io. Run!"

Chapter Thirty-Five

Samantha ran until she thought her lungs would burst, dragging her mother along behind her. It did no good against an airborne celestial being. In only moments, a whoosh above them showed just how futile their flight had been. Huge feathered wings cut through the air, the armored being banked and dropped to the ground a dozen paces ahead of them. The wings folded, shimmered, and disappeared entirely, leaving the still-glowing angel standing ahead, one hand resting on the pommel of his great, glowing sword. Beneath a white hood, eyes shimmered, radiating power.

"If you're looking for me to be cowed, Karael, you've chosen the wrong person. My family doesn't bend knee to those that proliferate on evil. You're the fallen angel, not Ioviel."

"I'm pleased you feel that way," the angel replied, tipping back his hood. The glow faded, the skin of the angel now ebony as it lost its shine.

"Io?" Samantha ran to him, hurling herself into his embrace. The relief flooded through her as Io squeezed her tightly in his steel-like arms. Stepping back, she admired him, no longer a vagabond in used jeans and shirt. Instead his armor, silver and white in a feather pattern across his torso. "I see you found your mojo." She was impressed at how magnificent he looked.

White teeth broke out in a smile. "We did it."

"How?" Eva asked. "What?" She twisted to take in the reactor. "Are we safe?"

Io's hand passed over his breastplate, revealing a glowing fist-sized silver gem in the middle.

"Is that—"

"The Phaethon Stone," Io finished Eva's question. "The only such stone successfully created."

Mesmerised, Eva stepped close. "May I hold it?"

"You may if you want to be instantly vaporised," Io warned. "This stone is your nuclear inferno condensed into one small orb. It forms the core of my armor, fills me with what I am. Only a celestial being has the power to wield the Phaethon Stone. It is a perilous balance. Remove it from me and the radiation will burst forth once more."

"Is the reactor safe?" Samantha asked.

Eva held up the Geiger counter. It emitted nothing more than a couple of scratchy blips. "Background radiation only. Nothing more than you'd find occurring naturally."

"You saved us, Samantha," Io said. "Drawing back the escaping radiation and sealing it in allowed the corium to finish its work. And as an added bonus," Io flexed his shoulders and the most enormous pair of wings shimmered into existence, folded neatly behind him, "My wings are back. More accurately, I become custodian of Metatron's wings."

"His feather?"

Io nodded. "Correct. A hoped-for side effect of the Phaethon Stone. Wings are bestowed only at the cost of great power. He pulled the feathers from His own flesh for us all."

"So, this is a promotion of sorts?" Eva asked.

"Indeed, for as long as it lasts. If I should make it through the doorway, I may find the heavenly host waiting on the other side, ready to strip my wings. They may still consider me fallen."

"Even like this?" Samantha took another moment to drink in the sight of him.

"Why, do you believe there's still peril?" Eva didn't sound convinced. "Did you defeat the other angel? Is the way not open for you?"

"There's still that thing inside Nina, Mom. Porter Rockwell isn't without strength of his own. Who knows what Aeon Fall have sitting over the horizon?"

"There is no better time to discover what lies in waiting," Io decided. "Samantha, wait here." He flexed once more, the mighty wings flashing into view, grabbing Eva and launching into the sky before she had a chance to object.

Samantha was now alone with only the noise of distant helicopters for company. Io had disappeared from sight in a streak of light. Then, just as impressively as before, he returned, landing on one knee, his head bowed.

"Show off," Samantha mocked.

Io broke into a grin. "Much more acceptable than sitting on a plane."

"I'll bet you turned a few heads."

"Your friends are safe. I let them read me with one of their meters. Those who didn't faint remained to hear me tell them of our plans. Your mother is taking charge now but they are following us to the place of sacrifice."

"Thornfalcon?"

Io looked skyward. "It is not far, as the angel flies." He clenched his fist and the hole in the distant reactor building repaired itself. "My brother will not escape that prison easily. I removed his ability to be summoned by his glyph. Gone are the days of Karael hunting us."

"Us?"

"Yes, Samantha. Now he knows what you are, he would kill you over me, given the chance."

"Io, my sister said we are both different. What am I?"

"At first I thought of you as a Nephilim, the offspring of an angel and a mortal. As such they are very powerful, an unforeseen consequence of my Fathers creations."

"But Madden hadn't become Satan when Mom had Nina. Nor when I was conceived. Mom made sure we very clearly knew those dates. It was important to her that no matter what else happened, we knew the truth about our parentage."

"Yet he had a demon in him when your mother conceived your sister, and also you. An abomination in the eyes of Heaven."

"You mean a Hellbounce?"

Io's face lost any trace of humor. "I would not name it as such, but yes. It appears you inherited more than your father's carefree nature. You are greater than Nephilim, both of you. Yet your nature is beyond my understanding. For where we're going next, you could make the difference." Io pulled her close.

Samantha squealed in surprise as he squeezed her tight. "Really, Io? Here?"

Io smiled. "Let me show you what it's like to really fly."

He held her close and Samantha felt the muscles of his thighs bunch. "Shouldn't you have your wings?" Her last word became a scream of terror turned pure exhilaration, drawn out as Io's pinions burst forth. They rocketed skyward.

Held in the cradle of Io's arms, Samantha finally understood. True flight was freedom. Io's wings didn't flap like a bird. With them he soared like a hang-glider. The power plant disappeared from view almost immediately, along with the gathering of people she had seen. They could nearly touch the highest clouds when he turned south.

Samantha tried to shout to Io, but the wind took her breath away.

Do you know where you're going?

I can feel the location of the doorway. The place of sacrifice is not far. Thirty miles or so.

Strangely, Samantha felt complete security in his embrace, as if hanging several hundred metres up in the atmosphere were commonplace.

What happens when we get there?

It is just the site of sacrifice that matters. I can raze everything to the ground with a thought.

"No," Samantha shouted aloud.

Io pulled up, hanging in the air. "What do you mean no?"

"Aeon Fall have my aunt, and Tricia. If you flatten everything you'll kill them. They aren't stupid. Rockwell, this thing that has my sister. They have a contingency at hand if you survived Hinkley. Karael wasn't their only gambit."

"Returning to Heaven is my mission now," Io declared. "I have to inform my brethren the truth behind the apathy."

"That's not the Io I've come to know speaking." Samantha reached up, running the palm of her hand down the side of his face, stroking his beard. "I hear the angel but I know the man is still in there. These people need our help. They need you. Be their champion, Io."

Io's face softened. "They need you more, Samantha. You're the one who should be saving the world, but for that to happen you need to save yourself. To forgive yourself. Perhaps you are right. We are all in this together, after all. But, how can I claim divinity after what we have been through if I willingly allow mortals to die for my goals?"

"Just don't destroy it all, not until we're sure they're safe. Let's exercise a little caution."

Io smiled. "I will of course be guided by you, as always, my saviour."

They soared once more, passing roads packed with cars still fleeing the perceived disaster. A major town gave way to several small villages, all of which were emptied judging by the total lack of cars. In only moments Io hovered above one tiny settlement. "The gateway lies beneath."

"That's it?" Samantha peered at the landscape below, a maze of tiny twisting lanes amidst fields of crops. "It's just four or five houses at the base of a hill."

"The portal doesn't require a building," Io replied. "Just a sacrifice, and beneath us lies the evidence for that. In Thornfalcon." He began a rapid vertical descent.

Samantha swallowed to keep her stomach under control, her ears popping as they dropped. "Well at least we don't need to worry about anybody seeing you land," she said, looking about them. If anybody from the main road bore witness to their landing, they would likely dismiss it as a bird from this distance.

"There's Benjamin Ferrey's church," Samantha pointed as they neared the ground.

"The church is our destination," Io replied.

"Typical. It's always religious."

"You can let go now," Io said with a smile.

Samantha hadn't noticed they were back on terra firma, on a lane bordered by great oaks; she was still focussed on Io's face.

"Quaint," she said, beginning to walk up the lane toward the church. The trees crowded overhead blocked out the daylight, creating a chill in the air. She stopped. "Do you hear that, Io?"

"Do I hear what?"

"Exactly. This is the middle of the countryside. Where are all the birds?"

"Like the jungle in Papua New Guinea," Io observed.

"True, but this time there is no plane to frighten everything away. Nature's fled this place. Does it have a sixth sense or what?"

Io looked distant for a moment. "Your mother knows we have landed. She will join us soon."

"With half the world's army and all of the media behind us, I expect. Do we wait?"

Io stopped at a gap in the wall. The church sat on the other side amidst a field of gravestones. "I am at full strength. I don't see any reason to wait. This area is deserted, or else I would know."

"You've still got a lot to learn about walking into traps," Samantha warned, "but it might be safer for the rest if we go in now. They're here, you can count on it. I think we need the backup."

"There's too much at risk," Io insisted. "We need to open the portal before Porter Rockwell gets here. Let me share with you a saying among my kind. The wisest warriors walk away from confrontation. They fight only because there is no other way. This time, there is no avoiding the confrontation. Here at the threshold of Heaven we must make a stand."

He turned and crossed to the doorway.

Samantha looked around. Her skin crawled in the eerie silence; it was as if many eyes watched her from the shadows. "Io, wait!"

The church was small, as befitted a place of worship for an isolated community. One arch separated the dais from the pews, the room lit by minimal light through heavily-coloured stained glass windows. "Not much, is it?" Samantha observed, wondering this church could possibly pose a threat with nobody inside.

"His Kingdom is inside us, and all around us. Not just in these halls of wood and stone," Io replied.

Samantha took a moment to consider this, perching on the nearest pew. "True," she admitted. "That's a good line."

"One of Metatron's best," Io said, walking down the aisle to the dais. "He put it down in writing and delivered the Word to those he saw fit."

"I wonder what ever happened to them."

"Your ARC has them. Metatron delivered the Word in the form of scrolls at a place called Nag Hamaddi."

"The lost scrolls? The ones that retell the Book of Revelation?"

"The very same. You should read them, Sammy. You might learn a lot more about yourself, such as why we are here. Leviathan featured heavily in that particular tale. I can sense his bones beneath us. This is most definitely not a normal church." Io pointed. "Look at the backs of the pews."

Samantha stood and joined Io, following his finger. "A carving of a glyph?"

"Indeed. Many of my brethren are here. Locien, Laylah, Joshua, William, Turiel. Their glyphs are all carved into this pew. Strange it was those particular five."

"Are there more?" Samantha crossed to the pews on the other side of the room. "Front row only. Another five."

Io joined her, running his hand over the glyphs. "Jessica, Samuel, Andrael, Zerachiel." Io stopped reading.

"Who's the last one?"

Io stepped back from the pews. "Metatron."

"Even stranger?" She watched his face. Conflicting emotions played across it. His brow furrowed in anger, jaw clenched with frustration, head shaking in disbelief. "Io, I understand why you might be torn up about Metatron, but why were these significant?"

"There were ten angels responsible for guarding my Father's most treasured Word. The orders he laid down for humanity to abide by each had an angel to enforce the meaning."

"The Ten Commandments, you mean? Those given to Moses on Mount Sinai to pass on as man's laws to abide by."

"They weren't for Mankind but for Moses: ten angels to guard him against himself, ten rules for him to abide by. Moses wasn't a slave child who became a prince of Egypt by chance. He was the first Nephilim—the very embodiment of sins angels were not meant to create. He worked miracles never meant for mortal man. This is a Holy place."

"Who was his father?"

"Leviathan. That he fell is not the entire truth. My Brother escaped from Heaven's jail, the Fearvent. He destroyed many of my brethren before he descended. Karael led us to believe he pursued our fallen brother with several of the Ten, those that were left."

"So why is their safety got you so spooked?"

"The Ten are the keys to what you call The Godmissile. As one falls, the Seals weaken. I knew of their number and heard rumours of who protected the seals, but I did not know their names—until I saw this. Now that I know, I have to get home."

"To find them?"

"To protect Zerachiel. With Metatron gone he's the only angel of the Commandments still alive. All these names—they perished in Leviathan's descent. I find your mother's explanation of Leviathan's existence more plausible as I now stand here. Karael should be taken home and brought to account for his version of the truth."

"Thou shalt not bear false witness against thy neighbor," Samantha quoted one of the commandments. "Which one of them bore that particular line?"

"Metatron," Io replied. "I can feel it from his essence. Truth was everything to him."

"Seems from what Mom told me, he was pretty good at omitting facts when it suited him."

Having evidently decided on a course of action, Io moved to a doorway to the right of the altar. "An omission is not a lie."

"That's a technicality and you know it, Io. Don't play semantics with me. Stick to the truth and honor Metatron's memory. Now what's got your attention?"

"This is the way down to the portal, but it appears to be barred. I don't want to leave anything out of place lest the ritual be either disturbed or utterly ruined. Everything is here for a reason."

Samantha peered at the sign. "It says no smoking."

Io frowned, asking, "What does that mean?"

Samantha smiled. "Io, in church, that's the eleventh commandment." She lifted the bolt and slid it across, the heavy metal clanged as it hit the stop. "Come on down. Let's find your demon."

Chapter Thirty-Six

The stairs were steep and narrow, winding back upon themselves more than once. Io took them at pace, Samantha struggling to stay close in the darkness.

"How are you doing that?" she asked. "I can't see a thing. If there were no railing, I'd be slipping all over the place."

"I can see my way down. You can't? You have the ability should you choose to use it."

"Maybe I'm not quite used to my new-found superpowers just yet." Samantha pulled a small flashlight from a pocket on the combat suit, switching it on. The light was so bright she had to shield her eyes.

"Just because the solution isn't easy and obvious, it doesn't mean you shouldn't try." Io's tone was that of an instructor, one who gently scolded her for taking the easy way out.

"I'm sorry, Io. Time is of the essence. Plus I wouldn't know where to begin."

"At the beginning. Consider how you felt the first time you raised an image of your father. What did you do?"

"I painted the pattern on the floor and spilled my blood onto it."

"But there was more to your efforts. You reached deep down, both inside yourself and through the earth."

Samantha stopped. "How do you know that?"

"In the instant you prayed to me, I came to know you, past, present, and potential future. If you don't take the easy way out, I can see what you might become. Think about how you felt that day. Consider how you felt earlier, reaching for those minuscule particles. I simply showed you the way. The power has always been yours."

Samantha looked inside, searching for the spark. It was there, but just out of reach. She chased after the feeling but nothing came. "It's too hard," she gasped.

"Nothing worth doing is ever easy, Sammy," he replied. "Stick with your light for now."

She shone the light around the catacombs. Smooth carved stone buttresses arched up to the ceiling. "This is much bigger than the church above, as if the church were merely a doorway to something greater." She considered her point. "It's always a church, isn't it?"

"Yes. These are often places of unexplainable events. They become shrines to something bigger, places of worship taken over by formality. The ceremony replaces what can't be explained. A church represents the human spirit's connection with this. It gives a focus. Your mother believes the same."

"She saw a church in Hell, atop the Tartarus portal."

"Or did she just think she did? Was it a visual expression of the connection between her mind and the reality she was presented with?"

"Are you saying I could be imagining this?"

Io stopped at a casket, placing his hands on the stone. "I am saying most people dream and, in doing so, escape reality. For you, reality is the dream, and you need to wake up." He frowned. "This is incorrect."

"Who's in there?"

"I'm meant to believe this is the tomb of Leviathan, but I feel the essence of Beelzebub. He is not here, though he is very close by. We need to get out. This whole construct is a trap."

"What do you mean? It's just a catacomb."

Io pushed her toward the stairs. "To a mortal perhaps. There is an energy at play here almost beyond my own comprehension. Get out, Sammy, while you still can."

Samantha began to climb the stairs. "While I — isn't this for you?"

"No, it is not. Whoever did this has constructed an intricate and elaborate trap for a being far more powerful than an angel."

"What's more powerful than an angel?" Samantha asked.

"I intend for you to live to find out," Io said. "Wait here."

He pushed past her, up the stairway, and out of her sight.

She paused only for a couple of seconds before following. Her flashlight seemed feeble against the darkness, coupled with her own uncertainty. "You're not leaving me down here alone Io. Io?"

Samantha took the stairs two at a time as she sought to catch Io. The door was ajar in the wake of Io's passage. To her right, Io stood on the dais, unmoving. His hand thrust back at her, his whole arm trembling as he fought an invisible force. A warning.

Samantha took stock of the situation, concentrating. She couldn't summon the will to augment her eyesight, but she felt an uncommon tingling, *perhaps prescience*, she wondered. A shimmer in which Io was caught spreading across the whole church formed in front of her. She stepped sideways, around the edge of the flicker. A scuff behind the altar caught her attention. *She was not alone.*

"Welcome," Porter Rockwell purred. "Nice to see you once again, Sammy."

She turned. "Aunt Clare?"

Rockwell held her aunt, gagged and bound, by a fistful of hair, his hand twisting with malice. No emotion showed on his face, those cold eyes bringing back memories of the warehouse in Port Moresby. Clare moaned through her gag.

"She's really not well," he said, a contented smile spreading across his face as if his sole purpose was to cause both of them misery. "I had to pull this little contraption off her. Made this really annoying beep." Rockwell threw a small gadget with tubing attached past Io. It landed at her feet with a crack of plastic.

"Aunt Clare's insulin pump?" Samantha said, bending down to retrieve it, not taking her eyes off of Rockwell. "You bastard. I'll—"

"Do nothing. You move and I'll give your aunt to my friend over here." Rockwell remained staring at her as a figure moved onto the dais from an alcove. Bald, reeking of violence, the polar opposite to Rock-well, Christopher Lanier hulked over everybody in the church. "Bet you never thought you'd see me again, eh missy," he said, his strong South African accent as clipped and cutting as she remembered it.

"Well I reckon a hail of bullets would be too easy a death for you, though I could always hope it was that easy."

"You little bitch," Lanier spat, surging forward.

"Stop," Rockwell barked.

Lanier obeyed, his mouth locked in a grimace. The skin of his head moved from beneath. Something was being contained.

Samantha concentrated, trying to examine the shimmering. "Not just an angel trap," she assumed aloud. "If your pet can't cross the boundary then it holds demons too."

Lanier baulked at the word 'pet' but made no further movement.

"Look about you, Samantha," Rockwell said. "This is no place of worship." Outside, the sky was darkening. Flashes of light filled the stained-glass windows and Samantha focused on the details. The window nearest her featured a horned figure bound with circles of light around its wrists and ankles, sitting amidst a cloud of bodiless heads, all of them screaming. On another, a flame-haired monstrosity with eyes of madness and curved fangs clawed at the bars that trapped it.

"But this is not new," Samantha began. "Benjamin Ferrey con-structed this church—"

"Without the slightest idea of what he was bringing into creation. The ultimate trap, a prison for a beings so powerful nothing else can hold them."

Did they know about her too? Were Io's suspicions widespread? Surely the creature holding her sister hostage told them. Samantha willed herself to remain calm.

"And here he is," Rockwell announced, "bound in a prison from which he cannot escape, surrounded on all four sides by evil, carrying the means to end you all. Look around you, Samantha. This is not a place of sanctuary. This is no portal. This is a trap to take his essence.

Yet thanks to you we no longer need it. Say goodbye to your tame angel, girl. He's outlived his usefulness."

"But the portal. Beelzebub."

"Not here, but close enough that the Phaethon doesn't degrade when I rip it from Ioviel's charred corpse."

Samantha turned away, concentrating. The map. Where was it? Her head throbbed as she sought the spark within, still just out of reach. Behind her, she felt a glow from the barrier and turned, catching only a glimpse.

"I won't let you," she said.

"Then by all means, step beside your companion. Pull him from where he stands, and you can both walk away."

Samantha stood her ground, closing her fists and taking in a deep breath of the musty church air between her teeth.

"No? I didn't think so. Your father may rule absolute in Hell, little girl, but it is just one realm. He has no sway over what we do now. As much as Tartarus is a lock, it is not the only lock. There are bypasses."

"You won't get to Zerachiel," Samantha growled.

"And by your own words, you condemn him," Rockwell spat back. "We didn't know the name of the Last Commandment. Now we do." He shoved Clare into the ungentle embrace of Lanier and turned to retrieve a cloth-wrapped bundle from the altar. Folding the material back he lifted a large knife and held it, admiring it as light glinted from the obsidian blade's countless lines. "It was a trial to retrieve this from under your father's nose. Yet, He does not see all. Hell is full of His enemies. Do you know this blade, girl?"

"Can't say I've had the pleasure," Samantha replied. The blade sang to her from across the room, resonating with a glowing red hue. She realised the blade was responsible for her sensing the trap. Now that she was cognizant of the source, Samantha was able to put the trap into focus.

I can see the trap, Io. How do I get you out?

You don't. Get out of here. Your sister is on the hill nearby. This whole church is the map, the needle in a compass, pointing straight to her. Save her. Save us all, Sammy.

No, Io. Don't give up!

"This blade is connected to your family, on a cellular level. It's tasted your mother, your father, your sister. I can feel it hunger for more. It knows you're here. You and your aunt."

"The Well of Souls," Samantha realised aloud.

"You do know it."

"That blade created monsters."

"Yes, when used by amateurs like Asmodeus and Belphegor. Creating an army of self-destructive nightmares, that's all they did. They were so blinded by their petty ambition they never stopped to wonder why this blade existed in the first place."

"It's a part of the key to Tartarus," she said.

Rockwell sneered as he said, "To all sorts of locks. The souls stored in here give this weapon exponential power. Your family's blood is special, holy even. You've been linked with this blade since long before you were born. Some might call it destiny."

Lanier held Clare rigid as Rockwell freed her arm and held it straight. The blade began to hum, the frequency revealing the trap as a dome over the dais. Rockwell began to carve.

"No!" Samantha screamed.

Clare screamed too, the knife slicing through her flesh as though it were insubstantial. Blood spattered to the floor as Rockwell continued the grisly task. "Perfect," he said as he stepped away, admiring his work.

On Clare's arm a six-pointed star had been carved. Clare stared in terror as the blood pouring down her arm dripped off her fingers.

"Aunt Clare, it'll be fine," Samantha tried to reassure her aunt.

"Oh no, it really won't," Rockwell countered.

Lanier took a step forward to the edge of the trap, pushing Clare ahead of him. "First her, then the angel, then you," Lanier said through a rictus grin. He forced Clare's arm into the trap, her screams now all the louder. Stepping back, he left Clare suspended by the force, the star carved into her forearm glowing as it made contact with the trap.

For a second nothing happened, then Samantha flew backward, propelled by the force unleashed within the trap. Landing on her back she rolled into one of the pews, the wood of the leg catching her back and making her gasp. "Io." Climbing to her knees, she shielded her eyes. Lightning pulsed into Io from the four pillars at each corner of the trap. Beams of red intersected them from the stained glass windows. The trap was revealed.

Io was a mere shape in the middle, his back arched, head thrown back, arms wide. His wings materialised as he hovered six inches above the floor, suspended in the energy. At his core, the Phaethon Stone throbbed on Io's chest, in sync with the lightning pulsing through the trap, but brighter than all. Its radiance filled the church with an ethereal glow beyond which everything was hidden. Samantha could no longer see Clare or the two demons.

Helpless she watched as Io began to smoulder, the sweet stench of burning flesh assaulting her nostrils.

"What do I do?" she said aloud, to be answered only with the crackle of the lightning.

Use your power, Io urged.

How? Io I can't and you're dying.

Think back to the beginning. Hurry. If my host is obliterated they have nobody to stop them. Everything ends.

Fretting, Samantha paced in a small circle. "Back to the beginning." She began to envisage a book, a spell written on the page, and her disbelief that such things were even possible. Yet when she carved the *sigil* and it worked, she believed.

Samantha grabbed a crayon from a basket of half-finished children's drawings and began to draw on the floor. The pattern she knew from memory; if Lucas had done one thing right it was to obsess over her learning the summoning spell. As complicated as the intricate patterns were, she was done in moments. Only one more ingredient: Blood. The Helltech blade was at her waist. She unsheathed the weapon and ran it along the heel of her palm. Droplets of blood welled from the cut and Samantha squeezed her hand into a fist. The blood dripped free of her hand, falling to the pattern on the floor.

"No!" Rockwell's terrified voice yelled from beyond the barrier.

Call to him, Io urged.

The pattern began to glow. Samantha knelt close to the glowing portal and screamed into it, "Father!"

From far below, in the depths of a place so vast and beyond her comprehension it was impossible to imagine the connection as anything other than magical, a roar answered.

The glowing portal erupted into a red shaft of light, throwing Samantha backward almost as far as the trap had done. She skidded to a halt, curling into a ball to protect herself, and then jumped up.

The beam ripped up through the roof of the church, leaving a gaping hole. Falling masonry hit one of the pillars emitting lightning, and the trap faltered, the lightning blinking out as the construct collapsed. Birds poured in through the hole in the roof, winging their way in a tight circle around the edge of the trap, squawking and shrieking as they did so. Io dropped to his knees, wings closing about him in a protective shield. The birds swirled down about him, landing in a pattern. A glyph.

"What have you done?" Rockwell wailed.

"She's summoned an angel," said Io's voice from beneath trembling wings. The birds waited, nervous and agitated, yet compelled to remain. "Our fight is not yet done."

"That's not Karael's glyph." Samantha replied. "That's not the Thornfalcon."

"It represents the truth," Io said, still covered. "It is what she will become. They answer to you, Sammy, not to me. Summon the fallen one. Let us see an end to this."

Samantha closed her eyes, letting her consciousness reach out. *Karael.*

The wait did not take long. With a scream the roof shattered as a bloody and torn Karael plummeted headfirst toward Io, sword seeking his throat.

Chapter Thirty-Seven

Io was immobile, unmoving as his enemy dropped an arrow—straight onto the broken trap.

Samantha closed her eyes. *Not like this,* she thought.

The clang of metal on metal filled the church, a noise so rapturous Samantha had to look. She stifled a cheer. Io stood, a step away from his previous position, his blade held out to one side blocking the thrust Karael aimed at Io's head.

"You can stop this, my brother. All is not lost. There is still time to undo what was done."

Karael grimaced, using brute force to battle Io. The body once filled with life by Lucas had not healed from the recent battle in the reactor core. Flesh hung in tatters from his face. Part of his jawbone was visible. Burns streaked his arms where veins were crisped under his skin. His wings, the only part not of Lucas, hung in tatters from his back, feathers slick with black blood.

"Time to undo it all, you say? Time to bring back our brothers? Time to send these back to the hole they crawled out from under?" Karael pointed at Rockwell and Lanier.

There was no sign from her aunt.

"Time perhaps to bring back the mortal who sits on the Throne of Hell and pretends to be one of us?"

"He is one of us," Io countered. "He passed the trials. He sacrificed himself with a pure heart and Father raised him up just as he fell. The blood chose him."

"Their blood?" Karael thrust one charred hand out at Samantha. "A diluted strain of a degenerate race?"

"That is not so, brother." Io's voice was calm, in control. "The Line of David runs pure and uncorrupted, culminating in his two ultimate progeny."

Karael began to laugh, a gurgling noise that resulted in a fountain of black blood spilling down his front. "So pure and uncorrupted one of them stands on the hill nearby waiting for you to open the gateway back to Heaven?" Karael disengaged, swinging his sword overhead.

Io parried once more. "They will never make it."

"Neither will you. I see it in your eyes, brother. The anguish of coming so close just to have your strength sapped away by the trap. You think you aren't exactly where Crustallos wants you to be? You're stalling. The Ten are all but extinct and one weak angel isn't going to halt an army."

Karael moved to strike once again with his sword but Io twisted to counter his attack. Instead of continuing, Karael twisted and grabbed Io, taking himself and Io through the wall of the church.

The building began to crumble around them. Samantha watched as Io regained his feet. The sky was now dark; flickers of lightning lent a malevolent aspect to the scene. Beyond the tussling angels stood innumerable bodies, unmoving, shadows almost as dark as the sky above. Io passed close to one. A bolt of lightning jumped from the dark being. Io screamed.

"The twelve tribes of Israel!" Karael shouted. "All for you, brother. This portal will send everyone home. It's time to end Father's mistakes."

"Not as long as I draw breath," Io roared, launching into the sky.

With a scream of rage, Karael followed him, the dark spirits rising into the air behind him. The church quaked in the aftermath of the angels' ascension; the noise of clashing swords echoed throughout the sky. Lightning flashed every time they came together. The clouds boiled the countless spirits surrounding the angels as they fought.

In the gloom of the church there was a nearby movement. Porter Rockwell and Christopher Lanier emerged from the deeper recess to stand atop the defunct trap. Outside, the shadows of men turned, rising in the wake of the angels' violent ascent. Rockwell raised a hand. Those that had not risen aloft, stopped and turned.

"There's no way out, girl," Rockwell purred. "They surround us. One hundred and forty four thousand life-sucking soul magnets. Touch just one of them and they will drain your life away. They are the anti-beings. Accursed and hungry."

"And for sale to the highest bidder," Samantha shot back. "I've heard the tales of them following the demon Iuvart in Egypt. They're puppets under someone's control. Perhaps even yours."

Samantha sensed a movement in the shadows. It was Clare crawling slowly along the base of the wall, avoiding the attention from the demons. She was injured. Her arm cut and her ribs broken by the way she winced. Her own body rallied against her with no source of insulin. Samantha knew Clare wouldn't last long, but she kept her eyes on Rockwell.

He remained still, unconcerned. "It's a shame you weren't the one caught in the trap. Stektes is more than Ioviel's match. With Karael keeping him distracted you've all but sealed the fate of this world. I'd have liked to watch the tribes chase you until you fell. Still, it falls to me to take pleasure in doing what they can't." Rockwell crossed the seal on the middle of the dais, closing on her. Lanier hulked at his side.

They wouldn't get to Clare, Samantha decided. Calming her mind she sought the feeling of elation that came with the portal opening. The red beam of her father had long since winked out with the church's destruction yet it granted her a legacy, the means to find her power.

Rockwell raised his hands to grab her.

Eyes closed, Samantha held up one hand, palm out. "Not today."

Only a step away from her, Rockwell stopped. "What is this?" He struggled against her, but Samantha's will was ironclad. He was locked within it. "What are you?"

Samantha looked inside herself. *What am I?* Samantha asked herself.

Get to the hilltop and find out, Io replied. *Just hurry.*

Snapped from her reverie as two gunshots rang out, Samantha felt the bullets pass her, one hitting Rockwell in the shoulder, the other felling Lanier like a redwood.

"She's my daughter, you son of a bitch." Eva said.

"Mom!" Samantha turned, leaping into the arms of her mother. Charlotte and Jim, each wielding one of the Helltech guns, stepped past them.

"This might not kill them, Sammy, but it'll hurt like Hell. Get out of here," Charlotte ordered as she loosened the Helltech rope, holding it like a whip.

Lanier took a step closer. Charlotte lashed the cord at him, striking his face. He screamed in pain, a burn down one cheek, and leaped forward.

"Stop," Samantha whispered, holding her hand up.

Lanier froze mid-air, dropping to the ruined church floor.

Samantha did nothing more than watch.

"What is it, love?" Eva came to stand beside her.

"I can see inside him. Mom, I can see down to every single twisted fiber. His soul. It pulses with an evil so deep and alien it's beyond this reality. There's no fire here, only ice. Lanier is a demon, but he's not from Hell. He's from somewhere darker." She turned to Rockwell. "Did you know this?"

For the first time since she had seen Porter Rockwell on the screen at Hunters' Ridge, his icy composure cracked. The demon had no answer.

"You didn't. You thought he was just another demon. Tell me, Porter. Do you know exactly what you've gotten into?"

"We're taking back heaven," he declared, his voice wavering.

"Who is 'we'?"

"Demonkind."

Samantha shook her head. "Sorry. Won't wash. I've spoken to my father. He's quite content returning Hell to what it should be. Do you even know what Stektes is?"

"A means to an end. The tool of my ascension. A stronger being than a bastard Nephilim."

"Is that what you think I am?" she replied, plucking the Well of Souls from his hand and tucking it into her belt.

Rockwell began to laugh. "You thought all it would take to end this was a bit of brute strength? A wave of the hand?" His eyes glanced to one side.

Samantha turned her head. The shadowed forms were closing in, filling the broken gap in the wall and spilling into the church. The closest reached for her.

"Sammy!" Her mother yelled, jumping in front of her.

The shadow brushed her mother and she screamed in agony, the skin charring black on her arm where contact was made.

"No!" Samantha twisted, thrusting her mother back into the arms of Charlotte. Eva hung limp and unresponsive as Charlotte lowered her to the ground.

Jim fired a shot past her. A moment later a searing pain erupted along her shoulder. It was Samantha's turn to scream, but her voice wasn't filled with agony. It was rage.

"You hurt my mom," she growled through clenched teeth, turning to face the shadow. Lanier stepped closer and she flung the two demons back into the wall, holding them there.

The shadow paused momentarily, as if considering its next move, then with both hands, it reached out toward her once more.

Samantha took a breath. "Time to find out what I can do." She stepped into the embrace of the shadow, clasping at its wrists with her hands.

"Sammy, no," Charlotte shouted from behind but it was too late.

Samantha was committed. The shadow struggled against her. Pain radiated down her hands, into her arms, but it was manageable. She remained silent, fighting the searing agony, refusing to give in. She believed this creature couldn't harm her and so she forced her will upon it.

A strange thing began to happen. As Samantha dominated the shadow, it became more pronounced, features beginning to appear where the darkness occluded the face. At the same time the golden-flecked cord on her twist began to glow.

Io, I'm doing it! The bracelet the old woman gave me in Dubrovnik. It's alive!

There was no response. In the sky above another lightning bolt accompanied the clash of sword on sword. On the hill beyond, a light pushed back at the darkness. She was on her own.

Squeezing tightly onto the shadow, she imposed her will, pushing it down. The cord pulsed and a golden light shone forth. The pain disappeared. The darkness evaporated and blackness became pale skin. A pair of brown eyes stared back at her from a face wrapped in a shawl. White robes flowed out underneath, falling back to the elbows where frail arms were held in Samantha's death grip. The shadow fell away, revealing a slender woman not much older than herself. The woman looked at her in awe, as if she were some sort of saviour. Her arms dropped.

"Anee hoff-she," the woman said, staring at her hands. "Anee hoff-she!" The woman looked up at her and smiled, tears rolling down her face.

"I don't understand. What does that mean?"

The woman stroked her face, still crying, and began to speak in what Samantha presumed was Hebrew.

"I'm sorry, I don't know what you're saying."

"She's thanking you," Charlotte said, still holding onto Eva's limp body. "You lifted her curse."

"What did you do to my mom?" Samantha demanded.

Charlotte translated and the woman responded. "It was the curse. The twelve Israeli tribes believed they were being protected from the apocalypse, but in truth, they were being enslaved. She asks if you can do the same to the rest of the tribes?" Charlotte paused for a moment, laying Eva onto the ground. "Sammy what are you? What happened at Hinkley?"

"She's a Nephilim," Rockwell spat from the back of the Church. "An abomination in the eyes of your God."

Io, you said I was something more…

The Hebrew woman caught sight of one of the pillars used to trap Io and began to speak rapidly, her voice urgent.

Samantha looked at Charlotte once again.

"She says there's a way to unbind the curse and set them free? Sammy, my Hebrew's pretty rustic."

The woman pointed at the pillar. "Hirsi et ha-amudim!"

"Break? No. Destroy. Sammy, destroy the pillars. Look! Three symbols on each."

Samantha followed Charlotte's gaze. The fallen pillar had three Hebrew inscriptions on it, as did the other she could see. Samantha nodded at the Hebrew woman and closed her eyes. Just like at Hinkley, she reached out. This time instead of radiation, she sought the darkness trapping the woman. The sky boiled above, as the angels fought. Samantha began to strip the shadow from the tribes.

At first there was resistance, similar to grabbing her opponent. There was agony too, a searing pain lancing through her middle that grew and grew as she reached outward. Yet, the shadow lifted. Above her, sooty spots became lighter as the spirits under the shroud of darkness were revealed. As each spirit was cleansed, it glowed briefly and disappeared. Samantha spread her arms wide and pulled. The shadow tore free of a hundred and forty-four thousand souls and coalesced above her head, a vortex of boiling violence. The darkness reached for her.

"Sammy," Charlotte warned.

"Just stay where you are," Samantha replied. "Protect Mom and whatever you do, don't move. Don't touch me, don't even breathe."

"What're you gonna do?"

"Take one for the team. I was meant for this."

There was approval shining from Charlotte's face. And pride.

Eva stirred, her eyes opening. "Sammy? Whu … what're you doing?"

"Don't worry, Mom. It's my time to do the right thing." Samantha felt good. Great even. There was no panic, no fear. Just belonging.

Tipping her head up, she invited the darkness in. The cloud plunged at her seeking vengeance for being deprived of its souls. Narrowing into a point, it struck the top of her head.

She screamed. The pain magnified a thousand-fold, yet inside, Samantha knew it was only a sensation. Nerve endings flared, chemicals reacted, as the dark continued to fill her with power. She redirected the cloud into four streams, each aimed at one of the pillars. Holding her hands open, she allowed the darkness to burst forth. Yet instead of black, purest white light erupted from within. Mixed with the gold from the glowing cord on her wrist, she radiated energy.

"No!" Rockwell screamed again.

The beams hit the pillars, the light filling the stone and fracturing it from within as it absorbed the power.

"Get Mom out of here," Samantha yelled above the roar of the wind. "I don't know how long I can hold this."

The pillars now pulsed with light. Her heart thumped in time with the glow, connected as a conduit to power. She was the nexus, erasing the curse. The vortex surged through her and into the pillars, refusing to allow her to break contact. It sucked the very breath from her lungs, and she saw spots in front of her eyes.

Just as Samantha thought she would pass out, the vortex ceased. White-hot stone hummed with the power contained inside, shaking her bones. She took a massive heaving breath, staggering away from the dais and out into the graveyard.

In the air not twenty metres from them, both Io and Karael paused, swords in hand, wings spread.

"What have you done?" Karael screamed.

Io laughed, a joyous sound in the darkness. "That's my girl."

Samantha joined her mother, Charlotte, and Jim in the lee of a stone sarcophagus in the graveyard. The humming increased in pitch, the vibration shaking every blade of grass around them. She put her hands over her ears. "I can't let go."

Sammy, the curse is within you. Release it and end their bondage.

She looked up to the distant angels. *Just as easy as flicking a switch?*

Io nodded. *Like snapping a twig. Break it, Sammy. Break it, and duck.*

She felt for the curse, stewing in the back of her mind, pulsing with the pillars, reaching to pull the power back.

"Oh no you don't," she said. Imagining it as a solid bar of black, she snapped the curse apart. In a shaft of white light, the church exploded.

Chapter Thirty-Eight

Still standing, Samantha was thrown back by the force of the explosion, landing face first on the grass. Pushing herself up, she scrambled over to her mother. "Mom? Mom!"

"She's breathing," said Charlotte. "Better since you worked that trick with the shadows."

"Look after her," Samantha replied. "We aren't done yet."

"Wasn't that the portal that just went up?" Charlotte indicated the remains of the church.

"I don't believe so," said Jim.

"Why not?"

Jim pointed to the top of the hill behind them. "Because that just switched on."

Above a line of trees another shaft of light now pierced the heavens, tapering to a point somewhere in the roiling cloud base above them. Unlike the blast from the church, this light rotated, causing the cloud to swirl and flicker red around its edges.

"The real rune is on the hilltop. The church wasn't the grave of Beelzebub, rather a trap intended for anybody who tried to open a doorway to Heaven. Aeon Fall may only be twenty years old, but those behind this are much, much older. The church contained a map, so Io said. I believe the church was a pointer, directing us up there. What

Mom achieved was only a setback for them. I've got to get up there. Where's Clare?"

"She's safe," Charlotte replied.

"How?"

"You don't think they came alone?" a voice called out from within the trees—a voice she should have never heard again. John Wolverton stepped into the graveyard, his face serious as he stared past her. "Good to see you, kid. You're working the family miracles again, I see, just like your old man. What do you say? Shall we go shut the bastards down?"

At a loss for words, Samantha nodded, walking alongside him. She glanced back to the ruined church.

"Don't worry about those two. If they aren't incinerated, our boys will get 'em. Helltech all around nowadays, and a good thing too."

They crossed the graveyard into the woods, following the path uphill.

"How?" Samantha finally asked.

"Thorsten can't stab worth a damn, and Alexander certainly can't break necks." John grabbed his shoulder, wincing. "Doesn't mean it don't hurt like hell though. We needed to expose the mole. We suspected Thorsten and put Alexander in a position to help him. While Thorsten was busy with me, Alexander put most everybody else down with an injection. Except Sejal, whose heart gave out. It was too much for the old guy. His heart was weak to begin with, and the action was too much for him before Alexander made it with the injection. And Swanson, of course. Thorsten didn't like his cousin and went after him. Nobody was meant to die, but in taking out the power, the act that saved the Chateau, it meant Thorsten got the jump on us. Even the most noble of actions have consequences, Sammy. Sometimes you just can't save 'em all."

Conflicting emotions raced through Samantha. Relief at knowing so many of the council were still alive. Guilt at the loss of Swanson and Sejal. "I don't believe that. You could have held Thorsten."

"On a suspicion? Sammy we don't work that way. Alexander had one job: to make Thorsten feel comfortable in his role as betrayer. Now we have to make sure Swanson's sacrifice was worth it. We've got to find a way to shut that down."

The portal continued to rotate, the cloud above spinning and growing darker as descending layers pushed out above the hilltop. Late morning soon became twilight under the trees.

Samantha hurried to keep up with Wolverton. "You can't close this doorway. Io needs to get home. All life on earth could suffer if he does not."

"It's not an option. Ask yourself what happens if it's not Io that goes through? Or if he makes it to Heaven and they don't like his message?"

"It's a risk they're going to have to take. Someone up there needs protecting and Io's the only one who can do it. You see those wings on his back?" They both watched Io slam into Karael, sending the avenging angel plummeting to the ground ahead of them. "They once belonged to Metatron. You remember him, don't you? And what he did for you all in Hell?"

"I remember," the old man grunted, "but we can't take that chance."

In the field ahead Io stood over Karael, sword tip touching his foe's throat. When they were about ten metres away, Wolverton held out his hand to stop her moving closer. Ever the protector.

"It is done," Io said without a trace of pride in his voice. If anything, he sounded abashed that he was in this position. "We are going home, you and I, brother. You have to answer for your crimes."

Karael laughed, torn wings flapping on the ground like a broken bird. "You'll never get through that portal, Ioviel."

"I have the Phaethon Stone. I'm the only one that can complete the activation. The orders need to know about Metatron. About Stektes. Humanity is innocent."

"Not all humanity." Karael fixed his gaze on Samantha. "Some of it is barely human, let alone innocent." Knocking Io's sword away, Karael leapt to his feet, one hand outstretched for her.

"Brother, no!" Io yelled.

In an instant Karael was on Samantha, hand wrapped around her throat, lifting her off the ground. "Ioviel you take one step toward me and ill rip her head from her body. You too, ape." He pulled her close. For a moment she recalled the face of Lucas as Karel regarded her from within the body of his vessel, sneering, black blood oozing from gashes on his face. The man who once tried to dominate and abuse her talents was the perfect container for this insane angel. "I see why you feel so protective of her. Indeed she's not a Nephilim. She's something more, about to be a memory."

"Karael," Io pleaded. "She could be the answer."

"The answer lies behind us. When Stektes crosses to Heaven in the body of her sister, then you will find the answer revealed. It's time for our Father to retire. A new God will rise from an ancient line." Karael began to squeeze her throat.

For a moment Samantha flailed, helpless. Then she remembered the knife at her side. The Well of Souls. Pulling the blade out she rammed it into Karael's chest underneath his outstretched arm, burying the blade to the hilt.

A look of confusion passed over his face, his eyes flashing. Black blood bubbled from his mouth. The hand holding her throat went limp and dropped away. From behind her, John Wolverton stepped up, pushing Karael away from her. "Ever hear about the time I killed a demon, Sammy? It's time I completed the set." With a right hook to the jaw, John sent the angel staggering back up the dirt track. "Nobody does that to one of my girls," he said, pursuing the angel. "Especially not one wearing the meat suit of that creep Lucas."

Io moved to trap Karael but Samantha held up a hand.

Let him have his fight. He's dead already. The blade takes all.

You're mistaken. My brother is gravely wounded but he will heal. He's still dangerous. There's only one way to end an angel.

Samantha examined the blade. Black blood disappeared as the knife absorbed it.

"John, leave him," Samantha croaked, her throat painful. "Please."

"Not this time. The Shikari will have one last hunt." Although he was in his sixties, the vigor of the man had not dimmed as he pursued the wounded Karael up the track toward the portal, kicking him to the ground. The light glowed through the trees ahead, making the underside of the clouds a freakish light blue.

John picked the angel up and held him much like Karael had held Samantha by the throat. "You're not so special. I can—" His words were cut off abruptly as Karael punched through his chest, the hand reaching out through the broken ribs of his back.

"John, no!" Samantha screamed.

Karael grinned in triumph. "One last hunt. One last failure." John's limp body slid off of Karael's arm, crumpling to one side.

His smile was short lived. Samantha stepped forward, her mind on fire as she prepared to obliterate her foster father's murderer.

Karael recognised the threat she posed and stumbled back.

"No, please. Sammy." The voice that came from Karael's mouth sounded different, a higher pitch, that of her recent companion and eventual tormentor.

"Lucas?"

"Spare me, Sammy. Only by sparing him do you keep me free."

Samantha closed her eyes, feeling the pressure build.

"Sammy?"

"No, Lucas. What you did was wrong, and you paid for it. Karael is the perfect match. You belong together." She raised her hand, intent upon wreaking revenge on the angel in the exact way he killed her foster father. An eye for an eye.

As she lifted her hand Karael's face appeared to register surprise. He looked down. Six inches of gleaming silver protruded from his chest. His eyes rolled back in his head and Karael slid off Io's blade.

Robbed of her target, Samantha screamed, a wordless sound full of anguish and rage. She focussed on Karael's body, still ready to obliterate it.

"Sammy, don't. Pause for just a moment and think through your actions. You were told you would use power for the right reasons, were you not? You did that. You saved everybody at the power plant and the millions who would have been infected by radiation. At the church you saved me. A time may yet come when your actions may be costly even if you consider them correct. Don't let that time be now." Io thrust his sword into the ground, leaving it wobbling, and approached her. "Don't let a petty act of vengeance stain your soul."

"But why, Io? He killed John."

"And he wanted you to kill him in return, to become a dark soul, like that in your sister. I spared you that fate. If he is not to come home and face justice then it is better I ended him than you. Save your rage for what's behind us. We still have to open the portal."

"Well what's that?" She waved at the prism of light beyond the trees.

"The conditions being met. The grave, the stone, the sacrifice. It activated when we stepped into the church. This moment has been long in the planning. Our enemy expected a trap and a procession."

"Instead they got an intact angel and a pissed off ... whatever I am. Karael recognised something in me. I saw it in his eyes. Io, what am I?"

"I still can't be sure. You may be something very rare, and very special. You certainly have power. Let's just describe you as a Legacy. If we survive the next ten minutes maybe I can work out a way to find you the answers."

After Samantha moved John's body to a position of some composure, with his arms across the chest, she watched as Io strangely did the same for Karael. They each bowed their head and then they climbed the hill through the woods.

She was eager to see an end to this chaos and win her sister back. The trees gave way to a strange field where Samantha came face to face with the doorway to Heaven. Patterns revolved within patterns, carvings shining from the ground as light beamed upward from dozens of points, creating the shaft of light that pierced the boiling cloud. The air reeked of ozone. It was all wrong.

"It's one giant glyph," she said.

"And you could have created such a pattern at any time," said a voice from the other side of the portal. Nina walked out from behind the light, Thorsten beside her, dragging a bound and gagged Tricia Pellirojo.

"Didn't your tame angel tell you such a thing was possible?" Nina sneered. "He doesn't need a sacrifice, or a grave, just someone with the power to call forth the pattern. As luck would have it, when we powered the satellite, his fall led him straight to you. Once the Phaethon Stone was complete, what was your reasoning for coming here, Ioviel?"

"To stop you. To end your ascension to Heaven. You will not activate the Godmissile and doom humanity."

"A noble gesture, but one doomed to fail. Do you believe for one second my master is concerned with the creatures infesting this rock? There are other worlds, other beings to worship Him. Crustallos will ascend straight to Heaven and there He will take the place your God usurped. Then mankind ends." Nina held her hands aloft. "See as life powers this doorway." Birds began to flock toward the portal. As each bird touched the light, a streak of red shot out from the pinnacle of the prism. The glyph began to glow red.

"No," Io said, shocked. "What have you done? What has this portal been activated with?"

"The life of an innocent," Nina replied, triumphant. "Birds are faster but all life will be drawn toward this portal until it closes. See why for yourself." Nina stepped aside.

At the centre of the prism, a body could be seen rotating. "Alexander," Samantha said. "Why?"

"No path is truly innocent, sister. Sometimes a little sacrifice is required."

"I'm not your sister," Samantha stated. "Nina is my sister. You're a parasite feeding off of her."

Nina smiled. "I'm the same person you grew up with, played with and fought with, Sammy. What difference does it make that in the back of my mind lurks a weak and pathetic child? Join with me, sister. Let us ascend together and place the final key in the lock. Your tame angel has mentioned it, yes? There are few, if any in Heaven, who can stand against only one of us. Together we will be unstoppable. I can teach you to unlock it. Your power combined with mine terrifies them. I know what you are, what we are. Join with me and I'll tell you. He," Nina pointed at Io, "would keep you ignorant of this knowledge. Up there, we could rule. Up there, we will be gods."

She doesn't know what I can do.

"And him?" Samantha indicated Thorsten. "He killed Swanson."

Thorsten grinned, with wide psychotic eyes. "I would do it again just for the pleasure. Alexander confessed before I threw him in. I know about the ARC council still living. Well, most of them. I understand you couldn't keep old Wolverton alive. I'll enjoy hunting them down again."

"Old Wolverton went doing what he loved, something meaningful," Samantha spat Thorsten's words back in his face. "He'll be remembered as a hero, unlike you. You're a traitor, nothing more. Not even worthy of the name you bear. An insult to your ancestors."

Thorsten roared aloud, his rage making him drag Tricia closer and closer to the portal. "I will be remembered as the man who changed life as we know it, a warrior prepared to make the difficult choices and sacrifice in the name of mankind."

Tricia Pellirojo tried to scream through her gag. The red-headed ARC finance director squirmed against her bonds, her movements frantic and desperate. Nina looked on, approving, as more and more birds hit the prism, turning the sky blood red.

Io, forgive me if this is wrong.

Uncomprehending, Io turned her way.

"Thorsten, if you're gonna sacrifice someone, spare Tricia. Let it be me." Samantha dropped her pack to the ground, handed The Well of Souls to Io and stepped forward to block his way, the portal at her back. She felt the pull from behind, its purpose being twisted as each avian life extinguished. "I'll be your sacrifice."

His grip loosening on Tricia, Thorsten turned to his master.

"Do it," Stektes said through Nina's lips, the sound of her voice now crystalline and profoundly alien. "Throw her in. I'm still going to destroy Heaven."

Samantha took a step backward into the portal. "No. You're not."

Chapter Thirty-Nine

The energy of the portal enveloped Samantha. Extending her hands, she watched as tiny flecks of light were drawn into the glow above. Beneath her feet, the runes continued to swirl and with each creature that touched the portal, it flickered.

Outside the boundary of light, Nina had a look of pure horror on her face, surprising for a creature from a dark dimension.

"Why don't you join me?" She held out a hand. Nina looked at the invitation with horror, mouthing words neither of them could hear.

Io, what's she afraid of?

Io frowned, tapped his head and shook it. Samantha was alone in the portal. A miscalculation with good intent.

She turned to the slowly-revolving body of Alexander Steadman at the nexus of the light. Reaching out she touched his neck. There was the faintest flicker of a pulse.

"Alexander, can you hear me?"

There was no response.

Alexander? She threw the thought at him.

Who summons me?

"Huh?" The thundering response caught Samantha off guard and she spoke instead of thinking.

Alexander it's me, Samantha.

Samantha. There is no angel by that name.

This wasn't Alexander Steadman she spoke to. The portal was open. Judging by the responses that threatened to make her head explode, she was talking to an angel in Heaven. If she could speak to Heaven, maybe she could do more.

Not yet there isn't. I bear tidings of Metatron and Ioviel. But first, I need a little favor.

This gateway opens only for the fallen. We don't listen to the prayers of traitors.

Samantha stopped listening. Whoever was at the other end of the portal reeked of hostility. Raising her hands, she sought the spirit of Alexander Steadman, focusing through Alexander's dead body in front of her. She closed her eyes, imagining him standing in line before two giant white gates of purest alabaster. "Got you," she said, and pulled.

Nothing happened. Samantha felt herself rising as something tried to pull at her. This was a trap, not a doorway. But she was not an angel and the presence above was baffled. She took advantage of the confusion. Just like the tribes, she pulled Steadman's essence back, focused on settling it within his body.

Steadman's eyes popped open. He stared at her for a moment and his face registered intense pain.

Before he could scream, Samantha shoved him out of the portal where he stumbled into the arms of Io. Turning and pointing at her, Steadman began to shout at the angel.

Nina stepped back from the portal, her Stektes-controlled face showing the first signs of doubt.

Thorsten said something to Io and then turned. Eyeballing Samantha, he grabbed The Well of Souls from Io's hand and leaped toward her, his teeth bared in a snarl. His arm pierced the veil of light, the blade aimed for Samantha's chest. The rest of his body made it no further than the surface. Caught in the haze, Thorsten began to scream, a muffled noise that filtered through the portal's core.

Samantha remembered her sister trying to shout underwater when they were kids. This time the gurgling voice wasn't fun. Thorsten's face began to dissolve away as the portal claimed another mortal.

Samantha truly realised she was something more. Even in his agony, the disintegrating arm of Thorsten Guyomard stretched out, the obsidian blade reaching for her heart. She watched the blade, preferring it to Thorsten's slow and agonising death, coming to the conclusion that it was The Well of Souls itself keeping him from release. With the arm locked by the portal's edge, Samantha reached out and claimed the blade, plucking it from fingers, now little more than bone and sinew.

In an instant Thorsten's body evaporated, the portal swirling red as he merged with its energy.

"More than a weapon," Samantha called out to her sister and friends outside the portal. She raised the blade above her head and screamed, "Come back! I need you." Samantha closed her eyes and reached out to a hundred and forty-four thousand recently departed souls.

You shall not, the voice Samantha dubbed, *the Angel Alexander,* roared out of space and time, the power of the words forcing her to her knees.

And yet I will. You can't prevent my attempt. Nor their response. There aren't enough prayers in the world to stop me. Samantha pulled at the souls through the blade, her will amplified. She stood, resolute.

And they came. Willingly, twelve times twelve thousand souls shining above as nebulous lights, burning the cloud away as they passed through the portal. Focussed initially above her, the orbs spread all over the hillside.

The portal began to flicker; the light surrounding her was strobe-like. Io watched her, his face a mystery as the portal faded away and the runes flickered out one-by-one, and sat dark and still on the hilltop.

"What have you done?" Nina asked, her eyes wide with fright. She looked around the hillside with quick, jerky movements as if a fight for control within consumed her. As each glowing orb settled to the ground, it became the glowing image of a Hebrew man or woman. As each materialised, they became aware of the being inside Nina; faces of pale serenity filled with rage. The person closest to Samantha, a woman Samantha cleansed from the shadows, spoke loudly in Hebrew, her voice harsh.

"What's she saying?" Alexander Steadman asked Samantha.

"I'm not sure there are words in English that quite do it justice," she replied. "From the feeling of these people I would say Stektes had a direct role in entrapping them."

The ghostly tribe parted to allow Charlotte and Jim to escort Clare and Eva to the hilltop. The half-sisters stood watching Nina, eyes wide, staring in disbelief.

"It was all you," Eva said. "Everything. Aeon Fall, the kidnappings, Rockwell's return."

"It's always been me," Nina replied, unrepentant. "These are the movements of dust compared to the avalanche to come."

"Io, who is Alexander?" Samantha asked.

"The master of Heaven's prison, The Fearvent," he replied. "He is the one who taught me the angel trap."

"Alexander spoke to me when I was within the portal. I pulled the tribe from his grasp. He wasn't pleased. There was more, though. This portal led directly to him. I felt he was waiting for someone. Io, I think this was never a return to Heaven. It was another trap—one set by somebody who wanted to barter their way into Heaven using a fallen angel as a bargaining chip." She turned to her sister, held firm within a network of ghostly hands. "You've got allies inside Heaven."

Nina began to laugh. Despite being trapped, she seemed the only one truly at ease. "We have allies everywhere. We are everywhere. He is coming, and nothing you can do to me will prevent that."

Samantha concentrated, letting power flow into her sister. "I have some tricks yet to try." Using her newfound powers, Samantha stepped fully inside the landscape of Nina's mind.

Samantha stood on a barren wasteland, limitless, flat, the rocks beneath her feet black and cracked. In the far distance, mountains rose below a murky sky, the stars, the moon hidden. A glow came from all around her, the source just out of view. She walked toward the center of the light. "So this is what they've reduced your existence to," she said aloud, her heart filled with pity. "What have they let you become?"

It seemed that hours had passed as Samantha maintained a dogged pace. In time, a plateau rose above the desert. She climbed, the light now brighter. When she reached the top, the source became clear.

"Nina!" Samantha cried out, rushing forward to grab her sister. Nina shone with pure white light.

Nina looked up to her and screamed. There was a tentacle wrapped about her waist. It lifted her aloft, pulling her away from Samantha into the maw of a nightmarish creature.

Coils spun around coils, tentacles reaching out in all directions, around a series of crooked claws. One red eye glowered at Samantha from the centre of the writhing mass, above an arsenal of teeth. Where she imagined the other eye to be, there was only darkness. The creature rose up, slithering toward her.

"Stektes. So, this is the real you." Samantha stood, her feet firmly planted, her hands on her hips.

The creature appeared baffled by her indifference. It recoiled, unsure of her or itself. "She is mine," it roared. "You will not free her."

"Shall we pit the power of a hundred thousand souls against you and see what happens then?" The Well of Souls materialised in her hand and Samantha pointed it at the creature. A beam of light shot out from the tip of the blade, spreading to become a latticework of pure energy. The net wrapped Stektes tightly, squeezing the claws and countless scaly coils to the tip. Where it touched its skin, there was a hissing, emitting an acrid stench. The being's skin bubbled and decayed under the onslaught.

"Let her go!" Samantha commanded. The net closed tighter. The creature roared and screamed. Black ichor spread beneath the mass of tentacles that supported it. Stektes lashed out with tentacles trapping her sister. Samantha ducked, as it passed over her head with countless hungry mouths yawning and chomping. Nina screamed in its tip.

Hold on, Nina.

"That's a no, then," she decided. "Better death than to return to your master a failure, eh?"

The ground shook, and Samantha stumbled across the plateau. From within the net of souls, a guttural laugh rumbled. "Do you feel the world beneath your feet begin to disintegrate? Yes? What you feel is her body under assault."

The tentacle returned, Nina wrapped in the tip, hanging just out of reach. Her face was as pale as those of the Hebrew tribe. Blood dripped where the tentacle had speared her through her abdomen.

"My sister," Nina beseeched. "Kill it."

"But I'll kill you."

"I don't care. It's had me always. I have been a prisoner. I've watched you my entire life, Sammy, while this thing has abused my body and mind. Kill it. In here, before it does any more damage out there. You've got the strength to do what I could not. I'm proud of you, little sister."

Nina screamed as the tentacle twisted tighter. Blood fountained from her mouth. The ground shook so violently Samantha was forced to her knees. "I'll find a way to save you, Nina,"

Nina's face pleaded with her as she was drawn away into the air. "Noooooo," she wailed as Stektes moved her body out of sight.

Samantha couldn't be sure if Nina's plea was for her or for the creature in her mind. She collapsed to her knees as the world around her violently bucked. The plateau cracked, rocks falling into the valley below.

"Release me, or we all die!" Stektes' voice quivered.

Samantha had the power to deliver death to this monster. All around her, Nina screamed.

And then, she heard a distant voice. Her mothers.

"Sammy, let her go. You've suffered enough. You're killing both of you. Sammy. She can't be saved, but you can."

"Mom?" Samantha let the net of soul energy dissipate, the blade in her hand crumbling to dust as her will to destroy this abomination evaporated with the spark of a new idea. Take Stektes into herself, battle it on her terms. Free Nina. Myself for her.

Stektes paused in its' violent attack on Nina's mind, as if hearing Eva's words, considering them as an alternative. "Mine," it roared, reaching for her with countless tentacles. The already massive bulk of the monster swelled and grew, becoming an enormity that dwarfed the plateau. Nina was lost in the labyrinth of twisting arms.

"No." Samantha held up a hand, freezing the creature on the spot. "Your hold on her is too strong. I'll save her yet."

"You are welcome to try," Stektes rumbled, lashing out with a tentacle, smashing the plateau asunder. The ground fell beneath Samantha's feet and she dropped into nothingness. The pure black of a starless universe engulfed her and she willed herself away.

She opened her eyes. Nina still faced her. They were only a pace apart. Her sister's eyes had changed to a dark green, the colour of Stektes' hideous skin. Her face, or the face of the monster within her, was terrified. The tribes surrounded them in a wide circle, their hands linked, light pulsing for another attack.

"No. Enough." Sammy raised a hand to the tribe. "We can't beat Stektes that way. Its hooks are too deeply embedded. If we destroy it, we kill Nina and I won't lose my sister. Mom, she's still in there, fighting. She's always defied the beast, which is why it doesn't have total control over her."

With the comprehension it was to be spared, a smug smile spread across Nina's face. "You touch me, she dies."

"A hollow threat. You still need her. But we can't have you running around causing chaos." Samantha put her hands to either side of Nina's head. A pulse of energy knocked her unconscious and Nina dropped to the ground.

"What have you done?" Clare asked, kneeling down to check Nina's pulse.

"Stektes has had my sister locked up inside her own head since she was taken to Hell. One might make it difficult to imagine there is any kind of symbiosis. My sister is the same as me, whatever that is, but Stektes is more of a parasite now. If it breaks free of her there will be chaos."

"What did it look like?" Eva asked, her arm bound in a sling. She leaned on Jim for support.

"Big, scaly. If whatever's waiting on the other side is like that we're in for trouble."

"It is," Eva replied. "It's bigger, and worse than you could imagine. And it's angry at us. We took away its chance of claiming Hell. There's a very good reason these Gods no longer walk among us. Hell would seem like a pleasant weekend break compared to what they would bring. We need to get Io home. His brethren need to know how close to disaster we all are.

"One problem there," Io said. "If the portal was one final trap to feed fallen angels into the Fearvent, then what hope do I have of returning home?"

"Can't you just fly?" Eva asked.

Io shook his head as he said, "My own garrison would be on me in an instant were I to reappear. I would have to follow the path of souls, where all these brave ones should have gone in the first place." He indicated the closest of the Tribe, surrounding them in a tight circle. Their faces were expectant, as if they knew something momentous was about to occur.

Then in her head the plan just clicked. Samantha smiled. "I think I know a way."

Chapter Forty

The group of six people, an angel and the small matter of one hundred and forty four thousand shining souls moved across the top of the hill to a flat area away from the trap. The sky was clearing, the clouds dispersing in all directions. A heavy mist enveloped them, moisture kissing Samantha's skin rejuvenated her, preparing her for the task ahead.

"Io, can you clear the ground, please? Make it nice and flat, about five meters across."

Io waved his hand and the requested ground cleared. "You could do that, you know."

"True. But I need to concentrate. I don't need another lesson."

"Another lesson in what?" Eva asked. "Sammy, what are you? What is she, Io?"

Samantha crouched and began to carve into the ground with the Well of Souls, directing a little energy through it as she created. "You know what most little girls want to be when they grow up: a princess when they're small—until they reach the age where they attain a skill—a gymnast, a horse rider, a musician. Their ambitions become more realistic as they grow up. All I wanted to be was the equal of my sister. To be seen through your eyes, Mom, the same way she was. I never understood until recently that you always saw me that way. I never realised until I found Io that we both had something special driving us. Io won't say, and I think nothing on earth is going to make him. He said the word 'Nephilim', the offspring of an angel, or in Pop's case an archangel. I don't think that cuts it."

"He wasn't Satan when we had either of you."

"It doesn't seem to have mattered, Mom. The spark was there and somebody important was watching. I think Madden was always headed in that direction. Now we are whatever we are. Not entirely human. I think we have a spark too."

"I have to be sure," Io protested.

Samantha stood, holding her clenched hand to her chest. "Deep in here there's something. A latent power. It's been awakened by Io. I've learned more in the past day than I could have ever imagined thanks to him. I have a purpose."

"But Nina has that power too. Stektes draws from it. She's never had the chance to be free, to learn."

Eva nodded, and squeezed her daughter's shoulder.

"Is that what this pattern is?" Clare asked.

"In part. Call it geometry, call it art. It's a bit of both. When I called my father, the pattern mixed with blood was the key. That won't work where you're going, Io. The grave of a demon would just send you to back to your prison. We need to fire up this gateway a bit brighter than that." She finished carving the pattern. Stars sat inside diamonds inside circles and more stars, all connected.

"Elaborate," Io approved.

"I'm glad you like it. Now I need you to think of a place to be sent. I doubt you want to go near the Fearvent. But wherever you decide, fix it in your mind and hold onto that image."

"I have it," Io replied. "Where I was patrolling when I was knocked out of Heaven. It's on the most distant edge. Nobody should be there, now." He turned to the small group of people with them. "I am thankful to have met you all. You helped me when you had no reason to trust me. You have shown me there is hope here yet. I'll convey that message."

"Will they listen?" Eva asked.

Samantha looked up as Io raised his head. His jaw was set.

"I shall make them listen, he said slowly nodding his head. "You, we are not alone. Humanity will remember this in the days ahead."

"Please step to the centre of the pattern," Samantha indicated with one hand.

"You sure this will work?" he asked.

"No idea whatsoever," she replied. "I just need that." Samantha reached up and plucked the Phaethon Stone from Io's chest before he could react. In an instant her hand was ablaze, the fire warming her but doing no damage at all.

Everybody around her threw their hands up at the light. Even the Hebrew ghosts appeared to wince.

"Amazing," Samantha said, squeezing the stone tight. "I can feel it all. This stone is alive. The energy from an entire nuclear reactor, bound up amidst Metatron's essence. I can feel him. I can see his memories." Samantha gasped. "Mom I can see the first time he let you see him. A barn with a demon speaking German? The portal opening. Tentacles." She frowned. "It was Stektes. Every time a portal opened near you, it was Stektes. He knew you, right from the start. They both did."

"It was Crustallos," Eva protested.

"No Mom, it wasn't. I've seen Stektes. One eye glowing, the other dark. You stabbed an eye out did you not? Do you imagine you could do that to a god and live? I fear Crustallos is an entity we have not yet encountered. We don't want the Godmissile let loose on the world."

Samantha stepped to the centre of the pattern. The glyphs glowed as she crossed them, circling her slowly, the outer rings clockwise, the inner counter-clockwise.

Io followed her to the centre of the pattern. "The Phaethon Stone won't be enough."

Samantha smiled. "I know. You'll be fine." She checked the rotation of the glyphs and nodded, satisfied. "You'll be needing this back." She pressed the stone into his armor where it clicked into place. "Guys you might want to step back for this."

Io's wings unfurled, reaching up above him as they shimmered. The light of the portal erupted, tapering to a point like the previous gateway did. He looked up.

Samantha watched him, all muscle and straining sinew as he waited for her. Io was ready to return home. She took his hands in her own. "It's been quite a journey since Dubrovnik."

Io tilted his head forward. Anticipation shone from his face. "I fear my journey's only just begun, Sammy." He leaned forward, brushing her lips with a kiss. "I won't forget you."

"Look in on me from time to time." She threw her arms around him, not wanting to let him go. Still, she did, stepping back.

"When I find out more about you, expect your prayers to be answered, Samantha Scott. I'll make Heaven believe in humanity again. I'm ready to make my exit." He spread his hands wide, arms parallel with his wings. In his silver scaled armour he was a regal paragon of purity. Her champion.

"This isn't an exit, Ioviel," she whispered. *It's an exodus.*

She sent out only one thought, and the twelve tribes of ancient Hebrews shone like the sun and launched toward the portal. Samantha had no searching for a clue, no quest for a familiar sensation. The spirits knew her invitation would send them to paradise. As one hundred and forty-four thousand glowing orbs bolstered the power of the Phaethon Stone, energy crackled around the base of the portal. As one Io and Samantha screamed, a release of pure unbridled joy. Light shone from within Io's body, and in an eruption of gold-tinged white the angel finally burst forth. Io surged heavenward, a streak of golden energy searing the sky with radiance. The spirits continued to swirl around inside the vortex, accelerating up in His wake. Beams of light shot forth in all directions at the pinnacle of the portal, piercing through the clouds, reaching for miles. Just for a moment Samantha felt something more—a connection with a higher plane of existence.

"Heaven," she breathed. "God's speed, my friend."

With a hollow boom the light disappeared, the portal fading to nothing. Io was home.

Samantha lowered her arms. Her eyes were still dazzled from the light. She blinked to try and clear them. Colours were blurry images which sharpened as she rubbed the tears away. She hadn't realised she was crying. At her feet rested a body. Black skin, heavy beard, dressed as she had last seen him in a worn top and trousers.

"He's still here?" Her mother asked.

Samantha kneeled beside the body, touching his throat. "No pulse. The vessel sacrificed everything to send the angel home."

"But that's him."

Samantha stood. "No Mom, that's just the body he used. Io is a being of light. What occurred here today … we may never see again."

"Well, we weren't alone," said Clare, pointing down the hill. A stream of people walked toward the woods that separated them from the tiny village beyond. As far as they could see, cars packed the roads beyond.

Charlotte reached for a radio, no doubt to call for whatever ARC security there was.

Samantha stepped out of the portal and lowered her hand. "Let them come. The entire hill is covered in burn marks, I'd say well over a hundred and forty thousand. Anybody for miles around will have seen the light show."

"And you don't consider containment necessary?" Charlotte was clearly sceptical.

Samantha recognised the dry scepticism in Charlotte's voice. "No." She felt at peace with the world. The direction her life was going to take now clear to her. "They're the first here. They need to know what happened."

"Why?" Charlotte thrust her hand in their direction. "Because it will justify our actions?"

"Because Heaven needs mankind to start believing again, and it all begins here. Aeon Fall took advantage of global disillusionment. People don't need to believe at first, but there are some things the eyes cannot doubt. One angel died, another ascended on this hill. Thornfalcon is a holy place. Perhaps the holiest since His son rose." She knelt down beside Nina's unconscious body, smoothing her hair. "I'll find you and free you. I promise."

Eva joined Samantha by her sister. Nina's face was calm as she slept. "What do we do with her, Sammy?"

"Keep her sedated. Heavily. That monster inside her needs the power we both have. If the body remains unconscious I doubt Stektes can do any damage. It's sealed in there. Bury her deep within an ARC facility, Mom. I will find a way to get that thing out of her. I'll get my sister back. We'll have a family again."

Jim and Charlotte moved the unconscious Nina away from the portal. Not long after, people began to filter through the trees, making their way to the peak of the hill.

"How close were we to failing?" Clare asked, as the three of them watched the strangers looking around the hill in bafflement and wonder.

"Close," Samantha replied. "I don't know what today's events mean. I just have a feeling Io will need my help again before this is all over. Stektes sought my power, but also feared it. The tribes surprised our enemy. We have to keep ahead of the curve. Mom, Aunt Clare, whoever is making the Helltech, you might want them to ramp up production. There's a war coming."

"Angels would destroy us?" Clare asked.

"No. This is bigger than that. An older God wants to reclaim the throne and He's but one step away. Humanity may just get caught in the middle."

"Excuse me?" A tall man, the foremost of the people beginning to swarm over the hill, called out. He held the hand of a redhead, three children in tow.

"I know you," Samantha said, stepping forward. "The guy from the airport with the lost daughter."

He smiled at being remembered. "Well I never. Samantha, isn't it? What happened here?"

Samantha shrugged. "An angel rose to Heaven. My friend went home."

"Well I never," he said again. "Sammy, how about that? Exactly what you said. It's all real."

His curly-haired daughter rolled her eyes at him and turned to Samantha. "He never believes me."

He smiled at his daughter and turned back. "What does that mean for us?"

"It means finally, Heaven will start to listen again. You'd better start praying. I think in the days to come, we'll need it." Samantha turned to Eva. "I miss him, Mom. He's only been gone moments."

Eva opened her mouth to reply when the hill began to vibrate, becoming a tremor. The people in front of them stared skyward. Samantha turned.

A shaft of light pierced through the cloud, touching down atop the hill. A sizzling bolt of lightning ripped down the shaft, hitting the hill with a jolt.

Wings folding behind him, Io stepped from the light. His armor was gold now, dented and broken. His sword, chipped and worn, hung from his side.

The light in his face faded and it became the face of the man lying atop the portal. He smiled for a moment, then became grim.

"What is it? You only just left."

"All Hell's broken loose. The forty-two have Him trapped in the Angelforge and Zerachiel's commanding an army. One of many. I need you. We all do." He held his hand out.

Samantha turned to Eva, who nodded. "Go, love. Save us all."

Three more impacts hit the hill, shaking it yet more.

"Ioviel, we can't hold the gateway much longer," said a woman's voice from within the light. "Hurry."

The people on the hill stared in amazement. Several dropped to their knees.

Samantha took Io's hand. "Look after them, Mom. Look after them all." To Io she added, "I trust you know what you're doing?"

"Giving us hope," he replied. "Hold on tight."

The light grew bright about them, a pearlescent glow. Samantha felt herself rise, rushing through the air at incredible speed. Rainbow colours around her merged to white and one word above all fixed in her mind. Destiny.

The End

About The Author

Matthew Harrill has lived all of his life in the South West of England. In 1997 he graduated from the University of Southampton with an honours degree in geology. This year he finally married his partner of eight years, Tricia. They have one son and another child on the way.

Books by the Author

The Focus Stone The Tome of Law Book 1)
The Path of Dreams (The Tome of Law Book 2)
Hellbounce (The Arc Chronicles Book 1)
Hellborne (The Arc Chronicles Book 2)
Hellbeast (The Arc Chronicles Book 3)
The Eyes Have No Soul
Thornfalcon

36904216R00211

Printed in Poland
by Amazon Fulfillment
Poland Sp. z o.o., Wrocław